Man in the Mirror

*A man finding himself
as he loses himself to Alzheimer's*

a novel

Zoe Murdock

H.O.T. Press

Published by
H.O.T. Press
Ojai, California 93023
www.hotpresspublishing.com

ISBN: 0-923178-29-5
ISBN - 13: 978-0-923178-29-1

This is a work of fiction. Names, characters, places, events and incidents are either the products of the author's imagination or used in a fictitious manner.

For Doc,

Without whom this book would not exist,

and without whom I would not exist.

For my father and all those with Alzheimer's

who long to be understood.

Acknowledgments

I am deeply indebted to the members of the Ojai Writing Workshop who gave me invaluable feedback and insight as I worked through the many drafts of this novel.

Man in the Mirror

Abruptly the poker of memory stirs the ashes of recollection and uncovers a forgotten ember, still smoldering down there, still hot, still glowing, still red as red.

William Manchester
Goodbye, Darkness:
A Memoir of the Pacific War, 1980

But when from a long-distant past nothing subsists, after the people are dead, after the things are broken and scattered, still, alone, more fragile, but with more vitality, more unsubstantial, more persistent, more faithful, the smell and taste of things remain poised a long time, like souls, ready to remind us, waiting and hoping for their moment, amid the ruins of all the rest; and bear unfaltering, in the tiny and almost impalpable drop of their essence, the vast structure of recollection.

Marcel Proust
Swann's Way: Vol. 1 of
Remembrance of Things Past
Translated from the French by
C.K. Scott Moncrieff (1922)

Chapter 1

Aaron woke up gasping and kicking wildly at the attacking vultures. Then he realized it wasn't vultures he was kicking—it was his covers.

When he finally got his legs unraveled from the bedding, he sat up and tried to remember the rest of his dream. It seemed like he was out in the desert. That's right. He was with Laura. They were hiking along, enjoying the sun and the beauty of the red rock desert. Then, suddenly, she was gone. It was as if she'd been whisked out of the air. He scrambled up through the slippery rocks, hoping he could see her from higher ground. But when he looked back down, it was himself he saw. His body was lying on a pile of rocks with those bloody-headed vultures picking the flesh from his bones. It felt so real. But it wasn't real. It was a dream. One of those damn nightmares again.

He yanked up the corner of the sheet and wiped the sweat from his face. Was Laura trying to tell him something? The dreams were always about her in some way. Sometimes they'd start out happy, and he'd be caught up in the joy of their life together. Then everything would change, and he'd be dragged down into the terrible sadness he'd felt when she was dying. Maybe she was afraid he was going to forget her, and that's why she was coming around in his dreams. Well, he wasn't going to forget her. He never would, but the dreams were making him too sad, and right now, he needed some joy in his life.

As he sat there staring at the narrow beam of light coming through the slit in the old curtains, he wondered if he should get rid of those damn things. Let the sun in. Brighten the room.

He got up and pulled on some pants. Then he went to the window and started yanking the old blue velvet material off the rod. The dust rained down, and he started sneezing, but he kept pulling until the curtains were in a heap on the floor. He picked them up and carried them out to the trash.

That felt so good, he decided to keep going.

He went back to the bedroom to see if there were other things he could get rid of. That old oak dresser had seen better days. Maybe he should give it away. The mirror had lost so much of its silver, he was never sure if it was himself he was seeing in there or some shadowy man drowning in water.

No. He couldn't get rid of that dresser. He and Laura bought it right after they got married, and they'd dragged it from one house to the next. Laura loved that dresser. And besides, if he got rid of it, he'd just have to buy a new one.

What else?

He walked around the room and ended up in front of Laura's closet. Maybe there was something in there he could get rid of. Maybe her clothes. He'd never been able to even think about it, but maybe if the clothes were gone, the dreams would stop and he could get on with his life.

As soon as he opened the closet door, his doubts came back. If he got rid of Laura's things, how would he remember their life together? And if he didn't remember that, what would he have left?

He was about to forget the whole thing, but he caught a whiff of Laura's perfume. It didn't seem possible it could still be there after all the years. But then he'd hardly ever opened that closet door, so maybe the scent had just gotten trapped in there. He went deeper into the closet and started looking through her clothes. Each item brought a flood of memories: the white eyelet dress Laura made herself for Easter, the blue and white-striped maternity smock she wore when she was pregnant with Michael, and later, with Sarah. Laura was so beautiful when she was pregnant. Beautiful and happy. They were both happy and had so much fun when the kids were young. Liberty Park on Sundays. Those long hikes up in the mountains to Secret Lake. Making homemade strawberry ice cream and those great big pancakes he liked to cook on the outside grill.

Laura's clothes brought back so many happy memories, he wondered how he could even think of getting rid of them. He was about to leave the closet when he caught sight of the warm blue coat he'd given her when he came home from the war. Salt Lake City had felt so cold and miserable after the warm humidity of India. He missed that humidity. In fact, there were a lot of things he missed about India. The intriguing temples and shrines that were scattered everywhere. The soft colors of the landscape. That sweet scent of incense that hung in the air everywhere you went. And somehow, the people of India had seemed more at ease than people back home in Utah. They didn't seem to have doubts about who they were; they were just living their lives. When he was in India, he didn't have so many doubts either. And he wasn't constantly worrying about what was right and wrong, according to someone else. That three year period during the war was the first time in his life that he didn't feel the presence of his father looking over his shoulder telling him how to be. It was like he belonged in India, and when he was there, it was okay for him to be exactly who he was.

That's what he needed now. To feel like he belonged and that his life had some fundamental value and meaning. But he shouldn't get thinking about that. He should focus on what he'd started. Pack up the clothes, air out the room, and get on with his life.

After retrieving some boxes from the garage, he came back and started pulling Laura's clothes off of the hangers. He worked quickly, loosely folding each garment before placing it in a box. He tried not to think too much about what he was doing, or what it meant. He just wanted to get it done.

Everything was going fine until he came to a long gray bag. He knew what was in that bag: Laura's wedding dress. There were so many intense memories associated with that dress, he was almost afraid to touch it.

He took a deep breath and forced himself to take the bag off the rod. He carried it to the bed and sat next to it. When he finally got the courage to pull the zipper down, he gasped. The small white beads sewn into the satin bodice were as perfect and polished as they'd been on their wedding day all those years ago. As he ran his fingers across the cool smoothness of the beads, he remembered how they felt on his hot skin that night when they were finally alone in his car. "Oh honey," he whispered, "I don't want to remember these things. It hurts too much."

The image of the first time he saw Laura in her wedding dress flooded his mind. It was up at the Salt Lake Temple grounds the day they were having their photographs taken. It was a glorious September morning in 1946, about a year after he got back from the war. He remembered how intense the colors of the flowers were that day. The reds and the whites. The purples and the yellows. It had rained the night before, and there were drops of water on everything. It made it look like someone had scattered diamonds everywhere. And there at the center of it all, was his pretty Lori with her beautiful dress and her sparkling green eyes. Her face glowed with such a sweet innocent beauty, it took his breath away. Even now, it aroused him. He remembered pulling her back into the trees and embracing her after the photographer left. Her body tight against his. The intoxicating scent of perfume in her hair. The way she responded when he kissed her in a way she shouldn't have been kissed until after they were married. Especially not there on the Temple grounds. There was such an urgent desire in her body, it had surprised him. Was a girl supposed to feel that kind of desire?

He pulled the wedding dress to his lips and kissed the beads one last time and then pulled up the zipper. What was he supposed to do with such an important symbol of his love for Laura? He couldn't just fold it up and put it in a box with all the other things.

Then, he knew what to do. He should give the dress to Sarah. She would want her mother's wedding dress, wouldn't she? Of course she would. Maybe she'd even wear it herself someday, if she ever got married again. That might happen. She was a lovely woman, just like her mother. He gave the bag a gentle pat and went back to the closet to see what else was there.

The only thing left were Laura's shoes. He sat on the floor and pulled them out, one pair at a time. It was odd that the shoes near the front of the closet were flat and practical, but those still in the boxes in the back were stylish high-heels with cut-out toes.

Laura used to wear those sexy high-heeled shoes when they went dancing out at the old Saltair resort on the Great Salt Lake. The two of them put on quite a show, waltzing out across the polished oak floor of the ballroom to the music of the big bands. Him in his black suit and starched white shirt, Laura in her long blue chiffon dress that moved so deliciously when he swirled her. He loved being on the dance floor with Laura. She was such a beauty with her dark brown hair in long silky curls. She wore lipstick and rouge, back then, and a light brush of mascara on her lashes.

He held up one of the high-heeled shoes and ran his finger along the length of it, feeling the smooth texture of the suede. He was surprised by how new it smelled. How could that be? It had been a lot of years since Laura bought those shoes.

He looked at the soles and was surprised to see that they were hardly worn at all. That was odd. Maybe they hadn't gone dancing as much as he remembered.

As he pulled out the last two shoeboxes, a blue plastic binder fell out from between them. What is *that*? He didn't remember seeing it before. He picked the binder up and flipped through the pages. Most of the pages were typed, but some were in handwriting that looked like Laura's. There was a date at the beginning of each entry. How odd. If Laura had been keeping some sort of a journal, why didn't he know about it? Or maybe he did know about it, and he just didn't remember. Was that possible? He *had* been forgetting a few things lately.

He read one of the passages from the middle of a page.

> Loneliness doth weigh me down
> Tis a burden to go on
> For life hath lost its meaning
> Now that love hath come and gone

The handwriting was definitely Laura's, but it didn't sound like her. Was it her poem? He'd never known Laura to write poems. He read the verse again and decided she must have copied it from a book she was reading. But when he glanced at the top of the entry, he saw her name beneath the title as the author. She *must* have written it.

He read the whole poem from the beginning.

> This Man that I Hath Loved
> by Laura Young
> November 5, 1980
>
> I have naught to give you now
> For doubt hath robbed my soul
> And left this aching pain
> To fill the widening hole
>
> And yet in years gone by
> I swear your eyes did glow
> Did I mistake your look of love?
> If not, where did it go?
>
> Loneliness doth weigh me down
> Tis a burden to go on
> For life hath lost its meaning
> Now that love hath come and gone

He had to stop reading and catch his breath. Obviously, Laura was writing about him. Who else could it be? There wasn't any other man in her life. So what was she saying? That he didn't love her? Of course, he loved her. How could she think such a thing?

He read on, slowly, forcing his brain to focus on each line.

> Then comes the morning light
> I pray that I will find
> That I've confused myself
> And love doth still us bind

I rise and find you've gone
Without a word to say
To give me hope or comfort
To help me through the day

But come the eventide
You sit before your meal
Without a word of gratitude
Nor smile to help me heal

Through all this disappointment
When I look upon your face
I pray the Lord will bless me
And open your embrace

And if I see your love
I'll give you back my heart
I'll take you in my arms
We'll make a brand new start

Overwhelmed by the accusation in Laura's words, he dropped the binder on the floor. He couldn't believe what he had read.

He went to the bedroom window and stared out into the backyard, trying to convince himself that the words weren't true, or if they were true, it was just a mood she was in. Sure. That's probably all it was. She'd get that way sometimes. Moody. Especially when she was having her menstrual period.

Somehow, he didn't believe what he was telling himself. The words in the poem were too explicit, as if she had been thinking them for a long time. Words couldn't just pour out of a person like that if they weren't true. Could they?

Still, it might have just been a temporary mood. Maybe she'd written it after they'd had an argument or something. Maybe there were other poems in the binder that were more loving, some that would make him feel less attacked and guilty.

He went back and picked up the binder. Feeling nervous and not so sure he should be doing what he was doing, he flipped to another poem and began to read.

Night Comes, and the Wolves are Howling
by Laura Young
August 17, 1979

Day becomes night and the wolves are howling
Not in the shadows beyond the glass,
but here within my wounded soul
Beneath this icy moon, I wait for some small sign
A look or sigh of passion that shows that you're still mine
The morning light won't shine without your love
The birds won't sing and chatter
The flowers wilt and rot upon their drooping vines
I'd give my life if I could feel your love just one more time

The poem shocked him. The images were so sexual and raw, her pleading voice hard to bear. He couldn't believe Laura had written those words, but she obviously had. Was that howling wolf supposed to be him? No. Laura was the howler. Like that night at Blue Lake. It was the first night of their honeymoon, wasn't it? Yes. They had stayed in a hotel in Wendover before driving to California the next day. There was a full moon, and they had hiked out to the hot springs at Blue Lake. He'd never forget that night: Laura standing totally naked in the steaming water, her head thrown back as she howled at the moon. Then the coyotes started howling too.

When the coyotes finally stopped responding, Laura sank down into the water and wrapped her arms and legs around him and made love to him with such an intensity he could hardly breathe. It was like she'd been waiting her whole life to make love like that. All that passion had scared him. He couldn't change that fast, couldn't stop thinking of all those times he'd had to pull back to keep them from committing a sin. He was pretty sure Lori would have gone all the way even before they were married if he had pressed the issue. But he could never do it. How would he have faced his father if he got a girl pregnant? How would he have faced the Bishop?

He read her poem again, feeling the full impact of the other, more disturbing, words. *Her wounded soul. Her willingness to die just to feel his love*. He couldn't stand the accusation that he had pulled away from her. And what did howling beasts have to do with love anyway? Love was gentle and enduring, wasn't it? And of course, he loved her. They were together all those years, weren't they? They made love all the time. Well, maybe not as much later on, but she was the one who lost her passion as the years went by. She was the one who started closing her eyes and turning away.

After reading the lines one more time, he slammed the binder down. He wasn't going to take on this load of guilt. It was outrageous. He'd always been there for Laura, living with her, loving her, having their children together. And he was there with her the whole time she was dying. The grief and sadness had just about destroyed him, but he'd done it willingly. How could she not know that he loved her?

He went back to the idea that she was having her monthly blues, as she called them. Those hormonal blues that always made her cry and get mad at him for no apparent reason. That had to be it. Why was he letting it upset him so much?

He tried to stand up, but there was a strange sensation in his head. It was like the words of Laura's poems were buzzing inside there. *The flowers wilt and rot upon the vine . . . The icy howling moon . . .* Was it really possible that he had made her life miserable? Had he somehow broken her heart without knowing it? It was a version of himself he couldn't recognize or accept, and yet there it was, staring him in the face like the murky reflection in the old dresser mirror.

The guilt was driving him crazy. He had to get out of there and go someplace where he could think straight and get some perspective.

He put on his shoes and socks, pulled on a T-shirt, and hurried out to his truck. He sat there gripping the steering wheel wondering where to go. How could he run away from Laura's words when they were still racing around inside of his head?

Once again, he tried to tell himself that the words weren't true. He wasn't blind. He would have known if things were that bad for Laura. He would have seen it on her face and in her eyes. He would have felt it in his gut. He smashed his fist into the steering wheel. "It's not true. It can't be true."

He got out of the truck and slammed the door so hard he wondered if he'd broken it. But so what? That didn't matter compared to this guilt he was feeling. If he couldn't find a reasonable explanation for Laura's poems, he was going to be haunted by them for the rest of his life. He had to figure out what she was saying, and why.

He walked out to the mailbox and then back to the house as he tried to think what to do. Then he remembered the forlorn look on Laura's face those last months before she died. Was he responsible for that look? Was it a look of loneliness and despair that she had written about in her poems? No! Damn it! It was the cancer that made her look that way.

Even the doctor said so. She couldn't keep any food down. She was dying. Anyone would look sad and hopeless in that situation.

Tears filled his eyes and ran down his cheeks. He looked up at the sky and whispered, "Oh, honey. Tell me it's not true."

Then he had a hopeful thought. Maybe if he read everything in Laura's binder, he would find something that would help him understand. The entries all had dates, didn't they? Maybe if he went back far enough, he could find some happy ones, and he could figure out what had happened later on.

He hurried inside and sat on the bed. He picked up the binder and held it against his chest as he tried to summon up the courage to open it again. But then he noticed the boxes of Laura's clothes scattered all over the room, and he realized there was no way he could be objective surrounded by all that. He had to read the poems somewhere else. Somewhere . . . safer.

Suddenly, he knew where to go. The cemetery. He'd take the poems to Laura's grave and sit by her side. Maybe there he could read the poems and she could help him understand what they really meant.

Chapter 2

Aaron drove the short distance to the cemetery and parked out on the road. He got out of the truck and hurried across the sagebrush field with the binder of Laura's poems tucked safely under his arm.

At the top of the ridge, he stopped short. He couldn't see the cemetery anywhere. Was it gone? Had one of those developers finally gotten hold of the land with its great view of the valley and the Oquirrh Mountains beyond? He knew their plan. They wanted to chop it all up into lots and sell it to a bunch of fancy pants with money. So far, the town committee had blocked it, but maybe some of them had caved in. Was it possible? Could they have bought the land and moved Laura without telling him? No. They couldn't do that. It wouldn't be legal. The cemetery had to be there.

He raced down the hill in the direction he knew it should be, and when he got to a flat spot, he stopped again. Finally, he saw the top of one lonely gravestone just visible above the weeds. So that's what the problem was: the cemetery had disappeared into the weeds. Somehow, he must have lost track of the time and forgotten to take care of Laura's grave. And no one else was going to do it. Why would they? She was the only one buried there, except for a few old pioneers. It was his fault.

Great. That's all he needed. More guilt.

Hurrying to the grave site, he found a flat rock to set Laura's poems on and started pulling weeds in handfuls, tossing them angrily across the field as far as he could. While he was working himself into a frenzy, an old worry hit him: maybe he shouldn't have buried Laura out here. She had told him that's what she wanted, but now that he'd read her poems, he wondered if she was just going along with what he wanted. Maybe the silence and isolation were too much for her. Maybe that's why she was showing up in his dreams.

Sweat streamed down his face and burned his eyes, but he kept pulling up weeds until the whole area was cleared. When he was finished, he stood back to scrutinize his work. With the weeds gone, the place had a kind of plowed-up look. Only five of the old pioneer markers were still visible, and some of those were broken or half buried. Before long there wouldn't be anything there except Laura's lonely headstone. That wasn't good.

He stamped the dirt down around her grave as best he could. It helped a little, but he knew the weeds would be there again the minute he turned his back. He could plant grass, but how would he keep it mowed and watered? It would be hard to haul a lawn mower down there, and he'd have to bring the water in by hand. It was too much to think about right now when he was still reeling from Laura's poems.

Retrieving the blue binder from the rock, he sat down in the dirt next to her grave and ran his fingers over the inscription on her headstone.

Laura Clemens Young
Cherished Wife and Mother
January 15, 1926 - September 15, 1982

Had it really been ten years since she left him? Some days, it felt like she'd been gone forever, but the grief was still fresh. Why couldn't he get over the grief? Or maybe it wasn't grief. Maybe it was just a deep sense of loneliness.

A withered bouquet, half buried in the dirt, caught his attention. He must have pushed it aside when he was weeding. Odd, he couldn't remember bringing those flowers, but he didn't know who else would have done it. Sarah maybe, but wouldn't she have come by the house to see him at the same time? No, it couldn't have been Sarah. He must have done it, and it couldn't have been that long ago because they were still intact. So why couldn't he remember? Was there something wrong with his brain?

He picked up the flowers and crushed them into a fine powder in his palm, then blew the dust into the breeze and whispered, "Dust to dust."

Is that all there was to life in the end? The body turning to dust? He didn't want to believe it. He wanted to believe Laura would be waiting for him when he died just like he'd been told all his life, but at this point, he just wasn't sure that was true.

Pressing Laura's book of poems to his chest, he closed his eyes and tried to see her face. The only image he could find was the way she looked in those last terrible months before she died. She was so shrunken and pale. So miserable, lying in bed with the covers pulled up to her chin. She was always cold. He would crawl in bed with her and wrap her up in his arms to give her his warmth. But it didn't help much. He'd still feel her shivering and hear her moaning with pain.

It hurt too much to think about all that. He wanted to remember Laura when she was happy. But *was* she ever happy? Her poems might be saying she wasn't.

But of course she was, at first. He was certain of that. Something must have changed over the years. Why didn't he know what it was?

He looked at the binder, wondering again, why he'd never seen it before. Did she hide it in the closet every time she wrote a new poem and put it in the binder? There was something not right about that. Did it mean she didn't trust him? And was that lack of trust his fault?

A terrible thought struck him. What if the reason Laura got sick was from being unhappy and feeling unloved? If it was true, it meant he was to blame for her dying as well. Was it possible?

There was a tight pain in his throat that made him want to cry. It was a familiar pain that he had pushed down after Laura died, and now it had moved up into his throat again and was stuck there. He could hardly breathe. He opened his mouth and gasped for air, but the aching pain only got worse. Calm down, he thought. You've got to calm down.

He focused on his breathing, pulling the air through the pain, taking deeper and deeper breaths until only a dull ache remained. That's right. Numb it out. That's the only way he could bear it.

He lay down in the dirt with his arm across his eyes and stared into the darkness, trying to think of anything Laura had said or done to indicate that she was hurting. All he could come up with was her moodiness. That was understandable. Women could be emotional. He had always had to account for that and not let it get to him too much. If he had, it would have ruined their relationship. But what if that way of thinking was wrong? What if discounting Laura's moods is what ruined everything? What if her moodiness was her way of trying to tell him that she was hurting, and that she needed his help? He should have listened, no matter how unfair her complaints seemed at the time. He should have listened and tried to understand.

A cold wind came up and made him shiver.

Was he really so different from Laura? He didn't have anyone to talk to either, especially during that time she was dying. That was when he needed it most. And now, it felt like he'd been alone forever. Pushing through the days, doing his drywall work, coming home each night to an empty house. No one to eat with, or sleep with. No one to wake up to in the morning.

Still, it must have been even harder for Laura because she really wasn't alone. She had him right there the whole time, but according to her poems, she still felt alone and unloved. What a shame.

He sat up and stared at her grave, feeling frustrated and depressed. If she'd just told him what was wrong, they could have fixed it. "Why didn't you tell me, Laura? Why didn't you make me understand?"

He brushed the dirt off his hands and looked at the binder. Her words were all right there. It was too late to fix anything, but he could read what she had written and try to understand. He could at least do that. Opening the binder, he turned to the first page.

> Journal of Laura Young
> 1974 to —

He tried to think what happened in 1974 that would have started her writing sad poems. Seventy-four. Wasn't that the year Michael left for college? That's right. And then Sarah got married. Maybe that's what happened. Maybe Laura didn't know what to do with herself after the kids were gone. He seemed to remember her complaining after the kids left, asking him why he had to work all the time. But, of course, he had to work. He was working six days a week, trying to pay for Michael's college tuition and catching up after Sarah's wedding. It was his responsibility to take care of all that, wasn't it? And then, while he was still trying to pay off those bills, Laura started going to that chiropractor all the time, complaining, like it was his fault her back hurt. How could he know that the pain in her back was coming from a problem in her colon that was going to turn into cancer? There was no way he could have known that, could he?

Maybe he just wasn't paying close enough attention. Maybe the signs were there all the time, and he just didn't want to see it. He thought back, trying to find something that he might have missed. Then he remembered. There was that day he stormed out of the house and left Laura standing at the door with a terrible mixture of pain and anger on her face. She had asked him to stay home from work. Asked if they couldn't go to a movie, or a hike, or something. Then they argued. He should have known something was wrong. He should have gone back and held her in his arms and asked her what was going on. Instead he yelled at her. "What do you expect me to do, quit working so I can take care of you all the time? Who's going to pay the bills?"

Thinking of those words he said stung him, just as they must have stung Laura back then. How could he have been so cruel? But truly, he hadn't meant to hurt her. It was just that he was working such long hours and coming home to Laura's complaints every night. He would have liked to cut back and spend more time with her, but he was determined to get free and clear from the bills. He had wanted to set up a nest-egg for them, and maybe even get to a point where he could do something besides drywall work. Something that used a bit of his mind, instead of only his hands. His ruined hands that were always cracking and bleeding and gradually being destroyed by the drywall dust. But he never did try anything else, did he? He was still doing the same damn thing. Nailing up drywall. Taping and pushing around mud. The only difference now was that when he came home, there was no one there to complain. There was no one there to say anything at all.

He sighed and turned to the next page in the binder. He was surprised to see this one was labeled as a song. So now there was something else he didn't know about Laura. Apparently, she also wrote songs. He wondered if she sang them too. Maybe to herself when no one else was around. He had never known her to sing much.

As he read the words, he tried to figure out the tune.

Is it so Hard to Say?
A Song by Laura Young
August 2, 1974

Today I saw a look of love on your face
I looked again and saw it wasn't clear
Maybe it was only a reflection
Of the words I've been longing to hear

I love you, I love you,
I love you, is it so hard to say?
I love you, I love you,
I love you, but I've lost my way

The evening sun cast a glow on your skin
I thought perhaps that mine was golden too
I whispered that you were a handsome man
You beamed as if you knew it was true

You're beautiful, you're beautiful
You're beautiful, is it so hard to say?
You're beautiful, you're beautiful
You're beautiful, but I'm on my way

Every night and day
I wait for your touch
A few kind words
To show me you care
But my heart's growing cold

And the nights are so long
I can't expect you'll ever be here

The week was full of difficult tasks
My anger filled the words that I spoke
I begged you to forgive the things that I said
You couldn't resist a vengeful joke

I'm sorry, I'm sorry
I'm sorry, is it so hard to say?
I'm sorry, I'm sorry
I'm sorry, but I just can't stay

He couldn't believe what the song said. Had Laura really considered leaving him? It was something he wouldn't have considered in a million years. How could she even think such a thing, let alone write it down? And it looked like she was saying he was all wrapped up in himself, and that he never said he loved her, or told her she was pretty. It was ridiculous. She was complaining about everything. Of course, he said he loved her. He said it all the time, didn't he? He *did* love her, so why wouldn't he have said it?

His guilt was building as he tried to remember some situation when he had told Laura he loved her, but he couldn't bring anything to mind. Was it true what she said, or was his memory just getting that bad? He hit the side of his head with his fist, trying to knock something loose in there, but it didn't help.

He looked around, frantic to find something else to focus on—the sagebrush, the sky, the clouds—but he couldn't get away from a growing feeling of panic. He squeezed his eyes shut, trying to push the words of Laura's poems out of his mind. But then he saw an image of her that startled him. She was wearing that lush green suit she bought for their honeymoon. Her dark hair all shiny and swept back into long smooth curls, her mouth moist with sexy red lipstick. They were in California. In that park. She was sitting on the thick lower limb of that tree they had found, a tree filled with extraordinary white and pink flowers that looked like huge tulips. And there he was, down below with his camera, using the lens to peek up her skirt.

She had laughed as he moved the camera upward, looking at each part of her body—her legs, her hips. He lingered on her breasts, then zoomed in on her face, her lips, and that teasing sparkle in her eyes. The image of that day was so remarkably clear he could almost touch the gardenia in her hair, could almost smell it. That was love. So why couldn't she feel it? "Don't you know how much I wanted you, Laura?"

He winced when he realized what his words really meant. He desired her. But did he love her? She wrote something about that, didn't she? Something about taking her body, but not loving her. He flipped through the pages until he found the poem he was thinking of.

> You take my body as if it were your own
> And never see the ache of my desire
> Your love does not belong to me
> I am just your mirror

He read the verse again and again, the words sinking deep into his heart and mind. He tried to reject them, but he realized she was right. Even on that first night of their honeymoon out at Blue Lake, he was thinking only of how it would feel to be inside her for the first time. To make love, not to give love. But he had never experienced lovemaking before, so of course, he wanted it. She had wanted the same thing. It was obvious. Hadn't she opened herself to him, and given him the gift of her body? That's what he had thought at the time. Now, he wasn't so sure. Maybe she had wanted something more . . . but what?

The wind was picking up, and now, it smelled like rain. He looked across the valley to the Oquirrh Mountains and saw a storm brewing, but he wasn't ready to leave Laura. Not yet. He was trying to think if he had ever satisfied her, or if he had ever even considered what their love-making was like for her. Why didn't he know?

Not knowing, made him feel dumb, like when he was a boy hanging around with his friends, watching the girls go by, wise-cracking about what it would be like to have sex with them. Back then, he didn't understand a thing about girls. None of the boys did. The thought that he hadn't changed after all the years left him confused and filled with doubt.

Again, his thoughts went back to that first night of their honeymoon. They had hardly gotten back to their hotel room in Wendover when Lori pushed him down on the bed. She stood in front of him, slowly undressing, letting him watch her every move, her shiny eyes never leaving his.

Her breasts were so beautiful in the soft golden light from the lamp. Those sweet tender nipples, the curve of her belly, her soft brown hair down below. She was exquisite. Almost overwhelming.

She came to him. She unbuckled his belt. She took down his zipper and completely undressed him. When he was naked, she ran her fingers over his body. It was like she was feeling his skin and his bones. She did it in such an inquisitive way it sent a shivering thrill to his groin. Even now, sitting in the dirt by her grave, he could feel it.

Then, he realized the *truth*. She wanted sex as much as he did. "You did, Laura. You always did. Remember how you chased after me?"

It was true. When they were very young, back when she called him Arni, and he called her his little Lori. She followed him everywhere. She showed up, even when he was with his friends. He got so sick of them making fun of him, he finally told her she was too young for him, and to go away.

It must have broken her heart, but she *did* leave him alone. Then when she was sixteen or so, she came up to him after the matinee movie at the church and said, "Hi, Arni, what're you doing?"

"What do you mean, what am I doing? I'm standing here talking to you. And my name isn't Arni, it's Aaron."

"Oh."

She was so pretty and innocent, looking down, pushing the dirt around with the toe of her shoe. Then she looked up and gave him a brilliant smile. "I thought maybe we could do something."

"Like what?"

"I don't know. Maybe go for a hike or something. It doesn't have to mean anything."

At the time, he hadn't thought much about it. He'd just said, "Okay."

But maybe he'd said yes because he was remembering when they were younger, how they used to meet up in different places, and he would tell her about his adventures and his thoughts. He had never forgotten the way her eyes shined, like he was telling her the most exciting stories she had ever heard. No one else had ever listened to him like that, and it was still true. If only he could talk to his little Lori now and see her green eyes shine.

Thinking about those early days, got him wondering if some of his youthful ambivalence about her age had remained with him after they got married. Before the war started up, he'd never thought of Laura as someone he would marry. Then, after he got called up by the Army Air Force and got his orders, he went ahead and gave her an engagement ring. He still didn't know why, exactly. Maybe he just wanted to know someone would be waiting for him when, and if, he got back. He didn't know where he was going, or whether it would be dangerous. It was

World War II, and all he knew was that he was being sent on some kind of secret mission.

He heard a loud crack of thunder and saw dark clouds moving across the valley towards him. There was definitely a storm coming, but he still didn't want to leave the cemetery. There was another disturbing thought forming in his mind: maybe he really didn't love Laura as much as he thought. At least not at first. Maybe he had married her to make himself feel more secure. It was even possible that it was just so he could experience sex without feeling like he was committing a sin. He was just a kid. What did he know about love? What did he know about anything?

A bee buzzed his ear, flew away, then came back and buzzed him again. When it flew away the second time, he noticed a low reverberating hum in the air. He scanned the area around the cemetery and saw bees everywhere, flitting across the top of the sagebrush, hovering over the wildflowers, their tiny bodies glinting gold in the sun. Had they been there the whole time?

The humming of the bees seemed oddly familiar, like a sound he had heard before. But where and when was that? It felt important to remember, so he closed his eyes and searched for the sound in his memory. Finally, it came to him. The sound was from India. He remembered hearing a hum like that on his first trip out from the base into the countryside. He and a couple of air force buddies had gotten a pass to go into town. The other guys went straight to a bar, but he didn't drink alcohol, so he continued on alone, going deep into the city. Eventually, he ran into a passel of young kids who came at him from all sides. "You got bubble gum, mister? You got chocolate?"

The kids' eyes were bright and shiny, watching him, following his every move. They pushed and shoved, each little golden-skinned child trying to get close to him. It made him feel like a movie star. He laughed and walked along in the middle of his noisy little troop, loving every minute of it. It made him wonder what it would be like to have kids of his own, maybe a whole passel of them, swarming around him, waiting to see what he would say or do.

When he got to the edge of town, he kept going, but the kids turned back, yelling, "See you later, mister. You bring chocolate next time?"

He told himself, yes, he should remember to do that.

He lengthened his stride and headed down a dirt road, feeling exhilarated even though he was a little intimidated to be wandering off into the unknown in a foreign country. That day, it felt like if he just kept going, he might end up in some wonderful new life. It was the first time he thought about living in India, and the desire had grown from there.

After he had walked for an hour or so, he saw a group of people sitting beneath a giant tree at the side of the road up ahead. It was a special type of Indian tree. A banyan tree, they called it. And it was from under that tree that he heard that deep reverberating sound like the hum of the bees. "Aummm. Aummm. Aummm . . ."

As he got closer, he had realized it wasn't bees humming. The sound was coming from some people sitting under the tree in front of a wild-looking man with wild hair and a long disheveled beard. The man was naked to the waist and had a large round belly that didn't seem to fit with the rest of his thin bony body. His eyes were closed, and even though it looked like he was the leader of the group, he hardly seemed to notice they were there.

Aaron remembered watching the scene for a few minutes before sitting on the ground behind the group, a little off to one side. From there, he could see that wild-haired man was wearing a bizarre white cotton thing wrapped around his legs and abdomen, like some kind of elaborate diaper. That seemed silly, but there was something ancient and serene about the man's face that fascinated Aaron. He kept his eyes on him as he sat there listening to the group humming, "Aummm. Aummm. Aummm . . ."

Pretty soon, the sound got inside Aaron's head, and he started humming too, softly at first, then louder and with less reserve. He closed his eyes, matching his breath to the rhythm of the sound, As he did it, he felt himself melt into the deep resonant tones. Then the most amazing thing happened. It was like the sound was coming from everywhere and penetrating everything, including him. He had never felt so much a part of the world before. Had never had the feeling that he belonged exactly where he was. What kind of spell had been cast on him? Was it the place? The people? The sound?

The bee at the cemetery came back and buzzed him again, as if to remind him that India was just a dream. It was true. India was a far away dream that he would never see again. But that day he sat humming in front of the wild looking man, he thought his life had been changed forever. He believed that after the war, he would return to India and live there. It was the place he knew he should be.

He should have known it was just a dream. When he got back to the base that day, he tried to tell the other guys what had happened, but they just laughed and said he must be drunk.

He kept his thoughts to himself after that, silently dreaming of living in India while he went about his duties, loading the planes, keeping his eyes on things in the fuselage while the pilots flew the planes over the Himalayas into China. Sometimes the weather was so bad, it was impossible to think about anything, except whether or not they were going to survive. Flying the Hump was never easy.

Whenever they weren't flying, he'd get a pass and go out alone to the countryside to see if he could find that wild man again. He never found him, but sometimes he'd end up at the Brahmaputra River where he'd swim. There were snakes in that river, and he'd often feel their slick bodies against his skin while he swam. For some reason, he was never afraid of them. Maybe it was because he wanted to experience everything he could while he was in India, and that was an experience he knew he'd never have anywhere else. After the war ended, and he was back home, he kept thinking about India and wondering if there was any way he could get back there. Turned out, he got married instead, and he wasn't sorry about that. Not really.

As he ran his fingers through the loose dirt over Laura's grave, it occurred to him that he had never told her that much about his experience in India, and about wanting to live there. Actually, he hadn't told her much at all about the war. Why was that? His time in India was one of the most important experiences of his whole life, and yet he hadn't shared it with her. Were there other important things he hadn't shared with Laura? Things that would have brought them closer and maybe changed how she felt about him and their life together? If he had shared more, would she still be alive?

No. It wouldn't have made a difference. To believe that he had the power to change things, and he hadn't done it, was too unbearable to even consider.

The sky got darker and the smell of rain even stronger. When a flash of lightning streaked across the sky, followed by a quick burst of thunder, he knew he had better get out of there, and quick. He tucked the binder with Laura's poems under his T-shirt and made a dash back up through the sagebrush to the truck.

He dove into the cab and pulled the binder out to see if the pages had gotten wet. Some of them were damp across the top, but thank God, they weren't ruined. He could still read the poems.

Chapter 3

By the time he got home, the rain was coming down even harder. Not wanting Laura's poems to get any wetter, he left the binder in the truck and made a mad dash for the house. He ran through the house opening all the windows. Then he went and stood in front of the window in the living room feeling excited by the storm. It reminded him of the drenching monsoon rains in India when the kids would run out into the streets stark naked to play in the rain and the mud, twirling around with their arms in the air like those whirling dervishes he'd seen when he was over there. That's what *he* felt like doing now. Something outrageous and free.

Tearing off his wet clothes, he raced outside and ran barefoot across the lawn. He turned his face to the sky and opened his mouth to the downpour, like a man dying of thirst. Then he held out his arms and spun around like a dervish, going faster and faster until he could see the water flying off his fingertips. Pretty soon, his head was reeling, and he was gasping for breath. He sank to the ground and lay there feeling the cool slick wetness of the grass on his back.

He stayed that way until it suddenly occurred to him that the neighbors up on the hill might be watching him. The idea of them sitting up there watching the crazy ol' naked man lying in the rain got him laughing so hard his stomach started to ache. Then, suddenly, he was crying, and there was a loud wailing sound that he knew must be coming from him. It was like that terrible wailing he'd done after Laura died when he realized how utterly alone he was.

A few last sobs escaped him, and he closed his eyes and focused on the sensation of the splattering rain on his face. The drops were distinct, each one like a tiny knife. It made him realize how fragile he was. Emotionally and physically. For the first time in his life, he considered his own death. Even in the war, he'd never imagined himself dying. It just didn't seem possible. But now he felt it. Maybe it was that dream he had last night, seeing his bones being picked clean by the vultures. It seemed odd that the inevitability of his death didn't frighten him now. It didn't even make him sad. What it did was make him want to stop dragging himself through the days and start living again. If he didn't do something, he could die right now and there wouldn't be any loss.

The rain stopped. He opened his eyes and realized he was shivering cold. But he wasn't ready to get up. He stayed on the grass and watched the storm clouds blow by until there was nothing left but a clear, dazzling blue sky. When the birds started to chirp, it filled him with that joy he'd been missing and gave him hope that he really could change his life.

But where to begin? First he would have to deal with his guilt about Laura. And before he could do that, he needed to know if the things she'd written about him were true.

He struggled to his feet, feeling like he needed to talk to Sarah. She knew her mother, and she knew him. She might be able to give him some objectivity about the poems and help him understand what had happened.

He hurried into the house and sat on the loveseat next to the phone and dialed up Sarah's number. As the phone rang, he wondered what he was going say if he had to leave a message. Should he tell her that he'd been outside frolicking in the rain without any clothes on. No, she'd think he was crazy, and then he'd have to tell her the whole story about how he found Laura's poems in the closet and what he'd done down at the cemetery after that.

He was about to hang up when Sarah answered. He knew he had to say something, but he didn't know where to begin.

She said hello again, and "Who's there?"

"Sarah?"

"Is that you, Dad?"

"Uh, yes it is. It's me."

"You sound funny. Is something wrong?"

He heard the worry in her voice. "No, no, everything's fine."

"It almost sounded like you didn't know who you'd called."

"Oh, I was just . . . thinking."

"About what?"

"Oh, you know . . . just, uh . . . about things."

"Okay. Well, what have you been up to this rainy day?"

"I was cleaning up and—" A sob escaped him. He tried to cover it by clearing his throat.

"Dad. What's wrong?"

"Nothing. I was just—"

"What do you mean, nothing? It sounds like you're crying. Are you crying?"

Tears streamed down his face, and all the pain he had felt at the cemetery came rushing back. "I didn't mean to hurt her, Sarah. I didn't know."

"Hurt who? What's going on?"

"How could I know she felt like that? She never told me." The hard aching pain in his throat was making it hard to breathe again. He gasped for air.

"Dad, please. Calm down. Tell me what you're talking about. Is somebody hurt?"

"I . . . I . . . found it."

"Found it? Found what?"

He tried to answer her, but couldn't.

"Please, Daddy. Tell me what's wrong."

He took a deep breath and forced himself to say it. "I found . . . that binder. I found out how . . . unhappy she was."

"What binder?"

"Your mother's poems. She wrote things . . . terrible things."

There was silence, and then finally, Sarah said, "Where did you find it?"

The way she said it made him feel like she already knew about the poems. Was it possible? Had Laura shown them to Sarah, but not him? Had they talked about it behind his back?

"Dad, did you hear me? I asked where you found it."

He spit out the words. "In the closet. Hidden away like some terrible secret."

"What did you read that's got you so upset?"

"You don't know?"

"No, I don't. Tell me."

Now, he wished he hadn't called her. And why did he have to go and tell her about the poems? He was ashamed of what they said. It would be even worse if she found out what they said. What would she think of him? He was her father.

His shame made him realize he was naked, and that made him even more ashamed. What was he doing running around without any clothes on? He stood up and looked for something to cover himself with, but the only thing he saw was part of an old sweatshirt he had been using to dust. He held the phone against his shoulder while he tied the cloth around his waist, letting it hang down in front. When he sat down and pushed it between his legs, he realized it looked like those ridiculous diapers that old holy man in India wore. He thought of the man's eyes. The way they shone with such a penetrating light, as if he—

"Dad, are you still there?"

"What? Uh, yeah. I'm right here."

"You keep disappearing."

"I'm sorry. I can't seem to stay focused today. Got a lot on my mind, I guess. I'll call you later, okay?" He wanted to say goodbye before he revealed anything more. There was no use upsetting Sarah. It would only make things worse. He should deal with Laura's poems on his own.

"Don't hang up, Daddy. Talk to me. Tell me what Mom wrote that made you feel so bad."

"I'm sorry. I can't. I need to go now."

"But, Daddy, you called me. You must have wanted to talk."

"I don't know, I just . . ." A line from Laura's poem, popped into his head: *Is it so hard to say I love you.* He wanted to ask Sarah if what the poem said was true, but at the same time, he didn't want her to know what it said. He couldn't burden her with this. He should act like a father and be strong.

"Daddy, please let me help you."

It sounded like she really wanted to know, like she wanted to help. He blurted it out. "She hated me, Sarah. She said I gave her a miserable life, but I didn't know I was doing that. Why didn't she tell me? Why didn't she give me a chance?" He was sorry as soon as he said it. He should have hung up when he was going to. Or never have called her in the first place.

"That's not true, Daddy. She loved you. I know she did."

"Yeah, that's what I always thought too, but now I know different. She said I only thought about myself. That I was . . . self absorbed, and that I never said I loved her. But I did . . . didn't I?"

"Of course, you did."

"Then why would she write such . . . terrible things?"

"I don't know. Maybe she was just in a bad mood. You know, maybe she was having her monthly blues."

"That's what I tried to tell myself, but it had to be more than that. There are so many of those poems. All with the same terrible message."

"Well, you were working all the time. Such long hours. Maybe she thought you didn't want to spend time with her."

"But I had to work, didn't I? When was there ever time to do anything else?"

"I know. It's just that she—"

It sounded like Sarah was hiding something. "What did she tell you, Sarah?"

"Dad, we don't need to talk about this. It's too hard. It doesn't matter now."

"What do you mean, it doesn't matter?" he shouted. "I've got this crazy feeling I don't know who I am anymore. And that I never knew who she was. And now it sounds like you were in on it too."

"I don't think we should talk about this over the phone. I'll come to your house. Just give me a minute to change, and then I'll leave. Okay? I just got home from work."

"No! Don't come over. Just tell me what she said."

"No, Dad. I'm going to come. I'll get there as fast as I can. Give me an hour or so."

"Sarah—"

"Daddy, you should try to calm down now. Listen to some music or watch TV or something. Okay, I'm going to get changed and head over. I'll be there soon. Bye."

Sarah hung up and Aaron sat there staring at the floor worrying about what he had got started. When the phone started to beep, he slammed the receiver down and went to get his wet clothes from outside. He put them in the washer to do later, and then he went and got dressed.

While he waited for Sarah, he prowled around the house feeling a bad mix of anxiety and impatience. He knew he couldn't leave, but he felt trapped. He had to do something to distract himself or he might bolt from the house.

He went to the living room and sat down at the piano, his pride and joy, his baby grand that he had never completely learned how to play. As he fingered the keys, he tried to think of some tune he knew, something that would help change his mood. What was that old love song he used to know? *"Only love can make the darkness bright . . ."*

He tried to play the melody, but the notes sounded wrong. Had he forgotten how to play? Or was he just too sad and confused. He gave up. The song was just another accusation anyhow. *Only love can make the darkness bright*. But it hadn't worked for Laura, had it? And all that darkness was his fault.

His lungs felt short and tight, like his chest had the weight of the whole world on it, and he couldn't push through it. He jumped up and rushed outside to get more air. He had to find something, anything, that would give him some comfort and make him not feel so worthless.

When he saw his flock of quail perched on the rock wall, he knew they were waiting for him. Well that's something good, he thought. My little quail friends. At least they still love me. But how long had it been since he fed them? Had he forgotten to do that too?

He ran and got the bag of seed from the garage and went slowly towards the quail with his hand held out. They chirped and pecked at the bare stones in anticipation of being fed. He chirped with them as he scattered seed along the top of the wall. His little quail friends trusted him. Over the years, they'd gotten big and fat from his constant care and attention. He loved to watch them eat, their topknots bobbling excitedly as they pecked at the seeds. They weren't afraid of him, and they didn't judge him, and that's exactly what he needed right now.

Chapter 4

Aaron didn't hear Sarah arrive, but there she was standing near the back of the garage watching him. She was wearing blue jeans and a pretty blue T-shirt. He was taken aback at how much she looked like Laura. She was taller, but she had that same figure, the same dark brown hair, the same penetrating eyes that were hard to read.

She smiled as she walked across the grass to join him. "Wow, Dad. Those quail are huge. How long have you been feeding them now?"

He shrugged. "I don't know. Some of them were just babies when I started."

She gave him a nice long hug and then pushed back and gazed at him. Her eyes seemed worried. "Are you feeling any better?"

"I guess so. My little friends here have cheered me up some."

"That's nice. I'm glad you have them." She hooked her arm through his and said, "Hey, how about I fix us something to eat? I'm starving, and Annie and Sam will have already eaten by the time I get home. I've got one of my friends looking after them."

"Sure. But I might not have much to fix." He couldn't remember how long it had been since he had gone to the store.

She squeezed him around the waist. "I can see that. You're too thin."

They went inside to the kitchen, and Sarah opened the refrigerator. "Well, you're right about not having much. Looks like . . . milk, some butter, a couple of potatoes, a kind of shriveled up onion, and . . . eggs." She looked over at him. "Sounds like breakfast to me. "

"Breakfast sounds good. I'm not sure I had it."

She gave him a stern look. "You've got to eat, Dad. You've always eaten good food and taken care of yourself. But now you really *are* losing weight. It's not good."

He frowned and said, "Yes, dear."

She smiled at his joke, and as she began whipping the eggs, he saw the avocado on the counter. He grabbed it. "How about this?"

"Great. That'll give you a few calories"

"I can go out and see if there's anything in the garden, if you want. Most of it's past its prime, but there might be something."

She nodded. "A tomato and some kind of herbs would be nice."

He felt excited as he hurried outside. How long had it been since he sat down to a meal with Sarah? Had he *ever* done that, just the two of them, without her kids and her husband before he took off? Maybe he should invite her over now and then and not just wait for an invitation from her. That would be okay, wouldn't it? A daughter shouldn't mind if her father asked her over for dinner.

The garden was dying back, but he was able to find one nice fat tomato and a second one that was a bit misshapen, but that wouldn't hurt the flavor. He picked a bit of woody oregano and some parsley and headed back to the house.

As he entered the kitchen, Sarah looked up from the stove. He held up the tomatoes. "Will these do?"

"You bet." She smiled. "You know, it's your fault I can't stand tomatoes from the store. They just don't taste the same as yours."

He nodded. "I know. Too bad this is the last of mine for the year."

The kitchen was full of the scent of butter and garlic and herbs. He loved that smell. Living alone, he never did any real cooking. He just threw something together when he got hungry. Sometimes he'd just grab an apple and some nuts. Something like that.

As he chopped up the tomatoes and the avocado, he realized he was feeling quite relaxed and happy. He was glad that Sarah had come over. "It's been a long time since I did this."

"What's that?"

"Had dinner with someone."

Sarah looked surprised. "You don't ever have dinner with friends?"

"Well . . . they've kind of . . . disappeared."

"Really?"

He shrugged.

"What does that mean? Disappeared?"

Trying to dodge her question, he looked away and saw the loaf of bread on the counter. "I can make toast, if you want some."

Sarah turned to face him. "What's going on, Dad?"

"What do you mean?"

"I mean, why don't you have any friends?"

"I dunno. I guess, I'm . . . kind of a loner these days."

She shook her head. "That's not good. You need to interact with people."

"Why's that?"

"You know, to keep your mind active and alert."

"Well, it's not as if I've stopped thinking."

"I know, but you shouldn't . . . let yourself get so isolated. You have to keep engaged and keep learning new things. It's good for your brain." She shrugged. "Anyway, that's what I've read."

Why did she have to bring that up when they were all set to have a nice meal? Did she think he was going the direction his sister Miriam went? Is that what she was implying? That he couldn't read or think of any words? "I read too, you know. I always have."

"I'm sorry, Dad. I'm just watchin' out for you. I love you, you know?" She smiled and waggled the spatula at him before she turned back to the stove.

"Yeah, well, I love you, too. But you don't have to worry about me and my brain. It's fine. Couldn't be better." Sometimes he wasn't sure if that was true, but he didn't want her knowing about that.

He sat at the table where he could watch her. He could almost imagine it was Laura. How many times had he sat in that chair watching Laura fix him a nice meal.

Sarah did a quick toss of her head to get the hair out of her face. It was just like Laura used to do. It was such a familiar action, it made him feel like jumping up and giving her a hug. But he stopped himself. She would be surprised. Better not.

When Sarah brought the plates to the table and sat down, she looked like she wanted to say something. But she didn't.

That was fine with him, he didn't feel like talking either. They ate their omelets in silence, smiling and nodding to each other now and then. Nothing needed to be said. It was nice watching her eat and relish the food as much he did.

After they had finished, Sarah said, "Those tomatoes were heavenly, Dad. Remember how much Mom loved them?"

Aaron tried to smile. "Well, hopefully they grow nice tomatoes in heaven too. You know, heavenly ones." He meant it as a kind of joke, but she seemed to take it seriously.

"Do you believe in heaven, Daddy? Do you think Mom's there?"

"I want to believe it. I try to imagine her somewhere, but I don't know if there's a heaven or not. I can't . . . find her." He blinked hard trying to keep back the tears.

Sarah touched his hand across the table. "Even after all the years, it's still hard, isn't it? I think about her all the time."

"When she first died . . . I felt like she was still with me. I even heard her voice sometimes, or I'd get a sense of her behind me, or feel like she'd been in a room just before I entered. Sometimes, I'd wake up in the middle of the night and feel the warmth of her beside me. I'd hold my breath, not wanting to break the spell." The tears came back, and this time he couldn't stop them. "I guess that's when I . . . lost my friends. I didn't want anyone coming around. You know. Breaking the spell." He wiped his eyes with his sleeve. "But that's all gone now. I can't find her anymore, well, except in my dreams."

"And in her poems?"

He frowned. "Yeah. That."

"Can I see the poems?"

He realized he didn't know where they were. Had he brought the binder back from the cemetery? Or had he lost it out there? Or maybe he'd brought it home and put it somewhere safe. Why didn't he know? He panicked and looked to Sarah for help. "I'm not sure where it is."

"Well . . . where did you find it? Maybe that's where it is."

"I don't think so." He tracked back through the day. So much had happened: the rain . . . the cemetery . . . Laura's clothes. That's right, he still wasn't sure what to do with Laura's clothes. But he couldn't think about that. Where were the poems?

"Dad. Why are you looking so scared? You'll remember where it is. Just think about it. Where have you been today?"

"I've . . . I've been everywhere."

"Everywhere? What do you mean?"

"I went to the cemetery. I'm sure I had the poems there. And then I . . . I don't know. Maybe—"

"You went to the cemetery to be with Mom?" She took his hand and squeezed it.

"Yes, I did. But I know I brought the binder back here because it was wet."

"It got wet?"

"Not very wet."

"Well then, you must have brought the binder home."

"That's right. I did. I brought it home. But I can't think where I put it."

"Maybe you left it in the truck."

He let out a big sigh of relief. "Of course. That's where it is. It's on the seat of the truck. It was raining so hard, I left it there. I'll go get it now."

He hurried outside and got the binder from the truck. When he got back to the kitchen, Sarah was at the sink doing dishes.

"I'll just be a minute," she said.

He put the binder on the table and sat down to wait, feeling unsure. Did he really want Sarah to read the poems? Maybe he should tell her he'd rather wait for a while. Think about it more and talk to her later. No, she probably wouldn't like that. She'd come all that way.

While he waited for her to finish the dishes, he stared at his hands. They were dry and cracked from doing drywall all those years. What if that drywall dust was affecting his brain too, and that's why he was forgetting things sometimes, like where he put Laura's poems? But he generally remembered later, didn't he? It was probably just because he was distracted.

Besides, Miriam forgot things, and she was never around drywall dust. So it couldn't be that. Her memory just went. A little at first, and then after a while, she couldn't remember anything. She'd just sit in a chair and stare at the wall all day. He was nothing like that. Not even close.

Sarah finished the dishes and came and sat at the table. She opened the binder and slowly turned the pages. He watched her carefully every time she stopped to read a poem, but her face didn't give anything away. When she'd read several more poems, she closed the binder and narrowed her eyes. Her look worried him. Was she judging him, like Laura?

He focused his eyes on a smudge of strawberry jam on the table, and muttered, "I told you. She hated me."

"Don't say that. It's not true."

"Then why would she write such things?"

"Maybe the poems were just her way of . . . getting things off her chest."

"Well, it didn't work, did it? Those things she wouldn't say ate away at her, until she . . . died." He shouldn't have said that. But there it was.

"Dad, you can't blame yourself for that."

"Not blame myself? Of course, I blame myself. I might as well have put a gun to her head."

Sarah looked away.

He realized his hands were shaking, and he held on to the edge of the table so Sarah wouldn't notice. "Don't you understand what the poems are saying? It was my fault she got sick."

Sarah shook her head in disagreement, but she wouldn't look at him. Was she afraid of what he would see in her eyes?

"Tell me what you're thinking, damn it. I want to know the truth. Was it my fault?"

"It doesn't matter, Dad. It was a long time ago." She folded her arms across her chest and looked down at her lap.

"Please, Sarah. Tell me what you know. I've got to understand."

She sighed and looked into his eyes. "Mom was lonely . . . sometimes. She seemed to get more and more . . . depressed, I guess.

And after she got sick, you didn't have much time for her because you were always working. That hurt her a lot." Sarah looked away again. "When she died, I . . . I don't know. I guess I blamed you for a while."

It felt like she'd struck him in the face. He wanted to bolt from the house, but he felt dizzy. He wasn't sure if he could even stand up. He swallowed hard, pushing down bile that was burning his throat. "You're just like her. Both of you. Keeping your dark secrets. Why didn't you tell me?"

She gave him a hard look and shook her head. "No, Dad, I'm not like her. Not in that way. I *want* to tell you the truth. And the truth is, I did blame you at first. I was hurt and confused about why she had to die, and I knew she was upset with you sometimes. But then I remembered a poem I'd seen on her desk. Here, let me see if I can find it."

She flipped through the pages, and somewhere towards the middle of the binder, she found a folded sheet of paper. She unfolded it and said, "Yes, this is it. I remember the title, 'The Sin of my Discontent.'"

She looked up at him. "Do you want me to read it?"

"You may as well. It can't be any worse than what I've already read." He braced himself as she sat back and began to read.

> The Sin of My Discontent
> by Laura Young
> October 15, 1976
>
> Here within this hidden heart
> Where no one sees the trouble start
> Or sees the aching pain begin
> The anger grow, my secret sin
>
> I know the Lord would not condone
> My discontent, this dreadful moan
> I am a wife, I have a child
> My duty is to serve and smile
>
> Now all those men in coats and ties
> Would say to clear my soul of lies
> Just listen to the sacred word
> And let my questions go unheard
>
> I try my best to make them stop
> I pound my head, I find the mop

> I wash the floor, I dust the room
> With all that done, my thoughts resume

Sarah glanced up. "I'm sorry, Dad. I didn't remember exactly what the poem said. Are you okay? Should I keep going?"

He frowned and nodded. Everything was coming out. There was no use trying to stop it.

Sarah continued.

> Then walking on a summer's day
> With husband gone and child away
> I feel the urge to run and play
> And find a field where I can lay
>
> I think of how my life might be
> Perhaps beside the restless sea
> Where none can say what I must do
> And no strict censure will ensue
>
> Alone with just my own still mind
> In self-reflective thought I'd find
> A person I could know and love
> And some forgiveness from above
>
> The shadows dim and I must wake
> From this sweet dream my mind doth make
> I take myself back home again
> And hide away my sin

When Sarah finished reading the poem, Aaron looked at her in disbelief. "What does it mean?"

Her eyes were sparkling with tears. "I don't know, Dad. Maybe she was just saying she wanted more from life. More than you or I or Michael could give her."

"But what did she want?"

"Well, maybe she wanted to explore her own direction. You know, to feel free to speak her mind and to be valued for that."

"Why didn't she? I would have listened."

"I think she was doing what she thought she was supposed to do. I mean, isn't that what the poem says? That *the men in their coats and ties* would say she shouldn't pay attention to her questions and desires, that

God wouldn't like her discontent. But you and Mom were both just doing what you were brought up to do. What you thought God and the church expected you to do."

"What are you saying? That we had no choice in our lives? That we were just a couple of robots following along?" He felt like he was getting hit from all sides now. First, Laura's poems said he was insensitive, and now Sarah was saying he was a weak man who only did what he was told.

"I didn't mean it that way. I just meant you and Mom each had a role set out for you by your parents, by society, by the church, by . . . everything. We've all been taught to be the way we are. We're all like that."

"Not you. You do whatever you like." He stared at the table. He hated the idea, but maybe what Sarah said was true. Except for that period in India, he had never had any *real* doubt about what he had been taught, until Laura died. He felt so wonderfully free in India, like when he was a boy, before he got filled up with everyone else's ideas. He questioned everything when he was in India—his patriotism, his religion, his beliefs. But then he'd come home and all that somehow got buried. Maybe that's what Laura wanted. To be free, like he wanted to be free. To not have someone judging him all the time and weighing him down with their expectations. What would have happened if he had shared his feelings with her? What if he'd told her that he too felt controlled by those *men in their coats and ties*? Would she have realized they both felt the same and talked to him more?

But what if she thought *he* was one of those men? Was it possible? He shook his head, hard, trying to escape the idea.

Sarah touched his hand. "Daddy, what are you thinking? You look so worried."

"I'm just . . . trying to sort all this out. I feel like her poem is saying I was one of those men in their coats and ties, that I was controlling her life in a way she didn't like. But there were plenty of things I wanted to do with my life too, that I didn't get to do."

"But she was a woman. You were the patriarch, the man of the house. She felt like she should listen to you."

"I listened to her too, you know."

"Yes, but you had a life beyond this house. She had to stay home and be a wife and a mother and try to be satisfied with that."

He put his head in his hands, trying to understand. Then he knew what had happened. It was *those men in their coats and ties*. The men at church. They were the ones that told him he was the patriarch of the family, the one who was supposed to make all the decisions and guide his family back to God. He'd fallen for it hook, line, and sinker. They had convinced him that Laura was supposed to listen to him and stand by him through thick and thin. Her duty was to comfort him, feed him, and bear his children. He just assumed she was happy doing all that. He had never even thought to ask if she wanted something more. "It's true," he said. "All I thought about was me, me, me. I was a stupid, arrogant fool!" He slammed his fist on the table, and then he jumped up and went to the kitchen sink to hide his face.

"No, Dad. You're not arrogant, and you're not stupid. Not at all. Just about everyone lives according to what they've been taught. It's hard not to. You took on the role of the patriarch like you were supposed to, and Mom took on the role of your wife like she was supposed to. You worked hard out there in the world, and she took care of the house and me and Michael. You were both doing what you thought God wanted you to do. For some people that's fine, but Mom wanted more. There was a creative side to her that she needed to express. And she was smart. She could have done a lot of other things with her life."

Aaron took a deep breath and tried to push down the tension in his shoulders. "She should have told me, Sarah. I would have understood. Nobody's life should be that miserable. Look what it did to her."

Sarah stood up and took his hand. "Come on. Let's go sit in the living room. We'll be more comfortable."

He let her lead him in to the couch

"What am I going to do, Sarah? I feel like my whole life has been a sham. I didn't understand a thing that was going on around me."

"You're just human, like the rest of us. I'm sure Mom has forgiven you." She wrapped her arms around him. "Really, Dad. I think she's okay now."

He hoped with all his heart that was true. He couldn't bear to think of Laura resenting him for all eternity.

Then, he remembered something that gave him a little hope, something he hadn't thought about in years. He whispered, "Maybe it's true. Maybe she *did* forgive me."

"What are you thinking?"

"It's something she did that last night before she died." He closed his eyes, trying to remember every detail.

"What, Dad? Tell me."

"It's so clear in my mind, but it hurts."

"Tell me."

"It was . . . getting dark, and I went into the bedroom expecting her to be asleep, like she almost always was those last few weeks. But she was awake. Her eyes were almost completely black, and they had a shine to them that I hadn't seen in years. I didn't know what to make of it. I asked her how she was, and it surprised me when she said, 'I want a bath.'"

"Really? She wanted a bath?"

"Yes. I went to start the water, and then I came back to sit with her while the tub filled. She didn't say a word. She just watched me and held my hand. And then the most amazing thing happened."

He paused, trying to bring back the details of how he undressed himself, and then took off her nightgown and carried her in his arms to the bathroom. She was as light as air, hardly anything left of her by then, but she had an astonishing look of desire in her eyes.

Sarah touched his hand. "What happened, Daddy?"

"I . . . I was carrying her to the bathroom. She was a feather in my arms. And then, just like that, she kissed me. The most . . . sensual . . . kiss. You know, like we were young lovers again." He found himself crying again as he remembered that kiss, the passion, the longing, the pain it brought to his heart.

Sarah whispered, "See. She *did* forgive you."

He nodded. "Maybe. Maybe so."

"And then you gave her a bath?"

"Yes. I got in the bathtub with her, and she leaned back against my chest, and I wrapped my arms around her. We stayed like that until the water started to cool down. Then I wrapped her up in a towel and carried her back to bed and lay down beside her." He put his hand over his eyes and whispered, "She died that night."

"That's so beautiful, Daddy. You never told me that."

"It was so . . . private, you know. Such a special gift she gave me."

"And you gave her too."

"Do you think so?"

"Yes. I do."

She held his hand, and after a moment of hesitation, she said, "I don't know if you remember, but I came to the house that day. The day before Mom died."

"You did?"

"Yes, but I never told you what happened either. I didn't know how to explain it. It was so strange."

"Something about your mother?"

"Yes." Sarah shook her head. "Even now, I can hardly believe it happened. But it really did."

"What? I'd like to know."

"You were outside in the garden when I arrived, so I went to the bedroom to sit with Mom. It was like you said; her eyes were almost entirely black, with an amazing shine to them. I'd only been with her for a few minutes when she leaped out of bed. She got down on the floor. On all fours. It was so unexpected, I didn't know what to do. When I tried to help her get back in bed, she almost growled at me. I mean, it really sounded like an animal growling. I reached towards her arm to help her up, but she said, 'Get back!' The way she said it scared me, and all I could do was back up against the wall and watch. It was as if she was in a battle for her life, as if she was a tiger, or something, and she was fighting some terrible beast. She crawled around the floor, striking at the air. I could almost see the thing she was fighting, the way she'd go at it until it struck back, and then she'd retreat and wait for the right moment to strike again, all the time making those growling sounds."

Tears streamed down Sarah's face. "I think she was battling death, Daddy. That's what it was, and there was nothing I could do to help her."

Sarah began to sob, her whole body was shaking. Aaron held her. Why hadn't they talked about these things before? Maybe it would have helped them both. Why was it so hard for people to talk to each other?

Finally, Sarah sat back and wiped the tears from her face. "Do you think that's what it was, Daddy? Do you think it was death she was fighting?" Her lip quivered as she spoke.

"I don't know, honey. I don't know much of anything right now. All I know is that I wish she was here with us. There are so many things I want to say to her. So many questions I want to ask."

"I miss her too. Even now, there are things I can't talk to anyone else about."

He let out a strained laugh. "I used to talk to her all the time. After she was gone, I mean."

"You did?"

"Yeah. Mostly when I was driving. People probably thought I was crazy."

Sarah laughed. "Nah. They probably just thought you were singing along with the radio."

"Well, I do that too sometimes."

"Me too." She nodded toward the piano. "Do you ever play that anymore? And sing?"

He shook his head. "Not much."

"You really should. You have such a wonderful voice."

That surprised him. "I do?"

"Of course, you do. Don't you know that?"

"Well, maybe. I just sing to myself."

"You can sing for me any ol' time."

He smiled. "Maybe I'll practice up and do that one of these days."

"That would be nice. I'd love to hear you sing again."

They gazed at each other, and Aaron felt a warmth between them he wasn't sure he'd ever experienced before. If only Laura could be there to see how much she meant to both of them. If only—

No, he wasn't going to think about it anymore. He had been asking himself those "if only" questions all day. Now, he was exhausted and needed to be alone. He patted Sarah's knee. "You know, it's getting late, honey. Your kids will be wondering what happened to you."

"They're okay. I asked my friend Julie to watch them. But you're right. I probably ought to get going. Will you be okay?"

"Yes, I think I will now. Thank you for coming, honey. You really helped me."

They sat silently for a few more minutes, then he walked her to the door. When they were outside, he said, "Maybe I'll go down to the desert."

"Really?"

"I think I might."

"When?"

"I don't know exactly."

"You'll tell me before you go. Right?" She gave him that look that he knew was a warning.

"Sure. Why wouldn't I?"

"I don't know. Sometimes you forget things like that."

"I do?"

She nodded and smiled. "Yeah. Sometimes."

They gave each other a final hug, and as she drove away the exhaustion hit him even harder. So much had happened that day it felt like it was going to take a very long time to sort it all out. Laura's poems had made him feel fragile and unsure of himself, like he didn't know who he was anymore. It made him think he might be headed for a change of some kind. He wasn't sure what it was, but it felt like there was nothing he could do to stop it.

Chapter 5

Aaron lay in bed that night telling himself that from now on he had to pay attention to what was going on around him. If he had been doing that with Laura, maybe she would still be lying there beside him, and he wouldn't be struggling to understand what had happened and how much of it was his fault.

Well, he didn't have Laura, but he had her poems, and if he was going to read them all, he might as well get started right now before he found some excuse.

He sat up and turned on the lamp next to the bed and grabbed the binder. As he skimmed through the pages, he kept hoping he would find a poem that would tell him Laura wasn't always unhappy. It wasn't there. Either she was miserable the whole time, or she only wrote poems when she felt miserable. There was no way he could know which it was, and he was worn out from the long day of trying to understand.

He put the binder aside. He needed sleep. He needed to go to sleep and wake up in the morning and get on with his life. There was nothing he could do about any of it now, except feel guilty, and that wasn't going to help. Not Laura. Not him. Not anyone.

As he lay there, rolling from side to side, trying to escape his miserable thoughts, he decided he had to get away. If he went down to his property in the desert for a while, he could be alone and think. Yes. That's what he should do. He didn't have any drywall work lined up, and he needed the peace and solitude of the red rock desert now more than he had ever needed it. Not to escape Laura, but to make sense of everything in a place where he could do it without all the guilt.

The next morning, he woke up with a headache, but he wasn't about to let that keep him from going forward with his plan. If he stayed home, he'd end up moping around, maybe for the rest of his life.

He went to the kitchen and splashed cold water on his face. Then he wolfed down a banana and a handful of almonds for breakfast and hurried back to the bedroom to dress. That's when he saw the boxes of Laura's clothes. He'd better take care of those on his way.

Working quickly, he carried the boxes out to the truck, forcing himself not to think about what he was doing. He would drive the clothes down to the thrift store, pick up some food, and then head for the desert.

When the boxes were all loaded, he added his sleeping bag and the cooler. He was almost ready to leave when he remembered he might want some tools down there. He grabbed an ax, a rake, a sledge hammer, and a shovel. He would need those if he decided to start digging out the foundation for the little house he'd always planned to build. A big project like that would be good right now.

He put the tools in the truck and went back inside for a last look around. When he got to the bedroom, he saw the binder with Laura's poems on the table. He hesitated, but then he decided once he got his head clear, he might want to read more of the poems. They weren't going away, that's for sure.

He grabbed the binder, and when he got back out to the truck, he put it on the seat right next to him. He patted it and said, "I'm not going without you, Laura. I never will. I promise."

As he drove down the hill and across town to the thrift store, his old guilt started up again. Maybe he should've kept aside a few of Laura's clothes to remember her by. When he got to the thrift store, he should go through the boxes and pick out some of her special things, clothes he wouldn't want anyone else wearing.

No, he couldn't go through all that again. He had her poems, didn't he? Those said more about her than anything. And he had all of their special treasures back home in Laura's cedar chest. That should be enough to keep his memories strong.

When he got to the thrift store, he worked quickly to get the boxes inside. As he carried in the last one, he saw a greedy girl already picking through the clothes. He yelled. "What do you think you're doing?"

The girl looked shocked. "Well, I'm just—"

"Why can't you at least wait until I'm gone?"

The girl's eyes told him his anger was unfair. He dropped the box and ran out of the store. He sat in the truck trying to calm down. What was wrong with him? Laura was gone. She didn't need those clothes anymore. He told himself to stop thinking about it. You were going to the desert. Remember? Now go buy some food and get on the road.

Having a purpose helped, and it got him thinking maybe he should go to that little farmers market he knew. It was a bit out of the way, but he was sick of eating that crappy produce they sold at the grocery store. He wanted the quality of fruit and vegetables his father used to sell off his produce wagon, something that hadn't been picked too soon and had some flavor.

When he got to the farmers market, he bought things that would be easy to eat on the road, peaches and nuts, apples and pears. He kept out an apple and some nuts, and put the rest of it in the cooler in the back of the truck. Then he drove across town and got on the freeway. The morning rush hour was just about over, which was great. He should be able to get down to the desert before dark.

As he drove along in the fast lane, he noticed how blue the sky was. Shimmering blue. And the whole valley was speckled with the gold and red colors of autumn. There was even a bit of snow up on the top of Mount Olympus. What a perfect day to start living a new kind of life.

At the south end of the valley, he leaned into the windshield to see if the hang gliders were up there flying around. Sure enough, there were several of them soaring on the updraft above the cliffs, speckling the sky with their bright canopies of red and blue and yellow.

Those hang gliders always made him think about his parachute training before he was sent to India. What a thrill that was. The exhilarating freefall, the lift when you pulled the cord. Hang gliding would be even more fun. You could stay up there and play in the air forever, if you wanted to. He should try it sometime.

He had to pay attention as he drove through the congestion in Provo, but once he was though there, he entered the kind of rural landscape he loved, fields of golden grass and old farm houses set back from the road. Just about every one of them had a row of poplar trees on one side to block the wind. Poplar trees were special to him. Like old friends. He remembered climbing them when he was a kid, remembered how they swayed in the wind once you got way up there in the top branches.

Just past the turnoff to the little town of Santaquin, he saw a man on a horse leading a lively colt. It put him on his guard. It reminded him of that time they were on their way to Yellowstone. A man on a horse leading a colt. The colt got spooked and bolted right in front of them. Then there was that terrible thud. That sound was embedded in his mind along with the pitiful cry of the poor creature bawling in pain. But there'd been no time for him to worry about the horse; Sarah and Michael were in the back of the truck in the homemade camper he had made, and they weren't strapped in.

Turned out, they were a little scared and little sore from the sudden stop, but they were okay. But that wasn't the end of it. The old man on the horse was furious, blaming Aaron for hitting the colt, instead of blaming himself. He growled obscenities and demanded that they stay with the poor thing while he went for his rifle. When he came back, he shot the animal in the head so quickly, he and Laura didn't have time to keep the children from seeing it.

He still felt sorry about that little horse. Sorry he hadn't seen it in time to get the truck stopped. Sorry the kids had to see it die. He had told Laura there was nothing he could have done to avoid it, but now, he wondered if that was true. Maybe he just hadn't been paying attention, like he hadn't paid attention to Laura.

But that was the past, and this was the day he was trying to get away from all that. Now, if he could just force his mind do it.

He saw the sign indicating that the little town of Nephi was just up ahead. That helped. He could stop and get gas and change his focus.

He took the exit and pulled into the first station. After he filled up, he checked the oil and found out it was low. He was about to head inside to buy a quart when a scraggly looking guy with long dirty blond hair and intense blue eyes limped over and said, "Hey, man. You headed south?"

Aaron wasn't so sure he wanted to answer. The guy reeked of alcohol, and he obviously hadn't washed in a long time. Still, he was wearing green military camouflage, so he might be a vet. He should help a vet.

The guy came closer. "I had a ride with a trucker, but the jerk took off when I went to the john. What a fucking asshole."

Aaron winced. Didn't the guy know using that kind of language made him seem crass and out of control. No wonder that trucker left him behind.

Aaron tried to think of an excuse to get out of taking him on-board, but the guy said, "Please, man. I don't wanna get stuck in this place. You gotta help me."

Aaron thought about it. Well, why not? It wouldn't be the first hitchhiker he had picked up, and if he had somebody to talk to, it might keep him from thinking about Laura's poems. He shrugged. "Well, I can take you south as far as the exit to Hurricane. I've got to turn off there."

"That'll do. I'm headed just down the road from there. To Saint George." The man threw his duffel bag in the back of the truck and got into the passenger seat real quick, like he was afraid Aaron might change his mind.

Aaron went into the station and paid for the gas. He stood at the counter thinking there was something else he was supposed to get. Was it something he needed for out in the desert? When he couldn't remember what it was, he let it go and went back out to the truck. He couldn't believe what he found there. The dirty guy had Laura's binder, and he was snooping through the pages.

He grabbed the binder, and said, "Hey, that's none of your business." He put it in the side-pocket of the door next to the driver's seat.

The guy just shrugged. "Didn't mean to pry, man." He stuck out his hand. "By the way, my name's Daniel. What's yours?"

Aaron eyed him for a minute, then stuck out his own hand. "I'm Aaron."

As they shook hands, Aaron noticed black dirt under Daniel's nails, and the ends of his fingers were yellow, probably from smoking. So he was a drinker and a smoker. Oh well, he had picked up some guys like that before. They weren't all bad.

He started the truck and as he headed back to the freeway, Aaron mustered a smile. "So, where you headed?"

"I just told you. I'm goin' to Saint George."

"Oh, that's right. You said that. You got a job down there?"

"A job?" The guy laughed and pushed the dirty blond hair back from his face.

"I mean, well . . . you must have some reason for going there."

"Winter's comin', man. Gotta get down there and stake out my claim before everybody else does."

His claim? What did that mean? Was he a gold digger? "Uh, what kind of claim you got?"

"You know . . . my place to camp. They won't let us sleep in the damn park anymore, so I have to find a place out on the edge of things. Makes it hard, though. No place to wash up, or . . . " He looked down at himself and scowled. "Come to think of it, I haven't washed up in a while. Guess I'm pretty stinky. Sorry, man."

Aaron shrugged and gave him a wry grin. "I've smelled worse."

"Oh, yeah?"

"You're not the first person I've picked up out here, uh . . . what was your name again?"

The man stared straight ahead. "The name's Daniel. Daniel. Like I said."

"Sorry, Daniel. I'm not so good with names."

The man looked out his side window. "Yeah. Well, whatever."

Aaron glanced over. The guy wasn't bad looking, just a little round in the face from the extra pounds he was carrying. But there was a wariness in his eyes that told Aaron he should be careful. The way the guy had his elbows pressed against the sides of his body made it look like he was trying to hold himself together. Why was he so tense? Was it the way he was living, homeless, and outside? That could do things to a man. The cold. The isolation. Aaron knew about that part.

He decided he should go easy on the poor fellow and find out more about him. "Looks like you were in the Army. Where'd you serve?"

The guy looked over with an expression that made Aaron think he shouldn't have asked the question. But after a long pause, Daniel answered. "I was in Nam."

"Oh . . . so it's not just for show."

"What's that?"

"What you're wearing. You know. Lots of kids wear camouflage these days. I've even seen it on girls. It doesn't necessarily mean—"

"Oh yeah. Right. But it doesn't hurt to wear camouflage when you're livin' out on the edge of things. If you know what I mean."

Aaron wasn't sure he *did* know, but he nodded as if he did. He looked up the road to see where he was, but he wasn't sure. Probably halfway to Cedar City. If so, they were making good time.

He drove on in silence for a while, and then he looked over at Daniel and said, "Uh . . . what were we talking about?"

"My clothes."

"Oh. That's right. You're a vet."

"Yeah."

"Me too. Army Air Force. World War Two."

Daniel perked up. "Really? Where'd you serve?"

"India."

"India? We were in India?"

"Yeah. We were flying supplies into China for the ones who were fighting the Japanese. You know, after the Burma Road got shut down."

"Really? You were a pilot?"

"Nah. Mechanic and crew chief. You know, the guy back in the fuselage with the gasoline."

"Gasoline?"

Aaron laughed. "Yeah. Big barrels of hundred-octane gasoline. The real explosive stuff."

Daniel shook his head. "Sounds kind of dangerous."

"You're right about that. One time, I was keeping tabs on things in the back when I noticed one of the barrels was leaking. I hurried up to the pilot in the cockpit and said, real casual like, 'Hey Joe, you might want to put out that cigarette. One of those barrels back there is leaking.' Joe put his cigarette out real quick, in the palm of his hand." Aaron chuckled, remembering the scene.

"Funny. So you know how to fix planes?"

Aaron shrugged. "Well, C-47s. But it's been a while."

"I've got an uncle who served in World War Two. He told me those C-47s were great planes."

Aaron nodded. "They really *were*, but we didn't have the best of them in India. More like the bottom of the barrel. After a while, they started falling apart. To keep them running, we had to cannibalize the ones that had crashed, or just plain couldn't fly anymore. Kind of scary when you're flying the hump."

"The hump?"

"You know, the Himalayas. That's what we called them. The hump."

"Oh man. You were flyin' over the Himalayas? That'd scare the hell out of me, even in a good plane."

Aaron accelerated so he could make it over the top of the next hill without shifting down. As they reached the summit, he turned back to Daniel. "What were you saying?"

"*You* were sayin'. You were tellin' me about flying gasoline over the Himalayas."

"Oh yeah. The Himalayas. They're the most beautiful mountains in the world, and the highest. But that's not so good when you're trying to fly over in a storm, or at night without navigation. So many of our planes crashed and went down into the jungle. We started calling it the Aluminum Trail because you could see the sun reflecting off the metal when you flew over." Aaron realized he was talking a lot, and he was talking fast, but he hadn't talked to anyone like this for a long time and it felt good.

Daniel cleared his throat and coughed. "You come out of it okay?" His voice sounded strained.

"Thankfully, I did. Just one bad slash on my knee when we were loading cargo. We were short on coolies that day and had to do it ourselves."

"Coolies? You had the enemy loading cargo?"

Aaron was surprised by Daniel's lack of knowledge. "They weren't the enemy. They were Chinese. We were helping the Chinese. You know, against the Japanese."

"That right?"

Aaron shook his head. "You saying you don't know about that?"

Daniel gave him a disgusted look. "Well, I never really heard about that part of the war. Guess I could ask you some questions about Nam that you wouldn't know."

The man was getting edgy again, like when he first picked him up. He shouldn't have made him feel dumb. "I'm sorry, my friend. I didn't mean to judge you. Hardly anybody remembers World War Two, especially not what we were doing in India. And I guess people want to forget about a war once it's over."

Daniel turned toward the side window and muttered, "You got that right, brother."

Aaron realized he had been talking so much about himself, he hadn't considered that Daniel might have his own stories to tell. "What about you? Were you in the thick of it? Over there in Vietnam?"

Daniel frowned. "Yeah. I guess you could say that."

"Were you wounded?"

He hesitated, then said, "Yeah, I'm wounded, all right. Got hit by shrapnel. Ruined the shit out of my hip."

"I'm sorry to hear that."

He glanced over and saw Daniel staring at him with his intense blue eyes "But I got lots of them, too. Killed the shit out of 'em!" He started squeezing his hands together in a strange way.

Aaron was startled by the amount of venom in the man's voice. He waited for him to say more, but he went quiet.

"That must have been hard," said Aaron. "It was dangerous flying the hump, but I never had to kill anyone. We weren't the ones dropping the bombs or shooting down Jap planes. The Flying Tigers did that. We just carried supplies, and tried to—"

Aaron heard a little moan, and when he looked over, Daniel was squeezing his hands again, and his eyes had a frantic look. "Those people I killed . . . they were just kids. You know? They were . . . hell, you don't want to hear about that."

"War's a terrible thing. I know that."

"So why am I alive and they're dead? Can you tell me that? If it wasn't for me, those kids coulda grown up. They coulda got married and had kids of their own. Shit, maybe even grandkids by now. I can't stop thinking about it. All those kids I killed." His voice cracked. "They shouldn't have made me do that. Nobody should have to live with that. Every day. Every night. I can't stop seeing them."

Aaron didn't know what to say to comfort the man, so he kept quiet.

Daniel continued to squeeze his hands, until finally, he threw them up in the air. "I don't know why I'm talking to you about all that crap. Screw it. Fuckin' goddamn war." He hit his legs with his fists. "Now, the damn doctors say I'm going to end up in a wheelchair because my hip's gettin' worse. How am I going to survive in a fuckin' wheelchair?"

"That's not good. Isn't there something they can do for you?"

"Sure, they'd be happy to cut on me again, but that'd just leave me worse off than I already am. I've been through enough of that." He rubbed his hip, as if talking about it made it hurt more. "So far, I can get by with my pills. Barely. Speaking of which, I could use one right now." He dug around in his coat pocket and pulled out a little plastic bottle. He took a pill out of it and swallowed it without water. Then he pulled out a pack of cigarettes, and his hands shook as he lit one. He inhaled deeply and blew out a big cloud of smoke.

So much smoke swirled around the cab, Aaron couldn't keep quiet. He hated cigarette smoke. It was nothing but pure poison. "I'm sorry, but it seems to me those cigarettes are doing you as much harm as anything. You could at least roll down the window and let some of that smoke out."

Daniel opened the window and faced into the wind as he exhaled. It didn't help. His smoke still filled the cab. Aaron coughed and Daniel swatted at it with his hand and muttered, "I didn't smoke these things before Nam. Fact is, I didn't do a lot of bad things before Nam."

Aaron wondered if it was true. Was he just a regular guy before the war? Had the war turned him into a broken homeless man, killing himself with his bad habits? One thing was obvious; the guy wasn't eating right. His face was pasty, and he was overweight. "What do you eat, Daniel?"

"What?"

"I was wondering what you eat. You don't look like you eat right."

Daniel glared at him. "Well, I ain't exactly rollin' in dough, ya know."

"Well, you must be eating. You're not wasting away."

"What of it?"

Aaron felt he shouldn't just stand by and let the man kill himself with his cigarettes and poor nutrition. "I'm just saying your body can't heal itself if you don't eat right. You can't survive on junk food. You've got to have some fruits and vegetables. You know, from a garden."

"What do you think you are, some kind of fuckin' nutritionist? You don't know nothin' about it. The last thing I need is some smart ass guy who got an itty bitty scratch on his knee in the war preachin' at me."

Aaron felt the heat rise to his face. "There's no need to insult me."

"Yeah, well, you insulted me. You don't know shit about my life."

This wasn't going well at all. Aaron decided he'd better hold his tongue and focus on driving.

Daniel wouldn't let it go. "Give a man a ride and ya think you've got the right to judge him. Bunch of shit. Why don't ya just pull over and let me out."

Aaron considered the idea, but that wouldn't be right. "I can't leave you stranded out here. What if you can't get another ride?"

"Who gives a shit?"

"Do you have to keep saying words like that?"

"Like what? Shit? You don't like me saying, shit? Well, shit, I guess, I oughta stop saying shit then."

Aaron focused on the road and tried to relax. He could understand a man cussing sometimes out of frustration or anger, but this guy's foul mouth felt like a physical attack. Maybe he shouldn't have said anything about the man's eating habits, but he was only trying to help. But then, maybe the guy was beyond help. Maybe there was nothing anyone could do for him. Could a person get to that point, where they were beyond help, where you just had to let them go? Yes, he knew that from Laura. In the end, there was nothing he could do except watch her die and then start crying.

He didn't want to think about Laura right now. And he didn't want to think about this hitchhiker's troubles. He'd left home that morning to get away from all that. It might help if he could get out of the truck and walk around for a minute. Maybe he should do it. He needed to pee anyway. He saw a ranch exit ahead and slowed down to take it.

Daniel shot him an angry look. "So you *are* gonna kick me out, eh? Just like that. What am I supposed to do way out here with my bad hip?"

"Calm down. I've just got to relieve myself. Maybe you should too. I'm not planning to stop again until we get to Cedar City."

Daniel rubbed his forehead so hard it left a streak of red. "Sorry, man. Shit. I'm so fucked." He held up both hands. "I know, I know. You don't like that kind of language. Sorry."

Aaron decided not to comment on that. He drove down the dirt road until they were away from the highway. Then he stopped and got out.

Daniel looked like he wasn't going to get out. Maybe he was still afraid he was going to be left behind. Aaron yanked open the passenger door and said, "Come on. Let's take a break."

Daniel didn't budge.

"Are you gonna just sit there and sulk?"

The man looked scared, so Aaron softened his tone. "Look. I give you my word, I won't leave."

Daniel still looked unsure, but he finally got out of the truck.

They walked off the road into the juniper trees. Daniel seemed to be moving all right, if a little unsteady. Maybe those pills really *did* help him. Aaron wondered what kind of pills they were. Some kind of narcotic, probably. He remembered what narcotics had done to Laura in the end. Made so she couldn't think straight or do anything but sleep most the time. It couldn't be good for a person to be taking those pills all the time, but Aaron knew pain like that was hard to live with.

They turned away from each other and neither spoke while they peed.

As they headed back to the truck, Aaron said, "What's in those pills you take? You seem to be moving better, but I'm wondering what else they're doing to you."

Daniel didn't answer, and Aaron didn't press it.

As soon as they were back on the road, Daniel fell asleep. His head was leaning against the window, and it made a little thump every time there was a bump in the road.

Aaron looked the guy over again, wondering how old he was. Probably forty or forty-five. It was hard to tell, but he'd have to be at least that old if he'd served in Vietnam. He looked younger than that, but maybe it was because of his round face. And he seemed innocent too, despite his foul language and all he'd been through. Maybe the war had just stopped him in his tracks and kept him from growing up. Now, it sounded like all he did was wander around doing nothing. It was sad to see a man waste his life like that.

It was obvious Daniel had a lot of self hatred from killing those people in Vietnam. Was that what kept his hip from healing? Could a person's mind affect their body that much? He wasn't sure, but it made him wonder again if that's what happened to Laura. She hid her feelings, just like she hid her poems. What if those trapped feelings festered inside her and that's what made her sick?

It was a disturbing thought that he didn't want to dwell on, especially not with a stranger sitting next to him, snoring away.

He glanced at Daniel again. His mouth was wide open now, and his heavy breathing filled the cab with the smell of stale alcohol and cigarettes. The odor wasn't pleasant, but Aaron couldn't help thinking how vulnerable and damaged the man looked. If only there was something he could do to help him.

He opened his window a crack to let in some fresh desert air. The sweet familiar smell of the sage gave him an idea. Maybe the hot springs out by his property would help Daniel's hip. Mineral water was supposed to be good for joint and muscle pain. In fact, it was good for all kinds of things, according to what he had read. It would be wonderful if his hot springs could keep Daniel from ending up in that wheelchair.

The idea excited him, and he wanted to wake Daniel to tell him about it, but then he thought maybe it was better to wait. The man was a handful. He should see how they got along the rest of the trip and decide later if he wanted to take him out to his special place.

Chapter 6

Aaron was amazed at how well Daniel could sleep with his head bobbing against the window. His snoring was annoying, and he wasn't very good company when he was asleep like that, but at least he'd given Aaron some compelling things to think about while he drove.

Daniel seemed like he had been totally ruined in Vietnam. Aaron hated to see that. He'd always been grateful for his own war experience. Not only had he found freedom from all the rules and restrictions of his life in Utah, he had been able to experience his own sensuality without guilt. He remembered the first time it happened. He'd gone out for a walk and ended up on a ridge above a tea plantation where young Burmese women were picking tea. They had on brightly-colored skirts, but they were naked on top, their breasts glowing in the yellow sunlight. He had never seen anything like it, and yet, in the steamy humidity of India, it had seemed perfectly natural. He'd felt like he had arrived in some kind of Garden of Eden. A place with no sense of good and evil where he could experience his feelings without worrying that he was under the influence of Satan. Later, when he thought about it, he realized how much he resented the religion he'd grown up with back in Utah, and how it had always made him feel ashamed of his body and his desires. How could God create a man capable of having those kinds of feelings and then command him to not feel them? It never made sense to him after that day.

The scene of the tea field and the young bare-breasted women was still so vivid in his mind, it aroused him. He could almost smell the incense in the air. That sweet scent that permeated everything in India was inextricably tied to the sensuality of the place for him. And the spirituality. That was the thing that amazed him: how could sensuality and spirituality be tied together like that? His religion wasn't sensual at all. Compared to the exotic religions of India, it was stark and mundane.

Thinking about those pretty Burmese woman made him hot, so he rolled the window down a little further. As he took a deep breath of fresh air, he had a strange thought: what would Laura have been like if she had grown up in India, or in Burma? He tried to imagine her out picking tea with the young Burmese women, but the image didn't work. When she was young, she was more like that, more at ease with herself. More passionate and free. But as she got older, she became quite inhibited. If they had grown up in India, would she have held onto that passion she showed him out at Blue Lake that night? Or maybe it didn't have to be India. What if they had just moved to California? Or down to the desert where he was headed now? Any place that would have allowed them to live more spontaneously, away from all the rules and restrictions they'd grown up with. They should have done something like that. It might have made all the difference.

He frowned and shook his head. He had to quit thinking about Laura and how things *might* have been. Couldn't he just enjoy himself now and then? After all, he was on his way to his favorite place.

He decided to think about the desert. The red rocks. The blue sky. The deep silence. Then he saw the sign for Leeds just up ahead. It meant they weren't far from the Hurricane exit. He'd better wake Daniel up.

When he touched the man's arm, he lashed out. His flailing hand smacked Aaron in the side of the head and caused him to jerk the wheel. The truck went sliding sideways across the lanes.

Daniel yelled, "What the fuck?"

Aaron tried to correct the slide, but the back end of the truck came around and they started sliding the other way. He felt sure they were going to flip, but instead the truck slammed into the ditch, throwing him hard against the steering wheel. It knocked the breath out of him and left him feeling dazed with a bad pain in his ribs. He rubbed his chest where it hurt. He sure hoped he hadn't broken a rib.

When he looked over at Daniel, the man was staring at him with a wild look in his eyes. "What the fuck did you do that for?"

"What do you mean?" shouted Aaron. "You were the one that nearly killed us."

"Bullshit. I'm not driving. You are."

"I just touched your arm to wake you up, and you hit me in the side of the head."

Daniel's eyes grew even wilder. "Oh no. Oh God. I'm sorry, man. Shit. I'm so sorry." He grabbed both sides of his head and squeezed. "I'm such a fuck. Such a fucking fuck." He turned and started bashing his head against the window.

Aaron grabbed his arm. "Hey, stop that!" He felt the muscles in Daniel's arm tighten, so he let him go before he ended up with another whack to the head. "Try to control yourself. You're acting like a crazy man."

Daniel rubbed his arm and muttered, "Oh shit. I'm sorry, man. It's those damn war dreams. They've got me all screwed up. I can't always tell what's real."

Aaron was beginning to understand: the man really *was* crazy. Or, at the very least, unstable. He felt like telling him to get out right now. But he couldn't do that. The guy was obviously messed up. He needed all the help he could get. Aaron softened his voice. "Okay. Look. What's done is done. Forget it. We'd better get out and see what we can do about getting out of this ditch."

He got out and walked around to the front of the truck. He still felt a bit dazed, and his chest hurt, but he took a deep breath and tried to calm himself. Then he squatted down to look at the damage to the truck. The wheels seemed okay. They weren't bent, or anything. He looked underneath the truck. Nothing seemed broken there, but the chassis was hung-up on the dirt.

Daniel came around and stood next to him. "Whatta ya think?"

"It's hung-up underneath."

Daniel threw up his hands. "Ah, shit! Now what the fuck are we gonna do."

"Well, don't stand there cussing. Let's see if we can move it."

Daniel frowned. "I'm not gonna be much help . . . you know, with my bad hip and all."

Aaron shook his head. "You can still think, can't you? Or has your brain gone out on you too?"

Daniel stared at the ground, pushing the dirt around with the toe of his shoe. He gave Aaron a pained sideways look.

Aaron said, "I'm sorry, but we're in kind of a jam here." He led Daniel around to the driver's side of the truck to look at the situation.

Daniel snapped his fingers, and said, "I know. What if you dig it out in front so you can go forward? Then we can put something in back of the tires."

"What good will that do?"

"Well, maybe then you can rock back up onto higher ground, and that would get the chassis off the dirt."

Aaron wasn't sure what Daniel was even talking about, but he could see it was going to take some digging. "All right. I'll get the shovel."

Daniel sat on the edge of the ditch and took out a cigarette while Aaron started digging. Within minutes, Aaron's shirt was drenched and his ribs were aching. He sure hoped nothing was wrong in there. On top of the pain, he was darn thirsty. He couldn't remember when he had last had a drink. Before he left home? Maybe. All he wanted to do is have a drink and rest, but he knew if he didn't get the truck out of the ditch, he'd be spending the night at the edge of the road with this troublesome guy. He didn't relish that.

After digging some more, he got back in the truck and edged it forward. He gave it some gas, but the back wheels just spun every time he did it. That wasn't getting him anywhere, so he got out and went over to Daniel. "Got any other brilliant ideas?"

Daniel shrugged. "Beats me. Guess we'll have to flag down somebody to pull us out."

"I guess you haven't noticed how everyone heads for the other side of the road as soon as they see us."

"Well then, I guess you better dig some more."

Aaron stared at him in disbelief. "So you want me to keep digging while you sit on your bottom and smoke cigarettes?"

"Hey, man, I told you. I can't do anything with this bad hip. I used to be as strong as hell, but not anymore."

"Fine."

As Aaron went back to work, Daniel lit up another cigarette and laid back to look at the sky.

By the time Aaron had finished digging and scooping out the dirt on both sides of the truck with his shovel and his hands, he was exhausted, and now his back was aching as well as his ribs. He stood up to stretch, but that made him feel dizzy, and he had to hold on to the truck. That wasn't good. But maybe it was just because he was thirsty. Better get some water. He went to the back of the truck, but there wasn't any water. Had he forgotten to bring water? That was dumb. How did he think he was going to survive out in the desert without water?

He went over to Daniel. "Hey, uh . . . you don't happen to have something to drink in that bag of yours, do you?"

Daniel smirked. "Not anything you'd want."

"So how did you expect to survive out here on the road without water?"

Daniel shot him a nasty look. "Good question. How did *you* expect to survive?"

"Well, for one thing, I didn't know I'd be sitting in a ditch with a troublemaker."

Daniel blew a big puff of smoke in Aaron's direction. Aaron waved it away and muttered, "Oh forget it. You're no good for anything except smoking those damn weeds."

Daniel glowered at him and took another drag off of his cigarette. Aaron knew what was coming, and he hurried away before the cloud of smoke hit him. He got the shovel and put it in the back of the truck, then he got inside and started up the engine again. When he looked up, Daniel was standing in front of the truck, ready to push. That was a surprise, but it was an even bigger surprise when he pressed the gas pedal, and the truck drove out of the ditch.

Daniel let out a hoot and came hobbling around and got in the truck. He grinned and slapped Aaron on the shoulder. "Hey man, we did it. Jesus. I thought we'd never get outta there."

Aaron pressed his forehead against the top of the steering wheel, offering a silent prayer of thanks. He looked at Daniel. "Well, I guess we're not such a bad team, after all. Are you okay?"

"Yeah. How about you? That's a lot of exertion for an old man."

Aaron flinched. "Old man?"

"Just kiddin'. You're strong as an ox. I'm impressed."

"Is that right?"

"Sure. Who wouldn't be? A guy your age."

Aaron liked that. He knew he was strong, but no one had told him that in a long time. Maybe this guy wasn't so bad after all.

Aaron nodded and pulled onto the highway feeling good about himself. His ribs hurt, and he knew he was going to be sore from the exertion, but he was proud that he had been able to get the truck out of that ditch.

He gSaint Georgeot up to speed again, and as they headed down into a narrow valley the landscape began to change. A thrill of excitement ran through his body. They were getting close to the desert. Walls of red rock rose up on both sides of the highway, and he could see the blue peaks of the Pine Valley Mountains up ahead.

Twenty minutes later, he caught his first glimpse of the Virgin River. That was *his* river. The one that flowed behind his property. It was a nice river, slow and lazy in the winter, roaring in the spring. Right now, it should be somewhere in between.

The turn off to Hurricane and his property wasn't far now, and Aaron had a strong urge to take Daniel with him so he could show him the hot springs. The man was trouble, that's for sure, but it would be nice to have some company for a while. But would Daniel want to go? Probably not. He didn't exactly look like a man who would enjoy being out in the desert. Aaron couldn't decide if he should even ask. Finally, he blurted it out, "Uh, Danny . . . I was uh . . . wondering if you might like to come out to my property with me."

Daniel looked surprised. "Nah, that's okay, man. I've got to get over to Saint George and find my spot."

"But what if you don't get a ride? You'll be out here all night by yourself. If you don't want to come with me, I better drive you to Saint George."

"Nah. You've done enough already."

"But what about your . . . leg?"

"Don't worry about me. I've been taking care of myself for a long time."

Aaron looked away. "I guess so." He stared down the road thinking how he really didn't want to let Daniel go. Maybe it was because he had been feeling more alert since he had picked the man up. More stimulated and alive. Well, maybe not when he was skidding across the road and smashing his ribs into the steering wheel, but the rest of it was pretty good. He could understand how Daniel might not want to hang around with some lonely old guy, but living on the road like he did, he was probably lonely too. He could feel Daniel watching him, and he looked over.

Daniel said, "What's going on, man?"

"Uh . . . It's just that I'd really like you to come see my place."

"Why?"

"I don't know. It's . . . nice. Maybe you'd like it."

"You got a house there?" There was a spark of interest in Daniel's eyes which gave Aaron hope.

"No, I don't have a house, but I'm going to build one. Right now, it's just beautiful endless desert. You know, red sand and red rocks, and the wonderful smell of sage. And besides, there's a . . . special place I want to take you."

"What kind of special place?"

"A magical place. You'd love it. It might even make your leg feel better."

Daniel didn't seem so sure. "My leg? What the hell are you talkin' about?"

"There's a hot springs I could take you to."

"A hot springs? I don't know, man. I don't think I have time for that sort of thing."

"But it might help your leg."

"It's not my leg. It's my hip. It's my damn hip that's all fouled up."

"That's what I mean. Your hip. I bet that mineral water would make it feel better." Aaron could hear the urgency in his own voice. Now why was he trying so hard to convince the guy to come with him? He should just let him go, if that's what he wanted.

The sign to Hurricane was right ahead now. Aaron slowed the truck and pulled to the side of the road, trying to sort out his feelings. This man had almost got him killed, so why was he so desperate to have him come with him to his special place in the desert. It didn't make sense.

He didn't need Daniel out there. Actually, he'd be better off without him.

He tried to convince himself, but the truth was, he was fed up with being alone. He wanted to share something with another person, even if it was a man full of demons. "Look, Daniel, I wish you'd give that hot springs a try."

"I don't get it. You think you're gonna get me all fixed up with some kind of magic water?"

Aaron shrugged. "It couldn't hurt, could it? The springs aren't far, just over by my place."

Daniel took out a cigarette. He lit it and seemed to consider the plan. "Does it cost anything? I don't have any money you know."

Aaron felt encouraged. "No, no. You don't need money. It's in the middle of nowhere. We could camp out on my property and—"

Daniel's smoke hit Aaron in the face, and before he could stop himself, he coughed and said, "I thought I told you to breathe that poison out the window." Immediately, he wished he hadn't said anything, but the smoke really bothered his eyes and lungs.

Daniel flapped his hands at the smoke. "Oh, shit. I forgot."

Aaron sighed. "And could you please stop cussin'." He was feeling worn out and defeated. He should just forget the whole thing.

Daniel blew up. "You're crazy, man. You've been pissed off at me since I got in your truck, and you still are, but for some reason you want me to stay around. I don't get it."

Aaron shrugged and smiled sheepishly. "I don't get it either. Maybe I'm as crazy as you are."

Daniel flipped his cigarette out the window, and they eyed each other in silence until Daniel finally said, "Well, okay. I guess it won't hurt if I get to Saint George a few days later than I planned."

Aaron slapped the steering wheel. "That's great. I'm sure you won't regret it."

Daniel raised an eyebrow. "Yeah, but maybe you will."

"No. I'm sure I won't."

Aaron started the truck up again and took the exit to Hurricane. Just before they crossed the Virgin River, Aaron glanced over and caught a look of suspicion on Daniel's face. "What? Did I do something wrong?"

Daniel squinted. "I'm just wonderin'. Do you get involved like this with everybody you pick up? I mean, are you some kind of religious nut or somethin'? Some guy with a mission to save people?"

Aaron shook his head. "Nah, I'm not like that. I may be religious, and I may be a nut, but I don't usually put the two together."

"I thought maybe you had plans to try and save my soul."

Aaron chuckled. "I think I'd better work on my own soul before I start working on yours."

"So, you don't have any hidden . . . you know . . . agendas, or anything?"

"Nope. Not that I know of."

Chapter 7

Instead of heading straight out to his property, Aaron drove into Hurricane to get some water and some other supplies they might need from a little market he knew of. Daniel waited in the truck.

Once he was inside, Aaron went straight to the bottled water aisle. He put a 12-pack in the cart, then took a bottle out and drank the whole thing down, wondering how he could have forgotten to bring something as important as water.

He decided the easiest thing for him and Daniel to eat would be some kind of soup and a sandwich. He picked out some whole wheat bread and got a couple of cans of tuna fish for the sandwiches and some stewed tomatoes and beans for his soup base. Next, he went to the produce section and picked out some nice tomatoes and a few veggies. He grabbed a bag of ice and headed to the checkout stand.

When he got back out to the truck, Daniel said, "Jesus. I thought you got lost in there."

"Really? Was I gone that long?" Aaron handed over a bottle of water to Daniel and kept another for himself.

"Guess they didn't have any beer, huh?"

Aaron laughed. "'Fraid not."

"It's not back there in the cooler?"

"Sorry."

Aaron started up the truck, and as he pulled out of the parking lot onto the road, Daniel said, "Uh . . . . who's Laura?"

"What?"

"You know, Laura. The one who wrote you all those lovey-dovey poems I read while you were taking your time in the store."

Aaron slammed on the brakes. "You read her poems? Where are they?"

"Hey, calm down, man. They're right there where you left 'em."

"Where?" Aaron frantically searched the cab of the truck

"Don't get all riled up. They're right there." Daniel pointed towards the side pocket in the door.

Aaron was outraged. What kind of man snoops through your personal things while you're off in the store buying him dinner. "Why'd you do that?"

"What?"

"Don't play innocent. You know what I'm talking about."

Daniel shrugged as if it was no big deal.

"Those poems are private. You had no right."

"Geez, if I'd thought you were going to get your panties all twisted up, I wouldn't have done it. I mean, you'd think a man would be proud if someone wrote poems like that about him."

"What do you mean? Poems like that?"

"You know, all sugar and spicey." Daniel put his hand over his heart and gave Aaron a lovesick look.

Aaron was shaken by that. The poems he had read weren't like that at all. They just made him feel guilty. Was Daniel making fun of him? Or was it possible there were some sweet poems among the others that he hadn't seen?

He pulled the binder from the pocket, and shoved it at Daniel. "Show me."

"Show you what?"

"The one you read. That sweet one." He grasped the steering wheel and looked straight ahead, waiting.

Daniel took the binder and said, "Uh . . . don't you think you ought to pull off the road? You stay here, you'll be blocking traffic."

Aaron took his foot off the brake and let the truck roll to the side of the road. He turned off the engine and glared at Daniel. "Show me. I want to see it."

Daniel flipped through the pages. "I'm not sure where it was. Probably near the back, though. I always start books at the back. Kind of dumb, I guess, but I don't like surprise endings."

"Never mind that. Where is it?"

Daniel turned a few more pages and stopped. "I guess this is it." He held the binder out for Aaron to see.

"Well, go ahead. Read it."

"Read it? I don't wanna read it."

"Do it!"

"Why don't you read it yourself?"

Aaron wasn't sure why. Maybe he was afraid he would just see the same bitterness he'd seen before. If Daniel had an eye for sweetness, maybe he could help him see it too. He looked straight ahead and waited.

"Look, I'm not much of a reader."

Aaron wasn't about to let him squirm out of it. "That doesn't matter. I just want to hear it . . . from outside myself."

"Okay, but don't say I didn't warn you. It's not going to sound like her." He cleared his throat and began reading in a voice much deeper than his usual one.

In My Dream, You Listen
by Laura Young
May 21, 1965

In the nocturnal visions of my mind
With all the day's confusion left behind
I stand beside the place where we began
And wonder what became of my young man

I was just a girl who loved your eyes
Your golden skin, the longing in your sighs
You took my love to fill your ego's need
And I began my journey to concede

Now there's a battle in my heart when I'm awake
All that despair that follows my mistake
I let you take the power of my mind
And here I stay, pretending I am blind

Daniel stopped, looking uneasy. "Uh . . . maybe I should have read the whole thing. I just kind of scanned it, you know, the *golden skin,* the *longing sighs,* they made me think, well . . . you want me to stop?"

"No! Keep going. I want to hear it all." Aaron braced himself for what was to come.

Still in my deepest sleep, I see your soul
The young man that I knew, I still can know
If you set aside your manly need to rule
You'll be my darling love, my sweetest jewel

Daniel closed the binder and set it gingerly on the seat between them. He shot Aaron a sideways look. "Well, it's obvious she loves you. Maybe she wants you a little different, but all women want that from their man. Just make her think you've changed like she wants, and she'll be right there with you. I guar-an-tee it."

Aaron shook his head. "There's no chance of that."

"Why not? You don't have to do it all the time. Just give it to her now and then."

"You don't understand. She's not with me anymore."

Daniel looked uncomfortable and pushed back his hair. "Oh, man, that's too bad. I'm sorry. Did she take off with somebody else?"

"No, she didn't take off! She's gone. She's dead. Look. I don't want to talk about this. Least of all with you." Aaron grabbed the binder and stuffed it angrily back in the pocket of the door.

"Hey, don't blame me, man. You're the one that made me read it."

Aaron gripped the steering wheel, feeling angry and confused. He needed time to think. Time to read the poem by himself. Maybe if he read each line carefully he could figure out what she meant. Did she love him, or did she die hating him? He couldn't stand it. Why didn't he know?

My darling. My love. My sweet jewel. Those were the words his mind wanted to hold on to, but the other words were stronger and more insistent: *Mistakes. Pretending. His manly need to rule.*

Daniel muttered something, and Aaron turned on him. "What?"

"Sorry to disturb you, man, but are we gonna sit here all day? I guess I made a mistake. I should have gone on to Saint George like I planned."

Aaron had an overwhelming urge to get out of the truck and make a run for it so he could be by himself, but he forced himself to stay put. He started up the engine and pulled out onto the road. As he drove out of town and back to the highway, he thought about how bewildering it was the way Laura wrote sweetness in one line, only to take it away in the next. No wonder Daniel was confused. Why couldn't she have just said what she meant?

The idea of Daniel sitting over there watching him, probably trying to read his thoughts and examining his pain, made him furious. A man like that had no right to pass judgment on him, no right thinking he was a bad husband, that he didn't deserve Laura. He didn't know a thing about him and Laura!

He pushed Laura's poems out of his mind and tried to focus on the road and the landscape. That's when he realized he didn't have a clue where he was. They should have come to the turnoff to his property by now. Had he missed it? No. He couldn't have missed it. He knew that turnoff like the back of his hand.

After continuing on a little further, he knew he had to turn around and go back, even if it gave Daniel more ammunition to judge him.

Sure enough, as soon as he pulled over, Daniel started up. "What's the matter now?"

"Uh . . . I guess I missed the road."

"You missed the road to your own property?"

"I was distracted by your . . . snoopy nose." It was true, he was distracted, but it was still unsettling that he had missed the turn. He had never missed it before. Not in all the years since Laura and he first came down to look over the property to decide if they wanted to buy it. Maybe Sarah was right. Maybe his memory was worse than he thought.

He had to backtrack quite a ways before he spotted the little settling pond next to the turnoff. That was the landmark he should have seen before. It was right there where it was supposed to be, so how could he have missed it?

As they started off on the dirt road, the sun was sinking low in the western sky, turning the whole landscape a rosy hue. It was a scene he craved. The reason he loved the desert so much. He pressed the gas and let his worries fly away like the red dust spewing up behind the truck. He was going home. Home to his red rocks and sand. Home to the splendid smell of desert sage. Home to the deep silence and the magnitude of nature.

He took a deep breath and thought about building his little house. Maybe Daniel could help him get the foundation going. Laura and he had picked the spot for the house and staked it out a long time ago. It was up on a little hill with just enough of a rise to provide a great view in all directions, the best spot on the whole ten acres.

The truck hit a pot hole, and Aaron glanced over and caught a pained look on Daniel's face. That wasn't good. "Sorry. I shouldn't be going so fast."

As he slowed down, Daniel twisted around to look through the rear window. "Seems like we're gettin' pretty far off the grid, and it's almost dark. Is it safe out here?"

"Sure it is." Aaron grinned. "Nothin' out here but rocks and a few rattlesnakes."

Daniel's eyes widened. "Rattlesnakes? Are you shittin' me?"

"Don't worry. They'll want to steer clear of you."

"I sure as hell hope so. I hate snakes."

They kept going until the road curved south, and after they rattled over the washboard for a while, Aaron saw the pile of rocks marking the edge of his property. The sun had gone down, but there was still enough light to see that everything was just the way he remembered it. He pulled the truck to the side of the road and turned off the engine. Then, he rolled down the window and took a deep breath of the sweet air. It was wonderful to be back in the desert.

He turned to Daniel and smiled. "See, I told you it was nice. We've even got shade when we need it." He pointed towards a row of tall trees a short distance from the road. "They're the only cottonwoods for miles. Don't know why they grow here. Look at those fall colors."

When Daniel didn't respond, Aaron said, "Well, I guess we better get camp set up before it's too dark to see anything."

Aaron got out of the truck and carried the cooler over to the trees and put it where it would be in the shade when the sun came up in the morning. Then he went back for the groceries. Daniel was still in the truck, looking like he was afraid to get out.

Aaron called to him, "You'll be more comfortable over here by the fire pit. See. There's a couple of big stumps you can sit on."

Daniel slowly got out, but he stayed close to the truck, holding onto the door, as if he didn't want to lose contact with its security. Finally, he hobbled over to the fire pit and flopped down in the sand.

Aaron nodded his approval. "That's right. You take it easy. I'll get us a fire going."

Aaron worked hard, cleaning the ash out of the fire pit and carrying it over to where he planned to plant his garden later. Ash would be good for the soil. He came back and restacked the rocks around the periphery of the pit. Then he gathered dried branches and sticks and got a nice fire going.

When he had stacked up enough firewood for the night, he stepped back and looked around. The high mountains to the west had turned a deep blue-violet while the sandstone cliffs to the east were ablaze with the last of the sun. It made the red sand of the whole valley glow beneath the green-gray texture of the sagebrush. Aaron felt like he was standing on hallowed ground. The untouched beauty of it was so pure and perfect it was as if God had just finished creating it, and he and Daniel were the first ones to behold His work.

He glanced back at Daniel to see if he was enjoying the evening light. There was a warm glow on his face, and Aaron thought that was how he must have looked when he was a young man, before the war took hold of him. But the image didn't hold: the man started into a loud bout of coughing that ended with him spitting phlegm into the fire pit.

Aaron turned and walked away in disgust. The man was uncouth. He could care less about the beauty around him. Once again, Aaron wondered if he should have brought him out here. Daniel didn't seem to be enjoying himself anyway. He just kept looking around like he was afraid something was going to jump him. Aaron couldn't understand that. He never felt more safe and at ease than when he was out in the desert away from the noise and complications of the urban life.

He walked further out into the sagebrush-covered valley, and turned to look back. From there, Daniel was a small, sad silhouette, hunched beside the ring of rocks surrounding the fire pit. It was like an image from an old lonesome cowboy movie. A wave of compassion washed over Aaron.

He hurried back to the fire, determined to give Daniel a chance, to help him find some comfort and joy, if only for a few days. "Hey, what say we fix up something to eat?"

Daniel's eyes lit up, and he nodded eagerly. "That would be good. I'm starving. I could eat a horse."

Aaron laughed. "Afraid we don't have any horses. Unless you plan on catching one of those wild ones. How about some vegetable bean soup instead?"

Daniel grunted.

Aaron put another log on the fire and got the soup going in the pot he'd left out there. Daniel watched his every move. The man hadn't stirred from his spot next to the fire pit since he first sat down, but every now and then he would wince and shift his position, stretching out his legs and then drawing them back in again. His pain showed on his face. It was too bad a person had to hurt like that.

Aaron thought he should try to make him more comfortable. He went and got Daniel's duffel bag from the back of the truck and put it down beside him. "You might as well get out your sleeping bag, if you have one, and stretch out for a while. This soup will take a few minutes to make."

Daniel pawed through his stuff, and came up with a dirty old green army blanket. He laid it out on the sand, and then he did as Aaron suggested and stretched out and looked up at the sky. After a few minutes, he said, "There's a hell of a lot of stars up there. They're popping out all over the place now."

Aaron looked up and nodded. "I love the desert sky. You see stars out here you've never seen in the city."

"I wouldn't know."

"What do you mean, you wouldn't know? Who doesn't look at the stars?"

Daniel shrugged. "I don't know. I guess I've had other things on my mind." He rolled onto his stomach and began sifting the sand through his fingers.

By the time Aaron handed Daniel his sandwich and served up two large tin cups of the soup, it was quite dark with only the light of the fire to see by. Daniel didn't hesitate. He went after the soup as if he hadn't eaten in days, slurping it and splattering the front of his shirt with the broth.

He must have felt Aaron watching him because he looked up and wiped his chin with his sleeve. "It's not bad."

Aaron grinned. "It's my camping out spe-ci-ali-ty. Vegetable bean soup."

When they finished eating, Daniel searched through his pockets, and then he began to dig through his duffel bag again. When he couldn't find whatever it was he was looking for, a look of panic came over his face. He dumped the bag out on the blanket in front of the fire and started pawing through all of his possessions. Aaron was curious to see what a man like that would carry: a half bottle of whiskey, a couple of old ragged corduroy shirts, a pair of faded jeans, some dark socks, and what looked to be the jacket from a pin-striped dress suit, all rolled up. Now what in the world would he need that for?

Next came what looked like an inner tube from a bicycle tire, a small magnifying glass, marbles, a little orange tin that said *Grandma's Ginger Cookies* in green lettering, and a book. Aaron leaned closer to see what the title was: *Heart of Darkness*, by Joseph Conrad. He wondered what that book meant to Daniel, and why he would carry it with him when he had so few possessions.

He was about to ask that question when Daniel stopped looking through his stuff and threw up his hands. He yelled, "Now, what am I gonna do?"

"What do you mean?"

"I'm fucking out of smokes. You should have got me some back at that store."

It caught Aaron off guard. "You didn't say anything about that."

"Well, you should've known."

"How was I supposed to know that?"

Daniel's face had that twisted up rage on it again. "You know I smoke, doncha? You've done nothin' but complain about it."

"Now, just a doggone minute," Aaron said. "You can't blame me. I didn't get you addicted to those things."

Daniel struggled to his knees and held his hands together out in front of him like he was praying. "You gotta take me back to town, man."

"It's dark. Everything would be shut down."

"What about that gas station we passed? They'd have some."

"It's a small town. They'd be closed too . . . I think you'll have to wait until tomorrow. I'm sorry."

"I can't do that. Can't you see, I'm already feeling it." He grabbed a log from the fire pit and threw it, almost hitting Aaron in the leg.

Aaron got up and walked away. Then he came back and yelled, "You're all . . . screwy."

Daniel glared at him and began stuffing his things into his duffel bag. He struggled to his feet and slung the bag over his shoulder and headed towards the road into the darkness.

Aaron went after him. "Where do you think you're going?"

"I'm gonna hitch a ride to Saint George, like I shoulda done in the first place." He kept walking.

"There are no rides. We're too far out."

"I'll walk clear out to the damn highway, if I have to."

"Can't you wait until morning?" Aaron was pleading now, he didn't want to be responsible for the man wondering around in the desert lost.

"I can't wait. I'll go nuts, man. I gotta have a smoke. Now!"

Daniel stumbled on something and Aaron grabbed his arm. He felt bad for the man, but he didn't like the idea of driving him somewhere. His eyes weren't that good at night. He might hit something, or get lost on one of the side roads. It wasn't a smart idea. He tried to reason with Daniel. "You know . . . this could be your chance to get over it. You know? Go with the turkey."

Daniel jerked his arm away. "Yeah, right." He hurried away.

Aaron called after him. "If you're ever going to do it, it would be lot easier out here . . . in God's country."

Aaron stood still and watched Daniel disappear into the darkness. When there was nothing left to see, he called after him, "I think you should come back now."

Aaron held his breath and listened, but there was no sound except the popping of the fire. He stayed still, listening and waiting for Daniel to come back, and when he didn't, a wave of loneliness engulfed him. He didn't know why he felt so sad. He had always loved being in the desert alone, but now, for some reason, he felt deserted. All he had left were the gold flickering flames of the fire.

His excitement was gone. It was as if someone had turned off a light inside his heart. What was he going to do out here by himself? Go to sleep? Wake up in the morning? Try to build his house by himself? There wouldn't be any joy in it without someone to share it with.

Aaron turned away from the darkness and headed back toward the fire. Before he made it there, he heard a yelp and then a stream of obscenities. "Goddamn son of a bitch . . . shit!"

A few minutes later, Daniel came limping back into the light.

Aaron hurried toward him. "What happened?"

"Shit. It's so damn dark out there. I stepped on a fuckin' cactus."

Aaron couldn't help chuckling.

Daniel growled. "Oh, you think that's funny, huh?"

"No, no. I'm just glad you're back. I was already feeling lonely."

"Shit." Daniel let his duffel bag drop to the ground

Aaron was so happy to see him, he didn't even mind his cussing. "Here let me help you with that."

He picked up Daniel's bag, and they made their way back to the fire. The flames were dying down, so Aaron quickly threw on a couple of logs. "That'll bring it back."

Daniel dropped to the ground, took off his left shoe, and started picking at the cactus spines in his ankle and foot. "Oh, man. Where's a woman with long fingernails when you need her?"

Aaron sat down and examined his nails in the firelight. "My nails are kinda long. Guess I forgot to clip them. Maybe I can help."

"See what you can do. I don't want them getting infected."

Aaron pulled Daniel's foot onto his lap, but when he started prodding, Daniel yelped.

"Sorry. Guess my eyes aren't so good in this light."

Daniel rummaged through his duffel bag and pulled out the magnifying glass Aaron had seen before. "Here. Try this."

Aaron used the glass and carefully picked out all the spines. "I think I've got 'em all."

Daniel ran his finger over the skin. "Yeah, I think you did. But it still burns. There must be poison in those things."

Aaron thought about what he might have that would help. That's right, something cold. He headed over to the cooler and came back with some ice wrapped in one of the plastic produce bags from the grocery store. "Here. Try this."

Daniel placed the bag on his sore foot. "Oh, man. That doesn't feel good."

"Keep it there. It'll go numb, and you won't notice the cold so much after a while."

Daniel shook his head. "Oh man, why're you being so nice when all I do is give ya trouble?"

Aaron shrugged. "I don't know. I guess, I like your company."

"Aw, I'm just a no good wasted bum. Not good company for anybody."

Aaron shook his head. "Now, that's not true. You shouldn't say that."

"Oh yeah. I came real close to punchin' ya when you wouldn't take me for cigarettes. I even considered stealing your truck."

That surprised Aaron. He hadn't thought of that. "It must be real bad."

"It's terrible. I feel all . . . prickly, like there are bees buzzing inside me."

"I'm sorry about that."

"Bet you were never addicted to anything, were you?" He paused, and then he said, "Except maybe—"

"What?"

"Never mind."

"What were you going to say?"

"Nothin'. It's just more of my meanness comin' out. I'm sorry." He looked away, like he didn't want Aaron to see his eyes.

There was a definite jitteriness in Daniel. His body kept twitching, and every so often, he'd squeeze his hands together in that strange way, then he'd stretch them out. All the time he was doing that, he was moving his tongue across his lips, and then he would bite at them. Aaron watched him, amazed by all the contortions.

He didn't want Daniel to catch him staring, and when he looked down he saw Daniel still had the ice on his foot. Wasn't there something about doing it too long? "Better take that off now."

"What?"

"That ice. You shouldn't leave it on so long."

"Oh. I forgot about that. I guess it must have gone numb, like you said."

Aaron took what was left of the ice back to the cooler and looked up at the stars. It seemed quite late, and he was tired and achy from his long day and all the exertion. He walked back to Daniel, and said, "Maybe we ought to get some sleep."

"Sleep? Are you kiddin'? I can't do that."

"Why not?"

"I told ya, man. I'm too jittery."

Aaron shrugged. "Well, what should we do then?"

Daniel rubbed his arms. "Talk to me, or somethin'. Tell me some stories."

"Stories? What kind of stories?"

"I don't know . . . anything. Just keep me distracted, or I'll probably go crazy."

"What kind of thing do you want to talk about?"

"I don't give a shit! Somethin'. Anything. Tell me about that woman of yours. Why did she write those poems?"

"I told you, you shouldn't have read those."

"I know, but I did. So what does it matter if you tell me? I'm just trying to imagine what kind of woman she was. Was she pretty?"

Of course, she was pretty, but he didn't want to talk about Laura right now.

"Come on. Tell me about her."

"Leave me alone."

Aaron tried to recall the words of the poem Daniel had read, but all he could remember was the sweetness and the sour, the way she loved his eyes, but didn't like what he took from her in bed. Isn't that what it said? Or were all the poems getting mixed together in his head? He was going to have to read that one again to be sure.

Daniel punched him in the arm. "Come on, man. Say something. Talk to me. Before I go nuts. If you don't want to talk about your woman, tell me about your father."

"My father?"

"Sure. You have a father don't you?"

"Well, I did. He's gone now. Why don't you tell me about *your* father?"

Daniel threw up his hands. "What are we having, a fucking contest?" He shook his head and stared at the fire for a minute, then he looked up and frowned. "There's nothing to tell. He died when I was three. I hardly knew him."

Aaron felt bad about that. "Must have been hard."

"Yeah. I guess you could say that."

"So, were you just raised by your mother."

"Her and that mean old bastard she married. You could say he's the reason I ended up in Nam so early. But I don't want to talk about him. It'll just piss me off and make me more jittery. Tell me about your dad."

Aaron leaned back on his arms and stared up at the stars, trying to think what to say. After a minute, he looked at Daniel. "My father was a hard man to understand, and I never did get the chance to do that."

"Why not?"

"Well, he died young too. When I was in my mid-twenties. There was a lot to admire, but I never got over my anger at him. I would have liked to settle that, but—"

"What did he look like?"

"You know, just the regular, tall, dark and handsome."

"You mean like you, huh?"

That surprised Aaron. Did Daniel really think he was handsome, or was he just flattering him so he'd keep talking? It didn't matter, the guy had him going now. "Anyway, like I said, there was a lot to admire about my father. When we were young, he was quite playful with us, and he seemed happy most the time. Then the Great Depression hit, and it ruined him. You know, not being able to support us like he wanted to. He shouldn't have felt so bad. Everyone was going through it. But even after the Depression ended, and things were getting back to normal, he couldn't seem to get over it. He was angry all the time. Or maybe just aloof and critical. Not so much with Stevie and Miriam, but he was always getting on me for one thing or another. It seemed like I could never get things right."

Daniel rolled onto his back and tilted his head backwards to look at the sky. "It had nothin' to do with you, man. When people get hurt by life, they tend to pass that hurt on."

"So you don't think we should be responsible for ourselves and try not to hurt other people?"

"We can try, but that doesn't mean we're gonna be able to do it."

"Sounds like you're speaking from experience."

Daniel quickly rolled onto his side. "From the tone of your voice, you sound like you're not all that different from your old man, with his critical judgments and all."

"I didn't mean—"

"Sure, I know. That's what I was talkin' about. We are who we are, and we can't help it after a certain point. Your old man hurts you, and you pass it on . . . one way or the other. It's like kicking the dog."

"What?"

"Never mind."

"Well, I hope you're wrong about our ability to change, because I've got a fair amount of changing to do."

They were both silent. Aaron didn't want to talk about his father anymore. It was just another thing to feel bad about. He wrapped his arms around his knees and stared into the fire.

"So. That's it?" said Daniel. "You're not going to say anything else?"

Aaron looked over. "No, I don't think I will. Seems like anything I say, just brings trouble."

Daniel glared at him and started pawing through his bag. He pulled out his bottle of whiskey and took a drink from it. Then, he held it up with a sarcastic grin. "Don't s'pose you'd want some of this?"

Aaron tried not to show his disgust, but he couldn't keep himself from saying, "Another dose of poison, huh?"

"Watch out. Here comes the ol' judge again."

Daniel took a drink and then another and another, all the time looking at Aaron as if he was daring him to say something. Aaron wasn't about to take his bait.

Finally, Daniel's bottle was empty. He hurled it into the darkness and curled up in his blanket next to the fire. Pretty soon, he was snoring. That was good. If he stayed asleep, he'd probably be okay until morning.

Chapter 8

Aaron woke to a piercing wail. It was too dark to see, but he could hear some kind of ruckus on the other side of the fire pit. Was somebody there? There was another long wail, and then he remembered that guy he picked up. It must be him.

Struggling out of his sleeping bag, he crawled across the sand on his hands and knees to find out what was wrong with the guy. Next thing he knew, he was on his back with the man on top of him. He was being strangled!

Aaron thrashed his legs and tried desperately to pry the man's fingers off his throat, but the pressure just got tighter. The man was too strong, he was cutting off his air, and there was nothing Aaron could do about it. He was pretty sure he was going to die.

He kept kicking and struggling to get free, but then a strange blackness filled his mind, and he felt like he was all alone, falling through a dark tunnel of emptiness.

Then, something changed. The grip on his neck went slack, and he could breathe. He gulped at the air, trying to pull it through the awful pain in this throat.

He could breathe now, but he still couldn't move: the guy had him in a grip and he was rocking him back and forth and whispering, "Oh, Johnny, Johnny, don't go. Don't die, Johnny. Don't leave me."

There was such pain in the man's voice it filled Aaron with his own pain, an aching grief that swelled in his throat and made him feel like he *still* might die. He started to cry, and the man cried too, and they held each other and rocked each other like two dying men.

"Don't die, Johnny. Please don't die."

Then, suddenly, the man released him and rolled away. Aaron stayed perfectly still, taking deep breaths, trying to recover and figure out what had happened. He opened his eyes and saw a full moon floating up there in the sky. It was so bright it hurt his eyes, so he closed them again and listened. The night was alive with sound. The loud steady chirp of the crickets. The hoot of an owl. The rustle of a breeze through the trees. Then, far off somewhere, he heard the sad cry of a coyote. He listened for the reply, but it never came.

He opened his eyes again and peered through the shadows. The man who had tried to kill him was asleep now, lying flat on his back, snoring loudly beneath the glittering shine of the moon. It was extraordinary to see him like that after what had just happened. He looked so harmless and innocent.

The man snorted and rolled onto his side. Then, he groaned and pushed himself upright, but his head kept sagging down. Finally, when he got control of his head, he reached out toward Aaron and growled, "Give me a fucking cigarette."

There was an edge to his voice that put Aaron instantly on guard. Was he going to try to hurt him again?

The man jerked his head back and shouted at the sky. "I said, I need a fucking ci-gar-rette!"

The threat was straight on now, like the threat of a rattlesnake coiled and ready. Aaron tried to think what he could say to calm the man. "Uh . . . I wish I had one for you. I really do."

"I told you, I couldn't do it. I'm going nuts. Fuckin' crazy nuts."

Aaron scooted back. "You're right about that. You scare me."

"What do ya mean?"

It didn't seem safe to reply.

"Come on. Tell me what the fuck you mean. Tell me. Tell me. Tell me." His voice was getting louder and louder.

Aaron backed further away. "Uh . . . you . . . got me by the neck. Don't you remember that?"

The man's hands started flailing. "Oh, Jesus, God. No. I didn't do that again . . . did I?"

"Yes, you did."

The man scrambled backwards, putting more distance between them. "You better get away from me, man. Better take me out to the road right now before you get hurt. I don't care. I'll ride in the back of the truck."

Aaron didn't want to drive him anywhere. "Why did you do it?"

"I don't know, man. I can't remember. It's always like that. I just wake up feeling scared. Like I'm back in the war and they're coming after me. The shrink said it would get better, but it doesn't get better. It gets worse." He wrapped his arms around his knees and started to rock.

Aaron remembered the name the man said when he was choking him, 'Johnny.' Maybe that's what this was all about. "Who's Johnny?"

The man jerked his head toward Aaron. "Johnny? What do you know about Johnny?"

"You kept calling him. Who is he? Did something happen?"

The man put his hands over his face and wouldn't answer.

Aaron wasn't sure what to do. "You don't have to talk about it if you don't want to." He understood about not wanting to talk.

The man flung out his arm. "Don't want to talk about it? Shit, I don't want to even think about it, or remember it." He moaned. "I took speed once for a whole fucking month just to keep from sleeping and having it dredged up inside my damn dreams. But after I stopped the speed, it got even worse. I started thinking everybody was trying to kill me. That's when Sherry left me for good."

"Sherry?" Was he supposed to know who Sherry was? "Is she your wife?"

"Hell, no. No woman would ever marry me. They get scared, you know? I guess, you can understand that by now."

Aaron touched his neck and felt the rawness of the skin, but he didn't mention it. It was clearly nothing compared to the dangerous pain bottled up inside the man. "Uh . . . I think I'm okay."

The man scrambled to his knees and started throwing stuff into his duffel bag.

"What are you doing?" Aaron said.

"I gotta go get some cigarettes. That's the problem. I'm too wound up."

"But where?"

"Back to that town we were in."

"I don't think it's there. It's too dark."

"What do you mean? It's not there? The whole fucking town's disappeared?"

"Well, I mean . . . the people . . . they're sleeping."

"Damn it! I'm tellin' ya, I gotta have a smoke. Can't you take me somewhere?" It sounded like he was about to explode.

"Look, I could take you, but if everything's shut down, it wouldn't do you any good. Maybe we should stay where we are until the sun comes up."

"Don't you understand anything? I can't make it that long."

He could hear the meanness in the man's voice, but then he heard something else. Aaron held out his hand to silence him.

It was that owl. Hooting, and close by.

The man jerked his head to the side. "What's that?"

"Shhh," Aaron whispered, "It's an owl."

He scooted closer to Aaron. "What does it want?"

That was a surprise. How could a grown man be afraid of an owl? It must be the cigarettes. Not having one really *was* making him crazy. Aaron tried to think of something that might help and remembered the hot springs. "I know what you need. A good soak."

"What are you talking about?"

"There's a hot springs near here."

"Oh, yeah, that. That's not going to help."

"Sure it will. It will take your mind off of things. And it will make you feel good."

The man frowned and looked uncertain. "How far is it?"

"I don't know for sure. A ways over there." After being strangled, he was feeling a little muddled, but he pointed in the direction he thought it was.

"How would we get there? It's too dark."

"Nah. There's plenty of light. We've got that full moon."

"I dunno. My hip's not feeling so good. What if I trip and fall into one of those fucking cactus again?"

There was that meanness again. "Okay, okay, we don't have to do it. I just thought you might want to do something besides sitting here going crazy."

The man sulked for a minute, then he muttered, "You really think it would help?"

"Well, it couldn't hurt, could it?"

The man didn't move so Aaron tried again. "So what do you think, uh . . . my man?"

"Daniel. The name's Daniel."

"That's right. I knew that. Okay, Daniel, what should we do?"

"I guess I could try to get there, if I'm not too froze up from this hard ground."

Aaron waited.

"Maybe I could make it if I take one of my pills. That might calm me down too." He dug around in his pocket, pulled out his little bottle and put a pill in his mouth.

"Don't you need something to drink that down? We must have some water."

"Naw. I take 'em this way all the time. It's no big deal."

Daniel got up and paced back and forth, like he was testing his hip. Then he stopped and said, "I guess I can make it. But I sure do wish I had a cigarette."

"Can't you think of anything else? Take a look at the moonlight. See how it reflects off that white quartz over there." Aaron pointed. "Have you ever seen anything so beautiful?"

"Just looks dark to me. I'll probably break my freakin' neck out there."

Aaron got up. "I told you. It's not that far." At least, he hoped it wasn't.

"Are you sure you know where it is? I can't be wandering around the desert all night."

"Sure. I've been there . . . lots of times." It didn't seem right that he couldn't remember exactly where the hot springs were. He had never had any trouble remembering that before, but maybe he was still recovering from just about being strangled to death.

Daniel grumbled and started off across the sagebrush field, as if he was the one leading the way. Aaron hurried to catch up to make sure the poor guy didn't stumble into a cactus again.

They hiked along in silence and eventually came to the edge of a gorge. That was good. The gorge was where the river was and the hot springs were down there in the river. Daniel plopped down on a big rock and let out a moan.

"That's right," Aaron said. "We should rest for a minute before we head down. We're not in any hurry." He joined Daniel on the rock.

While Daniel snorted and complained about his cigarettes, Aaron watched the shadows in the gorge grow longer and darker. If they grew anymore, they wouldn't be able to see once they got down there. He stood up and held out his hand to Daniel. "We better get going."

They struggled down the hill through the loose rocks, with Aaron helping Daniel as best he could. When they finally made it to the flat sandy area along the river, Aaron was relieved, but now which way should they go? He looked in both directions, letting his eyes drift across the shapes of the rocks, the bushes, the sparkling water. Then he saw the silhouette of a lone cottonwood tree upstream. That seemed right. He pointed. "It's that way."

Daniel hesitated. "I don't know, man. You don't look that certain."

"Sure, I am."

"Yeah, well, I don't wanna be walkin' all over creation. My hip's starting to hurt."

"Now, don't give out on me, Danny boy. It's just a little farther." He didn't like Daniel doubting him when he already had his own doubts. But he and Laura had been to the hot springs quite a few times, and he had come back right after she died. Surely, he could find it again.

They continued upstream with the river gurgling alongside them. It was a playful sound that helped Aaron relax and focus on his surroundings. He took a deep breath. The air around the water was cool and sweet smelling and there were critters scurrying through the brush. Even in the deep of night, the desert was alive. He loved that.

As they came around a bend in the river, he saw a grove of low trees. He was sure he remembered those trees, and the gorge was getting quite narrow now: the rock walls towering straight up on both sides. That seemed right too.

A little further on, he smelled something that told him he was right all along. He stopped and touched Daniel's arm. "Do you smell that?"

"What?"

"It's the hot springs. You can smell the sulfur"

Daniel sniffed the air. "Oh, yeah. Stinky."

As they got closer, Aaron could see steam swirling up from the river, like dancing spirits. They sprung up, twisted and turned, and then melted into the darkness, only to spring up again somewhere else. The sight of the teasing dance made him feel kind of giddy. He grabbed Daniel's arm and whispered, "You're gonna love this."

As they got closer to the bubbling water of the hot springs, Aaron felt more excited than he had felt in years. He tried to pull Daniel forward, but he resisted. "Oh, come on now. You're not going to back out on me after coming all this way, are you?"

"It looks too hot. It'll burn me. My legs are real sensitive, you know."

"No, no. It's not that hot. It's just . . . nice. Here, I'll show you." Aaron stripped off his clothes and waded into the pool. He lowered himself down into the water until it was up to his chin. He sighed. "Oh, that's good. You have to try it."

Daniel sat at the edge of the pool and slowly took off his shoes and socks. He rolled up his pants to his knees and cautiously stuck one foot into the water, then he quickly pulled it out. "Damn! It's really hot." He scooted back as if he was afraid of the water.

Aaron tried to encourage him. "You've just got to get used to it. That's all."

"I don't know. Maybe I better not. I don't need anything screwin' me up any more than I already am."

"It's up to you, but it's a shame to come all this way and not get in."

Daniel pulled his legs up to his chest and started to rock like Aaron had seen him do before. Why was he so afraid of everything? It made him seem like a kid, but he didn't look like a kid. He looked beat up and worn out. Even in the moonlight his shadowy form looked defeated. That damn war had taken all the spirit out of him.

Aaron was sure the hot water would relax Daniel and calm his nerves, if he could just get him to try it. But how? He thought about different tactics, but decided there was nothing he could do; the man had to decide for himself.

While he waited for Daniel to make a move, he dipped his head beneath the water, came up, and then did it again. When he came up the next time, Daniel had scooted closer to the edge of the pool. He had his legs pulled up by his chest, like before, but now he was dipping his hand into the water and letting it run out through his fingers.

Aaron kept still and watched. Then, he paddled over and dipped his hands in the water and drizzled it over Daniel's bare legs and feet. Daniel didn't protest, so he gathered dipped up more water and did it again. "See. It's not that hot. You just have to get used to it."

"It's not *too* bad."

"I think if you get in, it might draw that pain out of you. I'm sure it will at least relax your muscles."

"I don't know."

"You should try it."

"Okay. Okay. Give me a minute, would ya."

There was that anger again, but not quite so fierce. Aaron paddled back to the far edge of the pool and looked up at the moon which was straight overhead now. When he glanced back at Daniel, he was standing by the edge of the pool. He had taken off his clothes and seemed to be working up his courage to get in. Finally, he sat down and let his legs dangle in the water up to his knees, then after a few minutes, he scooted off the bank into the water. The man held his arms out to the side and lifted his chest like a little kid who didn't want to take his bath. But then, gradually, he seemed to relax. He moved across the pool and when he was next to Aaron, he sank down into the water and let out a deep moan.

That's just what Aaron wanted to hear. "See. I knew you'd like it."

"Yeah. It feels good. Really good. Like a warm woman holdin' me in her arms."

Aaron laughed. "That's right. A good warm woman."

Daniel laughed too. "Guess that's kind of silly, huh?"

"No. Not at all. I like the idea. It's perfect."

Daniel looked at Aaron as if he had something else to say.

"What?"

Daniel shook his head. "Nothing."

"Tell me. What were you thinking?"

"I was just wondering why you're doing all this."

"All what?"

Daniel shrugged. "I mean, why'd you bring me out here? Aren't you afraid?"

Aaron could see Daniel's face in the moonlight. Now that he was in the water, there wasn't a hint of that meanness in it. "No. I'm not afraid.

I can see you've got a lot of anguish inside you. It's pretty explosive, but I can understand that after what you've been through."

"It's those damn pills. I take 'em for the pain, but they make me sleepy and then . . . well, you know what happens when I go to sleep."

"You need to get those demons out of you, Danny."

"Yeah. But how?"

"I don't know. Maybe you need to focus on things outside yourself."

Daniel let out a deep sigh and leaned back against the rocks. It told Aaron he had done the right thing by bringing him here. Maybe the water would help his mind, as well as his hip.

They both grew silent and Aaron became aware of the sounds of the night: the gurgling water, the crack of a rock as it rolled down the cliff.

They stayed in the water for quite a while. Then they got out to cool off, and got back in.

Aaron felt a cool breeze come up the gorge, and he realized they'd been in the water a long time. "Maybe we should head back to camp," he said. "It's going to be morning before long. I'll make you some breakfast."

They got out of the water and got dressed. Daniel took another pill, and they made their way down the river to where the trail led up from the gorge. It was slow going through the loose rocks, with Aaron pushing Daniel from behind. When they got to the top, dawn was waiting for them with glorious pink streaks of feathery clouds stretched across a pale blue sky. Aaron gasped. "Now that's beautiful."

As they headed across the sagebrush, the sun rose above the mountain peak, drenching the desert with yellow light. Daniel laughed and held out his arms like he wanted to embrace the whole world. He looked clean, almost golden in the morning light as he twirled around and laughed. "Jeez, I feel like I've been playin' with Mary Jane."

Aaron shrugged. "Mary Jane? Who's that?"

"You know. Marijuana."

"Oh yeah. I've heard of that. What is it?"

Daniel stopped twirling and stared at him in amazement. "You know. Dope. Weed. You saying you never tried it?"

"Uh . . . can't say that I have."

"Oh man, you should. It makes things look just like . . . this. The colors. The shine on everything. It's amazing!"

Aaron laughed at his enthusiasm. "But, Danny boy, why would you have to take some drug to see all this? It's right there in front of you."

Daniel frowned. "I dunno know. Guess, 'cuz my brain's half dead. You live with bad things for so long, and pretty soon you can't see the beauty."

"Seems like you subject your body to a lot of different poisons."

Daniel's frown turned into a grin. "Mary Jane's not poison, it's an herb. One of God's natural creations. You can appreciate that, can't you?"

"Really?"

"Sure. It's just like basil or oregano." He giggled.

"And you think it makes you . . . see things?"

Daniel shrugged. "Well, maybe it just breaks your mind open and lets the stuff that's already in there get out. Or shifts you around so you see things in a different way. Something like that." He frowned. "I used to smoke it a lot, but I'm afraid of it now."

"Afraid?"

"Of stuff I don't wanna see. Things that make me feel bad. Come on. Let's not get started on that again."

He headed off into the dazzling light of the sunrise and Aaron followed.

Chapter 9

By the time they got across the sagebrush field and back to camp, Aaron could feel the sweat dripping inside his T-shirt. He was tired and famished, but he felt good, and he felt strong. As he lifted his shirt to let the breeze in, he noticed a ring of white crust on the material around his armpits. What was that?

He touched the crusty stuff and brought his fingers to his nose and looked at Daniel. "Smells metallic. Like rusty nails. That's not good." He touched his fingers to the tip of his tongue. The taste was salty and kind of tart and bitter. He didn't like it one bit. That had to be some pretty bad stuff he had inside him.

Daniel stared at him as he ripped off his shirt and rubbed the crusty places together, then he held the shirt out in front of him and shook it hard. "There. Dust to dust. All that crap is gone."

He stretched his arms to the sky and looked at Daniel. "That's why I come down here, you know? To sweat all that junk out of me."

Daniel shrugged. "Just looks like you're dehydrated to me. Don't we have any beer?" He smirked.

Aaron shook his head in mock disgust. "How about some water and another one of my great sandwiches? I don't really have the fixin's for breakfast."

"Sure. That would be great. I'm so hungry I could eat a horse." Daniel smirked again and plopped down in the sand next to the fire pit, ready to be waited on.

Aaron headed over to the cottonwood trees and sat on the ground while he made a couple of cheese and tomato sandwiches on top of the cooler. He carried the sandwiches over to Daniel and went back for two bottles of water.

While they were eating, Aaron thought about what an odd couple they made, but it was okay with him. It had been a long time since he had participated in any kind of partnership, and he kind of liked it. "I feel lucky I found you, Danny."

Daniel seemed unsure of how to respond. He blinked and rubbed his eyes and took another bite of his sandwich.

Aaron tried to explain. "What I mean is, it's nice to have someone to talk to and someone to share a sandwich with. You're a good man. I enjoy your company."

Daniel's blue eyes shone, like he was hungry for the words he was hearing.

Aaron laughed, feeling a little embarrassed. "I don't know what's gotten into me. I'm not usually so sentimental."

Daniel grinned. "Yeah, and vicey versy."

Aaron laughed again and slapped his leg. "We're quite a twosome here. A couple of wounded heroes."

"Heroes?"

"You know . . . in the war and all that."

Daniel's eyes suddenly felt too penetrating, too full of a question Aaron wasn't sure he wanted to hear. To ward it off, he leaned back on his arms and looked around. The sun was higher and hotter now, and there was heat coming up from the sand. He loved that about the desert —how the ground took in the sun's energy and gave it back as a dry warmth that could work its way deep into your muscles and bones. He loved everything about the desert, really. If he couldn't live in India, this is where he wanted to be.

He turned back to Daniel. "Hey, did I tell you about my house?"

"What house?"

"You know, the one I'm going to build here."

"Oh yeah, you did. But isn't it kind of crazy to build a house out here in the middle of nowhere?"

Aaron frowned. "In the middle of God's creation, is the way I'd put it."

"Whatever you say."

"I've been thinking about it for a long time, and now it's time I put my shovel where my mouth is?"

"Huh?"

"You know. Dig the foundation."

Daniel looked around. "So where's it gonna be?"

Aaron pointed. "Over there on that rise. Laura and I already staked it out. Uh . . . a long time ago. What do you think? Is it a good spot?"

"Jeez, I don't know anything about that kind of stuff."

Aaron could remember Laura saying it would be a shame to be down here in all this beauty and not be able to see it from every room. He pointed to the coral cliffs in the distance. "See all the layers in those cliffs. The different colors of the rock. That's the passage of time, you're seeing there."

"Oh yeah?"

"Those cliffs would make a great view from the living room. Or maybe the bedroom. What do you think?"

"You put a window facing that direction, and you'll have the sun blazing in all summer. It'd be too hot."

"That's right, but you've got the cold winters too. You'd want the sun then, wouldn't you?" He was giving Daniel a test to see if he knew anything about building.

"Guess you'd want the sun in the winter months, but keep it out in the summer."

"That's exactly right. We'll need a hangover."

Daniel slapped his leg and laughed. "Now, that's a good one. I like that. I know all about hangovers."

Aaron scowled. "Don't get smart with me. You know what I mean."

Daniel nodded. "Yeah, I guess I do." He looked toward the ridge and said, "So what do you do about water?"

"That's right. Water. I guess we'll have to dig ourselves a well."

"We?"

"Uh . . . I mean. I guess you won't be here, will you?"

"No, I guess I won't." Daniel picked up a thin stick and started breaking it into little pieces.

Aaron realized he had been hoping Daniel might stay and help him build the house. But of course he wouldn't be doing that. Why would he? It made him sad to think about doing things alone again, so he tried to think of something that would bring back their happier mood. "Say, do you want to see if we can find some of that water?"

"What? You wanna dig for water now?"

"No, not dig. Here, I'll show you." Aaron hurried over to the cottonwood trees and searched the ground until he found a small forked branch that was still green and flexible. He stripped off the leaves and took it back to show Daniel. "See. Now we've got ourselves a witching stick."

"A what?"

"A witching stick. It'll show us where the water is."

"You gotta be kiddin'."

"No, no. I'll show you how it works. Come on."

Daniel got up and they headed through the sagebrush toward a little higher area west of where the house would be. When they got there, Aaron stopped and pointed back. "See. If we find water here, we'll have a natural flow back to the house. We might not even need a pump."

Aaron grasped the two ends of the witching stick, trying to remember how to do it. Palms up. Thumbs out. That's it. He pulled his elbows in to the sides of his body, forcing the end of the stick to tip upwards. "I think this is how it's done."

Daniel was staring at him like it was a crazy idea.

Aaron said, "You'll see." He started walking, holding the stick out in front of himself. He went slow, keeping the upturned tip of the stick slightly rotated towards the ground while he focused his mind on the task. As he walked back and forth, he wondered what he was going to do if he didn't find water. He couldn't live out there without water. He should have looked for water before. But maybe that's why he had put it off. Maybe he didn't want his dream coming to an end over water.

When he had covered about fifty square feet of land, he hadn't felt anything from the stick. He started over again, forcing himself to focus only on water, willing himself to feel some sensation from the stick, but there was nothing there.

Finally, after going over the area two more times, he got frustrated and stopped.

Daniel hobbled over and held out his hand. "Hey, let me give it a try."

Aaron shook his head. "There's nothing here. I've been over it four times."

"I'd like to try it, if you don't mind. Will you show me how?"

Aaron reluctantly handed Daniel the stick and showed him how to hold it. "Now focus your mind. Don't think about anything except water. Imagine it flowing down there beneath the ground, clean and sweet and pure."

He stood by and watched as Daniel started walking. Rather than going back and forth like he had been shown, Daniel made a large initial circle and then started slowly spiraling in. He was totally absorbed, his eyes never leaving the point of the stick. Aaron was amazed by his level of concentration, and there wasn't a hint of his limp.

When he got to the very center of the spiral, Daniel looked up all excited. He waved Aaron over. "It's right here. I'm sure of it."

Aaron laughed. "You just ran out of your circle. That's all."

"No, man. Really. I felt it. The stick pulled down. Isn't that what it's supposed to do?"

"That's right. But I didn't feel anything like that."

"Maybe you just never hit the sweet spot."

Aaron gave him a skeptical look, and Daniel's excitement instantly vanished. "You don't fuckin' believe me, do you?"

The hurt in his voice knocked Aaron back. "Uh . . . sure, I do. I mean . . . why wouldn't I?"

"No, you don't. You think I'm bullshittin' ya." He threw the witching stick at the ground and hobbled away.

Aaron felt awful. He had knocked the joy out of the poor guy, and just when he was starting to get that youthful excitement back in his face. He caught up with Daniel and tried to retract his words. "If you felt it pull, then it's there. It's got to be. I just—"

Daniel kept walking. "Aw, forget it."

Aaron was ashamed. Why did he have to go and spoil the man's pleasure, his feeling of success? He had the chance to make him feel good about himself, and he had spoiled it. That's just the sort of thing his own father would have done. He hated being like his father.

Aaron hurried over to the witching stick and picked it up. He took it to where Daniel had said there was water and gathered some rocks and piled them up. Then he stuck the witching stick into the rocks as a marker. Maybe there really was water there. Maybe Daniel was a born 'witcher'. Maybe he had that special knack that Aaron lacked.

He hurried across the field to where Daniel was sulking by the fire pit. "You know, I think you really did find it, Danny. There's got to be something under there, or you wouldn't have felt it. I marked it. I'll go back to that spot when I'm ready to dig."

"Oh, sure."

"I'm not lying. Some people feel it better than others. I was never any good at water witchin. My father made a point of letting me know that. But you've got the knack. I'm sure you do."

"Really?" Daniel's eyes lit up. "You really think so?"

"I'm sure of it."

"You wouldn't shit me, would ya?"

Aaron laughed. "No. I wouldn't shit you. I promise."

Chapter 10

By mid-morning, the desert was starting to heat up. Daniel's face was all red and sweaty, and he kept pulling up his shirt and flapping it around like he was trying to get a bit of a breeze going. Aaron suggested they go sit in the shade under the cottonwood trees. But even there, Daniel still looked hot and bothered. He got up and started pacing.

Aaron raised a hand to try to stop him. "What's wrong with you? Got ants in your pants?"

"Man, I can't sit around here all day. I gotta go find my camping spot."

"You can camp here all you want."

He kept pacing, dragging his one leg along like he couldn't get it going. "No way. I gotta get to Saint George. I got people waitin'."

"Your girl friend?"

"What? No. I told you, I don't have no fuck . . . uh, no girl. I just gotta meet some guys I know. They're probably wonderin' where the hell I am. Besides, I can't sit in one place like this. It's drivin' me nuts."

Aaron remembered that look on Daniel's face. And he remembered what caused it. "It's those cigarettes, isn't it?"

Daniel glared at him. "So what? You think 'cuz I don't smoke for a few hours, I'm all over it. You don't know nothin' about it."

"I guess not."

Daniel picked up a thick stick and threw it at the trunk of one of the cottonwood trees. It bounced back and almost hit him in the leg. He threw up his hands, and yelled, "So, you gonna take me over there, or not?"

"I guess I better. You look like you're ready to explode."

As soon as the words were out of Aaron's mouth, Daniel hurried to the fire pit, grabbed his duffel bag, and headed straight for the truck.

Aaron shook his head. He felt bad that he was going to lose the company of his new friend, but he could see the demon cigarettes were calling Daniel. Nothing else seemed to matter, not the time they had shared at the hot springs, not the fact that they had come to understand each other a bit. The man was going to have his cigarettes, no matter what.

Aaron picked up the cooler and put it in the back of the truck. Then, he rolled up his sleeping bag, and packed up the other stuff they had used. He leaned against the side of the truck and looked out at the landscape. He wasn't really ready to leave the desert, but Daniel was sitting in the truck waiting for him. He thought maybe he should go back to Salt Lake after he dropped Daniel off in Saint George. He could check on things there and buy the building materials he would need to go forward on his house: lumber, cement, nails—all that stuff. And he had better bring down his cement mixer and his generator too. He was ready to get started.

As they bounced along the rutted dirt road back to the highway, Aaron tried to start up a conversation to get back on friendly terms with Daniel. "I guess I'll probably head back to Salt Lake after I drop you off. Pick up some stuff I'll need for the house."

"Why would you want to drive all the way back up there? Can't you get what you need in Saint George?"

"Uh . . . I dunno. Maybe, but I've got . . . machinery to bring down."

Daniel grunted and kept his eyes straight ahead. He held his arms tight against the side of his chest like he was trying to hold himself together. Aaron thought maybe the bumpy road was hurting his hip, so he slowed down and said, "Sorry. I guess I'm going too fast." Then suddenly, he felt like all this had happened before. Like he'd been on this road, and he'd said the same thing. Was it true? Or was his mind just going around in a loop?

Daniel didn't say a word until they finally got to the turnoff to Hurricane. Then he spoke up. "Damn, Aaron, I don't think I can make it to Saint George. How about stopping for cigs at that gas station we saw in Hurricane when we were there before?"

Aaron nodded. Might as well help the poor fellow out. He was going to have his cigarette sooner or later, so he might as well have it now.

They got to the gas station and Daniel was out of the truck and heading inside before Aaron could even shut off the engine. While he waited, he noticed Laura's poems in the side pocket of the door. Maybe he had time to read a quick one. He took the binder out and turned the pages until he found one that started with some words that he liked.

> My love, my love can't you hear me
> Calling within my dream
> My darling, my love won't you listen
> And give back my voice again

The loving words were nice, but there was that darn blame again. Didn't she have anything but blame?

He flipped through the pages trying to find something besides accusations. And then, he found one—a poem called, *My Secret Garden*. Surely, this was a happy one. Laura loved her garden. She'd spent hours out there, tending to her irises and roses and the annuals she'd plant every year. Even before the snow had completely melted, she'd be out in her little greenhouse planting her seeds and tending to the little buds.

He balanced the binder on the steering wheel and read.

> My Secret Garden
> by Laura Young
> June 17, 1978
>
> She slips outside the silent midnight room
> To meet her darling flower 'neath the moon
> While back behind his dark impervious screen
> Her sleeping man falls deep into his dream
>
> As the cadence of the crickets quicken
> The dew finds her skin and glistens
> Out to the shimmering water where no man ever goes
> Across the narrow path to where her perfect flower grows
> Ravens thrash the sky in strident warning
> As the moon fills her heart with restless yearning
> She cannot be denied
>
> It's not for a lover's touch she hungers
> It's not for a man who's kind and strong
> She wants to live in the heart of beauty
> And know that she belongs

When he finished the poem his head was reeling. What did all that mean? Crickets? Thrashing ravens? Her darling flower? Was she saying she had a secret lover? He wanted to read the poem again to try and understand why it upset him so much, but Daniel was heading back to the truck.

He slammed the binder shut and shoved it back inside the door pocket. He didn't want Daniel asking any questions about it. Not now, when he was feeling so bewildered. And above all else, he didn't want Daniel seeing the poem and making comments about its raw sexuality. Was it sexual? He wasn't sure. But if it wasn't, why did he feel so hot?

Daniel climbed in the truck with a cigarette already going. He glanced at Aaron. "Thanks, man, I owe you one."

Aaron shook himself, trying to recover. "Uh . . . yeah. It's okay. If you need it, you need it."

As Aaron pulled out of the gas station, Daniel settled back in the seat and blew out a big cloud of smoke.

Still upset and irritated by the poem, Aaron couldn't keep himself from taking it out on Daniel. He flapped his hand at the smoke. "Look. You may not be ready to quit, but I'm not ready to start, if you know what I mean."

Daniel winced. "Sorry." He rolled down the window and tried to blow the smoke out, but most of it came right back in. "I guess you'll be glad to get rid of me."

Aaron wasn't so sure about that. Besides, he shouldn't be blaming Daniel for Laura's baffling words. "Don't worry about it. I guess I'll survive."

"You just keep being nice, don't ya? You'll get me used to it, you know. Then, what will I do when you're not around?" The look on his face told Aaron he wasn't joking.

That was nice. At least, *Daniel* liked him. "You can always come visit me at my little house."

Daniel smirked. "Right. But then you don't really have one."

"Not yet. Just give me a few months."

After they turned onto the road that led to the freeway, Aaron looked over and met Daniel's eyes. "I hope you do come see me. We can go back out to the hot springs. It did you some good, don't you think?"

Daniel gave a slight nod. "Yeah. I guess so."

They crossed over the Virgin River bridge and soon they were on the freeway headed toward Saint George. Aaron thought about Daniel. It seemed like the man had changed out there in the desert, at least a little. Until he started thinking about his cigarettes again. He had stopped the constant bad language, and he didn't seem so wound up as before. Maybe there was a chance he could quit smoking and get healthy, if only he could be distracted long enough. It gave Aaron an idea. "Hey, my friend, what would you say if I asked you to help me build my house?"

"Me?"

"Sure. I could even pay you a little something. We could camp out together until it's finished. I'll pay for the food, and stuff."

Daniel wouldn't look at him. "Nah. I don't know nothin' about construction."

"Well, I could teach you. That would be good, wouldn't it? It would give you some skills you could use."

Daniel pointed to his hip. "What about my hip? You know I can't get around all that good."

"You seem to manage when you want to."

Daniel stared out the window.

Aaron said, "I've got to go back to Salt Lake to get the rest of my tools. You can come with me if you want. I've got a spare room up there."

Daniel looked at him. His blue eyes seemed shiny and interested, but then he quickly looked away. "Hell, man. I don't wanna go back to that shit hole. I just got away from there."

"Well, all right then. Stay in Saint George, if you want to. I can come pick you up there when I come back."

"How can you pick me up, if I don't know where I'll be?"

What was wrong with this guy? He was just trying to help. He banged his hand against the steering wheel. "Sounds like you're just full of excuses. Why don't you just say no, if you don't want to do it."

Daniel shrugged. "It's not that, man. I'm just kind of . . . I mean, I haven't done any real work. You know, for pay . . . in a long time."

"So, now's your chance. Why not? It'd be fun."

Daniel pulled his fingers through his long hair and seemed to think it over. Finally, he said, "Well, okay . . . I guess I could try."

"All right, then," said Aaron. "We have a plan." It was a great idea, and he wondered why he hadn't thought of it before. He liked the solitude of the desert, but maybe he wasn't ready to be out there alone just yet. And besides, he really could use some help. He would have to do all the heavy lifting, but if Daniel got stronger, maybe he could even help with that.

When they got to Saint George, Daniel said, "Uh . . . could you just drop me off at the park. It's just off the freeway. I'm supposed to meet my friends there. Anyway, if they're still around."

"Sure. I can do that."

When they got to the park, Daniel got out quickly and grabbed his duffel bag from the back. Then he came back to the open window and said, "Thanks a lot, man. I really appreciate you bringing me into town, and . . . uh, everything else."

Aaron nodded. "So I'll look for you here when I come back. Is that right?"

"Uh . . . yeah, right."

"You'll be here?"

"Sure. Or somewhere around here. I'll watch for ya."

Their eyes met for a brief moment, then Daniel shrugged and turned away.

Aaron watched him limp across the grass toward a group of rough-looking men who were sitting in a circle on the ground. Suddenly, he doubted that Daniel would be there when he came back. He would probably fall right back into his life of smoking cigarettes and staying drunk with his buddies. It wouldn't be long before he'd forgotten all about their time in the desert. It was sad, but if that's the kind of life Daniel wanted to live, there was nothing he could do about it. A man has to live his own life. That's something Aaron understood. He started up the truck and drove away.

Chapter 11

After the long drive from Saint George, it was late afternoon when Aaron got home. He parked the truck in the driveway, grabbed the keys from the ignition, and hurried into the house to use the bathroom. But something was wrong: there was something sweet, like perfume in the air. Or maybe it was that after-shave stuff. Had someone been in his house? He hurried and checked the doors and windows. They were all closed, and it didn't look like anyone had broken in. Still, he was sure somebody had been there.

After he used the bathroom, he took another look around the house and found a note stuck to the telephone. It said,

> Dad,
> Call me immediately!!!
> Sarah

Oh no! Did something happen to Sarah? Was she hurt?

He looked frantically through his stack of phone numbers and finally found her number and dialed her up.

She started yelling as soon as she answered. "Dad! Where are you? I've been looking all over for you."

"Why? Did I do something wrong?"

"I called and called, but you never answered. Then when I came over, it looked like you should be there, but you weren't. You can't do that, Dad."

"I can't do what? What did I do?"

"I thought something happened to you."

Now, it sounded like she was crying. Why was she crying? He hadn't done anything to warrant that, had he? "Well, I'm sorry, but I told you I was going down to my property."

"No, you didn't."

"I'm sure I did. You must have forgot."

"You didn't tell me, Dad. And anyway, why would you leave your bedroom window open if you were leaving town?"

"It was open?"

"Yes. And there were wet clothes in the washer."

"There were?"

"Yes. They were starting to smell. I had to wash them again."

"Uh . . . I guess I forgot to check. It's not the end of the world."

"From now on, you've got to tell me if you're going away. Okay? We've got to talk about it first."

Talk about it. Why did she think they needed to talk about it? He didn't need her permission to do things. "Now wait just a doggone minute, Sarah. I'm not going to tell you everything I do. It's ridiculous for you to be so upset. You better cool yourself off."

"Don't you understand, Dad? I was worried about you. We'd just been talking about Mom's poems, and you were really upset. Don't you remember that?"

"Well, I'm sorry, honey, but that's exactly why I needed to get out of here for a while. And I don't think I need to tell you when I do that."

There was a uncomfortable silence, then Sarah said, "Dad, are you having more trouble remembering things?"

"No. I'm not. Why would you think that?"

"Hmmm . . . I just noticed that you have the same phone numbers written down quite a few times."

Now, what was she going after? "Yeah, so what?"

"Well, you even have your own number written down a couple of times."

"I don't exactly call myself, do I? So how am I supposed to remember my number?"

"I guess that's right, but you *have* lived there a long time."

Now that was irritating. Sure, he forgot things now and then, he knew that, but it wasn't as bad as she was making out. "Well you might consider that I've had a lot on my mind."

"I know, Dad. That's another thing that worries me. I want you to be happy."

He didn't respond because he didn't know what to say. Sure he was unhappy sometimes. Laura's poems made him unhappy, but there was no reason for her to go on and on about it.

He wanted to hang up, but she said, "Look, Dad, I'm sorry. I didn't mean to get you upset. It's just that . . . I was worried. Promise me you won't take off like that again without telling me. Please."

"You might as well get used to it. I'll be coming and going a lot from now on. I've decided to build my house."

"What house?"

"Now you're the one forgetting. I've talked about building that house down in the desert for years. I'm finally going to do it. I'm going to build my house and move down there."

"But what about your work? Don't you still have jobs now and then?"

"My work? If I need to work, I'll work down there. They need drywall too, don't they?"

"In the desert?"

"You know what I mean."

"But how would we keep track of you if you moved down there?"

Oh great, now she was whining. He shook his head in frustration. "Damn it. I don't need anybody tracking me. I can track myself."

"I'm sorry. I didn't mean it like that. It's just that I'd . . . worry. If you were down there alone."

"I wouldn't be alone."

"What do you mean?"

"I met this guy. He's going to help me build my house."

"Really? Who is he?"

"He's just . . . one of those guys. I picked him up out there by, you know . . . down by Nebo."

"Oh no. You're not still picking up hitchhikers, are you?"

"Well, somebody's got to do it. We can't just let them stand out there on the road all day until they rot."

"Why does it always have to be you that picks them up? Why can't you let somebody else do it?"

He decided not to respond to that. He was fed up with arguing.

His silence didn't keep Sarah from going on. "That's the kind of thing that worries me, Dad. You go off, and I don't know where you are, and then you pick up strangers. What if you pick up some nutcase who takes you off somewhere and hurts you? How would we ever find out what happened?"

"Listen, Sarah, I've been taking care of myself for a good long time. I guess I'll just keep doing that, if you don't mind. Now I'm tired and hungry, and I think I'll go make myself something to eat."

"Wait a minute, Dad."

"What now?"

"I'm sorry. Don't be upset with me. I just want you to be safe. You know that. We can talk about this later, okay?"

"Fine." He hung up the phone, feeling deflated. What was the matter with her? Why did she have to go on and on about such a little thing? Maybe he did forget to call her, but so what? He was a grown man. He didn't have to answer to her. Why did she have to make mountains out of . . . moles?

His stomach felt like something was in there trying to gnaw its way out. Maybe he should find something to eat and try to calm it down. He went to the kitchen and looked in the fridge. It was empty. He stood there staring at the empty shelves. Then he remembered he had food in the truck. He went out and brought in the cooler. He made a toasted cheese sandwich with the leftover cheese and bread. He stood in front of the sink and ate the sandwich quickly before heading off to the bathroom to take a shower.

When he finished cleaning up, there was still a bit of light outside, but he felt exhausted. It was probably because of that darn talk with Sarah. Might as well go to bed and get some sleep.

For a long time, he lay awake staring at the ceiling, feeling agitated and depressed. He'd only been back in Salt Lake for a few hours, and his enthusiasm was already drained.

When he realized sleep wasn't going to come, he started thinking about Laura's poems again. Why wouldn't they leave him alone? Then, he remembered he hadn't brought the binder in from the truck. If he didn't get it now, he'd probably forget where it was, and then Sarah would be after him about that too.

He slipped his pants on and went out to the truck to grab the binder. Then he hurried back to bed to get warm. Knowing he still wasn't going to be able to sleep, he turned on the lamp and picked up the binder. Hadn't he read a poem about Laura and her garden? There was something about that one that had baffled him even more than the others. Maybe he should read it again to see if he could understand it any better.

He flipped through the pages until he found one called "The Wild Vines of My Garden." Was that the one? He wasn't sure, but it might be.

> The Wild Vines of My Garden
> Laura Young (August 1980)
>
> I search my garden damp with rain
> To find a flower to heal my pain
> A violet safe inside its nest
> A salvo for my aching breast
>
> But eyes befogged with silent tears
> Cannot escape the troubled years
> Nor see the healing flower grow
> Beneath the radiant sunlight glow

No, it wasn't the same poem. It couldn't be. He understood this one perfectly. It was just another sad poem full of pain. He put his arm across his eyes wondering how she could turn her treasured garden into a dreadful place of gloom. It didn't make sense, but if that's how she felt, that's how she felt. He should face it and try to find out why. He read on.

> Parasitic plants will cling
> And suck the hope from all life brings
> Within their greedy vines ensnare
> The flower's bloom cannot repair
>
> Then just when I have turned to leave
> I glimpse the lily 'neath the eave
> So white and pure in raindrop light
> A sign of hope, the world is bright

He closed the binder and held it against his chest. At least the end of the poem had a little hope. Still, it made him wonder if Laura was just unhappy for some reason that he didn't understand. Maybe it wasn't his fault at all. If she couldn't find joy even when writing about her garden, maybe she couldn't find joy in anything. But what would make a person feel like that?

He tried to reason it through, but the last lines of the poem had created an image in his mind that he couldn't escape. That pure white lily in raindrop light was a beautiful image that he knew well from walking in Laura's garden. As sad as they were, most of Laura's poems were beautiful. He had to give her that. He had never cared for poetry, or understood it all that much, but Laura's poems were different. Knowing her helped him to read between the lines more than he could with most poems. He could see how she took things from her world and used them in her poems to reflect what was deep and personal, and so often sad. He wasn't sure, but he thought her poems were probably quite good.

It occurred to him that it might have helped Laura if she could have gotten her poems out into the world instead of hiding them in her closet. If she had been given that opportunity, would she have still written sad poems, poems about the trouble and disappointment she had with him? Maybe if she was happier she would have written poems about love and beauty. And maybe all she would have needed to be happy was to share her poems with the world and have them be appreciated and valued. If only he had known about the poems, maybe he could have encouraged her to do that and helped her somehow.

Well, there was no use thinking about all that now. He couldn't go back and change anything, and now he was in the same boat she was in, feeling alone with nothing of value in his life. Oh, he had Sarah and his grandkids and his son Michael was off in California . . . somewhere. He loved them all, but a man needed more than that. He needed a woman to love. Someone who valued him as a man. Not just as a wife. Not just as the mother of his children. But as a friend and a lover, a companion who he could share things with. That's what he needed now more than anything. But he knew he wasn't going to find it. He was way beyond all that.

He put the binder down, turned off the lamp, and stared up into the darkness. This was the bed where he lay with Laura that last night of her life, the night she kissed him with such deep passion, that night when she had asked him to give her one last bath.

Suddenly, it occurred to him that she knew he would need those last bittersweet moments to hold on to after he found her poems in the closet. Perhaps that was her last gift to him.

Chapter 12

It took Aaron a week to purchase all the building materials he would need for his little house in the desert. He had it all packed in his truck, but before he could get on the road, an old friend called to say he had a drywall job.

"I'm sorry, Martin. I was about to leave town."

"No, no, you can't do that, Aaron. My son and his new wife are coming to live with us. We need to get a room ready for them."

"I'm sorry. I can't do it, but I can give you someone else's name, if you like."

"No way. I can't have one of those young bucks doing it."

"Why not? I trained every last one of them. They know how to do it."

"I need *you*. My wife needs perfection."

Aaron chuckled. "Well, if you're gonna butter me, I guess I'll have to say yes. When should I come by to see what we need?"

"Tomorrow morning?"

"Sure. Fine. I'll be there in the morning."

Three weeks later, he still hadn't left for the desert. He'd finished the drywall for Martin's room, and he was all set to go, but Martin said he had a friend who just had to have his basement done, and fast. Before Thanksgiving.

Aaron told him no, but when he found out how much the friend was willing to pay, he changed his mind. It seemed like he was back in the swing of it again. One job led to the next, and before he knew it, several months had passed. He kept wondering why he was so popular all of a sudden. Had somebody put out the word that he was trying to leave town? Were they trying to make him stay?

He hated the fact that he couldn't get down to the desert, but he thought he better do the work while it was there. He could use the extra money to pay someone to bring a backhoe out to his property to dig the foundation. It would be expensive to get somebody to come clear out there, but it would be a lot faster than digging it by hand.

When his drywall work was finally finished up, it was too late to go. Winter was in full swing. There was a foot and half of heavy snow in the backyard, and the valley had filled up with its usual depressing gray smog. He hated that smog and thought about leaving for the desert anyway, but then he came down with a bad case of the flu.

He couldn't complain too much because it brought Sarah to the house. She showed up every few days to bring him things like chicken soup and some kind of herbal tea she said would help him recover faster. He loved having her there. Sometimes she brought the kids with her, and he could hear their sweet voices and laughter echoing through the house. That's how a house should be, he thought. Full of happy sounds. That's what I've been missing.

One day, he felt quite a bit better, but when he heard Sarah arrive, he hopped back into bed and pretended to be asleep. When she came into the bedroom and touched his cheek, he let out a little moan before he opened his eyes.

"Hi Dad. I think you should come and eat in the kitchen today. Why don't you get dressed."

She must have known he was faking. Too bad. By tomorrow, he'd be back to cooking his own meals.

He got dressed and went to the kitchen. Sarah sat across from him and watched him eat the spaghetti she'd made. She had a weary look on her face that told him she was ready to get back to her own life. He ate slowly, and when he had finished, he looked her in the eye and said, "Well, I guess it's time for me to go down and start my house."

She threw up her hands. "Oh, no, Dad. I thought you'd forgotten about that."

"Forgotten about it? Why would I do that?"

She looked troubled as she reached across the table and took his hand. "Dad, I don't understand. What would you do down there all by yourself?"

"I'll build my house, and then I'll live in it."

"But it's so isolated down there. Wouldn't you get lonely?"

"I'm lonely here. So what's the difference?"

She frowned. He was sorry he had said that, especially after she'd been taking such good care of him. But that wasn't the kind of loneliness he was talking about. It was the loneliness he felt even when other people were around, especially when they talked about all the day-to-day things they were involved in. He didn't understand the feeling exactly. Maybe it was just getting harder for him to connect with the world because he spent so much time alone. It would be better to be in the desert where being alone was natural. He realized he never felt lonely down there. How could you feel lonely in the middle of such beauty?

Sarah squeezed his hand. "What are you thinking?"

"Oh, just this and that."

"You look sad."

"No, not sad. I'm just . . . ready."

"Ready?"

"Ready to do something different."

She looked away, and he realized she'd taken that as a rejection, but he didn't mean it that way. He tried to explain. "Don't you see. I've been doing the same things I've been doing my whole life. I want to do something different. I'm tired of rattling around this house. I feel like I'm one of those . . . uh, rabbits . . . on a wheel."

"You mean, a rat on a treadmill?"

"Yeah. Like that."

She squinted and looked up at the ceiling and then back at him like she was hatching a plan. "Maybe if you didn't have so much work, it would be better. What if that slowed down some? You could kick back and take it easy. You could do some reading. Or maybe take a class at the university, or help out in a community garden, or something. You'd like that, wouldn't you?"

"I don't know anything about all that. The last time I was at the university was before I went to the war, and that was just for a short time."

"Well, you could at least stop working and figure out what you'd like to do. You can live on your Social Security, can't you?"

"I don't get that much because I've always worked for myself." He looked around. "Maybe I'll sell this one. That would give me more money to work with."

"Sell this house? You can't do that. You and Mom built it."

He shrugged. "I might have to."

"But . . . but then you wouldn't have a place here in Salt Lake. Are you saying, you'd move down there permanently?" Her voice was shrill, but he wasn't going to let her change his mind.

"Why not? I feel good when I'm down there."

"Oh, Daddy. That would be terrible. What about Sam and Annie? They'd never get to see their grandpa."

"Well, it's not like I'd be on the other side of the world. You can come down anytime you want. I'll teach the kids how to rope a cactus." He smiled at his own joke.

"I just don't think it's a good idea for you to be all by yourself in the middle of nowhere. You wouldn't even have a phone, would you?"

He shrugged.

"Well, maybe you could build a *little* place, and you could go there *sometimes*. You know, when you get the wanderlust."

"A little place is all I want. I don't need this big one. And besides, what will happen if I'm not here to watch all this and take care of the yard? Yes. I think it's a good idea. I should sell this place."

Sarah turned to look around, like she was trying to find another angle. "What about your piano?"

"What?"

"Your piano? What would you do with a baby grand in a little house?"

That's right. What about the piano? He didn't want to lose *that*. "Uh . . . maybe you can keep it for me."

She gave him a stern look. "Think about this move carefully, Dad. Don't rush into it."

He frowned and looked away.

"Promise me you'll think about it, and don't do anything until we talk again. Okay? And don't be taking off without letting me know."

She was trying to take the steam out of everything again. He hated that. Still, she might be right. Maybe he *would* miss his piano. But if it was at her house, he could drive back up and play it sometimes, couldn't he? It didn't take any longer to drive one way than it did the other. It didn't make sense to keep a big house. He didn't need it, and he didn't want to be in the city anymore, even if he did lose the piano. And besides, he could get another piano. A small one. He could play it for the coyotes.

Sarah grabbed his hand across the table. "Listen, Dad. I have an idea. What if you sold this house and bought something smaller? Then, you'd have the money to build with, and you could have a place in Salt Lake too."

He thought about it. "Well . . . that might work."

"You could buy a place closer to me and the kids. That way, I'd at least be able to keep tabs on you when you're here."

He scowled.

She shot him a grin. "I'm just kidding about keeping tabs. Really, it would just be nice to have you closer. You know, when you come up to Salt Lake, I mean."

"Well, I guess I'd have to see how much they'd give me for this place, before I could do any of that."

He looked around, trying to imagine his house through other peoples' eyes. It was a large ranch style house, with three bedrooms and two baths. Laura had designed it, so it had some nice extra details, a mudroom next to the entry, nice crown molding in the living room, and beautiful wood floors in the kitchen. What he liked the most about the house was that it had lots of windows. He hated being cooped up in the dark.

Sarah said, "You know, Dad, it's a good-sized house, and you've got at least an acre of land. You should be able to get quite a bit for it."

"I'll do it, then. I'll put out a sign and see what they'll give me."

Sarah shook her head. "I don't think that's a good idea. You should hire a real estate agent, somebody who knows what they're doing. And you'll have to wait until spring, now. People don't like moving in the winter."

"Why not?"

"Well, most people don't like to move their kids to a new school in the middle of the year. And besides, who wants to move when it's cold and snowy?"

He let out a big sigh. "I guess you're right."

"So we'll wait until spring and talk about it then. Okay?"

He realized he shouldn't have let Sarah get going with her plans. Now she was going to try to twist his arm until it broke. He had to take a stand. "I can't wait that long to sell. I want to get down to my property and get going on things now."

"Well, you should think about it. You should try to get as much as you can for this house. It doesn't show as well in the winter."

He frowned and folded his arms across his chest, trying to hold onto what he had.

"Really, Dad. If you wait just a little longer, you'll end up with more money to work with. That would be nice, wouldn't it?"

Her face lit up with a sweet smile, and he caved in. "Okay. Okay. I'll think about it."

That seemed to satisfy her. She gathered up her stuff, gave him a hug and a kiss on the cheek, and then she left quickly, promising to call later.

When she was gone, Aaron went to his bedroom and took the calendar down from the wall. He flipped forward to March and put a big "X" on the first day of spring, adding the words, *BUILD MY HOUSE!!* Then, he remembered that spring weather never really came to Salt Lake until the end of April, or sometimes into May. It would be warm enough in the desert to start building by February or March, but he might have to wait until the end of April to sell his house. He didn't like it one bit, but he turned to April and marked another "X" across the third week of April. That's the longest he would wait to put the house up for sale, no matter what Sarah said. He'd get one of those house people, and let them take care of things while he went down south to get started building. By summer, his new place would be well underway, and he'd be living out there in the desert where he belonged.

Chapter 13

Winter had worked its way into Aaron's bones so deep it was hard for him to get out of bed every morning. His joints hurt and his muscles hurt, and he felt weak. He hated that feeling. He was not a weak man, he never had been.

One morning, he decided to stay in bed awhile longer. No point in even getting up. It was too cold and dreary. Why couldn't the days be like the winter days of his youth? Back then, storms would blow in from the Great Salt Lake, and a few hours later, the whole valley would be covered in glistening snow. Then, the clouds would fly away and leave the air so sparkling clean you could taste its sweetness.

It was nothing like that now. For weeks, the whole valley had been smothered under a thick blanket of dirty air that burned his throat. He was sure the toxins were working their way into his blood. He could even feel it in his brain, making him forget things. Sometimes, he'd walk into a room and he couldn't remember what he was after. Or he'd try to think what day it was, and wasn't sure. But maybe that was just because the days were too much the same. That's probably what it was. Besides, everybody forgets a few things as they get older, don't they?

He rolled onto his side, thinking how that sure wasn't true of his mother. She stayed sharp until the very last days of her life. His father was sharp too, but then he died young. There was no way to know how his mind would have gone had he lived longer.

The person he did know about was his sister Miriam. Not long after they locked her up in that terrible place, she didn't know where she was, and she didn't recognize anyone who came to visit her. He couldn't stand to think he might end up like her, sitting in the same chair every day, staring at the same blank wall. No. He wasn't even close to being like that.

He did *look* like Miriam. There was no getting around that. They both had that same long straight nose and high cheekbones. Maybe they had that forgetting thing in common too. Is that how it worked? If you got the good things, did you get the bad things too?

Thinking about all that was just making him anxious. Maybe he should go back to sleep.

He pulled the covers up tight around his neck and was starting to drift off when he thought of that night he almost got strangled. Was that a dream? Or was it real? It seemed like it was real. It was terrifying to think he was going to die. Then he remembered who did it. It was that crazy guy from the war that he picked up. The man with the messed up leg. He thought about it more, and it seemed like he was supposed to do something with that man. But what would he be doing with a mean guy like that? Maybe it *was* just a dream.

Lying there in bed was just bringing up more and more disturbing thoughts. He should get up and do something. But what? He didn't have any drywall jobs scheduled, and he didn't have any place to go. Maybe he should just stay where he was and read some of Laura's poems. He had been trying to read a few everyday. Even though it often left him feeling deflated, he still wanted to know what she had to say. He'd promised himself to read every last one.

He sat up and grabbed the blue binder from the table. After leafing through the pages, he came to a poem about love. He knew he couldn't count on it being happy. He had given up looking for that.

> The Tender Fruit of Our Love
> by Laura Young
> November 5, 1949
>
> Darling child at my full breast
> With dewy mouth and glistening eyes
> Transport me to our night of love
> When all our gentle words and sighs
> Our burning breath, our trembling thighs
> Began to meld our hearts

This poem was beautiful, and not unhappy at all. It made him think of all that passion he and Laura had when they were young. She was so . . . full of heat back then, with her dewy mouth and trembling thighs, like she said in the poem. He had almost forgotten about that.

> Within our nectar so sublime
> His soul took hold, began to shine
> A life emergent from our joy,
> Descended from our God divine
> Took balance on that human twine
> Within our melded hearts

It surprised him the way she mixed words about passion with words about God and the Divine. It felt like the poem was telling him that she felt the same as he did about passion. If God had made humans to feel passion, how could it be wrong to feel that way, even if that's what the church said? But maybe it was just a test God set up to see if you'd fail.

He read the poem again. He liked this one. Liked it more than any of the others because it gave him something he could recognize. Something that told him they weren't all that different.

The poem got him thinking about that first night of their honeymoon at Blue Lake, and all those days and nights after that when they only wanted to be with each other. When did that change? It must have changed. Laura's poems were the proof of that. But when did it happen? And what caused it?

Could it have started during that time when he was out of work and couldn't pay the bills? That was a hard time for both of them. Then, even after the jobs came back, he was all tense and worried, and he took every job he could get. That might have made Laura feel like he didn't have any time for her, and maybe even make her think that he didn't love her.

The idea that he might have let that rough time affect him in the same way his father had been affected by the Depression was almost too much to bear. It meant he had turned out like his father. Neither one of them could recover from something that only lasted a short time. It was crazy. He didn't have to work like a dog all his life. He didn't have to move his family from house to house, trying to get ahead, always trying to do better, do more. For what? So he and Laura would have a nest egg. As it turned out, it was a big waste. She wasn't there to enjoy it. And he couldn't enjoy it without her. So what was it all for? It was crazy what you could do when you got yourself all messed up.

He felt irritated with himself. What was he doing lying in bed all day dredging up the past? It was just a big waste of time. He kicked off the covers and quickly dressed. Then he hurried to the bathroom to wash his face. The mirror over the sink stopped him. Who was that sad looking man in the mirror? Could it really be the same man who made such passionate love to his Lori all those years ago? It didn't seem possible.

He turned away in disgust and tried to think what he could do to escape his bad mood. It might help if he could get out of the toxic air. And the only place to do that was up in the mountains. The air had to be better up there. Sure. That's what he'd do. He'd drive up to the mountains.

Afraid his lethargy might overcome him, he quickly found a sweater and his wool hat and gloves and headed for the door. On the way out, he grabbed an apple. That would have to do as his breakfast.

Once he was in his truck, he headed north along the foothills, then he turned east into Parley's Canyon. As he headed up out of the Salt Lake Valley, it felt like he was being chased by the bad air. It worried him that it might be bad everywhere, but then, halfway to the summit, he saw his first patch of blue sky.

Eager to reach that patch of sky, he pressed the gas pedal and moved over into the fast lane. Instantly, someone blasted their horn. He looked in the rearview mirror and saw a monstrous black truck riding his bumper. The truck was so close, it felt like the guy wanted to drive right over the top of him. Aaron darted back into the slow lane. The black truck flew by on his left, with the driver flashing his middle finger.

What in the hell was wrong with *him*? Was he crazy?

The confrontation left Aaron shaken. What happened? Was he so excited about that little patch of blue sky that he forgot to look before he changed lanes? Or had he forgotten to put his turn signal on? Maybe it was his fault. The bad air down in the valley must have affected him so much he was forgetting things. Maybe he shouldn't be driving. Maybe he should turn around and go straight back home.

No! He wasn't going to do that. He needed air. Good clean air. As much as he could get. He had to keep going.

When he had finally made his way up to the summit and saw the next little valley ahead, he gasped. It was even better than he had thought it would be. The countryside was covered with the same fresh sparkling snow that he knew as a boy. He opened the window and took a deep breath. The cool sweet air filled his lungs, and almost immediately, his mind felt clearer. This was *exactly* what he needed.

Shortly after he took the turn-off to the little ski town of Park City, he saw a gas station and looked down at his gauge. It showed less than a quarter tank. He decided he'd better get some. He pulled up next to a pump, but as he headed inside to pay, he reached for his wallet and found it wasn't there. Now where in the heck was his wallet? Had he forgotten to bring it? No, he wouldn't have done that. It must have fallen out of his pocket.

He went back to the truck and searched the seat, and the floor, and the space behind the seat. The wallet wasn't there. He *must* have forgotten it. But how could he have gotten in his truck and driven all the way up here without once thinking about his wallet? Now he was going to have to be careful and not go too far, or he might run out of gas.

Feeling exasperated with himself, he got back on the road. As he drove slowly into Park City, he tried not to look at the gas gauge. He didn't want his whole day being ruined by something as dumb as running out of gas.

When he had driven through town, and he was out beyond the houses, he remembered his father bringing the family up that way for a hike in the snow when he was about eight . . . maybe nine. They ended up tromping across some snow-covered field and following a long trail up into the pine forest. That was the day he fell in love with the smell of pine. It was a wonderful scent, like spice and mint mixed together. It would be fun to go find that trail again, see if he could make it back up to those pines. Now, if he could just remember where it was.

There were some higher snow covered mountains in the distance, and he thought that might be where it was. But as he drove in that direction, it didn't seem quite right. Wasn't he supposed to be in a narrow valley with a river on one side? He clearly remembered watching for the gray patches of light reflecting off the frozen river between the trees.

When he came to a side road, he took it, thinking it might get him to the right place. Soon the road narrowed, and it seemed right. It looked like it might be a private road, but it had been plowed, so they must be used to people coming through there. That was good. That's probably where they went before.

He drove slowly, and as he came around a bend he saw a place to pull off. There was a little farmhouse off to the right that he thought looked familiar. This was it. It had to be the place he had come with his father.

After he parked and got out of the truck, he saw an old rusted barbed-wire fence with a bent up "No Trespassing" sign that was sagging down towards the snow. Now, he was sure he was in the right place. He remembered that sign, and he remembered wondering if his father was going to ignore its warning. And of course, his father *did* ignore it. His father believed that nature belonged to everyone and that access to the mountains shouldn't be fenced off. Aaron felt the same way. Maybe they were alike in more ways than he thought.

As he approached the sagging fence, he felt just about as excited as he had as a child. He could almost see his father stepping over the fence with his long legs, and then stopping on the other side to hold the middle wires open while the rest of them ducked through. They were all there: Miriam and himself, and little Stevie. He tried to think if his mother was there too. Was she? It seemed strange that he couldn't remember.

He stepped over the fence and was heading across the field, when he realized he'd left his hat and gloves on the seat. He thought about going back to get them, but then he saw a small stream up ahead. Stevie had stomped through that stream in his rubber boots, splashing everyone. He remembered, his mother being mad. That meant she must have been there. That's right. She was wearing a dress under her coat, not pants like everyone else, and she had on black rubber rain boots, like Stevie, and her bare calves were showing. The image was as clear in his mind as a picture postcard. She *had* to have been there.

He jumped the shallow stream and went slipping and sliding through the half foot of fresh snow. His street shoes weren't the best choice for this kind of winter hiking, but he wasn't going to let a little thing like that stop him. He had come for the smell of pine, and he was going to have it.

The trail he was on was just barely visible in the snow, and he couldn't see any tracks. That meant nobody had come through since the last snowfall, which was probably last night. That was fine with him. He'd have the whole mountain to himself. He could probably thank the no-trespassing sign for that.

As he went along, he got to thinking about his mother again, wondering why she sometimes didn't go on the excursions his father organized. Did she stay home because she wanted to be by herself for a while, or would his father tell her to stay home so she could get dinner started? He couldn't decide which it would have been.

Aaron had always felt more comfortable with his mother than his father. He liked her sense of humor and her funny stories. Sometimes, when his father wasn't home, she'd call all the kids into the kitchen, and she'd make hot chocolate and cinnamon toast. The heat from the cinnamon and the heat from the fire in the old wood stove made everything toasty and warm. Then his mother would read from one of her books. Dickens or Steinbeck usually, or Gone with the Wind. She liked stories about interesting characters doing things in interesting places. In different times. He came to like those kinds of stories too.

Once in a while, his father would join them in the kitchen. He'd bring out his old violin and fill the room with his music. It was such an odd thing that he played the violin, and that he had taught himself how to play it. It was like he was a different person when he played his violin. It was the only time Aaron felt like they were a complete family, a special family he liked being a part of. Too bad it hadn't happened all that often. It might have made a real difference in his relationship with his father.

The trail dipped down into a grove of tall slender aspens that had lost their leaves. The tall white trunks of the trees reminded Aaron of his father. He was tall and slender like that, and he always walked with such purpose and strength. But then he died. Aaron could never quite believe how quickly his father had gone from being a towering force in his life, to that lifeless body in the coffin.

He died so suddenly. Of a brain aneurysm, wasn't it? Something like that. Aaron remembered how devastated his mother was, but then she'd pulled herself together and kept going, just like he kept going after Laura died. Maybe he got some of that strength from his mother.

Thinking of all that got him wondering again if she was up there with them that day. He couldn't remember her on this part of the trail, but he could clearly picture her with bare calves and black rain boots yelling at Stevie. But maybe that was a different day. She was always telling Stevie to quit doing things like stomping through mud puddles. It still bothered him that he couldn't remember for sure. Why would that be when everything else about that day was so clear?

As he passed out of the aspens into the warmth of the sun, he saw the pines just up ahead. He laughed and said, "There they are. Finally!"

He hurried forward, and when he got to where the pines were, he stopped and took a long deep breath of the spicy scent. This was what he'd been after all day. And now he realized why; it was because it reminded him of the sweet incensed air of India. The air in India had always brightened his senses, and he was hoping the pine scent would do the same thing for him now.

After he took in another deep breath, he headed deeper into the trees. The trail was getting narrow now, with the soft recent snow on top of an older icy layer below. It was so slippery, he had to use his shoes like skis to make any progress.

Every now and then, he saw animal tracks heading off from the trail. Most of them were old and indistinct, but then he came across a set that looked more recent. He stopped to take a closer look. The tracks were pressed deep into the snow, which made it impossible to know what kind of animal had left them. Maybe a deer, but that didn't seem right. Deer tracks were smaller than that, weren't they? He wasn't sure what other kind of critters lived in that part of the mountains, but whatever it was, it might be fun to see if he could find it.

He followed the tracks up the slope through the pines where the snow clearly hadn't seen much sun. It was deeper and more frozen which made it harder to push through. Soon his leg muscles and his lungs were burning. He had to keep stopping to catch his breath. Why was it so hard? Was it the altitude? Or was he weak from moping around the house all winter? He should make himself get out more. And next time, he should wear better shoes. His feet were getting colder by the minute.

It had been a warm winter day up in the mountains when he started out, but the long shadows between the trees made him cold and told him it was getting late in the day. But how was that possible? He hadn't been going that long. It must be because the winter days were so short. He should have remembered that and gotten an earlier start. He thought about turning back, but it was just a little further to the crest of the hill, and the tracks he was following still marked a clear path to the top. It wouldn't hurt to take a quick look before he went back down.

He kept climbing, and when he finally pushed out of the trees into a clearing at the top of the hill, he couldn't believe what he'd found. A huge mountain lion was basking in the late afternoon sun on an outcropping of rock. So this was the guy that had made those big tracks.

Aaron stood perfectly still, stunned at his amazing good luck. His heart was thumping so hard, he could hear it in his ears. He wasn't sure if it was from excitement or maybe a little fear.

But it didn't seem like he had anything to fear. The mountain lion acted completely unconcerned by his presence. It gazed at him in a nonchalant way, then stretched its mouth open in a big yawn, showing long yellowed teeth and an astonishingly pink tongue.

Aaron decided to take a closer look. He moved forward a little until he was about twenty feet away. The lion just yawned again and then blinked its big eyes. The scene was so unexpected, Aaron thought he might be dreaming. But he wasn't dreaming. This was real. As real and intense as anything he had experienced in a long time.

As he and the lion stared at each other, Aaron realized there was something unusual about the animal's eyes; they were steel blue, like his own eyes, and like his father's eyes. But weren't mountain lions supposed to have yellow eyes?

There was something disturbing about the scene, something that he couldn't quite put his finger on.

Then he remembered. It was in India. That day he watched a leopard take down a young deer. The leopard had the deer by the throat, and the poor thing was bawling and kicking frantically as it tried to get loose. Then all of a sudden, the deer stopped fighting and lay perfectly still. It had given up. It was waiting to die. There was a silence that came after that. Like the whole world had stopped. Then, the leopard lifted its head from its kill, and the world started moving again.

He wondered if the same thing could happen here. This big mountain lion could easily take him down, and if it came for him, there would be nothing he could do. No amount of struggling would save him. No amount of pleading with God. The fight would be terrifying, but in the end, it might not be a bad way to go. Up there in the mountains, no one would find him and have to worry about what to do with his body.

He felt a chill and turned to see the last rays of the sun disappear behind a peak in the distance. When he looked back at the lion, it had changed positions. Now, it was crouched, with its head low, and its back legs were bent and gently pulsing against the outcropping of rock. Was it getting ready to attack?

Aaron didn't feel all that afraid, but he suddenly realized how cold his hands and feet were. Even his ears felt a bit numb. That wasn't good. It would be dark soon, and then it would get even colder, and he had no idea how far it was back to his truck.

He kept his eyes on the lion and slowly backed away. When he had gotten far enough into the trees that the lion couldn't see him, he turned and started down the slope. He had only taken a few steps when he heard a sound, and he stopped. Was the lion tracking him? Should he turn around? He didn't dare look back. If he just kept going, maybe the mountain lion would understand that he was a human. Not its normal prey.

Despite the fact that Aaron was moving fast down off the hill, he was getting colder. He pulled his hands up inside the sleeves of his sweater and thought about his wool gloves and hat sitting on the seat of the truck. Why hadn't he put them on? And why hadn't he worn better shoes? It was crazy to go off into the snowy hills in street shoes like this.

There was nothing he could do about any of that now, so he pushed on through the snow, working his way down through the pine trees toward the trail he had come in on. In the last bit of light that remained, he could see his breath coming out in little white puffs. It had to be close to freezing now.

He tried to go faster by letting his feet slide along the slick layer of ice beneath the snow, but he got going too fast and slid onto his butt, right under the low branches of a giant pine tree. He lay there for several minutes, trying to catch his breath, but it was too cold to stay that still. He had to get up and get moving.

He gathered his strength and struggled to his feet. He was feeling the cold all over now, but what bothered him most were his hands. They hurt, and the aching pain was going all the way up his arms into his neck.

He continued on, but it seemed like it was taking too long to get down to the main trail. Had he gone the wrong way?

Finally, he broke through the trees into a narrow flat area that he thought must be the trail. But where were his tracks? There were only long narrow indentations in the snow. It took him a minute to realize that they were ski tracks. There hadn't been any ski tracks on the way up. Where the heck *was* he? He had to be in the wrong place, but how had he gotten off course? Had he come down the wrong way? Was he in a different canyon altogether? If so, he'd never be able to find his way back to his truck.

He turned in a circle, looking for something familiar. It was getting darker and colder. If he was in the wrong place, he could end up out there all night. He wasn't dressed for that. He could already feel his sticky sweat freezing inside his shirt, and now his feet were going numb.

His heart started to pound. It felt like there was bird in his chest, and it was trying to get out. He needed to calm down and make a decision. Do something. Anything. Just pick a direction and start walking.

He turned to his left and started out, but he immediately felt like it was the wrong way. He turned back and tried the other direction, but within a few steps, he had the same awful feeling. Nothing looked familiar. What if he was heading deeper into the wilderness? He went back to where he started and just stood there staring into the gathering darkness. Staying out there in the cold was crazy and dangerous, but he couldn't make himself pick a direction. What was the point of moving, if he didn't know where he was going?

Standing still made him realize how exhausted he was. He had been out there all day, never stopping, never eating or drinking. He was strong and had always done a lot of hiking in the past, but he didn't like this cold. He would rather be doing this down in the desert. He decided once and for all how much he hated winter. He hated what it did to his muscles and bones, and especially, what it was doing to his brain.

He sat down in the snow, just for a minute. When he was rested, he'd have to pick a direction and go.

A wind blew through, and he covered his face with his icy hands. It was so cold it made him feel like crying. But what good would crying do? He closed his eyes and tried to retrace his steps in his mind. But his thoughts were all jumbled and kept on circling back on themselves. It made him feel like his mind was as lost as he was.

He heard something behind him and opened his eyes wide. Was that a branch breaking? Was the mountain lion getting ready to pounce? It seemed like he was hearing all kinds of sounds, little pops and cracks. He held his breath and listened, but then all he could hear was his teeth chattering. Then he realized his ears felt like they were on fire. It didn't make sense. How could they feel so hot when they were so cold?

He shoved his hands up high under his armpits and waited. But what was he waiting for?

He decided he didn't much care what happened next. If he froze right where he was, at least he'd be with Laura again. Maybe she was already there. Watching over him. Waiting for him. He closed his eyes and whispered, "Laura. Are you here?"

No answer. She wasn't there. He might as well try to sleep.

A whooshing noise broke through his dream. He opened his eyes and saw a blinding light rushing toward him. Was he going to die? Is this how death came?

He braced himself, but the light didn't pierce him; instead, it stopped right in front of him.

Someone touched his arm. "Jesus, man. What the hell are you doing out here?"

Aaron wasn't sure. What *was* he doing there sitting in the snow? It was pitch dark.

Somebody's hands were patting his cheeks. "Wake up, mister. You've got to wake up right now!"

Aaron didn't know how to respond. He wasn't asleep, was he?

The brightness turned this way and that, and he thought he saw two people with lights on their heads. One of them knelt down beside him. It might be a woman. She rubbed his hands and squeezed his arms. Then she took her coat off and wrapped it around him. She lifted his hands to her mouth and blew into them. He expected her breath to be warm, but he couldn't really feel it. Why couldn't his hands feel the warmth?

The woman helped him get his arms through the sleeves of her coat, and then she turned to her man and said, "Have you got any spare gloves in your pack?"

"I have those mittens."

The woman pushed something onto Aaron's hands that made him feel a little warmer.

"Have we got anything for his feet?"

"I don't think so. But maybe if we get him up and walking, it will help."

Now, they were trying to pull him up. He wanted to help, but his legs felt all wobbly. When they got him upright, he held onto their arms and did a little marching step to see if his feet were still there. It seemed like there was a little bit of life left in them. He looked at the man and said, "I think they'll work."

The couple got on each side of him and pulled his arms over their shoulders. Then they were moving, and he started to think about home. If only he could just be there, without all the trouble. Wouldn't that be grand?

They moved slowly through the dark shadows of some trees. After a while, the blood in his legs started to warm up, and he was able to take more of his own weight. He was still all shivery and cold, but he felt less numb. Maybe he was starting to thaw out.

It seemed like they had been going for a long time. When they finally came out of the trees, Aaron saw a sky full of shimmering stars and a slice of white moon just coming up over the mountains. That's when he knew he was going to make it.

They came to a stream. Aaron recognized it. It was that stream where Stevie stomped through the water. That was a long time ago, so maybe that meant they were almost back to where he wanted to be.

The couple got him through the stream and helped him over the barbed wire, and that's when he saw his truck. "That's mine," he whispered. "My truck."

They didn't take him to his truck. Instead, they took him to a big white van. They helped him inside, and the man started the engine. The woman put a blanket around his shoulders, and pretty soon the air from the heater started to feel warm. But he still couldn't stop shaking.

The woman held a cup out to him. "Here. Drink this. It's hot chocolate. It'll warm you up inside."

He took an eager sip, but it was so sweet it almost made him throw up. Still, it was warm, so he drank some more.

The man said, "I think we better take him to the hospital, don't you?"

Aaron shook his head. No, he didn't want to go to the hospital. He hated hospitals. And besides, he knew he'd be fine, if he could just get warm, if he could just get some rest. His head sagged down toward his chest. He told himself, he couldn't let them see him like that, and he pulled his head up. "Just give me a minute. I'll be fine."

He rubbed his hands together, and then he slapped himself on both sides of his face, hard. That put some life back into him. Now, he just needed to get home and get into bed.

He reached for the door handle, but the woman grabbed his arm. "Really, mister. I think we should take you to see a doctor."

Aaron jerked his arm free. "I don't want to see any damn doctor. Just let me go home. I need to get home."

"But, sir," she said, "you were so cold. Look at you. You're still shaking. We've got to make sure you're okay."

Aaron focused his thoughts and tried to soften his tone. "I know you're trying to help me, and I appreciate that. But I'd really like to go home. I'll be fine now. It's no big deal. I wasn't cold that long."

She looked over at her young man and looked back. "Where is your home?"

"It's down there . . . in the city."

"You mean, Park City?"

"Yes, that's the one. I know how to get there." It was a lie, but he didn't want them knowing he had to go all the way to Salt Lake.

She looked doubtful. "Are you sure?" She touched her man's arm and said, "What do you think? Can we let him drive?"

Aaron said, "It's not your place to decide. It's mine. I'm going now."

The young man shrugged. "We can't stop him, I guess. Let's see how he does."

They let him out of the van, and he focused all his attention on staying straight and tall as he walked back to his truck.

The man got out and followed him and stayed close by while Aaron fumbled around in his pockets and found his keys.

At the last minute, Aaron remembered the coat and gloves he had borrowed. He took them off and gave them to the man. Then once he was inside his truck, he put on his own gloves and his hat, but he was still shaking so bad, he could barely get the keys in the ignition.

The man leaned in. "Are you okay."

"Uh . . . yeah. I'm fine. Thanks, my friend. I owe you one." He kept his voice calm and nonchalant. He didn't want the guy coming up with any problems.

The man eyed him for a minute, then said, "You want us to follow you. At least 'til you get to Park City."

"Uh . . . sure. That would be okay. Uh . . . maybe I could follow you."

"Okay. Let me get back to the van."

Aaron started the engine and turned the heater on full blast, but it was so cold, he turned it back off. He was going to have wait for that.

The van started down the road, and Aaron followed it. He hoped the man knew where he was going, because he sure didn't.

After a while, the heater got warm, and then Aaron started to get warm too. He wasn't as bad off as he thought, but it could have been really bad. He could have died out there. How could he have been so stupid?

Finally, he saw the lights of Park City up ahead, and that made him feel even warmer. When they got into town, the van pulled over, and Aaron followed it to the curb.

The man came back and tapped on the window, and Aaron rolled it down. The man said, "You sure you can find your way home from here?"

Aaron nodded. "Sure, I can. I do it all the time."

He could see doubt in the man's eyes, so he hurried and said, "Don't worry about me. Take that young lady of yours home. It's too cold to be out here."

"Well, okay, if you're sure. I'm glad we found you out there, Mister . . . what was your name?"

"Aaron. My name's Aaron."

"Okay, Mister Aaron. You drive safely now."

"I will. I promise. I will."

Chapter 14

Aaron lay beneath the thick layer of blankets he had piled on top of himself. Somehow, he'd finally made it home, even though the gas gauge was on empty. The experience had left him feeling like he couldn't trust himself. He could have died out there in the snow, and no one would have even known where he was. It would have been devastating to Sarah for him to disappear like that. He had to be more careful.

He squinted into the bright morning sun streaming across the room from the window. The golden light looked warm, but it didn't make him feel warm. He wasn't sure if he would ever be warm again, except maybe down at his place in the desert. If he was down there where the red sand and rocks captured the heat all day, maybe, finally, he could get warm. But he wasn't there, he was here, and the winter was just getting started.

His ordeal in the mountains had worn him out, but the thing that worried him was how careless he had been. Leaving his wallet at home on the dresser. Not wearing the right clothes. Staying out there far longer than he should have. Was it all part of the same thing? Was he going to start making serious mistakes like Miriam did? Getting lost? Leaving the stove on like she did?

From now on, he'd better watch himself like a hawk. But, really, what good would it do? Even if it was true that he was headed the same way as Miriam, there was nothing anyone could do about it. With Miriam, they said there was no pill she could take, and they couldn't transplant her brain.

At least Miriam wasn't alone. She had her husband, while he lasted. That's what really scared Aaron. Being alone. If he ended up wandering away, who would be there to find him? Or remind him? Who would be there to love him back into the world?

Sarah, maybe. But he wouldn't want to take over *her* life and ruin it. So what would he do, if his forgetting got worse? Could he manage on his own? He might be able to do it if he was down in the desert. Life was simple down there. There weren't that many things to remember. But if that's the place he should go, he'd better get down there and get his house built so he'd have a place to live when it was time.

He stared at the ceiling and wondered how it was even possible for your mind to go away like that. He could imagine himself dead, his body unmoving and lifeless. He had seen that with Laura. But he couldn't imagine his mind being gone. What would that be like?

He put the pillow over his eyes and tried to silence his mind to get a feel for how it might be. It didn't work. His mind immediately filled up with words.

Pushing the pillow aside, he tried to silence the words by focusing on what was outside of himself: the yellow light spilling across the room, the blue and white quilted bedspread, the golden veins in the oak dresser. But everything he looked at brought words. Words that named things. Words for the colors. Words for the shapes. Everything in the world had its own word. But if all the words were gone, what would he see? Would he be able to see anything? Would he be able to find his way anywhere?

He tried to imagine himself being lost somewhere. No, not in the snow. In a familiar place, like down at the nearby creek. Walking along the dirt trail. Bees buzzing all around. And maybe he would see little white flowers nodding in the wind. And bugs, digging in the wet brown earth. Maybe worms would be coming out because it had been raining and there were drops of water on everything, like diamonds. That's right. Raindrops like diamonds. The way it was that day he and Laura had their wedding pictures done. That day when there were drops of sparkling water on everything, and the air smelled so fresh and clean, and when he kissed Laura, she kissed him back with such passion, it made him wonder—

He slapped the bed. "Stop thinking about that. Making love and being with Laura has nothing to do with you anymore. She's gone, and she's not coming back."

An alarming thought occurred to him. If he was forgetting things, what if he forgot Laura? What if he forgot everything about their life together? Their passion. Their love. If that happened, he wouldn't have anything of value left.

It was unthinkable, but how could he stop it? He looked wildly around the room. Was there anything there to remind him of her, something that would always be there that could bring his memory of Laura back, no matter what?

He saw her binder, and he knew that was it. He had to keep her poems with him no matter where he went, and he had to read every last one of them, again and again, until they were set in his mind like steel. Not only that, but he should put her picture beside the bed and look at it every morning and every evening before he went to sleep.

He went and got their wedding picture from the dresser, then found a felt pen in the desk drawer and wrote her name on the glass across the white of her dress. But what if he forgot what that name meant? What if he lost that too? He wrote: "My wife, my love, my little Lori, my Laura." The big black words ruined the picture, but that wasn't important. He couldn't let himself forget Laura.

Now that he was out of bed, he decided he might as well stay up and do something to keep his mind off his sad thoughts. But what could he do when it was so cold outside?

Maybe he should call Sarah. Not that he was going to say a word about his getting lost in the snow, but maybe he could test her to see how bad off *she* thought his memory was.

He got dressed and headed out to the living room to turn on the furnace. Next, he found Sarah's number in his stack of notes by the phone, he started dialing, but noticed his hand was shaking. Now why was he doing that? There wasn't any proof he was losing his memory. It was just the winter and the bad city air. If his brain hadn't been so full of that bad air, he would have remembered his wallet and his warm clothes. And the only reason he got lost, was because he got too excited about being out there, and then he saw the mountain lion and—

What's wrong. Did he dial the wrong number? No one was answering the phone, and there wasn't any voice asking him to leave a message.

He was about to hang up, when he finally heard Sarah's voice. "Hello."

"Hi Sarah."

"What's up, Dad?"

"Uh . . . not much. I was just wondering . . . " Now how was he going to say it?

"Yes?"

"I mean, I was wondering . . ." Might as well spit it out. "Do I uh . . . forget things a lot?"

"Well . . . sometimes."

"I do?" Oh no. Even Sarah had seen it happen. That wasn't good.

"Sure, but we all forget things now and then."

"Yeah. That's what I thought too. It's no big deal."

"Are you worried about it?"

"No. Not really? It's just so darn cold . . . I feel like my brain's frozen sometimes."

"I know you've never liked winter. Well, except when Michael and I were kids. You didn't mind it so much then. We were always doing stuff in the snow."

"Yeah. Well, it was different then. The air was clean. Anyway . . . I was wondering, uh, if you'd like to come over here . . . sometime. I'd like to see you."

"Sure. I'd like to see you too. How about Sunday?"

"Okay . . . when is that?"

"Well, today is Thursday."

"That's right. Okay, then. Sunday."

"I'll bring the kids."

"Great. That'll be great."

After she hung up, he stayed by the phone, wondering if her words about him forgetting meant more than she said. Had she been watching him and keeping track of when he made mistakes? Maybe she didn't want to come right out and say he had a problem, not when they both knew what they knew about Miriam. She wouldn't want to make him worry.

He decided he'd try to find out more when she came over with the kids on Sunday. But what in the world was he going to do with himself until then.

"Stop it," he told himself. "Your brain's not dead yet. Get going on something."

Chapter 15

Early Sunday afternoon, Sarah arrived at his house with the kids. Annie came in carrying a bucket of Kentucky Fried Chicken.

Before Aaron could complain about "junk food," Sarah grabbed the bucket of chicken and said, "I know. I know. It'll kill us all, but I knew your fridge would be empty." She gave him a quick hug and headed for the kitchen.

His fridge was empty? How did she know that? It must be true. She *was* keeping an eye on him.

Annie grabbed his hand. "Grandpa, can we see your fat birds?"

"Birds? What birds?"

"Your quail," Sarah called from the kitchen. "I was just telling them how big and fat they are."

He patted Annie's head. "I'm afraid my birds only come around later on when it's time for their dinner. But if you're still here, you can help me feed them."

"I hope we are here. I really want to see them. I really do." She went skipping into the kitchen.

Sam stood in the middle of the living room with his hands in his pockets. He looked uncomfortable, so Aaron said, "What's wrong, Sam. Cat got your tongue?"

The boy rolled his eyes.

It surprised Aaron. What did that look mean? It seemed too . . . critical for a boy his age. "So, what are you now, Sam? Seven?"

"I'm just about nine. How old are *you*?"

How old am I? The boy was a feisty thing, wasn't he? "Uh . . . around seventy, I'd guess. I stopped counting a while back."

"Oh yeah? Why'd you do that?"

"When you get my age, you'll understand."

"Whatever." Sam shrugged him off and went to join the others in the kitchen.

Aaron felt like he had been reprimanded, but he wasn't sure why. Maybe just for being old. He wouldn't have gotten away with that kind of behavior when *he* was nine. He had to respect his elders. His father made sure of that. But then Sam didn't have a father anymore. Maybe that's why he acted that way.

Aaron went into the kitchen and found Sam sitting at the table waiting to be waited on while Sarah and Annie got things ready for lunch. Aaron went to the corner and leaned against the wall where he could watch. Annie was such a pretty girl with her strawberry-blond hair and her happy green eyes. She didn't seem that hurt by the divorce. Maybe it was because she was a girl, and she still had her momma. She might not miss her father in quite the same way that Sam would. It made Aaron feel bad for the boy. Made him think he should take him under his wing and get him involved in something. He went and stood next to him and said, "Hey, Sam. Want to help me get some wood so we can have a fire later on?"

The boy stayed right where he was, staring at the table.

Sarah came over and gave the boy's arm a little nudge. "Do it, Sam. It'll be fun."

Sam scowled, but he stood up and went to get his coat. Aaron got his coat too, and they both went outside and around to where the wood was stacked up behind the garage.

As Aaron brushed the thick snow off the logs, it brought back the memory of the lion he had seen up in the mountains. "Listen, Sam. Can you keep a secret?"

"What kind of secret?"

"A good one. But you can't tell your mother."

Sam's eyes lit up a little, and he came closer. "Okay. What is it?"

Aaron whispered, "I saw a lion."

"A lion?"

"Yes. A really big one."

"Where was it?"

"Up in the mountains. He was just sittin' on a rock, all golden and proud, like he was king of the world."

Sam's eyes got big. "Really? How far away was he?"

"About as far as that wall." Aaron pointed toward the rock wall where he fed his quail.

"Wow! Weren't you scared, Grandpa?"

Now he had the boys attention, and he didn't want to lose it. "Nah. I wasn't scared. And that lion wasn't scared either. We just looked at each other for a while, then we went our separate ways. I wish you could have seen him, Sam. He was a beauty."

"I've never seen a lion . . . well, except at the zoo."

"Yeah, well, that's different, isn't it? When they're in a cage behind bars."

"I know. It must be great to see them out there where they're free."

The shine in Sam's eyes encouraged Aaron to keep going. He loaded some logs onto the boy's arms and said, "You know, Sam. I've seen those guys before."

"What guys?"

"Those tigers."

"Tigers? I thought you said it was a lion."

"Well, yes. I did. What I meant was, I saw tigers . . . over there in Burma."

Sam scowled. "Where's that?"

"Over there . . . you know, on the other side of the world. Between India and China. Do you know where China is?"

"Sure, I do. I'm not stupid, you know."

"No. No. Of course, you're not stupid. Nobody could say that."

Sam leaned back against the garage, balancing his armful of logs. "So what were they doing?"

Aaron didn't know what to say. They'd been talking about something, but when the boy got riled about not being stupid, he forgot what it was. "Uh . . . what were we talking about?"

"You were telling me about the tigers over there in that Burma place."

"Oh, right. The tigers. They were like ghosts, Sam. They'd come out of the jungle at night and sneak around the streets. You could hear them rustling around outside the basha, and sometimes, if you were quick, you'd see them skulking away."

"Wow."

"There were elephants too. In India. I rode one of those guys. It was really something to be sitting way up there, lumbering down the road."

"Really? You rode an elephant? That's pretty cool."

"Yes. It really was. I wish you could try it. Maybe you will some day."

Aaron gathered up his own armful of logs, feeling good about how well he and Sam were getting along.

As they started toward the house, Sam said, "Why'd you go to India anyway? Were you on vacation?"

"No. No. It was the war. World War Two. Remember that?"

"Not really."

"They didn't teach you about that war in school?"

"Well, there were a bunch of wars, weren't there?"

"That's right. I guess there were."

Sam stopped at the door and looked back at him with an excited intensity in his eyes. "Did you kill anybody?"

Kill anybody? Why did he want to know that? "Uh, what do you mean, Sam?"

"I mean, did you shoot any people in that war?"

Aaron shook his head, no, and frowned.

Sam frowned too, and he looked disappointed. "Why not?"

"I was support. We flew supplies to the front and brought back the sick and wounded soldiers from China. It was—"

Sam burst in. "Really? You were a pilot? You flew airplanes?"

Aaron could see what the boy wanted, but he couldn't lie. "No, I wasn't the pilot. I was the crew chief. The guy in the back with the barrels of gasoline."

"Oh."

There was that disappointment again. The kid was like a roller coaster, full of expectations that Aaron couldn't fulfill. He wished he could. He would have liked to keep that interest in the boy's eyes, but now it was gone.

Sam turned away and went in the house.

Aaron stayed outside for a minute, thinking. He didn't quite know what to make of Sam. The boy seemed to be living in a world where everything had to be fantastic, or it wasn't worth anything at all. Maybe the boy had seen too many movies. Is that what it was? Was he living in a fantasy world?

And why was he so keen to know if his Grandpa had killed anyone. Was that just a boy thing?

Maybe that's all it was. Aaron remembered how exciting it was to arrive in India, and that didn't change even after he saw how it was going to be. The life and death reality of flying over the hump in such terrible weather conditions. The wounded Chinese soldiers coming in. Their dead bodies in the body bags. The downed planes. It was frightening, and terrible, but thrilling too. He had to admit it.

So maybe he wasn't all that different from Sam. Maybe the boy just wanted to be part of something bigger than himself, and he was hoping to do it through his Grandpa. Too bad he had to be disappointed.

Aaron realized he was standing outside in the cold snow with his arms full of logs. It sent a chill seeping into his bones, like when he was up in the mountains. It was the kind of chill he didn't really want to remember.

He hurried inside and stacked the logs next to the fireplace. Then he went back into the kitchen to see if it was time to eat.

After they finished their meal, the kids went outside to play fox and geese in the snow. Sarah did the dishes, while Aaron went into the living room and got a fire going. He pulled up a couple of chairs so he and Sarah could be warm by the fire while they had a nice talk. He sat in one of the chairs and tried to think what he wanted to talk to her about, but for some reason, he couldn't remember.

Sarah came in from the kitchen and joined him next to the fire. She touched his arm. "Is anything wrong, Dad?"

He sat up straight. "What are you talking about? I'm fine." He tried to sound nonchalant.

"You look like you're worried about something."

He frowned, and then tried to turn it into a smile. "What are you, some kind of a mind reader?"

"So, it's true? You are worried?"

He shrugged. "Well, maybe." He glanced out the window at Sam and Annie running around in the snow. That made him think of something he wanted to ask. "Uh . . . do you think Sam's okay?"

Sarah looked surprised. "Why?"

"I don't know. He seemed disappointed when I said I didn't kill anyone in the war."

"Really? I didn't think he knew anything about you being in the war."

"I was telling him about the tigers."

"The tigers?"

"Uh . . . . yeah. The tigers . . . in India, I mean."

She stared at the fire, then looked over at him with sad eyes. "I think he misses his dad."

"That's what I was thinking too."

"You were?"

"Well, he's a boy. It might be hard not having a man around."

Sarah nodded. "I know. It's too bad you don't live closer. It would be nice if he could spend more time with you. Maybe that would help."

"Maybe, although he seems kind of frustrated with me." He caught her eye. "I guess there's no chance you and Patrick will get back together."

She shook her head and frowned. "No, Dad. How can you say that? It's been over a year. And besides, he's getting married."

"He *is*?"

"I just got an email from him last week. She's got three kids, and he's moving to Texas. That's where she lives."

"Texas? How will the kids see him if he moves to Texas?"

She shrugged. "I don't know. We haven't talked about that yet."

Aaron touched her hand. "What about you? That must be hard that he's getting married."

"Dad. I was the one who left him. Remember? We weren't a good match. I told you that."

"Yeah, I know." He said it as if he understood, but he really didn't. Nobody matched these days. They didn't have any endurance. They split up without even trying to work out their problems. What if he and Laura had split up every time they had a fight, or every time he felt like being responsible for everything was too much? Sometimes being married meant you had to put your head in the sand and pretend like nothing was wrong. Like a damn octopus . . . or whatever it was. But maybe staying married wasn't the right approach. Maybe it was better if people moved on if they couldn't get along. Maybe if they did that, they wouldn't end up hurting each other so bad they couldn't ever recover. Is that what he should've done with Laura? Moved on?

No. That was impossible. He loved Laura. There was no way he could have ever left her. He hoped she had felt the same way, but what if she hadn't? He shook his head, disturbed that he didn't know what was true anymore.

"What's wrong, Dad? What are you thinking now?"

He kept his eyes on the fire.

"Come on, Dad. It's me, Sarah. You can talk to me. We always talk." Her voice was gentle, and when he looked over he saw real concern in her eyes.

"I don't know. It all seems so . . . impossible."

"What does?"

"This relationship . . . stuff."

She raised her eyebrows. "Are you thinking about me, or you?"

"I don't know. Both I guess."

She held his arm. "You're still hurting over Mom's poems, aren't you?"

He nodded. "I guess I'll always be hurting over those poems, but that's not my main problem now."

"No? Then what is it?"

He shook his head. "I don't know. I think, I'm starting to . . . Well . . . maybe I'm just getting old."

"You are *not*."

She said it so loud, it startled him.

"You don't look a day over sixty. Well, maybe . . . sixty-five. At the most."

He laughed. "That's quite a range."

"Well, you look really good, and you're healthy, aren't you?"

"I guess so."

She turned her chair towards him. "Are you trying to tell me something's wrong?"

"No, no, nothing like that. I just . . . you know, forget things . . . sometimes. Make mistakes." There, he had said it. He hadn't meant to, but there it was.

"Why are you so worried about it, Dad? Did something happen?"

He stared at the fire, not knowing how to continue.

"Anyway, I know you forget things sometimes. Like eating, for example." She wrapped her fingers around his wrist. "I keep telling you, you're getting too thin."

Was he getting thinner? He didn't know that.

"But then I think about that and realize if I didn't have Sam and Annie to feed, I'd probably forget to eat too. It's hard when there's only you."

He nodded to keep her going.

"And sometimes you don't know what day it is, but that's understandable too. When you don't have a schedule to keep, one day starts to seem like the next. I never understood how they could ask that question on those mental health exams. Old people, especially ones who live alone and don't get out much, don't have any reason to remember what day it is. It's crazy to think they would."

He smiled a little, feeling better, now that she was defending him. "Old people? I thought you said I was young."

"I wasn't talking about you."

"You weren't?"

"No. I've been reading about Alzheimer's and dementia . . . that sort of thing."

"Alz . . heimer's? What's that?"

"Don't you remember? It's what they said Aunt Miriam had."

That put him on guard. "Oh yeah. Why are you reading that stuff?"

"Well, I watched Aunt Miriam go through all that and . . . " She trailed off and gazed into his eyes.

What was she doing? Was she trying to see if there was any of that Alzheimer's stuff going on inside him?

Finally, she sat back and said, "Look, Dad. Don't worry about it. Worrying only makes things worse. If I think you're having a problem, I'll tell you. Okay?"

He wasn't sure how to take that. Did she really think he was okay, or was she just trying to keep him from worrying? And was it true what she said? Did it really make things worse to worry? He was going to have to think about that, because he'd been worrying a lot.

Sarah leaned forward again and took his hand. "I promise, Daddy. I'll tell you if I think something's wrong. *Really*. You can count on me."

He nodded and decided to let it go. He got down on his knees and added a couple of logs to the fire.

As he sat back in his chair, Sarah said, "So what about Sam? Do you think he's okay?"

"He's kind of . . . tough. Maybe that's all it is."

She sighed. "You mean his meanness? He was tormenting a cat the other day. Chasing it around. Cornering it. I wasn't sure what to make of it. Then, I remembered I did a few things like that when I was a kid . . . well, not me, but I watched some boys blowing up birds with firecrackers, and I didn't do anything about it."

Aaron was shocked. "Blowing up birds? They did that?"

She shrugged. "It seemed really mean, but maybe they were just experimenting. You know, testing the world."

"Sounds pretty mean to me. I love my birds."

She nodded. "Yeah, I know you do." She stared at the fire for a minute, then turned to him. "Remember when Michael and his friends busted up the bathroom in that vacant house? What was he, fourteen, or so?"

"Yes. I do remember. It was really disturbing to think he'd do that."

"And there was that time you chased him around the yard with a pipe after he threw a baseball through the basement window on purpose."

"I did not."

"Yes, you did. I was out on the lawn watching clouds, and I saw the whole thing. I was amazed by how fast he could run. He wasn't even Sam's age yet, was he?"

Aaron caught a flash of little Mikey dodging right and left through the apple trees. It scared him that he didn't know what happened next. "So what did I do?"

"When you finally caught him, it was like you were shocked to see that pipe in your hand. You threw it down and started crying."

Aaron looked at the fire, trying to get away from Sarah's eyes.

"I think all of that, especially when he was older, was just Michael's attempt to get your attention."

"My attention?"

"Well, you were working so much, it didn't leave you a lot of time to do things with us."

"What do you mean? We *did* things. Lots of things." He tried to think what. "We went to the park for Sunday picnics, didn't we? And we went swimming up at the municipal hot springs. And hiking in the mountains. I know we did. We did . . . *lots* of things."

She gave him a sideways look. "We only did that when we were little. After you had that hard winter without work . . . well, you took more jobs and didn't have much time for fun after that. It was especially hard on Michael because he was missing time with his dad, you know, like Sam is."

Aaron was stunned. Hadn't he been thinking that same thing about work and how he got all messed up. Still, he wasn't ready to admit it to Sarah. "But I was there the whole time, wasn't I? How could he miss me?"

"Now don't get upset, Dad. I'm not blaming you. You were working hard, trying to take care of us. Financially, I mean. I know that. Anyway, it doesn't matter now. Michael turned out okay. And so did I."

"He did, huh? I wouldn't know. I never hear from him."

Sarah frowned. "That's because of what you said to him during that big fight you two had the Christmas after Mom died."

Aaron couldn't believe what he was hearing. "What do you mean? What fight?"

She looked away and shrugged.

He jumped up and yelled at her, "Come on. Tell me. You started this. Now finish it."

She stood up and wrapped her arms around him. "I'm sorry, Daddy. I didn't mean to upset you. I was just . . . thinking about Sam, and then I remembered how Michael was when he was that age. It doesn't matter now." She touched his cheek with the back of her hand. "Anyway, you did the best you could."

He met her eyes. "You know, the way you describe me, it could be *my* father you're describing. He was like that. He wasn't there, even when he *was* there. I can't stand the idea that I'd end up like him."

"No. You're not like that. Not at all. You're a sweetheart, Dad. You really are. I love you. We all love you."

He frowned. "Well, I love you too. And I love Michael. He must know that."

She gave him another hug. "Come on. Don't get hung up on all that. If every child blamed their parents for ruining their lives, that blame would go all the way back to Adam and Eve. Unfortunately, we don't get instructions on being parents. We all do the best we can with what we've got. Right?"

Aaron shook his head and looked away.

"Well, you may not agree, but what good does blaming do? At some point, we all have to be responsible for ourselves. I think it's outrageous for Michael to blame you for his inability to have a relationship."

Aaron felt his blood rise. "He blames me?"

She winced. "I'm sorry, we should stop talking about this. I keep saying the wrong thing. I was just saying he should take some responsibility for himself. That's all I meant to say." She gave his hand a long squeeze, then she patted it, and said, "You know, I really *would* like Sam to spend more time with you. I think it would be good for him."

He couldn't believe what she was saying. "You'd trust me with Sam, after what you just said?"

Sarah smiled. "Sure I do. Maybe he could come out and stay with you for a week or two. You know, this summer when school's out."

Aaron thought about it for a second. "Sure. That would be . . . fun. I'd like that." He was telling the truth, but the idea scared him a bit too. What if they didn't get along? What if the boy didn't like hanging around with an old fogey? If Michael had bad feelings about him, the last thing he wanted was for Sam to have those bad feelings too.

The children came back in the house bringing a cold breeze with them. After they had warmed up by the fire for a bit, Sarah said, "Come on, kids, time to go home."

She got her coat and herded Sam and Annie to the door.

Aaron followed them outside, and Sarah gave him a long hug and whispered, "Don't worry so much, Daddy. Everything's fine."

Aaron watched them drive away, wishing he could believe that everything was fine, but he wasn't so sure. It wasn't enough that he had to worry about his memory going, now he also had to worry about what he said to Michael that might have driven him away.

Chapter 16

Aaron sat at the kitchen table poking at his oatmeal with his spoon and trying to not look at the dreary weather outside. He had a disturbing worry in his mind. Was it true what Sarah said yesterday? Had he really driven Michael away with something he'd said? And if he had, why couldn't he remember what it was?

Maybe Sarah was wrong. Maybe she had just seen them arguing, like they did sometimes, and she'd made more of it than there was. She had a tendency to do that sometimes.

Still, something was obviously wrong between him and Michael. He could hardly remember the last time the boy had come home. The only time he could remember was that day he stopped by to pick up some old family photos before he moved off to California. When was that? Five years ago? Something like that. There wasn't much of a conversation that day. No "I'm going to miss you, Dad," or anything like that. The boy just came and got what he wanted and left. So whatever happened, couldn't have happened that day.

He went to Michael's old room, hoping that might knock something loose. As he walked around, he noticed Michael's old map of California pinned to the wall. He traced his finger over the coastline trying to remember where Michael lived, but he wasn't sure. Somewhere south. Maybe Los Angeles. Or was it San Diego? It seemed strange that he didn't know. But maybe Michael had never told him. Or maybe he forgot. He didn't know which of the two would be more disturbing.

It occurred to him that he should go to California and see Michael. Maybe they could work things out. No. He couldn't do that. He'd never received an invitation, and he would never go without one. If Laura was alive, they'd have a standing invitation. He was pretty sure of that. She and Michael were very close. She would have known all about the boy's life and what he was doing and how he felt about things. Why was that? Why would a boy be closer to his mother than he was to his father? That didn't seem right.

He sat down on Michael's old bed, and suddenly, he remembered what happened. It was just like Sarah said. It was that Christmas after Laura died. The memory hit him so hard he got up and hurried out of the boy's room trying to escape it. When he stopped in front of the couch in the living room, he realized that's where Michael was sitting when he told him to leave and not come back. And that's exactly what Michael did.

It was a terrible thing to say, but the whole thing was Sarah's fault. He'd told her he didn't want to have Christmas at the house after Laura died. He knew it would be too hard. But Sarah said it was important for them to stick together and that Laura would want them to be together.

There was nothing he could do but go along with her.

It was unbearable waiting for everyone to show up that day. He'd paced the house, trying to escape Laura's absence, but it screamed at him from every corner. Then, he saw her hairbrush in the bathroom, and he broke down and cried, like he hadn't cried since the night she died. There was something about that brush. It looked so . . . useless.

Even Christmas day, he had wanted to back out of the get-together, but then Sarah arrived with her husband Patrick and their little baby Sam. The child was just a few months old. Somehow he gave Aaron hope that he might survive his grief. Laura was gone, but here was this precious little boy with shiny eyes.

Those good feelings didn't last. Michael was so late, everyone had already finished eating and the presents had all been opened. He came strolling in, not even offering an excuse. Just sat down and put his feet up as if everything was fine. Aaron was outraged by his impertinence. He blew up and yelled something about if he was going to come that late he might as well not bother to come next time. They could do just fine without him.

So that was it. That's what ruined his relationship with Michael.

But why? Michael had to know those weren't his true feelings. He was suffering from the loss of Laura. They all were. Emotions were very close to the surface. So why would Michael hold onto his resentment all this time? There had to be something else going on.

It had never been easy to talk to Michael. Even at Laura's funeral, he had felt some kind of accusation coming from the boy. Michael hadn't said what it was, but Aaron had seen blame in his eyes. He'd never wanted to think about it, but now he wondered if Michael blamed him for Laura's death? What if that's what was wrong?

He went into the kitchen and got himself a glass of water. Why did he keep on going over all this negative stuff? He was wearing himself out, and he couldn't do a damn thing about any of it. He was just a man. He did the best he could.

As he sat down at the table with his glass, an odd thought hit him. He and Michael were the same. He had been closer to his mother too, and he had blamed his father for being cold and judgmental. But what if that wasn't judgment he had seen in his father's eyes? What if it was hurt, the same kind of hurt he was feeling now with regard to Michael?

And what about Sarah saying how he spent less time with her and Michael as they got older. His own father was like that too.

But was that really so unusual? When kids were young, they were more fun, and they were always showing you how much they loved you, and needed you. They made you feel important and smart. Then, as they got older, they didn't think you were all that smart after all. Like when Michael was a teenager. He was always so damned sure of himself. It didn't matter what Aaron did or said, Michael would come back with a challenge. It wore Aaron out, especially after a long day at work. Eventually, he'd learned to tune the boy out.

But wasn't that how a boy claimed his place in the world? By challenging his father? *He* was like that too, as a boy. He challenged his father to no end. But it was only because he wanted his father to recognize him and be proud of him.

Suddenly, his relationship with Michael looked different. He should have known from his own experience what the boy was up to. If he hadn't turned away from Michael when he was trying to prove he was grown up, maybe they wouldn't be at such odds with each other now. Maybe they could have talked through their problems.

If he could fix things with Michael, it would mean so much. But how could he do it?

Then, he realized, if his own father had ever said, "Look son, I know I've made some mistakes, but I love you," it would have changed everything. So maybe that's what he needed to say to Michael. He should go call him right now. Tell him that he understood things better, and he hoped they could be friends.

He hurried to the phone, but then he thought Michael might be at work. He hated those message machines. But so what? It wouldn't kill him to leave a message. If Michael wanted to talk, he'd call back. If he didn't call back, well, that was his business.

He found a paper with Michael's name on it, but it was in Laura's handwriting, so that couldn't be right. Michael went to California after she died. There had to be a different one.

He searched through all the little papers again, but he couldn't find another one with Michael's name. He was going to have to call Sarah and ask *her* what it was.

So tomorrow, he'd call Sarah, and then he'd call Michael. First thing.

Chapter 17

Winter dragged on like it was never going to end. Then one morning, Aaron went to his bedroom window and was amazed to see that spring had arrived. It was like it had blown in overnight, melting the snow and exposing a big yellow patch of dead grass in the backyard. That grass would be green within days.

He hurried outside to take a closer look. When he saw a little daffodil sprout poking its head out of the circle of dark mud around the apple tree, he laughed out loud. And when he examined the tree a little closer, he saw tiny pink buds forming on the limbs. It really *was* spring. It was time to start planting his garden.

He hurried to the garage to get a shovel so he could start turning the soil, but when he got there, he saw all his building tools stacked up along the wall like they were waiting for something to do. That's right. He was supposed to go down to the desert and get started on his little house. Maybe he should plant his garden down *there* this year. He could start work on his house and do the garden at the same time. Kill two of those birds with one stone. It was a good plan.

After he got all his building tools in the truck, he knew he'd better call Sarah. If he didn't, she'd get all upset, and then he'd have to deal with that.

He went back in the house and dug out her number. As soon as she answered, he said, "I'm going down there now."

"What?"

"You know, so I can plant my garden and start building."

"What are you talking about, Dad? Building what?"

"My house in the desert. It's spring. I'm going down there to get started."

"It's not spring."

"Sure it is. The daffodils are up."

"But Dad, it's supposed to snow again tomorrow. You know how it is in Salt Lake. You can't count on spring until at least the end of May. Besides, you said you couldn't afford to build your new house until you sold the one you've got."

"I didn't say that."

"Yes, you did. And we talked about you getting a smaller place close to me."

"We did?" Now why did she have to suck the wind out of his sail? And just when he was feeling good for the first time in weeks.

"I told you, Dad, people don't like to move while their kids are in school."

"What's that got to do with me?"

"Because no one will be looking to buy your house until their kids have finished school."

"Well, when will that be?"

"Not until the middle of June."

"June? Not until then?"

"Yes, and it's only the beginning of May."

"Oh no. What am I going to do until June? I'm going crazy here." He felt a tightness take hold of his throat. It was an achy tight feeling that he was pretty sure he had felt before.

"Don't you have any drywall work to keep you busy?"

He shook his head and stared at the floor.

"Dad?"

"What?"

"I said, don't you have any work?"

"No, I don't!" he yelled.

"Well, don't get mad. I was just asking."

"I'm sorry. I just can't stand the idea of hanging around here for another minute." He jumped up and started pacing, dragging the phone cord after him.

"Have you thought any more about getting a house closer to us?"

"I have a house."

"I mean after you sell that one."

"I'd rather have my house in the desert where the air's clean, and it's warm."

"But you don't want to spend all your time down there alone, do you?"

"Why not?"

"Because you'd get lonely. You need to be closer to us."

"I do?"

"Dad, are you feeling all right?"

"What do you mean?"

"You sound a little . . . funny."

"I'm no funnier than I ever was. I'm just tired of this damn endless winter. It makes me all agitated and fuddled in the head."

"Did you have breakfast?"

He stretched the phone line to look in the kitchen for dirty dishes, but he couldn't see any. "Maybe."

"You don't know?"

"Well, I expect I did. Why wouldn't I?"

"I don't know." There was silence on the line, and then Sarah said, "Look, Dad. I'm sorry, but I've got to get to work. I'm late. How about if I call you later, and we can talk more about this?"

"I don't want to talk about it more. I want to go to the desert."

"Please, Dad. Can't you wait and talk it over with me first?"

He let out a big sigh. "I guess I could, if I have to."

"Okay, then I'll call you this weekend when I have more time. Or maybe I'll just drive up there and see you."

"Fine! Fine!"

"Now, Dad, don't you go taking off without telling me. Okay? You promise?"

He slammed the phone down without saying goodbye. There she was throwing water on his plans again. It was his life, wasn't it? What gave her the right to tell him what to do? And besides how did she know it was going to snow? He went out to the patio and looked at the sky. There were some dark clouds hanging around, but there was some blue sky too. It didn't look like snow all that much. He should just pack up some warm clothes and go down there anyway.

He tromped out to look at the daffodil sprout again. That little guy wasn't going to like it one bit if it snowed, and neither were those tender buds on the apple tree.

As he headed back to the house, a chilly wind hit his face. That worried him a bit. Maybe it *was* going to snow. If it did, and he was on his way to the desert, he might get stuck going over one of those tall passes, like he did with Laura that time. They almost froze in their car before a trucker finally stopped to help. Maybe he'd better wait and see how things turned out tomorrow, and then he could get an early start if it turned out okay. He could have everything ready, and just go.

The next morning, there was already a good two inches of snow on the ground when he woke up and looked out. He pulled on some pants and an old sweatshirt and went out to shake his fist at the sky. "Stop it, damn you. I'm sick of this!"

The freezing air drove him back inside. He paced the living room, trying to calm himself down, but he was so angry he could hardly keep himself from yelling at the walls. Now what was he going to do?

As the day dragged on, he refused to look out at the snow. He didn't want to see it, and he didn't want to think about it. He didn't care if he never saw snow again. He went from room to room, trying to find something to occupy his mind, but nothing worked. It could all go to hell as far as he was concerned.

Wandering into the bedroom for the umpteenth time, he spotted Laura's old cedar chest. It gave him a little hope. Maybe there was something in there that could take his mind off his misery. When he got down on his knees and opened the lid, the smell of incense washed over him, and he let out a little cry of joy. India. That's what it was. The undeniable smell of India.

As he pawed through the chest, his hand touched the edge of something hard. When he dug it out, he saw it was an old sandalwood picture frame. He knew immediately what it was. It was that photograph of him riding the elephant. Now that was something worth remembering. What an extraordinary experience that was to sit way up there above the crowd with the immensity of the elephant beneath him. And wasn't he just telling somebody about that elephant? Who was that?

He held the picture up to the light to get a better look, but the glass was too murky to see it clearly. He turned the frame over, removed the backing and carefully took the photograph out. When he saw the image, he gasped. It wasn't a live elephant at all, it was just a statue of an elephant. He was sitting on top of an elephant statue made out of some kind of white stone. The shock of it made him dizzy. How could it be a statue? He was sure he had ridden a live elephant. Hadn't he? He remembered the rough texture of its skin against his legs. The expansion and contraction beneath him as the elephant breathed, and the way it swayed back and forth as it lumbered down that dirt road. He remembered feeling so majestic up there, like he was the king of the pharaohs. But now, the photograph was telling him none of that was real. Could he really have made the whole thing up?

Stuffing the photograph back into its frame, he threw it into the cedar chest and quickly closed the lid. He felt sick. What did it mean to believe something most your life and then find out it wasn't true? It was just like those words in Laura's poems. Everything was telling him he couldn't trust his own mind. He hated to think his memory was that bad, but if it wasn't his memory, what did it mean? Had he been making things up his whole life? Had he been living his life in a dream?

He got to his feet and went to his bed and lay down with his arm across his eyes. How could he have transformed a statue into a live elephant? It didn't seem possible. But maybe he had ridden a live elephant at a different time. It could have been one of those elephants that helped load the gasoline barrels on the planes. No. That couldn't be true. They weren't allowed to ride those elephants. They wouldn't have let him do it. So when did it happen? He kept working it over in his mind, trying to remember a different time when he might have ridden an elephant. But he couldn't find it. There was just that one time, and the picture said it wasn't real. It was almost impossible for him to accept, but what else could he do? There was no other answer. The elephant wasn't real. He had to stop thinking about it. He already had a blazing headache. He should shut off his mind and try to go to sleep.

The next morning, he woke up feeling like he'd had a bad dream that he couldn't remember. Or maybe it was something real that he was trying to forget. Whatever it was, he'd woken up with a headache, and there was still a lingering pain.

He got dressed and shuffled down the hall, rubbing his forehead. When he got to the living room, he was amazed to see sunlight shooting across the floor. He ran to the window and pressed his nose against the glass. The sky was blue, and the snow that had fallen the day before was already melting.

He ran outside and scooped up a double handful of snow and threw it high into the air. "I knew it. I knew it. Spring has sprung and the grass has risen. I'm almost out of this terrible prison." He laughed at his version of the old song the kids used to sing about school, but that's exactly how he felt, like a kid who had been let out of prison. It meant he could go do what he'd wanted to do before. He could go to the desert.

As he rushed around the house, putting together everything he'd need for his trip, he caught sight of Laura's blue plastic binder on the dresser in the bedroom. He'd better take that. He stuck it under his arm and carried it out to the truck along with his work clothes and a few things to eat from the refrigerator.

He discovered that the tools he'd need were already in the back of his truck. When had he done that? No matter, they were there and it was good. All he had to do is grab his sleeping bag and put the food in the cooler.

Just as he was ready to leave, he thought about calling Sarah. But then he realized she'd just put in a roadblock. That's all she did anymore. Well, not this time. He was going to the desert, come hell or fire water.

Chapter 18

Aaron had driven all the way to Beaver when he decided to stop for gas. As he was headed back to the freeway, he saw a van pull over and drop off a young woman near the on-ramp. Something about her colorful clothes caught his eye. She had on a pretty rainbow colored skirt, a soft white blouse, and a sky blue jacket. Odd, but it all seemed to work together somehow. The thing that didn't fit, was the big, over-stuffed camouflage duffel bag she was carrying. It was a lot like the green duffel bag he had when he was in the service, only this one had blue and white splotches instead of the usual colors.

As the van pulled away, the girl dropped her big duffel bag at the side of the road and stuck out her thumb. So she was a hitchhiker, huh? Aaron didn't usually see girls out on the road and never one this young. He decided he'd better pick her up before someone else got a hold of her.

He pulled his truck alongside her and said, "Are you going my way, young lady?"

She flashed him a pretty smile. "I don't know. Which way are you going?"

"Uh . . . thata way." He pointed south.

"Wow. That's *so* amazing. That's exactly where I'm going." She bobbled her head, and that set her mass of crazy gnarled braids bouncing in all directions. It was a peculiar hairdo, but it looked good on her.

He got out and helped put her bag in the back of the truck next to his tools. She thanked him and gave his truck a little pat. "You know, I really love trucks like this. Is it an antique?"

He wondered if she was *really* asking if *he* was an antique, but there wasn't a hint of meanness in her pretty face. "It's about . . . uh, maybe twelve years. Does that make it an antique?"

She shrugged. "I don't know, but it's a really cool truck. I just love blue."

That was nice. Laura loved blue too. And there was something else about the girl that reminded him of Laura. Not her appearance, but the way she looked at him, meeting his eyes straight on with her shiny green eyes, showing a lot of interest in him like his Laura used to do . . . back when she was young.

The girl cocked her head to one side, and smiled. "So . . . do you think we should get going now?"

"Oh, sorry, I was thinking about . . . something." He opened the passenger door for her to get in, then he ran around and got in himself.

When he was up to speed on the highway, he glanced over and said, "Looks like you're goin' somewhere for quite a while."

"How'd you know that? Are you psychic?"

"Psychic? Uh . . . I don't think so. It's just that you seem to have a lot of . . . stuff in that bag." He tilted his head toward the back of the truck.

She giggled. "Oh, yeah, Jigger says it shows my deep attachment to the material world. He says I'm like a turtle, destined to always carry everything on my back. But Honeysuckle doesn't agree. She says it's just an expression of my pride, and everybody's got that, so I shouldn't let it worry me."

She raised her shoulders and let them drop before she started going again. "I tried to follow Seth's advice, you know, to wean myself from my material attachments, but it got to be winter, and I almost froze to death running around without any clothes."

Aaron glanced at her and then quickly back at the road. "You did that?"

"Well, it was a dare. From Jigger. I guess he wanted to see if I would do it." She shook her head, wobbling her dark gnarled braids. "Well, I couldn't do it for very long. I like my clothes. And I like being warm." She pulled her jacket more tightly around her and sighed. "I'm so needy, sometimes I wonder if I'm ever going to reach nirvana. Do you think that's bad?"

He scratched his head and shrugged. He didn't have a clue what she was talking about.

"I mean, do you think it's keeping me from being my true self? Guru Bara Bhai said we can only know our true self when we're free from our materialistic attachments."

Aaron stared straight ahead at the white lines flashing by on the highway as he tried to figure out her words. She *seemed* to be speaking English, so why was it so baffling?

From the corner of his eye, he could see her hands flying like birds as she talked, and her braids were jiggling again and making a kind of clacking sound. He glanced over to see what it was. No, it wasn't the braids clacking, it was those colorful beads she had woven into the braids. Small red and blue and purple beads. They made a sound sort of like wind chimes clacking in the breeze.

He glanced over again and realized she didn't have a bit of makeup on. None of that black goop around her eyes like a lot of young girls wore. No rosy red on her cheeks. She was just a pure natural beauty, like Eve in the Garden of Eden, the way God meant her to be. He liked that.

She shot him a look that made him think she knew what he was thinking, and it caused a sensation like something was coming alive between his legs, something that had been asleep for a very long time. He tried to ignore the feeling by pointing out the window. "Uh . . . it's a beautiful day, isn't it."

The girl let out a big sigh and stretched her arms above her head. "It really is. It's an absolutely perfect day for an adventure."

"An adventure, huh? Is that what we're on?"

"Yep." She took off her pretty blue jacket and dropped it on the seat between them.

"Uh . . . where's this adventure going?"

"Zions Park."

"Hmm . . . Why there?"

She let out another long breath, and he noticed that her soft white blouse was a little bit transparent.

"Well . . . I would've rather gone to India, but I don't have any money right now, so I heard about this job up at the fire tower. You know, where you watch for smoke so they can come and put out the forest fires before they get too big and burn all the trees and everything. Anyway, I thought if I went up there for the whole summer it would almost be like going to India."

"India?" Was she thinking about going to India? They were a mighty long way from India.

"I know, it's not exactly the same as India. I mean, there aren't any gurus or monks or anything, but I'll be up there on top of the mountain all by myself, anyway, most of the time, and that's kind of like retreating to a cave in the mountains like the holy men do. You know, to get enlightened. And there might even be mountain lions and bears and snakes. And other things." She took a quick breath and continued. "If I meet anything scary like that, I have to remember that they're just symbols of the demons I'm facing right now. If I don't meet them straight on, I'll always be controlled by fear, and I'd really hate that."

Whatever she was saying, it made her frown. And then suddenly, she was smiling again. Her face changed so fast, Aaron didn't know what expression he was going to catch when he looked over at her.

"Anyway," she said, "if I meditate every day while I'm in the tower, I might actually find my true self . . . or something."

She was quiet for a minute.

The silence surprised him. Was she waiting for an answer or some kind of response from him? If so, he wasn't sure what the question was. All he could think to say was, "I was in India."

She squealed and reached over and grabbed his arm. "No way."

He straightened the truck from her pull, and said, "Well, yes, I was. It was wonderful."

She squealed again and bounced up and down on the seat. "Tell me. Tell me. I've just got to know. Did you meet any gurus? Did they give you their wisdom?"

He wanted to please her, but he wasn't sure he had what she wanted. He thought about it. "Well . . . there was that one guy in some kind of diapers. He was under a tree with a lot of people. He might have been one of those . . . goos, like you said."

She clasped her hands together and pressed them against her heart. "Oh, wow! That is so cool. Was he a Buddhist monk?"

"Uh . . . I'm not sure."

Now she was bouncing again. "Did you happen to meet Swami Aakashvani? Did you?"

"Uh . . . Vani swashy who?"

"Oh man, he is the most amazing guru. I mean, anyone who ever comes in contact with him has some kind of really incredible metaphysical experience. I want to meet him sooo bad. If I can save enough money, I'm going to India next fall. For sure." She scowled. "Except that I might not make enough money. They're not actually paying me to watch for fires. I mean, it's sort of a volunteer position, but I don't have to pay rent or anything, and you should see how cool the place is where I'll be staying. I saw pictures, and it's just one big round room with a peaked roof, almost like a teepee, you know, and there's a fireplace and a bed and . . . other stuff."

He kept glancing over at her as he drove, hoping her face might help him catch up with her words. It didn't. She changed subjects so fast, there was no way he could follow. But he liked the music of her voice, the way it started sad and changed to happiness before she took a breath. And she was so pretty. So—

She caught him looking at her and cocked her head. "What?"

Not wanting to reveal what he had been thinking, he looked quickly back at the road.

"Come on. *Please*. Tell me what you were thinking." She was like a little kid begging for a cookie.

"I was just . . . uh . . . wondering about your hair." No. That was a lie. It wasn't her hair. It was *her*. Everything about her made him feel sensations he hadn't felt in a long time. But he was too old to be having feelings like that, wasn't he? He didn't feel all that old. He could at least look at her, couldn't he?

She bobbled her head and made the beads clack. "I know. Isn't it cool? It hardly took me any time to get them going."

"Going? That's right we're going somewhere. Where did you say we're going?"

She gave him a puzzled look. "Well . . . we were talking about my hair. My dreadlocks." She shook the beads again. "You know, some people can't make dreadlocks work, no matter how hard they try. But my hair's fine and kind of curly, so it worked really good." She turned her head from side-to-side, so he could take in the full effect.

"Uh . . . is that the way it's supposed to look?"

She gave him an exasperated stare. "Sure. What did you think?"

"I don't know. I thought maybe you got caught up in a hard wind, or something." He winked to let her know he was having fun with her.

She giggled. "Oh, you're just being silly. Everybody knows about dreadlocks. Bob Marley had dreadlocks." She raised her shoulders and let them drop in her exaggerated way. "I guess you know he's dead now. I felt so bad when he died. I cried for almost two days. Jigger laughed at me and said I was being melodramatic. He said I'd never even met Bob Marley, so how could I be so sad about his dying? But you know, that's the thing that confuses me about Jigger. Sometimes he's so nice, so . . . philosophical and wise, but then other times he'll turn around and be real mean. I don't know why he's like that. Sometimes, he'll sit in his lotus position all day and then stand up and say, 'Shit, my back's broken.' I don't think it's very spiritual to talk like that, do you? I mean, it makes me wonder if he's really as enlightened as he says he is."

"Who is this . . . bigger bugger . . . or whatever it is? Is he your boyfriend?"

"No. Not really . . . but sometimes we, well, I mean . . ." She giggled and straightened her skirt.

Was she saying that they had sexual relations? And he wasn't even her boyfriend? "Uh, what do your parents think about that?"

"My parents? Are you kidding me? I'm almost twenty-two, you know. I've been on my own since I graduated from high school."

"A long time, huh?" He said it like a joke, but he was seriously worried, the same kind of worried he used to get with Sarah when she was young and she'd get all flirty around boys.

The girl did that thing with her shoulders again, and her breasts moved gently beneath the soft white material of her blouse in a way that made it hard for him to keep track of what he was thinking.

"Anyway, Jigger's a lot older than the rest of us, but it's his house and he's really cool . . . most of the time. He lets us stay there, and we don't have to pay rent or do anything except a few chores and . . . other stuff . . . sometimes."

She lifted her rainbow skirt and let it float down several times, like she was trying to cool off. When she settled, she said, "So . . . what were you doing in India?"

That caught him off-guard. He didn't want to tell her about the war. About people dying and planes crashing. He didn't want to think about that part of India *himself*. And it seemed like it would be hard to tell her what it meant to him to be there. How he felt so free, for the first time in his life.

"Did you hear what I said?"

"No . . . what was it?"

"I asked what you were doing in India. What did you see there?"

"Well, like I said, there was that one guy out there . . . with all those people sitting around him buzzing like bees."

"You mean the one wearing the diaper thing?" She grinned, like she was making a joke.

"Well, maybe it wasn't a diaper . . . exactly. More like some kind of white cloth wrapped around his waist and legs. He was skinny, but he had a big belly. That's for sure. And come to think of it, his hair was about as wild as yours."

She tilted her head and tugged on one of her braids, looking serious. "Don't you know why they wear their hair like that?"

"Not really."

"To show they've given up the world. That's why I do it too. I'm trying to live like the gurus do."

"You are, huh?"

"Yes. I am. I think it's important." She looked out the side window for a minute, then turned back. "Do you know why his belly was big?"

"He ate too much, I guess."

"No. It's not that. It's because all gurus have big bellies. It's their hara. It's where they store their pranic energy."

"Is that right?"

She nodded, as if she thought he understood. "I started working on my hara one time, but then Jig said it was giving me a pot belly, so I stopped. He's so mean. Why does he have to be like that?"

She scowled, and continued. "Anyway, I think I'm going to work on it again when I'm up in the watch tower. The hara is ethereal. It's a sea of energy right beneath your belly button. It can be really powerful once you build it up with meditation. I mean, I saw this guy on TV once. He started a fire using his hara energy. He focused his mind and kind of rubbed his hands together, and this newspaper he was holding just burst into flames. It was so amazing. And then, one time, this other guy . . . he pulled a tumor right out of a woman's stomach."

The girl lifted up her blouse and pushed her fingers into her belly and pretended to pull out something icky, and then she shook her hand to get it off. "I couldn't believe it. He didn't use a knife or anything. He just reached inside her and pulled out this horrible bloody thing. There wasn't even a hole in her, or any sign at all that he had reached inside her body. Can you imagine a person doing a thing like that?"

Aaron shook his head, thinking it sounded pretty far-fetched. "Maybe he didn't."

She stared at him in disbelief. "Really? You don't think so?" She looked like she was going to cry. Then she turned away from him and stared out the side window.

Now why did he have to go and say that? He knew how it felt when someone took away what you believed to be true. That's what Laura did with her poems. And there was that elephant that turned out to not be a real elephant. Was that true? No. The elephant had to be real. Didn't it?

She looked upset. "You're exactly like Jigger. You think you know everything. But maybe I know some things too. You just don't believe in that kind of pranic energy, so you close off your mind and try to convince me that it's not real. Well, I don't care what you say. That's why I'm going to the fire watch tower. To get away from people telling me what I'm supposed to believe." She folded her arms across her chest and got a defiant look on her face.

Aaron tried to think how to make her happy again. "I'm sorry. I didn't mean to say anything . . . bad."

She kept her arms folded across her chest, but her face softened, and that encouraged him to keep working on getting her smile back.

"Listen . . . " What was her name. Was he supposed to know? Had she told him? Maybe he hadn't told her his name either. Or maybe he had. "Uh . . . do you know my name? Did I give it?"

"What do you mean?"

"I mean, did I tell you my name?"

"No, you didn't, but it doesn't matter. I feel like I know you anyway." Some of her smile came back, but her voice was still harder than it was before, and he wished it wasn't.

"Well, in case you want to know, it's Aaron . . . Aaron Young. What's your name?"

She paused for a minute, then smiled mysteriously and said, "I'm Maya." She cocked her head and waited for him to respond.

"Uh . . . that's a nice name."

She beamed. "Really? Do you like it? I chose it myself."

"You did, huh?" It made him remember when Laura decided to be Lori, and she started calling him Arni because she wanted them to have special names that nobody else knew. And now, here was this girl telling him her special name. Was he supposed to share his special name too? Maybe he should. "My other name is Arni."

"Arni. Oh, I like that. It's a gentle name. Do you know what your name means, Arni?"

"Uh . . . no. Not really." It felt a little funny for her to call him that name, but at the same time, he liked it too. It made him feel young, like before, when he was with Lori.

She was looking at him now. It seemed like she was waiting for him to say something, but he didn't know what she wanted, so he just smiled and shrugged.

"Well?" she said.

"Well, what?"

"Don't you want to know what *my* name means?"

"Uh . . . sure I do. Now, what was it?"

"I told you. It's Maya." There was a little edge to her voice.

"That's right. Maya." He repeated it silently to himself, trying to make sure it would stick.

"It means, well . . . it's kind of like . . . like an illusion. You know, how we think everything in the world is real, but it's really not."

"The world isn't real?" How did she come up with this stuff?

"No, not at all. Everything is just . . . well, kind of like a figment of our imagination, you know?"

"Uh . . . not really." How could the world be a figment? Is that what she said? What did it even mean? A figment. What was a figment?

She broke through his thoughts. "Well, if you want an example of that, Jigger says the only reason I worry a lot is because when I was young someone wanted to have power over me so they told me to do certain things, and if I didn't, they told me I'd be punished. That kind of thing makes you worry, you know, when you're little, because you never know when you might do something wrong and get punished."

That sounded familiar, but when he tried to respond, she held up her hand to stop him. "The thing is," she said, "all those rules are just a grand illusion. They're just your parents, or society, or all the other people who are trying to make you believe that some things are right and some things are wrong so they can control you. In reality, nothing is right or wrong. They're just two ends of the same pole."

"What was that about poles? What kind of pole?" He took a quick breath and focused on the road, trying to find his equilibrium.

"It's all about the yin and yang of things. How nothing is really black or white, or up and down. There's just the constant movement back and forth between the two extremes. But that's perfectly natural. Some people want to gain power by getting in the middle of everything, so they start telling us that one thing is good and the another thing is bad. It gets all confused, and that's when our suffering begins."

He couldn't control a nervous giggle. "Uh … your talking makes me feel like I'm . . . on some kind of roller coaster or something."

She nodded. "I know. It always feels like that when you're caught in the duality of things. You think everything is real, but you have to remember it's all just the manifestation of the ever changing pluralistic phenomena of the Tao."

His head felt like it was swarming with bees, and he had an ache in his temples. He glanced around at the landscape and realized he didn't have a clue where he was. How far had they come? How far was it to his turnoff? A nervous sweat washed over him. How could he not know where he was when he'd driven this road a thousand times?

He searched for something familiar. There was that range of blue-tinged mountains on the right where the sun was. That was familiar, wasn't it? And there were glowing red rock cliffs to the left. When the red rocks showed up, it meant he was close to his exit. But how could they have gotten there so fast? It had to be wrong. He realized he really *didn't* have a clue.

He rolled down the window and took a deep breath. The air blowing in was almost hot. Wasn't it just snowing before? He was sure it was snowing.

Suddenly, he felt sick. Worried he might throw up, he clamped his hand over his mouth. Then, he glanced at the girl to see if she had noticed. She hadn't. She was still talking a mile a minute, moving her head and hands in a rhythmic way that matched her speech. He tried to focus on her words again, but they floated by so fast he couldn't catch enough of them to make any sense of what she was saying. If he didn't get a break from her, his head was going to explode.

He pressed the brake and slid to a quick stop at the side of the highway.

The girl looked shocked. "Why'd you do that?"

"I've gotta have a . . . drink." He stumbled out the door and groped along the side of the truck to the back. Why did he feel so dizzy? He opened the cooler, but there was nothing in there to drink but a carton of milk. Milk was the last thing he wanted, but it was going to have to do. He took a big mouthful and spat the terrible sour goop on the ground. Of course, it was sour. There wasn't any ice in the cooler. Why hadn't he gotten some ice at the gas station? And why didn't he have any water? He always kept a gallon jug of water in the back of the truck, but for some reason it wasn't there.

Knowing that there wasn't any water scared him. Maybe he hadn't had any water for days. In fact, he wasn't sure when he had eaten last either. Maybe that's what was wrong with him. Maybe he was running on empty.

He looked up and saw the girl standing on the other side of the truck, watching him.

He tried to explain. "I think I need water. "

"I have some Sobe Elixir 3C."

"What?"

She dug through her big duffel bag and pulled out a large bottle of orange liquid and held it up. "The three Cs stand for Vitamin C, Chro . . . something, and Carnitine. Whatever that is. Anyway, it's got orange and carrot juice in it, and it's supposed to be really good for your mind."

She came around the truck and gave him the bottle.

He drank more than half of it before he considered that she might be thirsty too. He handed it back. "Sorry. I shouldn't have drunk so much."

"It's okay. I've got another one. I've got some energy bars, too. And some brownies. Special brownies, but I don't think you'd want any of those. Do you want an energy bar?"

"I guess so. Maybe I better."

She went around and dug through her bag again, then came and handed him the bar and gave him a uncertain look. "Uh . . . don't you think we should get going again? I mean it's getting kind of late."

"I feel dizzy."

"Maybe if you got back in the truck and sat down it would help."

"Maybe."

He got in like she suggested and sat behind the steering wheel eating the energy bar. The bar was kind of hard and hurt his teeth, but it tasted pretty good. He must have been hungry.

The girl sat quietly while he ate the bar, then when he had put the last bite in his mouth, she said, "Are you okay now? I mean can you drive?"

Some of the crumbled bar had stuck in his throat. When he tried to talk, it made him cough. He pointed to his throat and croaked out the word, "Drink."

She handed him the orange drink, and he finished it off.

"You know mister . . . I mean, Arni. I can drive if you want me to."

"You can?"

"Sure, I know how to drive a stick shift. My dad always let me move the truck when he was throwing cow manure on the vegetable garden. I'm sure I can remember how. All you do is push in the clutch and then put the shifter in the right place, right? I watched Jigger do it the whole time we were driving down to Phoenix that time. In fact—"

"Shush!" The word came out loud, but he couldn't help it.

She looked startled, as if she had been slapped.

He was sorry about that, but when she talked so fast, it made him feel like putting his hands over his ears. He needed some peace and quiet, so he could think.

She put her hand over her mouth and sat there staring at him. Her eyes got bigger and bigger, like her covered up words were trying to escape. Finally, she pulled her hand away from her mouth and whispered, "I'm sorry. Sometimes I can't stop talking. It's a nervous thing." She clamped her hand over her mouth again and looked at him with her big green eyes.

He almost got lost in those eyes, but then he remembered it was getting dark, and he didn't know where he was. He had to figure it out. Maybe she knew. "Uh, where are we? Do you know?"

She looked at him oddly. "What do you mean? We're on the highway, aren't we?"

"I mean, where . . . exactly?"

She looked around. "I don't know *exactly*."

"Then what are we going to do?"

"What do you mean?"

"How are we going to get where we're going, if we don't know where we are?"

She looked at him blankly for a second, and then her face lit up. "Oh, I get it. It's a koan?"

"A what?"

"A Zen koan?"

He shook his head. More confusing words.

"You know, a kind of riddle that helps you gain spiritual awakening."

He let out a short laugh, trying to keep back the panic.

"What's so funny?"

"I just can't seem to keep track of what you're saying."

"Oh, don't worry about that. Nobody can." She sat quietly for a minute with her hands in her lap. Then she said, "So, do you want me to drive?"

"You're sure you know how?"

"It's easy. I did it when I was just a little kid, didn't I?"

"Well, I guess it's all right. If you're sure you can do it. I wouldn't mind taking a break for a few minutes."

"Oh, boy," she said. "This'll be fun."

She jumped out and hurried around the truck while he scooted across the seat to the passenger's side.

When she got back in, she looked over at him and grinned. "Okay, what do I do?"

He realized this was going to be a driving lesson.

Chapter 19

Aaron did his best to tell Maya how to get the truck started, and then, just as he expected, the truck stalled when she let out the clutch

She squeaked. "Oops."

He forced himself to keep quiet as she tried again. This time she gave it too much gas, and the truck lurched forward. She hit the brake hard, and the truck stalled again. She giggled and shot him an apologetic look. "Oh dear, I guess it's not as easy as I remember."

Aaron smiled to encourage her. "You're doing fine. Try again."

She restarted the truck, and the engine roared.

"Too much," he yelled.

"Sorry."

A thin bead of sweat appeared above her lip, and her cheeks flushed a pretty pink.

He tried to think how to explain what to do, but decided maybe she just needed a little more encouragement. "Do both of them at once. You know . . . a little bit of one and a little bit of the other."

She shot him an exasperated look. Then, like always, her eyes lit up. "Oh, I get it. You mean I've got to take the middle road."

"No, no. You can't drive there."

She giggled. "I didn't mean that, silly. I meant the place of . . . perfect equilibrium. Is that the right word?"

"Well, I guess so."

"Okay. I'm going to balance my mind and start over."

She pulled the truck to the side of the road and stopped. Then she let her hands fall softly into the rainbow colors of her skirt. Her eyes fluttered shut, and she took long deep breaths, letting the air out each time with a low humming sound. As he listened to her breathing, he watched the movement of her breasts beneath the translucent fabric of her blouse. It almost took his breath away. Then, immediately, he felt guilty.

He looked away, but then he thought, why should I feel guilty? It's just God's beauty I'm seeing. That's all.

The girl was still concentrating on her breathing, and he found himself watching her again. Something about her innocent beauty and the intense passion she had for everything reminded him of his little Lori, back when they were both young. No matter what subject they talked about, Lori's eyes would be shining, and she'd listen to him like he was the most brilliant man in the whole world. It had made him feel good about himself in a way he'd never felt before.

Maya's eyes popped open. "Okay," she said, "I'm ready."

She started up the truck, and this time, she got it almost right. As the truck limped down the highway, she looked over and beamed. "You know, you're a really good teacher, Aaron Young. Is that what you do for a living?"

He liked what she said, but he had to think for minute if it was true. "Well, I guess I did teach a bunch of those guys how to sling mud."

She stared at him. "Sling what?"

The truck jerked and the engine chugged, and he yelled, "Shift down!"

She tried to scrunch the shifter into gear, but she couldn't do it. The truck lurched and coughed and finally rolled to a stop. "Oh, no. I'm so sorry, Aaron. I'm going to ruin your truck. Maybe you should drive."

A semi flew by rocking the truck so violently Aaron grabbed his chest and burst out laughing from the shock and absurdity of the whole situation.

Maya looked at him like he was crazy, but he couldn't stop laughing. Then she started laughing too, and then she was shrieking, as she held onto her stomach, gasping for air. Her gnarled braids bounced up and down and every which way, and pretty soon there were tears streaming down her cheeks. She looked so comical, it got him going again.

He couldn't believe it. Here they were at a dead stop in the middle of the interstate, with trucks roaring by, and he was having the time of his life.

"Don't stop driving now," he gasped. "Go, go. You've almost got it."

She was still giggling and snorting, but she managed to get the truck in gear, and they started down the road again.

Once they were moving at a reasonable pace, Aaron put the window down and let the wind blow in to cool his face. It was marvelous how good he felt—free and relaxed. He patted Maya's shoulder. "See there, all you had to do was relax and not think so much."

She wrinkled her nose. "It's only the shifting part that's hard. Why would anyone put a stupid shifter in a truck anyway?"

He thought about it and chuckled. "For the fun of watching you, I guess."

She stuck out her tongue at him and then grinned. "Well, I got the hang of it, didn't I? I think I was just being too self-conscious before." She frowned. "Jigger says I'm never going to amount to anything because of that. Do you think he's right?" She didn't wait for an answer.

"I mean, that seems so wrong. If you're really sure of yourself, doesn't that mean you're egocentric? And don't all the gurus say you have to get rid of your ego if you're ever going to find true happiness and reach nirvana?" She took a deep breath. "I do know that some people say you need to be confident and self-assured, and that you have to stand up for yourself or you'll get run over by everybody else, and you'll never amount to anything. But I don't know if I believe that. There's so much contradiction, I can't figure out what I'm supposed to do. Do you know, Aaron?"

He was baffled by all her words, so he just shrugged and said, "Maybe you think too much."

"Really?" She stared at him with her mouth hanging open.

The truck started to drift, and he pointed at the road to keep her from driving off into the weeds. "Why do you listen to those guys?"

She straightened the truck out and let out a big sigh. "Well . . . if I knew all the answers, I wouldn't have to listen to anyone, would I? And besides, the books say that you never know when you're going to meet the Buddha. For all I know, you're the Buddha."

That surprised him. "What? Not me. I'm Aaron. Who is this Buddha guy, anyhow?"

She looked shocked. "You don't know?"

"Well, I've heard of him. Some kind of idol or—"

She looked indignant. "He's not an idol. He's a . . . realized being. Not at all like the Christian God. You know, living up there in heaven while we live below wallowing in sin. I mean, what I've read is that everyone of us can be like Buddha and reach a higher plain if we just let our egos go and learn how to experience the one true reality." She frowned. "I want to experience that reality so bad, but Jigger says—"

Aaron held up his hand to stop her. "Not that guy again."

She shrugged. "I know, I know. I shouldn't listen to Jigger." She lifted up her skirt and let it float back down again, and then she sighed. "You know what? That's the exact reason I had to get away. I was getting too depressed from Jigger saying I wasn't ever going to amount to anything. I don't know what good he thinks it does to keep telling a person they're no good. But I guess that's just the way he is." She glanced at Aaron. "When I told him I wanted to leave, he immediately tried to talk me out of it. But then I found out I got the job in the Zions fire tower, and I just packed up my stuff and snuck out when he wasn't there. I'm sure he's really mad at me, but I don't care. I need to be out on my own right now."

Aaron didn't know who this Jigger guy was, but he was starting to have a real dislike for him. Why would he want to squash the passion of a sweet girl like her? Jigger? Jugger? What kind of a name was that anyway? Aaron decided *he* wasn't going to be one of those people trying to sway the girl to his own way of thinking. She should be just like she was. He reached over and patted her arm. "You know what? You're perfect just as you are. Don't let anyone tell you any different."

She gave him a dazzling smile and blew him a kiss. "Ya know, Mister Aaron Young. I really like you. You are sooo cool."

"Cool huh?"

"Yeah. Way cool."

He grinned and blew back a kiss.

She caught his kiss and held it to her cheek.

Her action was so spontaneous and sweet, it brought tears to his eyes. He hadn't felt that kind of affection from a woman for . . . well, for a very long time. He settled into the warmth of the feeling and gazed out at the red cliffs and the deepening shadows that were stretching out across the desert.

As they drove on in silence, he realized he was tired, and there was a dull ache in his temples. But it wasn't all that bad. Probably just from the effort of trying to keep up with the girl all day. He wasn't used to hearing so many words all at the same time. Now that she was quiet, it was nice to just ride along and enjoy the scenery. What a great thing it was to have company and someone else to do the driving for a change.

He fixed his eyes on the yellow light glimmering through the tall wheatgrass that was growing along the edge of the highway. Then, a memory filled his mind. The image was so clear it unnerved him. It was that half-buried temple he found at the edge of the jungle in India. It was late afternoon, like this, with not a soul around. There was a strange golden halo around the temple, and he could see monkeys coming in from all sides. Cast as black silhouettes against the halo of light, they ran back and forth along the temple's roof line, shrieking at him as if he'd done something wrong. It shocked him when one of the monkeys came to a stop at the peak of the roof and started masturbating. For some reason, it scared him and made him feel dirty. He knew he should leave, but he couldn't make himself do it. He'd leaned against the temple wall for support, but then he saw what his hand was touching, and he pulled it away. The entire face of the temple wall was covered with profane scenes carved into the stone. There was one sexual scene after the next, explicit sex between men and men, and men with several women, sex between a man and a horse, and direct masturbation. He had never seen anything like it. He had felt defiled, and yet he still hadn't been able pull himself away or keep himself from being aroused.

Remembering all that now, gave him the same dirty feeling he had back then. What was wrong with him? Why was he thinking about all that stuff? He turned away from the girl and grabbed the edge of the passenger window. Closing his eyes, he tried to force the sexual images from his mind, but they only became clearer. Then suddenly, he remembered the temple door. It was a huge teak door, with two giant, writhing cobras carved deep into the wood, compelling him to open the door and look inside. When he pulled the door open, a slice of light shot across the room and flashed in the eyes of a massive gold figure. The fury in those eyes had scared him to the bone, and then he'd heard a booming voice say, "What do you want?"

"I want . . . I want . . . to be free." That's what he'd said. He did want to be free, but at the time, he wasn't even sure what he meant.

As he ran from the temple and the shrieking monkeys, he had tried to convince himself that the voice wasn't real. But he hadn't been able to escape the thought that it was the voice of God he had heard. Maybe not the god he knew, but some other god, maybe a demon god, maybe Satan himself.

He wondered, now, if the whole thing had been a dream. Was there really such a temple somewhere in India? There were *definitely* monkeys. They were all over India. They ran around every temple and shrine, and they roamed the streets. Sometimes they would sneak into the bashas at night and steal food from the soldiers. But he had never seen those kind of sexual scenes before, or heard the monkeys shriek and masturbate like that. He had wondered for days what they were trying to tell him? Was it a warning of where his sensual feelings might lead him?

Right now, it didn't seem like a warning. It seemed more like an invitation. An invitation to be free, like the monkeys were free, like those sensual gods in the carved scenes were free to do anything they felt like doing.

He glanced over at the girl again, wondering if she had any idea how aroused he was, but she seemed deep in her own thoughts. Or maybe her mind was silent, and she'd been captured by the beauty of the red-rock landscape glowing in the late afternoon light.

He turned away and gazed at the clouds. They were turning pink and orange as the sun settled toward the mountains. He thought back on what he could remember of his day with the girl. What fun it had been teaching her how to drive the truck and hearing all that strange stuff she was saying. It was like he had been on some kind of magic carpet ride, floating through time with a pretty girl, unaware of the minutes and miles passing by.

The sun sank behind the mountains, and the landscape darkened. He felt the air get instantly cooler, and that made him feel like he was waking from a long sleep. What was he doing? He should be out at his property by now. He didn't like driving in the dark, and how was he going to set up camp if he couldn't see? Another thing was the girl. Was he supposed to take her somewhere? If so, would he have enough gas?

He looked over at her. "I was wondering, uh, what did you say your name was?"

"Maya. My name is Maya," she whispered it in a soft mysterious voice.

He nodded. "That's right. Maya . . . Maya. Where are you going to sleep tonight, Maya?"

She smiled. "I haven't really thought about that, Arni. I guess I've been living in the present moment."

"Yeah. Maybe I have to. But I think we're coming to my turn."

"Your turn?"

"The turnoff to my property. I'm going to stay out by my house."

Her face lit up. "Wow! You have a house down here?"

He frowned. "Well, not yet, but I'm going to build one."

"Really? You're going to build a house? From scratch?"

"Well, I guess I'd better. I've been talking about it long enough."

"That is sooo amazing. I've never met anyone who could build a house. Do you really know how to do it?" She looked at him like he was the most talented man in the world.

"Well, I expect so. I've done a fair amount of construction."

"Oh man, I wish I didn't have to go to Zions. I'd help you build it."

That surprised him. "You would?"

"You bet, I would. I'd love to learn how to build a house."

His mind rolled with the idea. She probably wouldn't be much help, but it would be wonderful to have the company of such a pretty girl. "Well, if you really want to help, I wouldn't mind."

"I really, really wish I could, Aaron, but I've got to go to Zions. I promised them I'd be there tomorrow, and I can't break my promise, can I?"

"I guess not." He looked away, feeling disappointed.

"But I'd like to stay with you tonight, if you don't mind."

"Really?" He hesitated. "There's not much out there, except desert and stuff. We'll have to camp out. Is that okay?"

"Sure it is. I've never camped out before. It'll be fun."

"It's just a little ways outside of . . . that town over there." He pointed vaguely in the direction he thought it was. "You know that place . . . what is it called?"

"I don't know."

"I can't think of its name. It's like some kind of storm blowing through. A big wind . . . or something. Darn it, why can't I think of the name?" He knocked on the side of his head to try to shake it loose.

She shrugged. "Don't ask me. They just told me to take the Hurricane exit and then follow the signs to Zions Park."

"That's it. Hurricane. The name of the town is Hurricane."

She rattled her braids. "Of course. I should have known that. You said a big wind. You meant a Hurricane. Your place is in Hurricane?"

"No, not there, but close. Over by the Virgin."

"The Virgin?"

"Uh . . . the river. The Virgin River." He felt flustered. He had been doing fine all day, so why was he forgetting things now? Maybe it was because the girl was going to stay with him, and he wasn't sure what that meant.

"Virgin's an interesting name for a river. Why's it called that?"

He thought about it and grinned. "Because it's, uh, fresh, like you."

"Like me? I'm hardly a virgin . . . I mean—" Her face flushed.

He realized what she meant and helped her out by changing the subject, "So, should we get something to eat first. I mean some food . . . at the store."

"Sure. That would be great."

It was wonderful how she decided things. She just made up her mind, and that was that. He leaned across her to turn on the headlights and caught the scent of her hair. There was a slight hint of perfume mixed with her sweet perspiration. He closed his eyes, breathing deeply, remembering how Laura's hair smelled like that after she'd been out working in her garden all day. He loved that smell.

Maya touched his arm and pointed down the road toward an exit sign. "You were right. There it is. The exit to that big wind." She laughed.

Was she making fun of him for forgetting Hurricane? How could he have forgotten it? He'd been coming down to his property for years. It made him wonder if he had forgotten other things during the drive. Did the girl suspect he had problems with his memory? It seemed like he'd gotten through the day pretty good, but maybe he had just forgotten what he had forgotten. Was that possible?

The truck lugged as Maya slowed for the exit, but after the turn, she got it going again, and they headed away from the sunset on the two lane road toward Hurricane.

As the darkness deepened, Aaron's thoughts turned back to his wonderful day with the girl. She was different from anybody else he knew. He liked that. Why did people always spend time with people like themselves? People the same age, the same race, the same church. That's why he loved India. There was so much difference over there. The different plants and animals. The different religions. The soldiers from different countries. And they all had their own ways. When he left Utah for the war, he had thought people were pretty much the same as he was. But he found out that wasn't true. They had ideas and notions he had never considered before. They looked different, they acted different, they even smelled different, probably because they ate such different food. He loved all that difference.

Maya touched his arm. "You're so quiet, Arni. What are you thinking?"

"Oh . . . I was thinking about people, I guess. How it's hard for them to be with someone who's different and doesn't think like they do. Why is that?"

She nodded. "Bara Bhai says it's because we don't want to live in the chaos of our differences. Seeing different ways forces us to realize that our own reality is an illusion. Then we start to doubt ourselves, and the world gets all shaky because we're not sure what to believe or what to do when we have to make a decision."

He wasn't quite sure what she'd said, but he knew how it felt to doubt yourself and get all shaky. That's how Laura's poems made him feel. He tried to explain. "I thought we were the same, but then I discovered all those . . . words of hers, and I felt like I didn't know a damn thing about myself or her."

"Whose words are you talking about, Arni?"

He mumbled. "Laura." Now why did he bring that up? He didn't want to talk about sad stuff right now.

"Laura? Is that your wife?"

"Well, she *was*."

"Oh, no. Did you get divorced?"

"No, not like that. She's . . . gone. She died. She went . . . to the other side."

Maya shook her head and sighed. "That's really sad. You must miss her a lot."

"Yes." His voice caught. "I really do."

"How long has she been gone?"

He shook his head. "I don't know. A long time." He turned away and wiped a tear off his cheek with the back of his hand. It had been so long since anyone cared how he felt, he wasn't quite sure what to do with it. They had just barely met, hadn't they? And already it seemed like they were friends. Were they friends? He hoped so.

The warmth she gave him, made him wonder how a person could live without love, without someone to talk to and share your thoughts with, someone to comfort you when you were feeling low. Then it hit him how isolated and utterly alone he had become.

He chided himself. Why was he sitting here feeling bad and missing the girl when she was sitting right there beside him? It shocked him that she had done that to him in such a short time. Maybe it was because she was so spontaneous and free, and he craved that kind of freedom. And for some crazy reason she seemed to like him.

She touched his hand, sending a shiver up his arm. "Are you thinking about her now, Arni?"

"Who?"

"Your wife. Laura."

No. He hadn't been thinking about Laura, he had been thinking about . . . the girl. It wasn't right. He *should* be thinking about Laura.

"You said she wrote some words that weren't like you thought?"

He frowned. "Yes. Terrible, accusing words. But she was already gone, so I couldn't do a damn thing about it." Tears filled his eyes, and he whispered, "I'm sorry. I shouldn't have said anything."

"Don't be sorry. It might help if you talk about it. I mean . . . if you want to."

He looked away, confused by his contradictory feelings. Talking about Laura at the same time he was thinking about the girl made him feel guilty, and now his skin was all hot and prickly. He didn't want to talk about that subject anymore. He didn't want to be sad, and he didn't want to feel guilty.

He lifted his shirt and flapped it, feeling the cool night air on his skin. If only he could recapture that happiness he'd been feeling before, but it was gone. He glanced over at the girl and said, "You okay driving in the dark?"

She gave him a smirk. "Sure. Can't you see. I'm an expert driver. It's just the shifting part I'm no good at."

"That's right. You're *quite* the expert."

She drove, and he watched the subtle colors of the evening landscape turn to black and white and thought about the golden sunlight on the girl's skin and how it had sparkled off her colorful beads. Now, in the dim light from the dashboard, she seemed older, and even a little sad. But maybe that was just his own sadness he was seeing.

She started glancing over at him, as if she was uncomfortable with the silence. Finally she said, "Are you missing her? I mean like right now?"

"Who are we talking about?"

"Laura."

He didn't answer.

She tilted her head in a kind of bashful way. "It's okay if you don't want to talk about it. I can understand that."

The gentleness in her voice made him want to explain, but he wasn't sure how to say what had happened between him and Laura. He wasn't sure he understood it himself. How did he live with Laura all those years and not know how she felt? As he thought about it, he wondered if the girl might understand better than he did. After all, she was a woman. Maybe women knew things about each other that a man could never know. He cleared his throat. "Maybe *you* can tell me how you can live with a person your whole life and not know who they are?"

"How do you know that? Is that what the words said?"

"Yes. She wrote . . . poems. Sad ones. Angry ones. Angry at me. I hoped that someone else had written them. You know, some poet in a book. But it wasn't true. They were hers, and they were all about me and about how much misery I gave her." He heard the bitterness in his voice and wished again that he hadn't spoken.

"That's really hard, Aaron."

"It's right there." He pointed to the binder in the side pocket in the door next to the girl. "She hid that book of poems in the back of her closet. It was a terrible secret for me to find after she'd been dead for so long. And that's it. I just have to live with it. She's gone, so there's nothing I can do."

Maya ran her hand across the binder and didn't answer for a minute. Then she whispered, "Maybe nobody ever knows anybody."

"But I thought I did. We were married . . . all those years. We had two children. How could I not know her?"

"Bara Bhai says that after you've known a person for a while, you start to see them like you think they are instead of how they really are. Maybe it was like that."

He shook his head. "I don't know. Maybe."

"Well, I think Bara Bhai was saying that you see some things about a person, and you like those things, so that's how you want to think they are. And maybe you see some other things you don't like, and you get stuck thinking that's how they are too. So you miss all the other things that don't match up with your expectations. And then, you can't see the real person, or the changes they're going through, because you've got those thought blinders on your eyes and over your heart."

What she was saying, seemed right, and he desperately wanted to understand, but her words were still coming too fast. "Could you tell me that last part again?"

"You mean about people not being able to see things like they really are?"

"Yes. Maybe that's what happened."

"You shouldn't feel too bad about it because everybody does it. I bet Laura did it with you too. It's really hard not to. Anyway, that's what Bara Bhai says."

"He sounds like a wise man."

"He really is. He's wise, and he's kind too. He'd never make a person feel stupid, or anything like that. He teaches in a very gentle way. I was amazed by his gentleness when I met him at that retreat in the Catskill Mountains. It was wonderful the way everyone gathered around him, and he—"

Aaron's mind drifted off as he thought about his *own* guy in India. He had been watching him, when suddenly, his eyes popped open, and it was as if the man knew everything about him. But how was that possible? They had never seen each other before. Still, the memory was there, and it seemed right. Maybe—

The girl's voice got louder and it pulled him back. He said, "Sorry. What did you say?"

"I asked if you knew about power spots."

"What's that?"

"You know, like the power spots in the Catskill Mountains where I met Guru Bara Bhai. What I've been talking about."

"Oh yeah, sure I do." It wasn't true, but he didn't really want to hear the explanation.

She started talking, faster, even more excited than before. He didn't try to go with her. He let her voice float over him like music as he gazed out the side window. There was still a dim halo of light above the blue mountains behind them, but stars were beginning to pop out across the sky. As he peered into the darkness ahead, he saw the sign for the turnoff directly into Hurricane. He pointed. "That's it. We'll get some stuff at the store there."

Maya drove into town and they went into the little local market. As they wandered around the aisles, she went for everything that was bad for your health: cookies, chocolate, marshmallows. He was about to tell her those things would kill her, but it was too much fun watching her excitement. He got some bottled water, some fruit and some whole wheat bread and cheese and a few tomatoes and lettuce. He figured that would be enough for supper, and it might help balance out her sweets.

When they got back to the truck, he felt alert and confident again, so he took over the driving. It surprised him that his brain had recovered some of its sharpness. Maybe it was the cool night air, or maybe it was being back in the desert again, or maybe, just maybe, it was being out there with a new sweet companion named Maya.

Chapter 20

Aaron leaned into the windshield, trying to stay on the narrow dirt road that led out to his property. It wasn't easy with the wild bouncing of the truck over the washboard surface and the way the bright headlights made the side of the road disappear into murky shadows

Maya said something, but he couldn't hear her over the noise of the road, and he was too focused to ask her to repeat it.

She spoke louder. "I said, how come you're going so fast on this bad road?"

"Uh . . . I didn't know I was."

"Well, maybe you should slow down. I don't know how you can even see where you're going. It's making me nervous."

He let off on the gas some and sat back slightly, trying to relax the muscles in his arms and neck. They should have gotten to the property before dark like he had planned to. It wasn't safe driving on this bad dirt road in the dark. What if he accidentally took one of the side roads? They could get lost. Maybe they were *already* lost.

Maya touched his arm. "Are you okay?"

He wanted to look at her, but he didn't dare take his eyes off the road. "I keep getting caught up in the lights. I mean . . . it's like water."

"Water?"

"You know, how it gets hold of your eyes, and you can't keep them from going with it."

She was silent for a minute, then she said, "Oh, I get it. You mean how you can't hold your eyes in one place when you're looking at a river, and the river of light from the truck is like that."

"Like what?"

"Like the river."

He didn't have a clue what she was talking about.

"It reminds me of that saying that you can't push the river," she said. "I mean, you've got to just flow with whatever life brings you and not get caught up in fighting it. You know?"

No, he didn't know. How could you push a river? With a paddle? Is that what she meant? He glanced at her, but he didn't know what to say.

She frowned. "I'm sorry. I better let you concentrate on driving."

He leaned into the windshield again, wondering if they had come too far. He had been so focused on staying on the road, he had no idea how long they had been rattling along. Maybe he should get out and see if he could recognize anything. He was just about to do that when he saw a large rock up ahead that had the shape of a bird's head. That's the kind of thing he'd been looking for the whole time. That old crow head was his friend. He was always there waiting for him to come back. "It's not far now," Aaron said. "We'll be there before you know it."

"I hope so. My bottom's sore from all the bumps."

He drove until he saw the silhouette of the cottonwood trees on his property. "Well, it looks like we made it." He pulled off the road and stopped the truck.

"Really?"

"Yep. This is my property."

"But there's nothing here."

"Nothing but us and the turtles."

"Turtles?"

He chuckled. Where did that thought come from? Were there turtles out here in the desert? It seemed like he might have seen one once.

He turned off the lights, and they made their way to the fire pit. Maya plopped down in the sand while he got started on the fire. He could feel her watching him, and he wondered if she was taking mental notes so she could do it later on by herself. "I guess you were never a boy scout, huh?"

"Hardly," she said. "I'm not exactly a boy."

He smirked. "Yeah. I noticed that."

After he had a nice fire going, he sat down next to Maya.

The girl stared into the fire as the flickering light played on her face. One minute she appeared as a wild child with sun-browned skin and crazy hair, and the next minute she was a woman of such beauty it took his breath away.

She glanced at him and let out a nervous laugh. "What are you staring at?"

"You. You're such a beauty."

She looked surprised. "Really? You think so?"

"Sure. Don't you know that?"

She laughed nervously again and turned to stare into the darkness by the cottonwood trees. "I don't know why, but I keep thinking there's a rattlesnake over there." She looked back at Aaron. "That's probably Jigger's fault. When I told him I was going to apply for the job in Zions Park, he told me there would be rattlesnakes and other dangerous things there. He said I was the kind of girl that snakes like. I don't know why he says things like that." She looked back toward the trees. "Seriously, do you think there could be snakes over there?"

He grinned at her mischievously. "Could be."

She looked shocked. "Really? Do you think so?"

"Well, it's possible. That's about the only thing that guy is right about. Snakes *do* like it out here in the desert. They like it hot."

"Oh, no. Don't tell me that. What if they sneak up on us while we're asleep?"

She scooted closer. When their knees touched, it felt like an electric current ran up his leg. He held perfectly still, thinking about the feeling. What was she doing, working some kind of magic on him to make him feel young again? He took a chance and put his hand on her knee. She didn't remove it. "Don't worry. I won't let any snakes get you."

"You promise?"

"Actually, I expect they're pretty scared of us."

She looked confused. "Really?"

"Well, I'd think so."

"Well, if that's true, I mean, if the snakes really are afraid of us, we should try to communicate with them. We should let them know we're their friends, and that we won't hurt them."

Aaron wasn't sure about that. "Uh, how would you do that?"

"Well, we could send them a . . . telepathic message."

He didn't know what she meant, so he just shrugged.

"Don't you know you can communicate with animals if you try. You can even communicate with things like plants and trees, if you get into the right state of mind."

He tried to not let his doubt show. "Uh, I didn't . . . know that."

"Anyway, we should try." She looked all around like she was searching for something. Then, she smiled mysteriously and said, "I know what we need."

"You do?"

"Remember, I told you I had some brownies?"

"Not really."

"Well, I told you before, when we were stopped by the road. Anyway, we can eat them now. I mean, if you want. It might help us get in touch with the snakes."

"I *am* pretty hungry. I'm not sure I've eaten much today."

She bobbled her beads. "Well, they're not exactly *regular* brownies. They're special. They'll open us up to the non-ordinary reality and let us overcome the tonal world of our social conditioning. That way, we'll be able talk to the snakes." She took a deep breath. "Carlos Castaneda talks about that. Have you read his books?"

"Who?"

"Carlos Castaneda. Oh, you'd love his books. They are sooo amazing. I've always wished I could meet a shaman like Don Juan. I know some people can't handle that sort of thing, but I really think I could. Maybe even better than Castaneda did. He was always doubting everything and asked so many questions it must have driven Don Juan crazy." She stared at Aaron and then hit herself in the forehead. "I'm so dumb. You probably don't even know what I'm talking about."

"It's okay. I'm getting used to it."

She looked at him intently, her green eyes shining in the flickering light of the fire. What was she trying to do? See inside his mind? He turned his focus to the fire so she wouldn't see how nervous she was making him.

He felt her hand on his knee.

"So . . . do you want to try one of my brownies, Aaron?"

"I sure could use *something* to eat."

She got up, ran to the truck, and scurried back to the fire with her duffel bag. She plopped down, breathing hard as she rummaged through the bag. She pulled out a plastic container, opened it, and carefully unwrapped a dark chocolate brownie. She broke off a tiny piece and handed it to him.

It was so small he knew it wouldn't do much for his hunger. "Uh . . . can't you spare a little more?"

She raised her eyebrows. "Are you sure?"

"Well, if you don't mind."

"Okay, but I think you ought to eat that piece first and see what happens. It's Jigger's special recipe."

"Jigger, huh?" Now he wasn't so sure he wanted to eat it.

"It's his recipe, but I made them myself. So don't worry."

She narrowed her eyes and was watching him closely as he put the piece of brownie into his mouth. There was a strange crunchiness to it that he wasn't sure he liked, and the intense sweetness made him cough. He pointed to his throat and tried to ask for a drink, but he couldn't get the words out.

Maya pulled a bottle of that orange drink from her pack and handed it to him. He gulped some down.

She started on her piece of brownie, concentrating on chewing for a long time. When she finally swallowed, she said, "Oh man. This is going to be great. Do you like it?"

He didn't want to insult her, so he just said, "They're a little . . . dry. But good. I was hungry."

She winked. "I'm glad you like them, but you're going to like them even better in a minute."

"Well, maybe," he said, "but we might need something more. I'm still pretty hungry." He took another drink trying to wash down the part of the brownie that was stuck in his throat.

"Oh, for sure we'll need something else. Before long, we'll get the munchies."

"The munchies?"

"You'll see. It's one of the best parts."

She was always saying things like that, things that baffled him, but he was getting used to just letting it go. If he questioned her, the answer would probably just confuse him more. He threw another log on the fire and stood up. "Maybe I should get our supper going."

She held up her hand to stop him. No, don't do that, Aaron. Not yet. We should wait. When you get the munchies you want to eat exactly what you want to eat. That's the best time to decide."

He frowned. "Well, how long will it take?"

"Not too long. Maybe a half hour or so. Just sit down and relax."

He sat back down, and they both stared at the crackling fire.

After a while, she closed her eyes and began to rock back and forth. She whispered, "It feels exactly like I'm back up there."

"Where?"

"In the top of the poplar tree."

"A poplar tree? I've done that."

"The wind is blowing, and the tree is swaying from side to side. It feels like it's going to break. I'm holding on tight to the main trunk, with the branches shooting up all around me, holding me in."

Aaron nodded. He knew poplar trees. When he was a kid, there was a row of them along the irrigation ditch that ran through the backyard. He had climbed those poplar trees lots of times, so he knew exactly how it felt when the wind blew while you were up there in the top branches.

She held her hands up toward the stars. "The whole sky is a red blaze, with strips of dark purple clouds and little swirls of lavender blue. The wind is blowing harder and harder, and the tree is swaying more and more. I'm about to let go. I'm about to fly." Her voice escalated into a shriek.

Aaron imagined her flying out across the sky, her rainbow clothes flapping in the wind, her hair beads sparkling like colored stars.

She let out a big breath and said, "Oh, man, that was fun."

"It would be fun to fly," said Aaron. "I used to fly in my dreams."

She looked amazed. "Really? Me too. Not everyone is lucky enough to fly in their dreams. It means you're a special person."

Aaron didn't know how to respond to that, but he was starting to really like the kind of things she was saying.

They both turned back to the fire and Maya began to speak in a low, sensuous voice. "You know, Arni, sometimes when I watch a fire like this, and I see how it licks the wood, I imagine that I'm the wood. I think about how it would feel to be tickled and licked that way until you melt down and turn into atoms that float away with the smoke and merge with the other atoms in the universe. It makes me feel like I'm a different form of myself, like I'm part of the electromagnetic field of the cosmos." She turned to Aaron and sighed. "Do you ever feel like that?"

Aaron rubbed his forehead. For some reason, he was feeling a bit lightheaded. "Well . . . I don't think so."

She looked disappointed, so he quickly added, "But I can see how *you* might. I mean . . ."

Something shifted in his mind. Or was it in his eyes? Maya's beads were glowing like Christmas lights, and there was a strange buzzing sensation near the top of his head. Were his memories trying to get out. He clamped his hand over the spot where the buzzing was and pressed hard to keep everything inside.

Now, the fire was glowing with the same intensity as the girl's beads. The way the golden flames were licking at the black skeletons of the logs made it seem alive. And there were bright yellow sparks flying out of the fire that looked like tiny butterflies fluttering away into the darkness. He laughed, but he felt scared. "What's happening to me?"

Maya touched his arm and giggled. "It's hypnotic, isn't it?"

"Uh . . . I'd say so."

"Did you feel it lick you?"

"Lick me?" What did she mean by that?

She giggled again. "Jigger did that once."

"Did what?" His voice sounded loud and brassy. Was he shouting?

Maya covered her eyes with her hand and peered out through her fingers like a little peek-a-boo girl. "Oh, no. I'd better not tell you."

"Why not?" Again, his voice seemed to boom.

"Because you'd think I was . . . naughty."

He shook his head. "No, I wouldn't."

"Yes, you would."

"No, no I wouldn't." He felt like he had to keep her talking, or he was going to get lost in the flames.

She pulled her blouse over her face. "No. No. I can't tell you."

He couldn't believe his eyes. Her sweet breasts were right there in front of him, fully exposed, begging to be kissed. Then, before he could even blink, they were gone, and he wasn't sure he had really seen them.

She rolled her eyes. "Anyway, he was just playing around."

"Who? What?"

"Jigger. He was pretending like he was a giant cat. A tiger."

"You mean like that one *I* saw?"

"Like a great big one," she squealed. "With a big rough tongue."

"I did. I saw one of those."

"You saw a tiger?"

"Well, that one, but another one too. A mountain kind."

Her eyes opened wide. "Really? A mountain lion? Where? Was it out here?" She looked around.

"No. Somewhere else . . . I'm not sure where. It was so close, I could almost taste it. No, not taste. I mean, its tongue was really pink. Like bubblegum."

She giggled. "Wow. That's so cool. I bet that lion is your animal spirit guide. Rhapsody taught me about spirit guides at that concert. In Liberty Park. As soon as she saw me, she knew my spirit guide was a dragonfly. She said it was because of the way my aura was always changing colors. I was really upset at first. I mean, a dragonfly isn't exactly an animal, is it? It's an insect, and who wants to be guided by an insect. I didn't really believe Rhapsody, until one day, I saw a whole bunch of dragonflies soaring around up on a trail in the mountains. They looked exactly like little helicopters."

"Helicopters?" What she was saying sounded interesting, but what did helicopters have to do with it?

"I know. Isn't that cool? Anyway, that's when I changed my mind and realized a dragonfly could be a powerful spirit guide. There really *is* something special about them. Don't you think?"

Her words felt like a waterfall pouring over his head. He couldn't think of a thing to say.

She met his eyes. "You don't know what I'm talking about, do you?"

"Well, maybe not, but I like the sound of it. It's like . . . bubbling water. Or maybe like music."

"Oh, you're just being silly."

"No. Your voice is . . . lovely. Like you."

"That's really nice of you to say, Arni. I like the idea of sounding like music." She shifted her knees up under her watercolor skirt and wrapped her arms around her legs. She looked at him in a way that filled him with such longing he could hardly bear it. He tried to think how he had come to be with her, but he couldn't quite remember. It must have been a miracle . . . or something. Or maybe she only existed in his mind. She seemed real enough, all golden and glowing in the firelight, but maybe . . .

She ran her finger lightly across the top of his hand, sending chills up his arm. "You look so . . . melancholy," she said. "What are you thinking about?"

"I'm trying to figure out where you came from."

She leaned close and whispered, "Don't you know? I came from the stars."

"You did?"

"Yes. Haven't you heard? We're all made of stardust. When the universe exploded at the beginning of time, it sent stardust flying out in all directions. That dust carried the seeds of life to the earth, and that's what started our evolution. You know? And that eventually led to the development of our consciousness. It's so incredible. I think about it all the time. It fills me with such awe. I mean, how did we get from being stardust to the point where we could think about things like atoms that we can't even see?" She gazed at him with her shiny eyes. "Jigger says that's abstract thinking. It's the key to us being human. If we couldn't do that, we'd just be animals. You know, we'd bark at the cat when it came in the yard, but we wouldn't remember the cat when it was gone away. What would that be like, to not remember things?"

He wanted to answer, but her words had already flown away like a scattering of birds. He smiled and nodded to let her know he agreed with whatever she'd said.

All at once, she started digging through her backpack. She looked like a pack rat, digging through its stash of treasures, throwing things out when they weren't what she wanted.

Finally, she stopped and held up something. "Here it is."

"What?"

"Popcorn. I told you we'd get the munchies." She giggled. "And I've got the jabbers too. I don't know why those brownies always do that to me. I hope you don't mind."

Aaron tried to focus on what she had in her hands, but there was an odd tingling sensation moving through his spine. It felt like he was melting into a pool of yellow light. He closed his eyes against the glare, but it entered his flesh, and he melted down into the warmth of it. He was floating along a narrow tunnel through rows of flickering candles, and there was a rattling sound, as if someone was shaking a dried gourd full of seeds. Where was the sound coming from? And what was that strange smell? Butter? It smelled like butter. But that didn't seem right. There couldn't be butter in the desert. It would melt. "What's going on?" he whispered. "Where am I?"

A soft voice told him to keep going, and he'd find out.

He glided through the candles until they ended in front of a large wooden door with carved monkeys and dragons and a terrifying man with snake hair. He felt like he had to open the door, but he could hear something breathing behind it, and he didn't want to know what it was. The door began to open on its own, and he tried to run, but his feet wouldn't move. Then he saw it, that angry glint of gold in the giant man's eyes. He had seen those eyes before, hadn't he? But where? India? It must have been in India. It must be that devil god behind the temple door. Was that god still angry with him after all these years? Why? What did he do that was so bad?

Suddenly, Aaron felt like he was being pulled backwards by someone who wanted to save him. Then, he was falling through a black tunnel, zigzagging past people he knew: his mother, his sister, his father and little Stevie. And there was Lori, and pretty little Sarah with her favorite doll. He tried to catch hold of each one of them, but they were all just out of reach. "Help me," he cried. "Please help. I'm falling."

"Hold on," he was told. "I've got you."

He tried to focus on his father, sitting high atop his produce wagon, so proud of his perfect fruits and vegetables. He wanted to tell his father that he missed him, but the horses reared up, and it all flew away.

Then, there was little Stevie, splashing through the stream in his red rubber boots. Where are you, Stevie? Why did you go? I need you to help me remember.

He looked sideways and caught the darkness of a rusted wire fence cutting across the stark whiteness of fresh snow. He was with his boyhood friends, and there was a pretty young girl waiting for him on the other side of the wire. He thought he might know the girl, but why was she crying?

There was a crack, like the sound of a tree branch breaking. He ducked and put his arms over his head to ward off the blow, but it didn't come. He opened his eyes and saw a fire and heard the sound of firecrackers going off. Pop! Pop! Pop! And there was a laughing girl with wild snakes in her hair. The snakes danced and sparkled with colorful lights. He blinked hard and looked closer. The girl was shaking a little pan with a sparkling, poofed-up roof. That was where the firecrackers were coming from. "What's going on?" he yelled above the roar of the fire.

"I'm making popcorn."

"Making what?"

"Popcorn. Why are you yelling?"

He put his hand over his mouth and watched in fascination as she placed her little silver pan on a rock and peeled back the puffed-up top with her long golden fingers. Inside, he saw perfectly formed buds nestled down inside the sparkling foil. The buds were like some kind of flower, or maybe pearls that had blossomed.

The pretty girl held the pan out toward him. "Would you like some buttered popcorn, Arni?" There was that musical voice again. It hung in the air for a moment and then dissolved into a fine mist.

He shook his head and turned it from side to side, trying to see things in the way he was used to.

The girl raised the foil toward him again. "You sure you don't want some? It's really good." Her voice was so seductive, he couldn't resist.

As he sank his hands down into the warm buttery blossoms and gathered up two big handfuls, the aroma of butter flashed him back to the candles in the dream. And there was something else. Something just beyond the candles, hiding in the dark. What was that? A face with the glinting eyes of a demon? Or maybe an angry god. Why couldn't he leave him alone?

A dull pain pulled at his stomach. He thought it might be hunger, so he stuffed all his popcorn into his mouth. He chewed for what seemed like forever. Finally, he swallowed and looked at the girl. "What happened to me?"

"I don't know. You floated away somewhere."

"I did?"

"You asked where you were, and I told you to follow the vision to see where it led. Did you do it?"

"I'm not sure. Maybe."

"You looked scared. Why were you scared?"

A chill moved up his spine into his neck. "I'm not sure about that either," he whispered. "It was like a . . . dream, or something. A nightmare."

"What did you see?"

"That buttery smell of the light, and all the rest of it." He rubbed his forehead, trying to remember what had frightened him.

"Don't be upset. It was just the popcorn. It's got butter on it."

"No. Something else. That angry gold gleam in his eyes. In the corner. Behind the door. "

"A door?"

"Yes. Who is he? What does he want?" He pounded on the side of his head with his fist, trying to remember.

She grabbed his wrist. "Don't do that, Aaron You're scaring me."

He closed his eyes to see if he could see anything, but there was only silence and emptiness inside his head. He started to cry. "I don't want it like that."

"Like what?"

"With the world gone and everything disappearing."

"But nothing's gone. It's all right here. Open your eyes, Aaron. Look around. You're okay. We're both right here exactly where we were before."

He did what she said, and the world came rushing back: the pretty girl was there, the flickering fire was there in the cool darkness of the night. He tipped his head back and saw stars twinkling blue and white in a black velvet sky. He held his breath and listened. There were crickets chirping, and an owl cried somewhere off in the distance. He heard a rustling somewhere. Maybe over under the cottonwood trees. Thank goodness, the girl was right: the world *was* still there. But the unbearable feeling that something wanted to hurt him was still there too. If he could just remember what it was, maybe he could make it go away. He closed his eyes again and felt himself falling back inside the dream.

Someone shook his arm. "Aaron! Open your eyes. Right now!"

He held his eyes open with his fingers and tried to keep his focus on the girl. She was searching through her bag

He tried to think only about her, but he kept slipping away.

When he looked again, she was holding a long purple cord strung with three brass bells. He knew those bells. He brought them home from India. How did *she* get them?

He reached for the bells, but she pulled them back and held up the smallest one. She commanded him to listen, and she started to ring the bell. The purity of the sound moved through him and made him feel like he was floating. Like the world was spread out around him, and he was the crater at the center.

When the last note of the chime faded away, he was left in silence that was so vast he thought maybe he had died.

He started to panic, but then he saw the girl. She moved her head from side to side, capturing his eyes. Then she began to ring another bell on a string. This one was bigger and had a deeper sound.

The tone settled into his chest, and it felt like his heart was pounding against his ribs. Or maybe it was some kind of creature in there, a creature who was in love with the sound of the bell, and when it stopped, the creature would die. Or was it his heart that would die? Somehow he knew the only way to stay alive was to focus his full attention on the pulse inside the creature. It grew stronger and faster until his whole body was pulsing. Pay attention, he thought. Pay attention to your heart, and it will keep you alive.

The last ringing note slipped away, and his pulse slowed. Was his heart going to stop? Was it going to fail him? No. They were friends now. He understood his heart now, and he knew what it needed.

He placed his hand on his heart, and whispered, "Thank you."

The girl smiled and began to ring a third bell that made an even deeper , more resonant sound. It found its way into his belly and made it growl so loud it startled him. He laughed and gave it a pat.

Maya laughed too. "Oh, that's good," she said. "That's really good."

"It is?"

"Yes. It means the bells are working."

She rang the bell again, and it got the muscles in his legs twitching. It was a strange, somewhat uncomfortable, feeling. He got to his feet and hopped around, trying to stop the twitch. When he sat back down, he looked at the girl and said, "Are you witching me?"

"Well, I had to do something. You had so much energy in your head, I had to drive it back down to your lower chakras so you wouldn't go crazy."

"Was I going crazy?"

"I think so."

"How did you fix it?"

"It was the vibration of the bells. Didn't you feel it?"

"I think I did. I've never felt that kind of . . . thing before."

"I know. The bells are really powerful. A man from India gave them to me. He said they were tuned to the exact frequencies of my chakras." She rattled her beads and rang the bells all at once. "I wasn't sure they were going to work for you, but by some miracle they did. It's so amazing. I think it means we're soul mates."

"Soul mates?"

She laughed. "Yes. Soul mates. That's exactly what we are."

He liked that he knew what she was talking about now. Maybe the bells really had helped him. Maybe he'd be able to remember things from now on.

Chapter 21

Aaron awoke to the excited chatter of birds. When he saw the yellow halo along the ridge in the distance, he knew what those birds were doing. They were calling up the sun. He tried to remember going to sleep, but he couldn't quite put it all together. Still, he was in his sleeping bag, in the desert by the fire pit, so he must have gotten there somehow.

As he stretched and rolled onto his side, he caught sight of that girl with the funny hair. She was in a sleeping bag too. Things started to come back, but they were still a little fuzzy.

The girl must have noticed he was awake because she looked over and flashed him a pretty smile. "Good morning, Arni. I've been waiting for you to wake up. Did you sleep well?"

He smirked. "I don't know . . . I was asleep."

She laughed and shook her beads at him. Her pretty arms emerged from her sleeping bag, and she stretched them high into the air. "What time is it?"

"I don't know. I don't have one of those . . . gizmos." Was he supposed to know the girl's name?

She stared at him. "What's wrong? You've got a funny look on your face."

"Uh . . . I'm not sure who you are. I mean . . . where did I find you?"

She frowned. "Oh dear. It must be those brownies. I'm sorry. I never should have given them to you. Do you think you'll be okay?"

"Well, I think so."

"I was really worried about you last night."

"Why? What happened?" Maybe she had the story about why his mind didn't seem right.

"You don't remember?"

He shrugged and shook his head.

"Oh no. That's not good. I hope it comes back."

He was trying to figure out what she wanted to come back when she disappeared inside her sleeping bag and wiggled around like she was putting on her clothes in there. It must mean she'd slept naked. And if *she* was naked, maybe *he* was naked too. He took a quick look and saw it was true. Oh dear. Had they been doing something they probably shouldn't have been doing?

As he looked around for his clothes, the girl's head popped out again. He said, "Uh, did we do something we shouldn't have?"

"No. Of course not. Why would you think that?"

"Well, I noticed you . . . I mean, we don't exactly have our clothes on."

"I told you last night that I can't stand to sleep in anything at all. I always get all twisted up in it, and then I can't breathe. You said you didn't mind."

"I did, huh?"

She looked worried. "Boy, I hope those brownies didn't make your memory worse. You seem to be having a lot more trouble remembering things."

What was it he was supposed to remember? Was it something he did, and she wasn't telling him? He tried to think what it could be, but all he could find was a scared feeling about something frightening behind a door in a dark room.

The girl crawled out of her sleeping bag, rolled it up and stuffed it into a duffel bag that looked like white clouds against a blue sky. Had he seen that before? It was the kind of material you would want if you were falling through a cloudy sky during the war over in India. Had he told her about that?

His brain took off, carrying him back to memories he thought he had left buried over there. He could almost see the parachutes coming down from the sky, the planes crashing into the jungle. But he didn't want to think about that. He wanted to think about the girl. She was right there, giving him a look that said she thought something was wrong with him. He sat up and smiled to show her he was okay. That's when he felt something balled up in the bottom of his sleeping bag, and he knew it had to be his clothes.

He pulled them up with his toes and dressed inside his bag like the girl had done. Then he crawled out, rolled up his sleeping bag, cinched the old belt around it, and looked around for somewhere to put it off of the ground. That's when he saw the truck. "Oh, there's my truck."

"Oh dear. Did you forget that too?"

"Of course not. I was . . . uh, just thinking we should put our bags in there so we don't find them full of bugs and critters tonight."

A sad look crossed her face. "I'm afraid I won't be here tonight, Aaron? Don't you remember? I've got to get over to Zions for my new job."

"Oh no!"

"I know. But I have to do it. They're expecting me."

"But what will I do without you?"

"What do you mean?"

"Well . . . I mean . . . there's nobody else here." He felt a knot of fear tighten his throat, but he didn't understand why he would be afraid. He had been in the desert alone before, hadn't he? Of course, he had. So why was he so scared of doing it now?

She looked worried. "What about your house? Won't you be busy building your house?"

"Oh . . . that's right. My house. I have to get that built." It sounded good, but he wasn't sure it was going to help him feel less afraid.

She looked around as if she didn't want to meet his eyes. He wasn't sure he wanted to meet her eyes either. She might see that he was just about to start crying.

As they sat in silence, he felt an overwhelming loneliness set in. He knew it wasn't right. He hardly knew this girl, but he didn't want to lose her. He had lost his little Lori, and now he was going to lose this girl too. Why did he have to lose everyone? Wasn't God supposed to be kind? It didn't seem like He was kind at all. He let those pilots die. He let Lori die. And now, He was going to take away this girl who was the only one who could make him feel happy and alive. He shouldn't have let himself fall for her. He should have never taken the first step. She was a wild girl who was just like a wild hawk that swoops down to steal your heart and then flies away. You can't hold onto any of them. You shouldn't even try.

He watched while she seemed to be deciding something. Finally, she shook her beads and said, "I'll tell you what? If you'll drive me to Zions later on, I can probably stay a little longer. It's still pretty early, isn't it?"

"Yes. Yes. It's very early. It's probably the crack of dawn." His heart fluttered hearing she might stay.

"Well, I don't think it's that early." She gave him a solemn look. "But I think I can stay a little longer, if you can drive me over there this afternoon."

He nodded. "Sure. I can do that."

"You promise? I absolutely have to get over there, Arni."

"No problem." He kept his voice nonchalant, like he didn't care, even though he did care, a whole lot more than he should.

Maya smiled. "Okay, then. That's what we'll do."

He let out a big sigh and told himself to not even think about later.

Maya stood up and stretched her arms, and then she bent from side to side. When she straightened up, she cocked her pretty head to one side and said, "You know what I'd really, really like?"

"What?"

"A bath." She raised her shoulders and let them drop. "I mean, is there a river or anything around here? Any kind of water?"

He thought about it. "Sure there is. I know a good place."

Her eyes lit up. "Really? That would be so great if I could clean up before I go to Zions. I'm sure I don't smell very sweet by now." She lifted her arm and sniffed at the armpit of her blouse "Yikes! I need a bath for sure."

He leaned toward her and sniffed. "You don't smell bad. In fact, you smell good. Like a peach."

She giggled. "A peach? What do you mean by that?"

"You know, sweet. And . . . juicy."

She tipped her head and said, "Well, that's very nice of you to say, Mr. Aaron Young, but I don't think even the bears would want to come near me when I smell like this."

He thought about the water. "You know. I think that water is hot."

"Really? Hot water? Oh, you can't mean it. Are you saying there's a hot springs around here?"

"Right. That's what it's called. A hot springs."

"Well, what are we doing? Let's go find it." She jumped to her feet and grabbed his arm and pulled him up.

"Wait a minute. Aren't you the least bit hungry?" He was hungry. In fact, it didn't seem like he had eaten anything in a very long time.

"Oh, that's right. We better eat something, and then we can go."

They stashed their sleeping bags in the back of the truck and had a cheese and tomato sandwich for breakfast. Then they headed across the desert in the direction Aaron thought the hot springs might be.

The girl raced ahead, dodging between the sagebrush and cactus, flitting from one spot to the next, her rainbow skirt billowing up around her pretty legs. Suddenly, she came to a dead stop and plopped down on the ground. When he caught up to her, she was sitting cross-legged in front of a sun-bleached skull. It looked like an old cow's head, but she was staring at it like it was some kind of holy object. He had seen bones in India that made him feel that way, bones of the men who had gone down in the planes years before. Bones of the wild animals the leopards had killed. For some reason, it made him think of Laura's bones. Is that what she was now?

He sat down next to the girl and ran his fingers along the thick bone between the cow's eye sockets. It felt rough and weathered, almost slivery, but the horns were as smooth as glass, as if they had been polished by time. It seemed strange that the horns had weathered so differently than the rest of the skull.

The girl sighed, and murmured, "It's beautiful, isn't it?" She ran her fingers across the skull in such a tender way, he could almost feel her touch on his own skin. He shivered and thought he saw her shiver too. Was she thinking the same thing he was? Did she know the affect she was having on him?

He quickly wiped away his tears, hoping the girl wouldn't see them. "What's wrong, Arni?"

"I don't know. I guess I'm . . . just feeling . . . sad."

"But why?"

"Because I'm so happy I found you."

"That doesn't make any sense. How can you be sad about something you feel happy about?"

He mustered a smile. "Yeah, I know. Maybe I just need a hot bath."

She jumped up and brushed the red dirt off her skirt. "Come on then, let's go find it."

By the time he was on his feet, she was skipping across the desert again, turning back every now and then to make sure he was coming. It wasn't long before she called back to him, "I see it, Arni. I see it. There's a river down there. That must be where the hot springs are."

He caught up to her, and they helped each other down the rocky slope to the river. The slippery rocks felt familiar, and he was sure he had helped someone else down that slope, and not all that long ago. Somebody with a bad leg. But who was it?

It worried him that he couldn't remember who the guy was, but maybe it happened a long time ago. He shouldn't worry about it.

When they got down to the river, he wasn't sure which way to go. He pointed. "It might be that way, but I'm not sure."

"Okay, well let's go see." The girl ran on ahead, and before long, she turned back and waved at him. "We're getting close. I can smell the sulfur."

She disappeared into the brush, and a few minutes later, he heard her yell, "It's here. It's here. I found it."

By the time he got to the hot springs, the girl's clothes were strewn across the rocks, and she was sitting chest deep in the steaming water. Her skin was already flushing red, and her pretty breasts were bobbing lightly just below the surface. She flashed her green eyes at him. "Don't be shy. The water's the perfect temperature and there's soft squishy mud that feels really good on your bottom."

Aaron climbed up on the smooth flat rocks that encircled the pool. Was he supposed to take off his clothes too? He hadn't thought about that. He glanced around. What if someone was watching? Should he be doing this with a naked girl?

As he stood there feeling unsure, she gestured for him to come in. "Don't be worried about clothes, Aaron. We're just two of God's creatures taking a bath."

She was right. They were like Adam and Eve, just two of God's children taking a bath in a beautiful Garden of Eden. How could there be anything wrong with that?

He stripped off his clothes, stepped quickly into the water, and sunk down to his waist before she could see too much. He paddled across the pond and settled in beside her. As he leaned his head back against the rock wall, he closed his eyes and let out a deep moan. There was no place in the whole world he would rather be than right here.

As he listened to the bubbling water in the river, he thought of that man he had been trying to think of before. Some of it was coming back. The man had a bad leg and the water had helped him. And then they'd gone back up, and he'd done the water witching thing. But where was that guy now? Weren't they supposed to do something else? If the guy found the water, maybe he was supposed to drill the well. But if that was true, where was the guy now? Did something happen to him?

He felt Maya wiggle her toes against his foot. When he opened his eyes she was watching him.

"What's wrong?" she said. "You look worried again."

"Somebody's gone."

"Who?"

"I don't know who he is, but I think he might be hurt."

"But we haven't seen anyone out here at all."

"I know, but I have this bad feeling that something is wrong. I just don't know what it is." He was angry with himself. "Why can't I remember! They're here, and then they're gone, and I can't do a damn thing about any of it."

"Are you saying people disappear?"

He waved his hand in the air. "People. Things. Words. Everything goes away, like smoke."

Maya leaned her head back against the rocks and sighed. "I know you forget things sometimes, Aaron. But I don't think it helps for you to worry about it so much."

"I'm sorry. I didn't mean to."

She shook her head. "No, don't be sorry. It doesn't matter to me if you don't remember things. I've been trying to learn how to live in the present moment for a long time. You do it so naturally. I guess because it's easier for you than trying to remember things. But it's not such a bad way to be, is it?"

He wasn't sure what she was asking, but it made him uneasy. He shrugged and focused on the lines in the rock wall across from the pool. The grain was interesting, the way it ran kitty-corner, like the whole thing had been forced up on one side by something really strong. A quaker, maybe, or maybe some kind of eruption. Seems like he remembered something about that.

The girl touched his foot again. "What I'm trying to say is, if I stay in the present moment with you, it's like we're the only two people in the whole world, and the world is only what exists around us right now. Everything else is an illusion. From the past, or the future. I mean, Zions Park only exists because I know I have to be there tomorrow. And Jigger and Honeysuckle are part of my past. But, what if I lost my memory, like you're afraid you're doing? Would they still exist? Maybe. But they wouldn't exist for me, so it wouldn't matter to me if they existed or not." She snapped her fingers. "Just like that. They'd be gone, and I could be someone else altogether."

It seemed like she was saying something important, but he'd gotten caught up in the melody of her voice, and that made it hard for him to make sense of the words. He frowned. "I don't know any of that."

"I know, Arni. I'm sorry. Sometimes I think you understand what I'm saying, but you just can't find words for your thoughts. I mean, maybe it's like Bara Bhai says: when you're living in the present moment, it's impossible to describe the experience in words. You understand, but you can't say it. If you and I stay in the present moment and only talk about what's right around us, we understand each other perfectly. Right? It's only when I get talking about every single thing that comes into my head, about the past and the future, that's when we lose each other. It's my fault. I know that."

Was she trying to confuse him? "But I'm *not* lost. I'm right here."

"I know. That's not what I meant. See, I did it again. I'm sorry. I'm going to try to not do that anymore. I'm going to see if I can live in the present moment, like you do." She disappeared under the water and then came back up and splashed him.

He splashed her back, and she went into a frenzy of splashing that left him gasping for air. He laughed. "Well now, you're quite the splasher, aren't you?"

She laughed. "I've had lots of experience splashing. My brothers—" She clamped her hand over her mouth, then she took it away, and said, "I'm sorry. I promised not to do that."

Before she could see what was coming, he ducked under the water and grabbed her foot. She kicked, but he held tight and pulled her under.

They both came up sputtering. "Okay, okay!" she shrieked. "I give up. You win."

While he was rubbing the water out of his eyes, she kissed him real quick on the cheek. It was just a soft touch of her lips, but it left him wanting to kiss her back.

She said, "I'm sorry. I shouldn't have done that."

He laughed. "Don't be sorry. I liked it. It was nice."

"Yes, it was nice." She paddled over and wrapped her arms around him and kissed his neck.

The touch of her face against his cheek and the feel of her firm breasts against his chest excited him, but it also confused him. What was going to happen next?

She wrapped her legs around his hips, and he felt a thrill in his groin that was so intense it made him cry out, "No, wait."

She hesitated. "What's wrong?"

"Nothing . . . I . . . . I don't know. Something." Before he could stop himself, he started to whimper.

She moved close again and held him, cooing and rocking him in a way that made his whole body tremble. He tried to concentrate on the rise and fall of her breath, her soft humming in his ear, anything but the painful urgency in his groin. Something about this was wrong. *Oh, Lori, we shouldn't. We're not married yet.*

She silenced his mind by moving her body rhythmically against him, swirling the hot water around them, slowly at first, then faster and faster. She made love to him with such intensity and passion he couldn't tell where he ended and she began. *Oh, Lori, my love. My sweet love. Where have you been?*

When it was all over and the sensations were melting away, he opened his eyes and ran his finger across her cheek. "Who are you? Where did you come from?"

She kissed him gently on the forehead, then brought her warm breath to his ear and whispered, "I've always been here. The stars made me, just so I could be with you."

Chapter 22

Aaron watched a shadow ease its way across the slab of red rock that surrounded the hot springs. When the sun had moved completely beyond the canyon wall, he paddled over to the edge of the pool and looked back at Maya. "I think I'll cool down in this shade."

"Oh, that's a good idea. I think I will too."

When they were stretched out on the rock next to each other, he found out he wasn't going to be cooled. The rock was quite warm. Still, the dry heat felt good on his waterlogged skin. He closed his eyes and sank into the nice feeling. Then suddenly, he felt exposed. What if someone was watching? He grabbed his shirt and draped it over his crotch.

Maya wagged her finger at him. "Now remember, Arni. We're just two of God's creatures cooling off in the shade. There's nothing wrong with that."

He didn't mind being naked. It was just that voice in his head telling him it was wrong to be naked with a girl. If he were alone, he'd be doing the same thing, and he wouldn't think a thing about it. He often shed his clothes when he was out in the desert. He felt more real without clothes, more the way God made him to be.

He looked down at his chest and stomach. He might be getting older, but at least he wasn't saggy. His muscles were still strong, and he didn't carry a bit of extra weight. He wasn't ashamed of his body. He'd never understood why people would be ashamed of their own body, especially if they took care of it. The human body was a creation of God. So why should you feel like it had to be covered up all the time? But maybe—

Maya screamed. "What's that?" She scrambled across the rock on all fours.

Aaron sat up. "What's going on? What's wrong?"

She pointed to a dip in the rock just beyond where she had been lying. "Right there! Quick! Get it!"

He saw the tarantula and laughed. "That little guy's not going to hurt you."

"Little? Are you kidding me? He's gigantic. And how do you know he won't hurt me? Look at him, he's all black and hairy. He's the biggest spider I've ever seen." She pulled her knees up to her breasts, and wrapped herself up tight with her arms.

Aaron had seen a lot of tarantulas out there in the desert, and he liked to play with them. "Look, he's just a little softie." He scooted over and put his hand in front of the tarantula and let it climb onto his palm. He slowly moved his hand toward Maya. "See. He's friendly. Wouldn't hurt a fly."

She looked doubtful. "Don't they *eat* flies?"

"Well, maybe." He smiled mischievously and gently stroked the back of the spider with his finger. "Don't worry little fellow. She won't hurt you. She's just scared."

Maya gave him an exasperated look. "You're just like my brothers. They always tried to scare me with bugs and snakes and things. In fact, one time they put a snake in my bed. It about scared me to death. Ever since then, I hate spiders and snakes."

"You can't hate this little fellow. Look at him. See how gracefully he moves his legs."

She leaned a little closer.

"Don't you want to hold him?" He held it up toward her.

"No," she shrieked. "Get it away."

He shook his head. "How are you going to live in the desert if you're scared of everything you see?"

She gave him a dark look, but then she nodded. "I know. I know. I've thought about that. It's part of the reason I've got to go to Zions. You know, to face my fears. But how can I ever get over being afraid of spiders."

"Try holding him. He won't hurt you."

She eyed the spider. Aaron could see her working up the courage to touch it. Finally, after several tentative tries, she lifted her hand and held it out with the palm turned up. Aaron used the edge of his finger to encourage the tarantula to cross over.

Maya's eyes grew wide as she watched it take a few tentative steps forward on her palm. Then she seemed to relax, and she laughed. "It tickles."

The tarantula moved across her palm, and when it got close to the edge, she cupped her hands so it wouldn't fall off. She started talking to it in a sweet whisper, "Hi, little spider friend. Will you be my teacher? Will you help me learn to not be afraid?"

Then, out of the blue, she leaned back and allowed the spider to step off onto her stomach. The spider seemed curious about this new landscape. It wandered here and there, stopping to check things out. It marched on down past her belly button, and when it paused to stroke her soft pubic hair, Aaron held his breath, waiting to see where it would go next. It took a wide turn and moved slowly up her belly and ribs, then it stopped to prod the edge of her soft breast before making its way up the incline to the sweet pink nub of her nipple.

Aaron glanced at Maya's face to see if she knew she was teasing him, but no, her attention was completely focused on the tarantula. He took a deep breath and told himself it was okay. They were just two of God's children taking an interest in a spider.

As he watched the play between the naked girl and the tarantula, he thought about how wonderful it was to be that innocent and free. As a child, he had been that way. Free and at ease with himself. Until they started putting the fear of God in him. Or rather, the fear of Satan. Why did they want to ruin a child like that?

This girl still had that child-like innocence. It was as if she had never grown up, never eaten from the Tree of Knowledge. No worries. No thoughts of sin. He wished he could attain that kind of innocence again.

He realized Maya was staring at him, and now, she was shaking her head.

He shook his head too. "What?"

"You're such a mystery, Arni."

"I am?" What did she mean by that?

"Yes, you are. Your expression changes so fast, I can't decide if you're happy or sad, or upset or worried. For example, what were you thinking just then?"

He tried to remember. "Uh, I was thinking about . . . you."

"Me?"

"Sure. Who wouldn't? I mean . . . " He looked at her breasts and suddenly remembered the spider. "What happened to your spider? Did you eat it?"

"Oh ick! I bet spiders taste horrible. Especially big black furry ones. No. I let him go. I think he was tired of playing." She rolled onto her stomach, exposing her pretty pink bottom. Aaron wanted to give it a quick kiss, but he restrained himself and waited to see what she'd do next.

She propped herself up on her elbow and gave him a serious look. "Arni?"

"Yes."

"Do you believe in reincarnation?"

"Maybe. What is it?"

"It's where you come back as a different person after you die, or maybe you come back as a butterfly, or—"

"A butterfly?"

She laughed. "Well, I wouldn't mind being a butterfly, fluttering around all the beautiful flowers. Wouldn't you like that?"

He shrugged. "Sure. Why not?"

"What I meant to say was, do you think we've had other lives? I mean, before this one."

"I don't know about that, but we'll have a next life. We'll have a whole eternity that'll come after this. At least, that's what they say."

"I don't mean heaven. I mean, multiple lives. On this earth. You know, coming back as different people? Do you think it's possible? I mean, I keep thinking you and I must have been together in a previous life, and that's the reason I feel so relaxed with you. Why I like you so much." She screwed up her face. "After all, you're quite a bit older than I am. In this life, I mean."

"I'm not so old."

She looked surprised. "Is that a joke?"

He thought about it. "I don't think so."

"Really? How old are you?"

"I don't know . . . seventy something or other."

"And you don't feel old?"

He shrugged and pressed his hand to his chest. "I'm the same in here as I've always been. I don't feel a bit different. I can still do things."

She sat up and brushed off the little pebbles and grains of sand stuck to her belly and breasts, then she looked at him. "Don't you ever feel like some of your memories don't quite belong in this reality, like maybe they came from another time?"

"Uh, no, I don't think so."

She frowned and looked away.

"Did I say something wrong?"

She shook her head. "No. I'm just feeling melancholy. I don't understand where I belong anymore. I can't be with Jigger, and I can't live with my mom and dad. I'm just too different from them. From everybody, really." She looked away and sighed. "Somehow being here with you makes me realize even more that I don't belong anywhere. Like who really cares if I come home at night, or not? I mean, someone who really cares about me because they know who I am and they value that."

"I do."

She frowned. "I'm serious, Arni. Sometimes, I feel so . . . I don't know. Lonely or something."

He nodded. "I understand *that*."

"So what are we supposed to do about it?"

He shook his head. "If I could go back to where we started, maybe she'd still be here."

"You mean Laura? Your wife?" Maya sat up cross-legged and faced him. "I wish you'd let me read her poems."

He sat up and faced her. "I called her Lori, you know."

"You did?"

"Yes, I did. She was young then . . . and kind of like you. All full of passion, and love, and . . . life. Then when we got older . . . she changed. Well, I guess we both changed. We must have if those things she said about me are true." He stared down at the rock, not wanting the girl to see how much the memory hurt him.

The sky darkened and a cold wind blew up the canyon. It made him shiver.

Maya touched his bare knee and that made him shiver again. "Listen Aaron, I know you feel bad about your wife's poems, but I'm sure there must be some love poems in there too. How could she not love you? I mean, you're an amazing person. You're handsome and you're kind and you're smart. She just *had* to know all that. You should let me show you the love in her poems."

The girl's high praise, made his head reel. Did she really think he was handsome . . . and smart and kind? Even if *she* did, he was pretty sure Laura didn't. Not later on, anyhow. She was hurting and feeling bad all the time, and it was all because of him. Isn't that what those poems of hers said?

"What do you think? Do you want me to try?"

"Try what?"

"I mean, do you want me to try to find the love in Laura's poems?"

What if the girl was right? What if he'd just missed the poems that had love? Or maybe he'd misunderstood Laura's words, and it was right there in front of him the whole time. Was that possible?

He was going to have to read all the poems again and try to hold onto the words long enough to figure out what they were really saying.

The girl touched his knee again. "So?"

"So, what?"

"Laura's poems. Should I read them?"

He looked around. "Well, you could, but I'm not sure where they are." That thought scared him. Had he lost Laura's poems? He stared at the girl. "Where are they? Where are Laura's poems? Did I lose them?"

"Don't worry. They're back in your truck. The blue binder is right in the door pocket where you put it."

"Are you sure?"

"Yes. I'm sure. They're safe in your truck."

He scrambled to his feet. "We've got to go make sure. Somebody could have taken them while we were down here messin' around. We have to go back now. Come on. Come on. Let's hurry!"

Maya got up and took hold of his arm. "Why would they be gone? I mean, nobody would come out here in the middle of nowhere to steal somebody's poems, would they?"

"Well, we've got to be sure. I can't lose them now. What if I've missed the best parts? The parts that say how much she loves me?"

"Okay. We can go back, but calm down. I'm sure they're okay, Aaron. You shouldn't get so worried about things."

He couldn't get his clothes on fast enough, and when Maya pointed out that his shirt was on inside out, he had to take it off and put it on right. "Hurry," he said. "Hurry. We have to go."

He watched impatiently as she pulled her rainbow skirt up over her legs and slipped her pretty feet into her sandals. Then she pulled her blouse over her head, and her beautiful breasts disappeared behind the fluff of soft white cloth. He already missed them. Would they ever come out again?

She looked at him. "Okay, we can go. I'm sorry we have to leave this nice place, but I have to get over to Zion's anyway. Don't forget. You said you'd take me."

"I did?"

"Yes, you did. And it's getting pretty late. Can you still take me?"

"Well, I guess I could, but why do you have to go?"

"I'm sorry, Aaron. I have to. I gave my word."

Everything was turning bad. First Laura's poems were gone, and now his pretty girl was going to go someplace else. Once again, he was going to be left all alone with absolutely nothing to hold on to. Why did God hate him so much? What did he do that was so bad?

Chapter 23

It seemed like it was getting darker by the minute as they headed back down the canyon. Then, just as they reached the top of the ridge, lightning flashed, followed by a loud clap of thunder. Maya yelped and started running. Aaron tried to keep up with her, but when he realized he couldn't do it, he slowed down and looked around. There were dark clouds filling the whole sky except for one place where a pearly blue light was shimmering down over the red cliffs in the distance. He was standing there lost in the beauty when the rain came. The huge drops hit the ground, making rusty splotches in the orange sand and filling the air with the sweet smell of sage. I love this land, he thought. This is where I want to be.

The rain came down harder, and he heard Maya yell from up ahead: "Run, Aaron. Run."

He pushed forward into the buffeting wind, feeling the power of it on his flesh and how it whipped at his clothes and tried to spin him around. It was slow going, but the fact that he could keep moving at all made him feel strong and alive.

When he finally made it to the truck, Maya was already inside. She pushed open the door for him, and he dove in. He sat there dripping water and gasping for air. When he could finally speak, he said, "Boy, *that* was fun."

Maya giggled. "I know, but it was scary too. I thought the lightning was going to get me, and those raindrops were so huge they hurt when they hit. She pulled her blouse down over one shoulder. "Am I bruised?"

He laughed. "No. But your shoulder is all splotchy, and your face is splotchy too. Or more like rosy. It's nice."

She shook her gnarled braids, spraying him with water. "I'm freezing. We should have stayed in those hot springs where it was warm."

"Why didn't we?"

She stared at him. "You wanted to come back here to make sure Laura's poems were safe." She pulled the blue binder from the pocket in the door and held it toward him. "See. They're right here. Safe and sound."

That's right. Laura's poems. He grabbed the binder and flipped through the pages, trying to see if anything was missing. But how could he know what was missing when he couldn't remember what was there in the first place? He kept going through the pages until he realized he was getting them all wet. Oh no. That wasn't good. He slammed the binder shut and looked around for a safe place to put it, but everything was wet. He looked to Maya for help. "I need to keep it dry, but where can I put it?"

She closed one eye, like she was thinking. "I know. We have a plastic bag from the store." She reached under the seat and pulled it out. "This should work, shouldn't it?"

Aaron nodded. "Sure. Good idea."

She took the notebook from him, put it inside the bag, folded over the top, and carefully placed it behind the seat. "You won't forget where we put it, will you?"

"I'm not sure. I won't be able to see it back there. What if I—"

She patted his leg. "I know. I'll put it back in the door when we get to Zions."

"Zions?"

"You know. Zions Park. You said you'd take me. And I think we'd better get going, if I'm ever going to get there."

"It's raining."

"I know, but there's no use staying here. Our stuff is all wet in the back of the truck, and we'd just have to stay inside here. If we start driving, maybe we can outrun the storm and things will dry out."

Aaron just stared at her, trying to think how he could keep her from going.

She stared back, and finally said, "So, are you going to drive me?"

"Well, you're in the driver's seat, aren't you?" He heard the grumpiness in his voice, but he didn't mind letting her know how unhappy he was about losing her.

She shook her braids at him and said, "That's right. I guess, I am."

"Do you know how to drive?" he said.

"You taught me, didn't you?"

"In the rain, I mean. Do you know how to drive in the rain? It's not exactly . . . the same."

She frowned. "Well, I wasn't born yesterday, you know. I've driven in the rain before."

He kept it up. "In slippery mud?"

"Well, maybe not in mud, exactly."

"Then we'd better not go."

Her face softened, and she touched his arm. "Look. I know you don't want me to go, but I have to. It's hard for me too, okay?" She sighed. "I'm going to miss you, Arni. I really am."

It helped that she said that. Maybe it meant she'd come back when she was done with whatever she was doing. He let out a big breath. "Well, I guess we'd better go then. But drive careful."

"Okay. I will. I promise."

As she started the truck and ground it into gear, Aaron settled back against the seat and tried not to think about the future.

The truck jerked a little as she pulled out onto the dirt road, but soon she was going along pretty good. He really didn't mind her driving, but he told himself he had better keep an eye on her, just in case.

They hadn't gone far when the clouds blew away and the sun came streaming in through the back window of the cab. It turned the girl's skin all golden and warm and made him remember the hot springs and the nice things that happened there.

The girl turned and gave him a dazzling smile. "See, I told you it would stop. Isn't everything fresh and beautiful after the rain?"

Her smile should have melted his heart, but it didn't feel melted, it felt broken. He stared at her. "What am I going to do without you?" As soon as he said it, he wished he hadn't. What if she was tired of hearing him complain? It might make her want to go away and never come back.

She drove on in silence, while he worried. Then she glanced over and said, "You know what I was just thinking?"

"No, but I wish I did."

"I just realized, I've never lived alone in my whole life. Not even for one day." She glanced at him. "Does that shock you?"

He thought about it. "Not really."

"Did you ever live alone? I mean, before Laura died."

He shook his head. "I don't think I did."

She looked surprised. "Really? You never lived on your own even before you got married?"

"Well, in India, but I wasn't really alone there. I mean, there were all those other guys. But I felt like—"

"Are you saying, you didn't fit in?"

"I didn't mind that. I guess, I'm kind of a loner. I liked going out on my own . . . whenever I could, but—"

"That's just like it was with me. I mean, when I lived with Jigger and all those kids that were always coming around. I wanted to know them and talk about serious things, but they treated me like . . . like I didn't know anything about anything, even though I've read a lot of books . . . and stuff. Anyway, I ended up going for long walks by myself, or I'd sit out under the big weeping willow tree in the backyard and think. And sometimes, I'd . . . weep."

She went silent after that, and Aaron started thinking about those guys he knew in India. He got to know them quite well, but he didn't know where a single one of them ended up. There was something wrong with that, wasn't there? After all, they'd shared a lot in the war. Maybe he should have tried to keep better track of them.

He felt the truck slide sideways, and he yelled, "Watch out!"

Maya coaxed the truck back on the road and smiled sheepishly. "I'm sorry, Aaron. I can't seem to concentrate. I keep thinking about being alone up there in the watch tower and wondering if I can handle it. Maybe you should drive."

He didn't want to drive. If he was driving, he wouldn't be able to look at her, and this might be his last chance. "You're doing fine. We're almost there, aren't we?"

"Almost where?"

"To the . . . hard road."

She frowned. "I don't know. I've only been through here once, and it was night, and we were going in the other direction."

Aaron looked for something familiar that would tell him how far they'd come. The rain had turned the sandstone rocks and the desert sand to a deep rusty orange, and there was a fresh dewiness to the vegetation. The normally gray sagebrush looked almost green, and the yellow flowers of the creosote looked especially bright. He didn't know exactly where they were, but it sure was beautiful.

Soon, he saw the settling pond up ahead. "That's it," he said. "We're here. We've made it."

"Made it where?"

"To the hard road. It should be right around that bend."

"Well, we still have to get to Zions. I wonder how far it is. Do you know?"

"I can't really say."

Maya stopped at the highway and looked over at him. "You know, Aaron, you don't have to take me all the way over there. I can hitchhike, like I was doing before you picked me up."

"No! You can't do that!" It surprised him how sharp his voice was. "I mean, It's not safe. And it could rain."

"It already *did* rain."

"Well, it could do it again, couldn't it?"

"I suppose, but maybe someone nice like you will pick me up. I don't want you to have to drive all the way over there, and then drive all the way back alone.

He didn't want to think about that. "I can take care of myself."

"Are you sure? Where will you go? Back out there to your property?"

"I might." He considered the idea, but it felt lonely. "Maybe I'll go back up to my other place."

"What place?"

"My place in Salt Lake."

She looked more worried. "That's a long ways from here."

"No longer than it ever was."

She looked unsure.

"Listen," he said. "If I take you to . . . that place you're going. Then I'll know where you are. Right? Maybe I'll come find you sometime."

She still looked unsure, so he waved his hand to tell her to get going.

She shifted into first gear, but hesitated again. "Are you sure you don't want to drive now that we're on the hard road?"

"No. I'd rather sit back and look at you for as long as I can." He meant it as a kind of joke, but it made him sad, and he had to look away.

"Don't be sad, Arni. We've had some really nice time together. We should hold on to that. Okay?"

He nodded and tried to smile. "Okay. Come on, then. Let's go."

They drove awhile, and as he watched the evening shadows stretch across the desert, a feeling of dread took hold of him. Sometimes it felt like there were shadows like that inside his mind, darkening the corners, taking away his words. What would happen if they took over completely? He had seen it happen with Miriam from the outside, but what would it be like from inside? If he lost all his words, would his eyes and ears still work? Would he still hear sounds and feel the wind on his face and see beauty. And even if he could experience all that, what would he do with it? If he didn't have any words to describe it, he wouldn't be able to share it with anyone. So what would happen? Would all that beauty just get stuck there inside him?

He told himself to stop thinking like that. He wasn't going to have anyone to talk to anyway, once his girl was gone. He should just stay in the desert and be satisfied with that. It was the perfect place for a man without words. He knew how to talk to the coyotes and the birds, and how to whisper like the wind in the top of the cottonwood trees. If he was surrounded by his wild friends and all the beauty of the desert, he'd be happy, and he'd be just fine.

Now, he was crying again. Why was he always doing that? He wiped his face with his sleeve and looked at Maya to see if she'd noticed. She seemed sad and lost in her own thoughts. He let his eyes linger on her face, the soft line of her jaw, the sweet swell of her breasts beneath her soft blouse. No matter what else happened, he'd never forget her breasts, and he'd never forget those crazy braids with the colorful clacking beads.

He looked forward and saw headlights in the distance. "Better turn on the lights so they can see us coming."

Maya did what he said and then glanced at him. "That's the first car we've seen out here. Is it always like this?"

"Like what?"

"So . . . desolate?"

"I guess rabbits don't drive."

She laughed. "Yeah. Or lizards and rattlesnakes either, but you'd think someone would come along now and then."

"You'd think so, wouldn't you."

She didn't say anything else, so Aaron leaned his head against the side window and looked all around to see if there were any stars coming out. What he saw instead were the clouds that had been chasing them all afternoon. Oh, no, was it going to rain again? They didn't need more rain.

He heard some kind of clicking sound in the engine, and wondered what that was all about. He was about to mention it, but then Maya sighed and said, "You know, Arni. I'm feeling pretty afraid about being alone up there in the watch tower."

"What are you afraid of?"

"I'm not so sure I can handle it. I've been around people my whole life. I mean, I guess I like people." She glanced at him again. "Anyway, certain people."

"I could use some people too."

"Don't you have any family or friends?"

"A few, but they don't come around much."

"So what do you do when you're alone?"

He shrugged. "I don't know. Nothing, I guess."

"Nothing?"

"Well, I guess I . . . " He had to stop and think about it. What *did* he do when he was alone? It was a question he couldn't seem to find an answer to, and besides, he was still hearing that strange clicking sound in the engine. What was that?

"I mean, do you read? Or listen to music?"

"I like music. I like to dance. Lori and I used to go out to—" There was that sound again. He held up his hand. "Wait. Did you hear that?"

"No, what?"

"That knocking sound. Quick! Pull over!"

Before she could do it, the truck started to shake violently. Then suddenly, it came to jerking stop.

Maya shrieked, "Oh, my gosh. What did I do?"

Aaron tried to think what it could be. Then, he remembered what he should have remembered before. "Oh no."

"What?"

"I forgot what to do."

"What do you mean?"

"Oil."

"Oil?"

"I told myself to do it, but I didn't do it. Now it's a wreck."

"The truck?"

"I should have checked it. The oil. I knew I was supposed to put it in. What in the hell's the matter with me? Now the engine could be ruined."

"Oh dear. What are we going to do? I mean, there's nobody out here to help us."

Suddenly, he felt hot, and he realized his armpits were dripping with sweat. How could he forget to put in oil? If he couldn't remember something as important as oil, what else was he forgetting? A truck had to have oil. He knew that. But could all the oil really have gone away that fast? Maybe that wasn't it. Maybe it just stalled for some other reason. Maybe the girl *did* do something wrong. He said, "Try it. Try to make it start again."

"Are you sure? Won't we just ruin it more?"

"Just try it."

"I don't think we should, Aaron. I mean, if it doesn't have any oil in there—"

"Okay then. I'll do it." He got out of the truck and hurried around to the driver's side. Maya didn't want to move over, so he gave her a little push. She squeaked and slid across the seat.

He got in, put the shifter in neutral, and held his breath. He carefully turned the key. There was a click, but nothing else. He tried it again. Nothing but that click. Maybe the engine really *was* ruined. Or maybe it was something else. He pulled the latch and got out to look at the engine. As soon as he lifted the hood, he smelled something burned. Damn.

Maya came around the truck and stood next to him. "Do you think it can be fixed? I mean, should we try to get a tow truck or something?"

"Where would we get that?" He could hear the impatience in his voice, but he was angry with himself and irritated at the whole situation. If he had just remembered to put in some oil, none of this would have happened. Dumb. Just plain dumb.

He saw a flash of lightning, followed immediately by a long growl of thunder. He looked up at the sky and felt the first drops of rain hit his face. "Oh, great. Now we've got rain." He slammed down the hood and they raced to get back inside the truck.

Aaron sat in the driver's seat shaking his head and chiding himself. A truck needs oil. It needs gas. It needs tires and water and . . . Oh, what's the use? He stared out into the growing darkness through the rain-streaked windshield. He couldn't think of anything to do. It was raining, it was night, and they were stuck out in the middle of nowhere. What could he do? Nothing. Absolutely nothing.

Maya let out a little giggle.

He looked at her. "What?"

"I was just thinking the gods must be trying to keep us together."

"The gods, eh?"

"You know, the forces of the universe. I mean, there's a reason for everything. Isn't there?"

He kind of liked that idea. "Well, if that's it, I don't mind keeping you."

She giggled again. "I don't mind either, but the gods might have picked a better place to do it. This is not such a great situation."

They sat there in silence as the sky grew darker. Then, Aaron saw a flash of light in the rearview mirror.

They both looked back, and Maya yelled. "It's a car. She put her hand on Aaron's chest. "You stay here. I'll get out and flag it down."

Before he knew what was happening, she was out in the middle of the road, in the rain, waving her arms and jumping up and down. But it wasn't a car; it was huge semi truck. It blasted its horn and swerved, rocking the truck violently as it went by. Aaron couldn't believe it. How could anyone pass up a pretty girl like that and leave her standing in the middle of the road in the middle of nowhere in a torrential rain?

Then he saw that the truck *had* pulled over just up ahead.

He looked back and saw Maya grab her duffel bag from the back of the truck. She opened the door and yelled, "Quick. Let's go."

Aaron got out. He hesitated, wondering if he should take his stuff too, but there was no use doing that. Everything was soaked, and he was going to have to come back for his truck anyway. He could get his stuff then.

As they raced through the rain, he focused on the red taillights of the semi. They were like beacons of light, but when they got to the big black truck, he saw a skull and cross bones on the door. What was that all about? Was it a truck from hell?

Maya didn't seem to care. She climbed up on the running board and pulled open the door. Aaron heard the trucker say, "Well, hello there, baby doll."

Aaron quickly climbed up next to her to let the trucker know she wasn't alone.

The trucker scowled, "Hey, who's the old guy? Your grandpa?"

Maya pushed her duffel bag onto the passenger seat and said, "No, he's my . . . friend."

"You're friend, huh?"

Maya looked at Aaron and then back at the trucker. "Do you think you could take us somewhere to get a tow truck?"

"Sure, honey. I'll take you anywhere you wanna go. But I don't know about that old geezer? There's not that much room in here."

She flashed the man a pretty smile. "Please. There's nobody else to help us. You can't leave us out here all night in the rain, and I'm not going anywhere without Aaron."

Aaron didn't like the guy's looks. He seemed kind of mean with that narrow band of spiky fake yellow hair stretched across the top of his head and all that messy black writing covering his big-muscled arms and even up the side of his thick neck. The writing was like an evil code, or something. Aaron got a hold of Maya's duffel bag and said, "Maybe we should just—"

"It's okay, Aaron," she whispered. "He's going to help us. Let's just get in." She pushed her duffel bag further into the cab, and climbed aboard.

There was nothing Aaron could do but follow. He wasn't about to let her go off with this guy by herself. He squeezed onto the passenger seat next to the duffel bag, which left Maya standing half-bent over in the middle of the cab.

"Uh, where should I put my stuff," she asked the driver.

The trucker hesitated, then pulled a rag out from under his seat and tossed it at her. "Wipe that rain off of it and then you can put it back there." He pointed towards a curtain at the back of the cab. "You'd better not get my bed all wet. I may be needing it soon." He laughed in a crude way.

Aaron didn't like what the guy was implying, and he was about to say so, but Maya shook her head at him. She carefully wiped off her bag, put it behind the curtain, and squeezed in next to Aaron on the passenger seat.

The trucker pulled down a little bench seat and patted it. "You sit right here next to me, baby doll."

Maya started to sit there, but then she let out a squeal. "Oh no! I've got to go back to the truck. I forgot something."

The guy yelled. "Hey, you think I got all day?"

Maya touched his arm. "I'm sorry, but it's really, really important."

"Okay, okay, go ahead. But move your ass."

The guy was really getting under Aaron's skin. There was no call for that kind of language. They should just forget the whole thing and try to get another ride. Surely, someone else would come along.

Before he could suggest that idea, Maya crawled over him and opened the door. She jumped down to the ground, and said, "I'll hurry, Aaron. You stay put." She slammed the door, and he watched her race back toward the truck in the rearview mirror.

When she was gone, Aaron noticed all the photos of naked girls taped along the dash. Seeing that made him even more sure they should get a different ride. But Maya had told him to stay put, and maybe she was right. What if they couldn't get another ride on this lonely back road? They hadn't seen any other vehicles. He didn't care about himself, but he didn't want Maya to be out in the cold rain all night. Why in heavens name hadn't he done what he was supposed to do? He'd seen the oil leak, hadn't he? So why didn't he remember to put in the oil?

A voice broke through his thoughts. "Whatcha doin' with that girl, old man? Are you some kind of pervert?"

He turned to meet the trucker's eyes. "What do you mean by that?"

"It don't seem right for an ol' fart like you to be with a pretty young thing like that."

"You watch yourself."

The trucker glared at him. "Oh, yeah. Whatcha gonna do, if I don't?"

Before Aaron could answer, Maya was back. As she climbed in, Aaron could see that she was protecting something under the lower part of her blouse, which by now was so wet and transparent her breasts were clearly showing through. Now that wasn't something he wanted the truck driver to see. It would just get him going even more with his dirty mind. Aaron wished he had something for her to put on so she could hide herself, but he'd left everything back in the truck.

Maya crawled across him and sat on the little pull-down seat. She shook the water from her braids and frowned. "Boy, that rain is coming down hard. I'm completely soaked."

The driver stared at her breasts. "Yeah, you sure are. I like it." He gave Aaron a look that dared him to say something, and then he ground the big truck into gear and pulled out onto the road.

Before Aaron could tell Maya to put something on to cover herself, she leaned towards him and handed him a plastic bag with something inside. She whispered, "I got Laura's poems."

It took Aaron a moment to realize what she was saying, and then he was shocked. What in the world was wrong with him? How could he have left Laura's poems back there with no one to watch them?

He took the binder and stuck it inside his own shirt so he wouldn't forget it again, no matter what happened. The last thing he wanted was for that trucker to get his hands on Laura's poems.

The trucker roared. "Hey, what's the big secret?"

"Nothin'," said Maya. "It's no big deal. It's just a notebook with some poems."

"Yeah well, I don't like whisperin' in my truck. If you're going to say something, say it loud enough for me to hear." He yanked the shifter back into another gear, and they picked up speed.

Maya touched the trucker's arm and smiled sweetly. "I'm sorry. We won't do it anymore, will we, Aaron?"

Aaron frowned and didn't say a word. He didn't like the way she was playing up to this filthy guy. Why the heck was she doing that?

She squeezed some of the water off her dripping braids and wiped them on her skirt. Then she held her hand out to the driver. "By the way, my name's Maya. What's yours?" Her voice was as sweet as sugar.

The trucker frowned. "Why do you wanna know?"

"Well, I just thought it would be nice for us to know each other as long as we're going to be riding together." She nodded towards Aaron. "This is my friend, Aaron."

"Yeah. You already told me."

Aaron didn't like being talked about as if he wasn't there. He decided to set things straight. "Listen, mister, me and this girl are good friends. That's all you need to know."

The trucker smirked at Maya. "He's a feisty one, isn't he? How exactly did you come by him?"

Maya hesitated. She glanced at Aaron, then back at the driver. "He gave me a ride when I needed it."

"I see. So you're a regular ol' hitchhiker, huh? A real pro."

She looked confused. "Not really. I just—"

"Anyways, my name's Tucker." He stuck out his hand.

Maya took it, and after they shook, he took her hand and pressed it against his chest and wouldn't let go. She yanked it loose and said, "Tucker's a very . . . interesting name, isn't it? It's really nice of you to help us, Tucker."

"Sure, I am. I'm real nice, especially when you get to know me better." He licked his lips with quick flicks of his tongue in a way that reminded Aaron of some kind of devil snake. How could Maya say this guy was nice? It was obvious he wasn't nice. In fact, Maya shouldn't even be sitting next to him. He should be sitting between them so he could protect her. He wanted to tell her that, but when he thought about actually confronting Tucker, he wasn't sure he could do it. It made him feel weak, like an old man. Especially after the driver had called him an old geezer. Maybe the guy was right. Maybe he was too old to be with Maya. The truck driver was closer to her age, but he was foul-mouthed, and had all those dirty black tattoos, and the naked pictures. Maya couldn't possibly like him, could she? Those smiles she gave him had to be fakes. What kind of name was that, anyway? Tucker? Tucker the trucker. It sounded like a name he had made up. Kind of like that other guy Maya knew. What was his name? Jeepers Creepers. Something ridiculous like that.

Maya didn't seem bothered by any of it. She chattered away, saying how she had always wanted to ride in a big rig truck. She pointed at all the gauges, asking what everything was.

Tucker was more than happy to explain. He was smiling now, obviously happy to have her attention.

It made Aaron wonder about Maya. Was she like that with every man she met? She seemed about as comfortable with this guy as she'd been with him. What did that say about what happened out at the hot springs? He stared at the windshield wipers going back and forth. The engine was so loud, it made it hard to concentrate. Were all big trucks loud like that, or did this trucker just like it loud? It felt like the sound was coming through his feet, sending a vibration up his legs in a way that made them bounce, like people do when they're nervous. He didn't feel right in his head either, it felt like the rain had seeped into his brain and was making him foggy about what was going on.

Things seemed very different on the other side of the truck. Maya and the trucker looked nice and warm over there. Had the guy shut off the heat on the passenger side? Was it some kind of plot to freeze him out? Maya's cheeks were all rosy, and the man kept on smiling at her. They were jabbering away about something or other, and Maya was laughing at everything the guy said. It was like she had forgotten that *he* was even there. Then, Aaron noticed something else: it was very suspicious how the trucker was shifting. He kept moving the shifter forward and back, forward and back, and each time he pulled it back, his hand ended up in Maya's lap. What the hell was he doing?

Maya didn't seem to notice. She didn't try to scoot back or anything. She didn't even look down when he touched her. Finally, Aaron couldn't stand it anymore. He reached over and grabbed the guy's arm. "You stop that, right now!"

Tucker pulled his arm away. "What the hell's the matter with you, ya old codger?"

"I know what you're up to, you devil. You stop this truck right now."

Maya put her hand against Aaron's chest. "It's okay, Aaron. He was just kidding around. Don't make trouble. We need this ride."

Tucker snorted. "That's right, old man. You got nobody but me."

Aaron ignored him. He was stuck on what Maya had said. How could she think the man was only kidding when he was obviously touching her where he shouldn't be touching her? He glared at her. "You're telling me you don't mind what he's doing?"

Maya met his eyes. They were telling him to stop talking, but he didn't care. He wasn't going to let her sweetness be spoiled by the likes of this dirty-minded guy. He yelled again, "I said stop this damn truck!"

Tucker flipped his middle finger at Aaron and sped up. The semi careened down the slippery road. What was he trying to do, kill them?

Aaron knew he had to stop the guy, but how was he going to do it? He looked all around the truck and finally spotted a wrench under Maya's little seat. He grabbed it and held it above his head, shouting, "I said, stop! Now!"

Tucker slammed on the brakes, throwing Aaron head first into the dashboard. He heard the wrench smash into the windshield, and there was an awful screeching sound. When he was finally able to gather his senses, he realized he was scrunched up on the floor with an excruciating pain in his head.

He heard angry voices, but he couldn't make out what they were saying, and he couldn't get out of the position he was in to find out what was going on. Then, he heard a scream. It was Maya. He wanted to help her, but for some reason he couldn't move, and he couldn't get his voice to work right. And why was it so dark? He needed to breathe, but his lungs felt squashed. He wanted to cry out for help, but he couldn't get enough air. A hopeless feeling of panic took hold of him. He was useless. He was making one mistake after the next. Maybe the trucker was right. Maybe he really was a ridiculous old fool.

Suddenly, someone grabbed his arms and jerked him out of the truck. They dragged him across the hard surface of the road and dumped him on the gravel. He lay there with rocks digging in his back and rain slapping him in face, but he couldn't move. Why couldn't he move?

There was such a sharp pain in his head, he couldn't think straight. So much pain and exhaustion. If only he could just sleep for a while. Maybe he'd be okay. But, no, he couldn't sleep. He had to find Maya. Where was Maya?

He heard a truck door slam, and he struggled to his knees. As the truck pulled away, he screamed, "Stop, you devil! Where are you taking my Maya?"

Chapter 24

As the red glow of the taillights vanished into the rain, a wrenching pain took hold of Aaron's heart. His girl was gone. It was his fault, and he didn't know if he'd ever see her again. He fell sideways into the mud, feeling utterly lost. What good was he, if he couldn't take care of his girl?

He lay there in the freezing rain wondering if a person could die from loneliness. Could it make your heart stop beating? He pulled his knees up tight to his chest and waited to see if it would happen. But no, it wasn't going to be that easy. His heart was beating faster than ever, and the raindrops were pounding his body like bullets. He was so cold, he knew if he stayed there in the mud, he could very well die. But it would be a slow and painful death.

He sat up and peered into the darkness. There wasn't enough light to see a thing in any direction. He knew he should start walking, but how could he do that, if he didn't know which way to go?

Maybe it didn't matter. If he walked, at least he'd be warmer.

He struggled to his feet and headed down the road splashing through mud puddles that soaked through his shoes and socks. His feet were feeling numb, but that didn't matter. The important thing was to keep moving. If he focused on the smoothness of the pavement and let that guide him, maybe he wouldn't wander off the road into the rocks and get lost in the desert. Sooner or later, somebody might come along and save him.

Taking action made him feel more confident, and after a while he *did* feel a little bit warmer. Maybe he wasn't going to die after all. His feet were quite numb, but they were still working, weren't they? The pounding rain hurt his head, but his mind was still working pretty good.

He thought about jogging, thinking it might help move his blood faster, and that would make him even warmer. But no, that might use too much energy. Not much in the tank right now. Not much . . . that's it. The tank. The oil tank! That was the thing he didn't do. That's why his truck broke down and why his girl went away. That dirty trucker took her in his big truck. Was he going to hurt her? Please God, don't let him hurt her. If he does, it will be my fault.

Worrying about all that wasn't going to help anything. The only thing that would help was to keep walking. Try to get to some place where there were people. Then he could tell them about the girl, and they could go save her from the bad man. In the meantime, he had to try to stay warm and keep thinking straight thoughts.

He kept going, but his feet felt completely dead now. And one of his legs wasn't working quite right.

Finally, that leg gave out completely. He fell back on his rump in a cold puddle of water. Well, that does it, he thought. Now what am I going to do?

He tried to get up, but his worn out leg wouldn't do it. And by now, he was too cold and too tired to care. He let himself sag to the side until he felt the hard pressure of the road. Sleep. That's what he needed. If he got some sleep, maybe he'd feel better, and he could go back to walking. He told himself to just take a quick rest. If he didn't wake up, so what?

It seemed like he had just gone to sleep when he felt someone squeezing his arm. A voice said, "Can you hear me, sir? You need to wake up."

He didn't want to wake up. He was too cold. Too exhausted. Why didn't they just leave him alone?

"Sir. Can you hear me? Can you talk to me?"

He wished they wouldn't yell like that. It made his head hurt. And his eyes were full of water. Why was that? Had he been crying? Was there something that made him want to cry? Of course there was. His girl was gone, and he didn't know how to save her.

"Can you move your legs, sir? Are you in pain?"

Yes, he was in pain. His head felt like it had been cracked wide open. And his heart hurt because it had been broken by a bad man. He tried to tell the person to go find his girl, but it only came out a whisper.

"What was that, sir? What did you say?"

"Please. Help."

"That's right, sir. We've come to help you. You're going to be okay now."

Was he going to be okay? He tried to focus on the voice, but the icy cold water trickled down his neck and made his mind trickle away too. Couldn't she do something to make it stop being so cold?

Now, he was being jostled. Something pressed hard against the back of his neck, something cinched tight around his chest. He struggled to get loose, but whatever had him wouldn't let go.

"Settle down, sir. We just want to make sure you don't fall off and hurt yourself."

Fall off? Fall off of what?

The rain was gone, but then the air raid started. He could hear the sirens wailing. Were the Japs coming in? Were they going to bomb the base and kill every last one of them?

He knew he had to take cover, but he couldn't move.

"Just relax, sir. We'll be at the hospital real soon."

The hospital? Why were they taking him to the hospital? He didn't want to go to the hospital. That was the place where people died. They cut them open, and they sewed them back up, and then they died anyway. Like his little Lori. They did that to her, and now she was gone. And the other one was gone too. That bad man took her. Was that Lori? No, it couldn't be Lori. Lori was gone. It had to be the other one. But she was gone too. He tried to sort it all out, but all he knew for sure was that his girl was gone. He started to cry and couldn't make himself stop.

"What's wrong, sir? Are you in pain?"

"We have to find her?"

"Find who? I don't know what you mean, sir."

"My girl. What did they do with my girl?"

"There's no one here but you. We're taking you to the hospital now. Just lie still. We'll be there soon."

He tried to do what the voice said, but he was scared. It felt like a wind had blown through his mind and left it hollow. Had he lost something out there in the rain? Had he lost every thing he ever knew? He tried to catch a thread of thought that might bring back the story of what had happened. The only thing he knew for sure was that there was a girl, and he had lost her.

He heard a moan and realized it was his own. Did it mean he was hurt? Had he done something bad and got himself hurt? He'd better call Sarah and ask her for help.

He tried to sit up, but they still had him tied up. He yelled, "Let me go. I've got to call Sarah."

"Who's Sarah, sir?"

"My daughter, Sarah."

"Sarah is your daughter? That's good. Can you give me her number?"

Number? What number? His serial number? He used to know what that was, but he couldn't quite remember. He started running numbers over in his mind, but it didn't do any good. He'd already forgotten it. And it wasn't coming back.

He opened his eyes. The light was too bright and there was a pretty girl at his side doing something to his arm. She smiled. "So, you decided to wake up."

He mumbled, "Where am I?"

"You're in a hospital, sir. Can you tell me your name?"

"My name?"

"Yes. We don't know your name. You don't seem to have any identification on you."

"I don't?"

"No. Can you tell us your name?"

He shook his head. He knew the rule. You don't tell them anything.

She smiled again. "You don't remember your name?"

He held firm, and didn't answer.

She squeezed his hand and smiled again. "The paramedic said you mentioned your daughter. Her name is Sarah, right?"

Sarah. Yes. That's right. Where was Sarah? He should call her. If he didn't, she'd be mad, and he'd have to go through all that.

"Do you have Sarah's phone number so we can call her?"

He decided he better tell. "They're on my notes."

"Your notes?"

"On the table."

"What table is that, sir?"

"Where they always are."

"I'm sorry. I don't know where that is." Her voice sounded like it was a million miles away, echoing through a long tunnel.

She folded her arms across her chest. "Where do you live, sir? Where's your house?"

"It's . . . up there." He nodded his head in the direction he thought it might be.

"Up there, huh?" Her pink lips were still smiling, but there was no smile in her voice.

He decided he'd better help her understand. But how? He knew he lived in a house, but where was it exactly? He closed his eyes, but the only house he could find was the one they lived in when he was four. A hot summer day. Four candles on the cake. His cake was in the kitchen, but he was outside running through the sprinkler. Then his father came and grabbed him by the arms and spun him around and around until his stomach was ready to come up. Was he going to let go? Was he going to send him flying off into space? Maybe.

It was almost like a dream, coming up from that dark murky swamp. He could have easily drowned. How long had he been under there?

He opened his eyes and found himself in a small white room with a bad smell. It was that smell of the plane's fuselage after they'd unloaded the body bags and washed it all down. That smell got into your skin, and you couldn't get rid of it. And there were those bags, the dead weight of the bodies, the poor soldiers inside. He started to cry. "Please, Captain. I don't want to die. I don't want to be put in one of those bags where I can't breathe."

"It's okay, sir. You're okay. You're not going to die."

There she was again, the pretty girl with the smile. She was leaning over him, brushing his hair back from his face. So soft. So gentle.

The lights went down and the girl went away. Too bad. He was alone again. The soldiers were going home in their bags. But what about him? Was he ever going home? And if he did, would anyone be there? His little Lori was gone. She was buried out in the field with the sagebrush. He could talk to her all he wanted, but she'd never talk back. She was on the other side talking with God.

He shut his mind to the loneliness in his heart and focused on the ground below. Was he flying? Yes. He could feel the coolness of the air around him. He could see the tiny trees down below.

Why was he so cold? Wasn't there anything that could get him warm? He needed his desert. His red rocks. The warm sun baking his skin.

Yes, he should go there. The desert would save him. "That's what I need."

"I'm sorry, sir. Did you say something?"

He tried to open his eyes, but they wouldn't do it. "Who's there?"

"I'm your nurse. Are you in pain? Do you need something?"

"I just need to get to the desert where I can be warm. Please let me go?"

"We need to find somebody who knows you, someone who can take you home."

"But I want to go now! Let me out of here!"

"I'm sorry, sir. I can't do that."

He felt a prick in his arm, and his mind melted away.

He woke up, thinking about Laura. "I'm sorry, honey. I didn't mean to hurt you. Please believe me. I didn't know what I was doing. Can't you forgive me."

The woman came closer. "Did you say, Laura? Who's Laura?"

"Laura. Is she here?"

"Who *is* Laura?"

"She's my wife, Laura."

"Can you give us her phone number so we can call her?"

He knew that wasn't right. "She's gone."

"Where did she go?"

"She's out in the weeds. I have to go over there and pull them up, or they'll take over everything."

"I'm not sure what you're saying, sir."

"You know, the weeds . . . on her grave. Nobody's gonna do it, but me. I've got to go now. I can't let her get lost in those weeds."

"Are you saying she passed away?"

"What?"

"Your wife. Did she die?"

"Yes. She's gone. She left me."

"I'm sorry. How long ago was that?"

He thought about it. "I don't know."

"Isn't there someone else we can call? A loved one who can come and take you home?"

A name popped into his head. "Maya. You should call Maya."

Chapter 25

Aaron heard a voice. A familiar voice. He opened his eyes and saw Sarah over by the door whispering with a man. Were they whispering about him?

He was pretty sure the man was a doctor because he had on a white coat. He waved his hand, trying to get their attention.

Sarah saw him and came running to his side. "Oh Daddy. You're awake. You're finally awake."

"I am?"

"I was so scared when we couldn't find you. I didn't know what to think. I thought something terrible had happened."

"Well, it *was* . . . uh . . . quite bad."

She squeezed his hand and gently touched his chest and his face. "Why didn't you tell me you were coming down here, Daddy? Why didn't you call me before you left?"

So there she was, scolding him just like he knew she would. And she was asking him questions that he didn't have the answers for. He couldn't remember leaving home, so how could he remember why he didn't call her? He must have had a reason.

He didn't want to fight with her now. He hurt all over and he was tired. He'd rather just go to sleep. He turned away and pulled the covers over his head.

Sarah uncovered his head. "I'm sorry, Daddy. I'm not trying to make you feel bad. It's just that I was so scared."

He could see that she was scared. Her eyes were wet and full of worry and love. All he could think to say was, "I'm sorry, Sarah. I don't know why I didn't remember to call you."

She was quiet for a minute, then she touched his cheek with the back of her hand and said, "You know, when we didn't find you out at your property, we got the whole police force out looking for you. It was quite a man hunt."

"Did you find me?" He tried a little smile to cheer her up.

"Yes. We finally did. But it was only because the people here at the hospital reported an unidentified man who was confused."

Confused? Is that what they thought? "So they found me, and here I am. And I'm not confused at all. That's good, isn't it?"

"Yes, it's good. Very good."

She held his hand and said, "What were you doing out there in the rain, Daddy? Where were you going?"

He shrugged. "There was a . . . place, I think. Somewhere we needed to go, because she had to get there."

"We? Are you saying someone was with you?"

"Sure. She was there the whole time. But then the mean truck man threw me out and took her away."

"Who are you talking about, Daddy?"

"My girl."

"Your girl?"

Tears filled his eyes. "I tried to stop him, but he took her anyhow. I don't know how to get her back. Will you help me."

"Who, Daddy? I don't know who you mean."

He tried to think of her name, but he couldn't find it. "My little chatterbox. The one with the wild hair and the pretty smile."

Sarah looked worried. "Are you sure there was a girl?"

Of course, he was sure. He just couldn't remember her name. He tried to think harder. If he could remember her name, maybe Sarah would believe him, and she'd help get her back. He closed his eyes and concentrated. What was her name? Lori? Was that it? Maybe. "I think it was Lori?"

"You thought Mom was there?"

"No. Not that one, the other one."

Sarah looked over at the doctor like she needed help. But how could the doctor help? He wasn't there when it happened. How could *he* find the girl?

Aaron grabbed Sarah's arm to get her attention back. "We've got to find her, Sarah. *Now*. Before that dirty man hurts her."

Sarah frowned and turned back to the doctor. "I don't know what's going on with him. He seems so confused. He's been having trouble with his memory, but nothing like this. Do you think his experience out there, you know, getting so cold, could have made it worse?"

"Yes, that is possible." The doctor came close enough for Aaron to see that he had brown eyes, but he couldn't tell if they were kind eyes or not. The doctor came even closer and pointed at Aaron's head. "He has this bad contusion here. Looks like he hit something hard."

"So, maybe that's making him more confused? Is that what you think?"

The doctor nodded. "Sure. If he was having trouble with his memory before, a concussion could worsen it. Or it could just be the stress of the situation. Being out there all night. The rain and the cold. Maybe it will clear up over time, but you should keep an eye on him. Have him checked out once you get him home."

Why were they talking about him like he wasn't there? He hated that. And besides, his memory wasn't that bad. So what if he forgot some words now and then? So what if he forgot his keys? Everybody did that sometimes.

That's right, his keys. Where were the keys to his truck? And where was his truck? Did he lose that too?

He grabbed Sarah's arm. "Have you got my truck?"

She shook her head. "I'm sorry, Dad. They towed your truck to the junkyard."

"The junkyard? Oh no. They can't do that." He pushed back the covers and tried to get out of bed, but there was something attached to his arm that wouldn't let him move very far.

He tried to pull the thing out, but Sarah stopped him. "Don't do that, Daddy."

"But I need my truck."

"Listen to me. Something went wrong with your truck. It's ruined."

"Ruined? It can't be ruined. What will I do? I can't get to work without my truck."

She patted his hand like he was a child. "You don't have to work anymore, Daddy. You just need to rest up and recover."

"But how will I get where I'm going?"

"I'll take you where you need to go, okay?" She patted his hand again.

No, it wasn't okay. How could he get by without his truck? He'd always had a truck. There were things he needed to do. Places he wanted to go. Like down to his house in the desert. That's right, he was going to build his little house in the desert. But how was he going to do that if he didn't have his truck?

He grabbed Sarah's arm again. "Please, Sarah, you have to help me get my truck back."

"I told you. The engine is ruined."

"Well then, I have to go get a new one."

She reached out and brushed the hair back from his face. "Look, Daddy, let's just think about getting you home and letting you recover, okay? Then we can figure out what to do next."

He looked into her eyes. "But I can't go home, Sarah. I've got to find my heart."

"Your heart?"

"That girl. The one that loves me."

"I'm sorry, Daddy, but you have to realize you were alone out there. Mom is gone. You have to face that."

He shouted, "No! I wasn't alone! And if you won't help me, I'll go find her myself."

He pushed Sarah back and almost made it out of bed, but the doctor helped her hold him down. He kicked and yelled, but it didn't do any good. Some other people came in, and they all got together and tied him down.

"Why'd you do that?" he said. "I wasn't going to hurt anyone. Let me go! Let me go!" He tried to kick lose, but his legs wouldn't do it. Everything he had was tied down.

He got scared. What were they going to do, lock him up like they did Miriam? He hadn't forgotten that much. He just needed some rest and some time to get over his headache. Then his memories would come back, and he'd be fine.

The commotion died down, and everyone went out and left him alone with Sarah. He didn't want to look at her. She should have stopped them from doing what they did. He lay there with his eyes closed, pretending to be asleep, hating the whole world and wishing he could just be alone. He was all tied up, and there was no way he was going to get loose unless somebody helped him. And nobody was going to do that.

He must have gone to sleep because he woke up, and Sarah was sitting beside him.

She smiled. "How do you feel?"

"I'm not sure." He tried to sit up. "What's going on here? Let me loose!"

"It's okay, Daddy. You're okay. They'll come take those off in a minute." She patted his hand. "You were trying to get out of bed, but you shouldn't be doing that yet."

"I promise. I won't do it. Can't you let me go?"

She got up and left the room and came back with a woman who undid the tie things. He gave the woman a mean look and said, "Don't try that again."

The woman frowned. "You stay put, and I won't."

Sarah sat back down and rubbed his wrists where the tie things were. "You know, I've been thinking about what you said, Daddy. Maybe it *was* Mom you saw out there in the rain. You know? Maybe she came to you in a dream, to watch over you and keep you safe. She loved you. I think she'd want to make sure you were safe."

Was it true? Was that Laura out there? Had he dreamed the whole thing about the other girl? It kind of felt like a dream. But what about his head? He was pretty sure it was that mean trucker that hurt him. And what about all that walking in the rain? That seemed so real and so cold. Was that part of the dream too? No, it didn't seem like a dream. The girl was there, and he knew it. "That's not right, Sarah. It wasn't her. It was the other one."

"Well, I don't know about that. I just know Mom loved you. I've been reading her poems."

"You have?"

"Yes. You had her poems under your shirt when they found you."

"Where are they?"

"Right here." She held up the blue binder. "When you're feeling better, I'll read you some of her love poems."

"She loved me?"

"She sure did."

"Then why did she leave me? And why did the other one leave me? What did I do that was so wrong to make everyone leave?"

Sarah pulled her chair closer. "Dad, are you saying you've been seeing someone? A woman that I don't know about?"

He tried to sit up. Finally, she might understand. "Yes. She was with me the whole time, and then the truck took her, and it rained. I tried to catch her, but I couldn't. It was too fast."

"What was too fast?"

"The truck."

She stared at him like she didn't know what to do with him. "Your truck is ruined, Daddy. I told you. They took it to the junkyard. It's gone."

"Oh no! They can't do *that*. What am I going to do without my truck?"

She sighed and looked away. "I don't know, Daddy. I just don't know."

Chapter 26

Aaron tried to sleep on the long drive home. Sarah had given him a pillow to help him do it, but he kept waking up with his head bouncing against the side window. Now he had a crick in his neck that hurt about as much as his head. He looked over at Sarah. "It's too hard. Can't you keep me awake?"

She gave him a worried look. "Okay, let's talk about what we need to do when we get home."

The way she said it made him think he'd rather sleep. He shook his head and turned toward the window, wishing he was home *now*.

"Do you feel okay, Daddy? Can you talk about that?"

"I guess so."

"Well, remember how we talked about you selling your house and moving in with me and the kids?"

"What? I never said that."

"Well, I think you should be closer to me now." She gave him a little smile. "I mean, it would be nice for the kids, you know. So they can be closer to their grandpa."

He knew exactly where she was headed, and he wasn't going to go there. He yawned and closed his eyes and pretended to go back to sleep.

She didn't care if he was asleep or not. She just kept talking. "That house is too big for you anyway, Daddy. And it's got that big yard. Wouldn't it be nice to not have to take care of all that?"

He opened one eye. "I like it."

"But you would have more time to—"

He opened both eyes and glared at her. "To what?" It wasn't her business to tell him what to do. Why was she pushing so hard when he wasn't feeling very good? Didn't she know he didn't want to live with her. He needed his own place. He knew that as much as he knew anything.

She shrugged. "I don't know. You could read. Or watch TV. Or play with the kids." Her eyes lit up on that one. "Sam and Annie would love that. Wouldn't *you*?"

Is that what she thought? That he wanted to play with kids all the time? "I'm not going to do it."

"But why, Daddy? It would be so nice to have you with us. We could —"

"I told you, no! I have my own things to do."

"Like what?" Her voice sounded soft, but she was still pushing.

"Like whatever I decide. I'm not going to sit around and waste myself." If he let her do this, the next thing she'd do is try to put him in that place with Miriam. He wasn't about to let her start down that road.

She frowned and let out a big sigh. "Well, I'm not going to twist your arm. I just thought you might like to spend more time with your grandkids." She touched his knee. "And besides, having you around would be a big help to me. You know? I could work a little more if I knew the kids were safe with you."

Now, he understood. "So you need a baby watcher, do ya? Is that what you're trying for?"

"No, Dad. I just—"

"Spit it out, why don't you!"

She looked shocked. "Spit what out?"

"Whatever your spitting."

When he saw the tears in her eyes, he knew he'd gone too far. He should have just kept his mouth shut and pretended to be asleep. But why was she trying to take over everything? It wasn't her job to be in charge. And what was she doing driving anyway? He was the man of the house, wasn't he? He felt like telling her to pull over and let him drive, but those tears in her eyes told him it would just make things worse. "Laura, I—"

"I'm not Laura. I'm Sarah. Your daughter, Sarah. Don't you know that?"

"What? Sure I do. Why wouldn't I?" A hot sticky sweat soaked through his shirt. Of course she was Sarah. His daughter, Sarah. Did he call her by the wrong name?

Desperate to escape her accusing eyes, he pressed his face against the side window and stared at the fence posts flashing by on the side of the road. Barbed wire, everywhere. Those barbs made him feel like he was in prison with no way out. If he could just be by himself in his own place, he wouldn't feel so tense and pressured. And he could be in charge of himself. Why was it taking so long to get home anyway? Was she going the long way around?

He started thinking about being home and wondering how long he had been gone. A few days? Weeks? He hoped his plants weren't all dead.

He turned to Sarah. "Did they water everything?"

"Who?"

"You know, the . . . pipes. The hose thing."

"I'm sorry, Dad. I don't know what you mean."

There was something in her tone that told him she was going to be upset with him again, but he wasn't sure why, and that scared him. Why was he having so much trouble knowing how to say things? Sometimes he forgot things before, but now he felt confused and his memory seemed a lot worse. Why? Was it that rain he'd been in? Had it washed out his brain?

He couldn't even remember why he'd been out there in that rain. And now, when he tried to focus on things that were right in front of him, it was like he'd never seen them before. Like the blanket on his lap. A dark red blanket with green and yellow plaid lines. Had he ever seen it before? He was pretty sure it wasn't his. So whose was it? The car wasn't his either. He should be driving his truck home, shouldn't he? It seemed like something might have happened to his truck. But what?

He wanted to ask Sarah if she knew where his truck was, but she still had that worried look on her face, so he turned back to seeing what was outside. There was grass and trees and mountains. He knew all that. It was all very familiar, so that was good. And there was snow high up on the mountain peaks. That didn't seem right. Wasn't it just summer? Maybe he'd been gone longer than he thought, and it was already fall. How could he have lost track of *that* much time?

A fire engine roared by giving him a jolt. He hoped they got to the fire before everything burned down. And he hoped it wasn't his place that was burning down. It was a random thought, but then he realized it might be true. What if it really *was* his house that was burning? The thought scared him, and he grabbed Sarah's arm. "You've got to go faster."

She jerked her arm away, and swerved the car back into place. "Don't do that, Dad. You almost made me hit that car."

"Well, hurry."

"What's the matter? Do you need a bathroom?"

"What?"

"I said, what's wrong with you? Why are you so urgent?"

"I don't want to lose it."

"Lose what?"

"My house!"

"Your *house*?"

"I want to make sure it's still there."

"Why wouldn't it be there? Please, Daddy, you're not making sense."

"I just want you to get going." He grabbed her arm again, and she jerked it away.

Instead of going faster, she slowed way down. "Dad, you're acting crazy. I don't know what to do with you."

Why did she say that? He wasn't crazy. Was it her way of getting in the driver's seat, so she could tell him what to do? Well, it wasn't going to work. He was her father. She should be listening to him.

He was about to tell her that when she looked over and said, "Daddy, I'm really worried about you. You're saying such strange things. I'm afraid you got more hurt out there in the rain than we thought."

"Me? I'm fine. You're the one saying strange things."

"Please, Dad. I want to help, but you're not making it easy. And why are you so angry with me?"

She was right. He was feeling angry. Well, why shouldn't he be angry? His head hurt, and he felt confused, and she was trying to take advantage of all that.

But what if there really was something wrong with him? With his brain. It was hard to tell when she blew everything up and tried to make him unsure of himself. Why did she want to do that, especially when he was so tired and ready to be home? Maybe if he closed his eyes, she wouldn't talk anymore. Then, if he fell asleep, he could wake up and he'd be home. He could get back to his routine, and everything would be fine. Then she'd have to leave him alone.

He glanced over. She was still going slow and holding on tight to the steering wheel. And she didn't seem to even know he was there, so he *did* close his eyes. He focused on the sound of the engine, the tires against the road, the slight vibration of the seat. He had a vague memory of something vibrating like that before, only bigger. Something that made a lot of noise, like a big truck.

Then it all came back. There *was* a big truck. With a mean man driving it. The man hurt him and took off with the girl.

He opened his eyes and yelled, "Stop! We've got to back!"

"What do you mean? Back where?"

"We've got to go find the girl before she's gone."

Sarah shot him an exasperated look. "Oh dear. Are you back to that again?"

"Yes. That's what I said. We've got to go back."

"We can't go back. We're almost home."

"But what's she going to do if we don't find her?"

"Daddy, was there really a girl?"

"Of course there was. We were in the hot tub. She was young, and she was pretty, and she—"

"But where did you meet her?"

"I don't know. I found her. I guess."

"Found her?"

"She was in that water."

"What water?"

"You know. The water. The water that comes out from the hot rocks."

"Do you mean a hot springs?"

"Yes, that's right! The hot springs." Now he was getting somewhere. "We've got to go back there and get her."

"At the hot springs?"

"No, I told you. The man took her in his mean truck."

"You never said that."

"I didn't?"

"No. What man are you talking about?"

"The man in the truck."

"He took her? Where did he take her?"

"That's what I don't know!" Suddenly, he felt drained. All the words flying back and forth made him feel like he was sinking in mud. He gave up and stared out the side window at the mountain. What was the name of that big mountain? Nemo? Nebo? Yes, that's what it was. Mount Nebo. See there, he could remember things if he really tried.

"Daddy?"

"What?"

"Are you sure there was a truck?"

"Of course, there's a truck. I've had it . . . a long time. I just don't know where it is. Do you know? Can you help me get it back?"

There she went, shaking her head again, looking like he'd said something really dumb. But why shouldn't he wonder about his truck? He needed his truck. How was he going to work if he didn't have his truck? How was he going to do anything?

She stopped talking and wouldn't look at him. Well, so what? If she wasn't going to talk, then he wasn't going to talk either. What were they doing driving all over creation anyway? He should have driven himself. He should have just left her at home. He closed his eyes and leaned his head into the pillow and went back to feeling the vibration of the road.

When he woke up, someone was shaking him.

"Dad. We're here."

He opened one eye and looked around. Something was wrong. This wasn't his place. "Where are we? I want to go to my house."

"I don't want you to be alone right now, Daddy. It would be better if you stayed with us for a while."

"I said no, didn't I?" He was sure he said no.

"You've been in the hospital. You need time to recover."

"I'm fine. Now, take me home! Right now!"

"I'm sorry. I can't do that."

"What do you mean, you can't? Just drive this car to my house and let me out."

She shook her head, looking fed up. Why was she treating him like a child? If he wanted to go to his own house, he should be able to do it. Well, fine. If she didn't want to drive him, he'd walk.

"Listen, Dad. Just sleep here tonight. Then, if you feel okay tomorrow, I'll take you home. That is, if you still want me to."

She took the keys out of the ignition and opened her door.

It was obvious, she wasn't going to change her mind, but he wasn't going to change his mind either. She came around and opened his door, but he wasn't about to get out. He knew if she got used to bossing him around, he wouldn't have a chance. She would end up thinking she was the man of the house, the boss of everything.

She pulled on his arm, but he didn't budge.

She pulled harder, but he reached over and got a hold of the steering wheel and held on with all his strength. No way he was going to let her win this one.

"Now you stop that, Dad. You're acting like a child. You'd think you were being kidnapped."

"I am being kidnapped. Call the cops!"

She quit pulling on him and stepped back. "Would you rather I come stay with you tonight? I can do that, if you want me to, but I'd have to make some arrangements."

"Nobody needs to stay with me."

"I'm not leaving you alone tonight, Dad, and you might as well get used to it." Her face softened. "Look, Daddy, I just want you to be safe. You gave me a bad scare, and now I know I have to keep a closer watch on you. It's because I love you. Don't you know that?"

All the resistance went out of him. He did need someone to love him, especially now. He had an aching sadness inside him, and his head was bursting with pain. In fact, he felt like he'd been beaten up all over. Something had gone wrong, and he didn't know for sure how it happened.

He tried to take a deep breath to relax, but it just made him aware of a hard knot in the middle of his stomach. That must be where the pain was coming from. He took more deep breaths, trying to make the knot go away, but it only pulled tighter and tighter, as if someone was squeezing him from inside.

"Dad. What's wrong? Why are you breathing like that?"

He looked over and saw who it was. It was Sarah, his daughter Sarah. Why was she standing outside the car looking at him all worried like that? "What?"

"You're breathing like . . . like you can't breathe. What's going on?"

"Uh, I was just . . . uh. What are we doing here?"

"We're at my house. Don't you know that?"

"I mean, what am I supposed to do now?"

She gave him an odd look. "Well . . . you're supposed to come into the house. Then, I'm going to make you something to eat. I'm sure you're hungry? Aren't you?"

Yes, he *was* hungry. Very hungry. "Uh, sure I am. What are we having?"

"Well, let's go inside, and I'll see what we've got." She smiled a little and reached for his hand.

He let her take it, and she held it against her cheek. Her face was wet with tears. Why was she crying? Had he done something wrong again?

"I can fix whatever you'd like, Daddy. We'll make you something really special."

She helped him out of the car, and they started up the sidewalk toward the house. Then the kids came flying down the sidewalk, yelling, "Momma, Momma, you're home. What happened to Grandpa?"

She bent to hug them, and he heard her whisper, "Everything is fine now. Come on, let's get Grandpa inside. He's hungry."

Chapter 27

Aaron woke up needing to pee. As soon as he opened his eyes, he knew he wasn't where he was supposed to be. It was too dark, and the air was too thick. Was he in a cave somewhere? He rolled onto his side and nearly fell off whatever he was on. It couldn't be that bed he had with Laura; it was too thin. More like some kind of cot, like in the barracks back in the war. Is that what it was? Had they taken him back there?

He pushed the covers off and planted his feet on the floor. There was just a hint of light coming from a little window up near the ceiling. He could tell he was in a room, but where was the door? Maybe there wasn't a door. Maybe he was in one of those rooms where they took the key and wouldn't let you out. Is that what happened? Had they put him in that place with Miriam?

The more he tried to figure it out, the more his heart raced. And the more his heart raced, the more scared he got, and the less air he could get to his lungs.

He told himself to calm down and think. There had to be a door. How else would they have gotten him in there? And if there was a door, he could get out. Now, he just had to find it.

He stood up and held his hands out in front of him and slowly moved forward until he bumped into something that felt like a wall. He felt his way along the wall, but then he bumped his knee, and said, "Ouch!"

A light flashed on. "Grandpa. What are you doing? Are you okay?"

Aaron turned. It was a boy. Was he locked up with a boy?

The boy said, "Grandpa? What's the matter?"

The boy sounded like Mikey, but it couldn't be Mikey. Mikey was all grown up. He lived far away in a place where he never called, and he never came to visit. It must be a dream. He turned back to see what he had bumped into.

"What are you doing, Grandpa? Are you sleepwalking?"

Aaron turned back to see why the dream was talking. "What? Where'd you come from?"

"I've been here all night. You're sleeping in my bed."

"I am?"

The boy went and turned on the ceiling light. He was in a dark room. It had carpet and a desk and pictures on the wall. And there was that little bed. It had to be the boy's bed, but if it *was* the boy's, why wasn't he in it? Aaron tried to clear his thoughts. "Uh, I'm feeling a little . . . foggy. Tell me again, who you are?"

"I'm Sam."

"Sam?"

"Yeah, Sam. You're my grandpa. What's the matter? Don't you remember me?"

"Sure, I remember. It's just that I thought I was in my house. But I don't think this is my house."

"You're at *our* house. Momma put you down here in my room so I could watch you."

So the boy was his watcher, was he? He wasn't sure he liked that. But first things first. Right now he had to pee. "Okay, Sam. Could you tell me where the bathroom is?"

"It's upstairs. You've already been there three times."

"I have?"

"Yes. How come you need to do it so much?"

"How would I know?" Now, he remembered. They were downstairs. In the basement. That's why the air was so thick. He hated basements. Being in a basement was like being in a root cellar, down with the carrots and the peas. Down where the rats and the spiders lived.

He went over and grabbed the boy's arm. "Come on. Let's get out of here."

"Wait a minute. Don't you want to put on your clothes? It's getting close to morning. Momma might be up."

"That's right. My clothes. What'd you do with 'em?"

"I didn't do it. You got hot and threw them all over the place. I put them right there." He pointed to a folded pile of clothes on the floor by the bed.

"Well, they aren't doing me any good down there, are they?"

Sam handed him the clothes, and Aaron sat on the bed to put them on. When he bent over to put on his socks, his back was so stiff he could hardly do it. He looked at the boy. "How come I can't bend?"

"I don't know. I guess you got hurt out there in the rain. How's your head feel now? Is it any better?"

Aaron ran his hands over his head. It did hurt, but it wasn't that bad. "It seems okay. I guess."

"Momma said you couldn't remember things, but you remembered a lot of stuff last night."

"I did?"

"Yeah. The first time I took you to the bathroom, we came back down and you told me all about that garden you had. You know, over there. In the war. You said you grew vegetables for the soldiers because there wasn't very much food."

"I told you about that?"

"Yeah. And you told me about the jungle and how the monster rains would come and all the kids would run out naked to play in the streets that were full of mud. And the vegetables got ruined, so you wouldn't do it anymore."

"I remember that. The lieutenant wanted me to grow all that stuff, but I wanted to be up there in the sky with the other guys, so that's what I did."

The boy sat down next to him on the bed, and said, "I bet flying in those warplanes was great. I wish I could do that."

"You do?"

"Yeah. I wish I could go up there with the clouds, like you did."

"Have you ever done it?"

"No. Not once."

"Well, that's too bad. Maybe you will sometime." He put his hand on the boy's knee and said, "Now, where's that bathroom?"

They went up the stairs, and when they got to the top, the boy pointed down the hall. "The bathroom's down there."

"Oh, that's right. I went there before."

Aaron went in the bathroom, and while he was peeing he saw some pale light coming through the textured glass. That must mean it was morning. He was glad for that. Maybe he could figure out why he'd slept over instead of going to his own house. Was it Christmas or something? He tried to remember the night before, but the only thing he found was a bad feeling that his truck wasn't there. But where would his truck *be*, if it wasn't there? He decided he'd better go outside and see.

Once he was in the hall outside the bathroom, he had to stop to figure out where the front door was. The light seemed brighter in one direction, so he headed that way. Before he could get there, the boy showed up and said, "Momma says come have some pancakes."

Momma? Whose Momma?

He followed the boy to the kitchen where he saw Sarah standing at the stove with a spatula in her hand. So that's where he was. He was at Sarah's place.

She hurried over and gave him a hug. "Did you sleep okay, Dad."

"How would I know? I was asleep."

She laughed. "Well, at least you still have your old sense of humor."

He was about to ask her what she meant by that, but then he saw a girl with pretty strawberry hair at the table. She was smiling and wiggling her finger at him. "Come sit by me, Grandpa."

She was a pretty young miss with green eyes and pretty freckles on her nose. "Sure, I'd be happy to sit with you . . . uh . . ." He sat down quick hoping should wouldn't realize he didn't know her name.

She looked at him like she was waiting for it.

"Can you give me a hint?"

She cocked her head and said, "Ummm, it starts with an 'A'."

That was easy. "Apple."

She shook her strawberry curls. "Nope. Try again."

He grinned and said, "Peanut butter."

She giggled. "You're just being silly, Grandpa." It seemed like he'd heard that line before, but who would have said it?

He stared at the girl, and she stared back at him, but her name wouldn't come.

Finally, she leaned toward him and whispered, "It's Annie."

He nodded. "Oh, sure, Annie. I knew that. I was just playing a fun game with you?"

She smiled, but she looked sad. "I'm so happy you're home, Grandpa. I missed you."

"I missed you too, sweetheart. Where were you?"

"Right here. We stayed with Julie while Momma went to find you. Are you okay?"

"Sure. Why wouldn't I be?" He didn't want to talk to her about the things she was asking. It was too hard a subject for a young one like her. Instead, he looked over at Sarah. "Say, aren't those cakes done yet?"

Sarah brought over a pitcher of milk and a platter of pancakes. She put them on the table and sat down. Aaron smiled at everyone. It was nice to have breakfast with the family. He had missed out on some of that. Always leaving early for work. Making money to pay the bills. Maybe he should have stayed home more. Maybe he should have helped with the dishes, or . . . something.

No one talked while they ate, but the little girl kept her eye on him, and so did Sam, now and then. A couple of times the boy looked like he was going to say something, but then he didn't. Aaron didn't mind the silence, but he wondered why nobody was talking. Did the cat have their tongues?

Then Sarah *did* talk. She waved her fork in the air and said, "By the way, Dad, I got you an appointment with the doctor at eleven."

That stopped him. "The doctor? What for?"

"That doctor at the hospital down in Hurricane said we should have you checked out."

No. He wasn't going to do that. "I don't need any checking."

"I think we need to do it, Dad. You got quite a bump on the head. You must have hit something hard. We'd better make sure everything's okay."

He put his fork down and licked the syrup off his fingers. He didn't need a doctor. What he needed was to get back to his own house where he could get back to normal and start thinking straight. He stood up, and spoke as firmly as he could. "Thanks for dinner, Sarah, but I'm going home now. See you later."

"No, Dad. I can't take you home yet. You're going to the doctor. Now why don't you go watch TV with the kids while I do the dishes?"

Annie wiggled her finger for him to come with her, but he stayed put. He didn't want to watch TV. TV was a big waste of time. He shook his head. "I'm not going to do it."

"I'm sorry, Dad, but I think it's important. It won't hurt to check things out."

"You do it if you want to. I'm going outside." He wanted to look for his truck. If he could find his truck, he wouldn't need her to take him home. He could take himself there.

As he headed for the door, Sarah said, "Fine. But stay in the yard. I don't want to have to come looking for you."

Once he was outside, he hurried around to the front of the house. His truck wasn't there, but maybe he'd parked it further down the street.

He felt better outside in the cool morning air. It told him if he could slow down and be alone with himself, his memory would come back, and he'd be okay. He just needed to find a way to do that, and that meant he was going to have to get past Sarah.

He headed down the sidewalk, looking at the houses and wondering why they'd want to build them like that. They were all the same, except some of the colors were a little different, and some had a little different front porch. If he'd been the builder, he would've put in some variety so you'd know where you were.

When he came to a house that was older than the rest, he smiled. He liked this one. It was set back from the street with a big pine tree shading the front yard. He stopped and stared at the house. Something about it seemed familiar. Then it hit him: it was just like the house he had grown up in. A little cottage-style house, with wood siding, painted white. And there was that little attic room where he and Stevie used to sleep, and the little window where they looked out and kept track of the moon.

As he hurried across the shaggy grass, he almost expected to see his mother waiting for him at the front door. The third step squeaked as he went up to the porch, and he laughed out loud. He remembered that squeak from before.

He pressed his face against the big front window and saw the splash of yellow sunlight spilling across the polished oak floor. He remembered that floor. He and Stevie and Miriam used to skate around on that floor in their stocking feet. That was a lot of fun.

He tried to go inside, but the door was locked, and he couldn't find the key under the doormat where he thought it might be. Too bad. Maybe the back door was open.

As he rounded the house into the backyard, he saw a big trampoline. Now, that was great. They used to have one like that. He'd bought it for the kids when they were still young. And he used to jump on it too. But that was a long time ago. He hadn't jumped on a trampoline in ages.

Something told him he wasn't supposed to be there, but he took off his shoes and climbed up on the trampoline anyway. As he walked out into the center, he felt the soft warmth of the rubber coming through his socks. It was nice.

He tried a few bounces, and when he got the feel for it again, he bent his knees and bounced a little higher. Then, just as he was starting to get some real height, he heard someone yell, "Hey, what do ya think you're doing?" It was a crabby voice, probably a woman, but he wasn't sure.

He climbed off the trampoline and hurried across the grass, trying to see where the old crab was, but he couldn't find her. When he was almost out to the street, he stopped and looked back.

She yelled, "Get yourself outta here, or I'll call the police."

That's when he caught sight of her. She was hiding behind a screen door on the long side of the house next door. But why was she yelling at him? He hadn't done anything wrong.

He was about to go tell her to mind her own P's and Q's when he heard someone behind him. "What are you doing, Dad?"

He spun around. "Uh . . . nothin'. I mean. I was just—"

"I've been looking all over for you. We're going to be late." She looked at his feet. "What did you do with your shoes?"

"My what?"

"Your shoes? Where are they?"

"Uh . . . I guess they're back there." He pointed toward the back of the house."

"Really? What were you doing back there?"

"I was just . . . uh looking at things. You know, they've got a bouncer back there."

As they went around to get his shoes, Sarah said, "This house has been for sale for quite a while. Do you like it?"

"Sure. It's the same one I lived in before."

She smiled. "Hey, that's right. I hadn't realized it, but it does look a lot like grandma and grandpa's house. I always loved that house."

"It was a good one." He sat on the grass to put on his shoes.

Sarah said, "It would be a nice place to live. Don't you think?"

"It always was."

"It could be fixed up."

He looked up at the house. "It's not so bad. It's got that great attic room." He pointed toward the little window up by the roofline. "Stevie and I slept up there."

She squinted at the house. "It's an interesting idea. I'll have to look into it."

What did she mean? "We're looking at it right now, aren't we?"

"Never mind. I was just thinking out loud." She took his hand and pulled him to his feet, and then led him out to the sidewalk. "We've got to hurry, if we're going to make that appointment."

"What appointment?"

"You know. With the doctor."

"Why? Is there something wrong with you?"

"No. Not me. We're just going to have you checked out. Remember?"

Remember? No, that wouldn't be something he'd want to remember. "I'm not going to let those guys get their hands on me."

"What do you mean?"

"You know . . . what they did to Miriam."

"Oh, Daddy. I won't let them do that to you."

He looked at her. It seemed like she was telling the truth, but what if she wasn't? What if she was just trying to get her own way? Or trying to put him some place where he wouldn't be so much of a bother now that his memory was getting worse. He was going to have to keep his eyes on her and make sure that she didn't try anything like that.

When they got back to her house, Sarah took him inside to the bathroom and started to unbutton his shirt. What was she doing that for? Did she think he was a child? He pushed her away and unbuttoned it himself.

She frowned. "I'm sorry. You go ahead and wash up, and I'll find you a clean shirt. There must be one of Patrick's around here somewhere."

He splashed water on his face and on his chest and under his arms. Then he grabbed a towel and dried himself off.

Sarah came back in and laughed. "My word. It looks like a wet dog has been shaking in here." She handed him a shirt. "It's probably too big, but it's better than that sweaty one you had on."

He looked at it. "I don't really like plaid."

"I'm sorry, but it'll have to do. We'll get you your own clothes later."

When he finished buttoning the shirt, she held onto his arms and tears filled her eyes.

"What's wrong with you?"

She shook her head. "I don't know. I'm just happy you're okay."

"Well I'm happy too, but we don't need to cry about it, do we?" He didn't want any more tears. It just told him things were wrong, and he was trying to forget that.

She let go of him and wiped her eyes. "That's right. There's no use crying. Are you ready to go?"

"Sure. I'll be glad to get home."

They went outside to the car, and after she drove down one street after another, she stopped at a place he didn't know. "What are we doing here?"

"Your doctor's appointment. Remember?"

"I keep telling you, I don't need a doctor. Just take me home." Why couldn't she do what he said instead of always trying some kind of maneuver? He needed to get home and take care of things. "Come on. Let's go. Quit stalling."

Sarah got out of the car and came around and opened his door. "Look, Dad. Let's go in, and then when we're finished, I'll take you home. Okay?"

He didn't know if he believed her. "You promise?"

"I promise."

He looked her in the eyes, hoping he could make her understand. "Look. I just need some time to myself. You know? So I can get back to where I was."

"I understand, Daddy. Let's just see what the doctor has to say. If he thinks you're okay, I'll take you straight home."

So it was going to be a test, was it? That meant he had to make sure the doctor knew he was all right. He'd have to keep things simple and keep things straight, and not answer any questions he didn't know the answer to. If he flubbed up, who knows what could happen.

When they got inside the building, they had to wait for a long time. Finally, a tall woman showed up and called out his name.

Sarah stood up. "Come on, Dad."

The woman led them down a hall to a small room. When she left them alone, Aaron looked around at all the doctor stuff. Again, he warned himself to be careful and not say anything he might regret.

After a while, the doctor came in and stuck out his hand. "Hello, Mister Young. I'm Doctor Mathews. How are you today?"

He shook the doctor's hand vigorously and said, "I'm great. How are you?"

The doctor sat down. "Fine. Fine." He cleared his throat and said, "So, I hear you had a bad experience down south."

Aaron wondered how the doctor knew about that. "Uh well, that's right, I did."

The doctor said, "Do you want to tell me what happened?"

"Uh . . . not really. I'd rather leave bygones be gone."

"I understand your truck broke down, and you were caught out in the rain all night. How did that happen?"

"Well, who knows how things happen? The rain was bad. I know that much. My truck stopped and—" He looked at Sarah. "Did we get my truck?"

The doctor leaned toward him. "So, you remember your truck?"

"Of course, I do. My truck is my truck. I can't work without it."

The doctor looked surprised. "So, you're still working, huh? What do you do?"

Aaron wasn't sure he wanted to tell the doctor what he did for a living, but he decided he'd better do it anyway. "I walk around on stilts and sling mud, if you've got to know."

"Mud?"

"You know. Drywall mud. We've all got to make a living, don't we?"

The doctor smiled and sat back in his chair. "Yes, of course. That's what I'm doing here."

"Right. So, how long have you been at it?"

The doctor looked confused. "What's that?"

"You know, sitting around here."

"Oh, I don't know. Twenty years or so."

"Nice, huh?"

The doctor laughed. "It's not so bad."

"I guess not. I bet you make a pretty penny."

The doctor looked at Sarah and raised his eyebrows, and then looked back at Aaron. "Maybe we should keep the focus on you."

Aaron shrugged. "Sure. Why not?"

"I understand you had a good sized bump on your head, Mr. Young. Do you remember how that happened?"

"Sure I do. Wouldn't you?"

"Did somebody hit you?"

"Something like that."

"Are you experiencing any pain in your head right now?"

"No. Not really."

"Are you sure? You haven't been having any headaches?"

Aaron felt his head with both hands. There was a deep achy feeling down in the center of things, but he figured he'd be smart not to mention it. He shook his head. "Everything seems okie dokie in there to me."

"Have you felt sick to your stomach at all?"

"Nope."

"Any dizziness?"

"Nope."

"How about confusion? Have you had a hard time thinking straight or remembering things?"

That put Aaron on his guard. He took a deep breath and said, "Nothing like that. I'm as clear as a bell."

"Well, I'd like to be sure of that. You hit your head pretty hard. You could have a concussion. Why don't you get up on the table there, and let me check a few things out." He pointed to a padded table covered over with white paper.

Aaron didn't budge.

The doctor nodded towards the table. "Do you mind?"

"I guess not. But I hope you can hurry. I need to get home."

Aaron sat on the table and the doctor made him look at things and listen to things, then he knocked on his knees with a little rubber hammer, and made him squeeze his hand as hard as he could. After that, he had him get up and do some kind of funny walking across the room. Then he had to stand on one leg with his eyes opened and then closed. It was all a bunch of crazy nonsense.

He kept checking the doctor's eyes, trying to see what he was finding out, but they didn't tell him a thing.

Finally, it seemed like the doctor was done with his checking. Aaron said, "Well, I guess I'll be going now. Thanks for everything."

The doctor glanced at Sarah and then back at Aaron. "You're ready to go, huh?"

"I can't hang around here all day."

"Can you hold on for just a few more minutes?"

"I'd rather not."

"Well, that was a difficult thing you went through out in the desert. We need to make sure you don't have any lasting effects."

"I told you, I'm fine."

"Well, maybe that's true, but I'd like to do a few more tests. You can sit in that chair, if you like." He pointed toward the chair next to Sarah.

Aaron frowned, but he sat down in the chair. "Sure. Go ahead. What do I care?" He was getting nervous, but he didn't want to show it. That's when they'd catch you and try to put you away.

The doctor sat down at his desk and took out a piece of paper and a pen. He held the pen over the paper and said, "So, Mister Young, can you tell me what the date is."

"Well, I've been a bit out of commission, but I'd say, it's spring. Or maybe a little later. Somewhere around there. I was planning on doing my garden, if I could ever get home."

"That's right. It *is* spring. Good." He marked something on his paper. "Do you know what year it is?"

Aaron stopped to think. "Nineteen hundred and something. Probably after ninety. Something like that. Or maybe a few more." He shrugged. "That sort of thing doesn't really matter that much anymore, if you know what I mean."

"Sure, I do. Do you know where you are right now?"

"I'd say I'm sitting right here wasting my time with you."

The doctor laughed. "Well, that's probably right, but do you know what state you're in? What city?"

"Well, I've lived in Salt Lake my whole life. You'd think I'd know that."

"That's right, you would."

"And do you know who the president of the United States is?"

"What?"

"The president? Of the United States?"

"What in the world does that have to do with anything?"

The doctor kept asking ridiculous questions and making him do things that a child wouldn't want to do. He thought he was answering everything pretty good, until the doctor asked him to count backwards with sevens. Why would anyone want to do that? Was it a trick?

He decided he wasn't going to do it anymore. "Look," he said to the doctor, "You can stay here and play these silly games all day if you want to. But I'm sick and tired of it. I'm going home." He stood up.

Sarah pulled on his arm. "Wait just a minute, Dad." She looked at the doctor. "So what do you think?"

"It's probably what you thought. But he may get back to where he was before this happened. Maybe not. Only time will tell."

"But what can we do about it? I mean, if he keeps forgetting more things."

"I'm sorry, but there's not much we *can* do. There are some drugs, but they're not all that effective. For now, just keep an eye on him. See how it goes."

Aaron glared at the doctor. "What do you think you're doing? I'm not invisible, am I? I'm standing right here."

The doctor frowned. "I'm sorry, Mister Young. That's not very nice, is it? I was just telling your daughter that some of the symptoms you've been experiencing, you know, forgetting things and feeling confused, could be due to that bump on your head. But there could be more to it. And a stressful situation can make things worse."

"Worse than what?"

"Well, if you've had trouble remembering things before, stress can compound that."

"Trouble before? Nope. Never had any trouble like that. I'm sure it will get better." He stared at Sarah daring her to say any different.

The doctor looked him in the eye. "Now don't get yourself all worried, Mister Young. You'll probably be just fine. Still, I think we should keep an eye on you. I'd like to see you again in three months. Is that all right?"

"Sure, sure." He turned to Sarah. "Come on. Let's get out of here."

She hesitated and gave the doctor a worried look. It was like she was trying to say something with her eyes that she didn't want to say out loud. Aaron didn't know what that look meant, and he wasn't going to waste any more time trying to find out. He was ready to get out of there, right now, and he wasn't coming back, no matter what the doctor said.

He opened the door and was heading down the hall before either one of them could try to stop him.

Chapter 28

As soon as Sarah pulled the car into Aaron's driveway, he bolted for the front door. He had a bad feeling that something was missing, and he wanted to get inside to see what it was. When he got to the door, he looked back and saw Sarah heading across the grass towards him. Damn it. Why couldn't she leave him alone?

He tried to get inside quick, but the damn door was locked. He searched frantically for the key: under the mat, under the rock by the door, inside the planter box. Where the hell was it?

He spun around and saw Sarah watching him. "What's going on, Dad? Are you looking for the key?"

"What if I am?"

She frowned and wagged her head. "Why are you so mad at me all the time? I'm just trying to help you."

"I'm not mad!"

"Then why are you yelling?"

"I'm not yelling!" Well, maybe he was yelling, but so what? It was his place. He could yell if he wanted to.

She wagged her head again and looked away.

He hated that. Why couldn't she understand that he just needed a little time to himself? Time to recover and get his mind back.

Now she had her hand over her eyes, like she didn't want him to see her.

"For crying out loud, Sarah. What do you want from me?"

She dropped her hand, and he saw she was crying.

Oh dear. Now what? "I'm sorry. I didn't mean to—"

"You don't have to be sorry, Daddy. You didn't do anything wrong. I just don't know what I'm supposed to do. You're the one who always helped me when I needed it. But you can't help me with this."

That shocked him. "I can't help? Why not?"

"Because, this time, you're the one that needs help."

"Me? There's nothing wrong with me."

"You get that lost look on your face, and you treat me like I'm the enemy. It scares me, Daddy. What can I do if you don't trust me?"

What could *she* do? He wasn't even sure what *he* was supposed to do. He just knew he needed some peace and quiet without someone asking him questions all the time and expecting him to know all the answers. He squeezed his eyes shut and took a big breath, then he opened his eyes and tried to go inside, but the knob wouldn't turn. Where was the damn key?

Sarah pointed toward the top of the door frame. "I think it's up there."

He walked his fingers along the wood and felt it. It was there all the time. How did she know where it was? Was she playing some kind of hide and seek with him? Well, he didn't want to play. There was something missing, and he needed to get inside the house and find out what it was.

He unlocked the door, but Sarah wouldn't let him go in. She said she wanted him to help bring in the groceries. Oh, that's right. They'd bought groceries on the way there. He should've remembered that.

They carried everything into the kitchen and put it away. Then Sarah sat down at the table. He stared at her. Why did she sit down? Did she plan to stay? He cleared his throat. "Uh, maybe you should get going now."

"I don't think I can let you stay here alone, Dad. Why don't you put a few of your things together, and we'll take some of those groceries back to my place. I'll make you something nice to eat." Her smile was sweet, but he wasn't going for it.

"I just got here. Why would I want to leave?" He looked around for something solid to hold onto in case she tried to drag him out.

"Just for a few days, Daddy. Until you get your bearings."

"My bearings are just fine." He poked at the side of his head. "They're right here, and they're humming away just like they're s'posed to."

She stared at him for a minute, then said, "The doctor said I should keep an eye on you. How can I do that if you're here, and I'm there?"

"It's none of your business."

She looked hurt. "It is *too* my business. I'm your daughter. I love you."

He held onto the counter with both hands, and yelled, "Go away."

"Oh, Daddy. What am I going to do with you?"

She looked like a sad dog, but he wasn't going to soften now. He pounded the counter with his fist and said, "Go home!"

"Please, Daddy, come with me. I'd stay here, but Julie can't stay with the kids all night."

He turned his back on her and walked out of the kitchen and down the hall. When he got to his bedroom, he closed the door. Not sure that would keep her out, he pulled the chair over from the desk and pushed it under the doorknob. Then, he sat on the chair to make sure it wouldn't budge.

Sarah knocked, just like he knew she would, and she begged, just like he knew she would, but he pretended he was a deaf man that couldn't hear a word she was saying.

He heard her crying, and he wanted to console her, he really did, but he knew it was just her way to get him to come out the door. He wasn't going to let her doctors lock him up in that place where he could never get out. He'd run away first. He'd find a place to hide where they'd never find him.

It seemed like Sarah had stopped crying now. He pushed his ear against the door to make sure. She yelled, "Fine. I'll leave you here. You can fend for yourself. Is that what you want?"

"Yes!"

He shouldn't have said that. Now she'd be waiting for him to say something more, but he wasn't going to do it. He put his hand over his mouth to make sure.

"Okay, Dad. I'm leaving now. There's nothing else I can do. I've got to go home and take care of my children."

He waited.

"You call if you need me. Okay? I'm going to write my phone number down and put it right on top of the phone. If you need anything, even if you just want to talk, you call me."

She paused like she was waiting for him to answer, but he wasn't going to do it.

"And I'm going to go over right now and talk to your neighbors. I'll ask them to come and check on you sometimes. So if somebody knocks, you answer. Okay?"

No, he wasn't going to answer.

"And I'm going to call Michael as soon as I get home and tell him he has to come out here to see you. Maybe he'll know what to do with you."

Michael? Oh no. More people asking him questions. That was the last thing he needed right now. He wanted to tell her to not call Michael, but that would let her know he was still there. He held his hand over his mouth even tighter.

"Okay. I'm going, but I'll make you a sandwich first. At least, you'll have something to eat."

"No!" he yelled. "I can make my own damn sandwich. Get out of here."

"Okay. Okay. I'm sorry."

She didn't say anything more, but he knew she was still there, probably with her ear pressed against the door, listening, just like he was listening. He held his breath and stayed perfectly still.

Finally, he thought he heard the hall floor creak. Maybe she was leaving. He kneeled on the chair and pressed *his* ear against the door. She rustled around a bit, and then he heard the front door open, and then close. He waited a little longer to make sure she was really gone, then he moved the chair back and opened the door just a crack. The house was silent. That unmistakable kind of silence that says you're completely alone. Did he really want to be alone?

He went out into the hall and called out, "Sarah. Are you here? Sarah?"

Nothing.

The silence was awful. It was so loud, it made him want to cover his ears. "Don't leave, Sarah. I was just . . . afraid." Yes, that's what it was. He was afraid. Afraid if she stayed she'd make him believe that something was wrong with him. Some kind of wrong that couldn't be fixed.

He hung his head and stared at the floor, feeling insecure and hopeless. What was going to happen to him now? Was he going to end up rattling around his house forever, alone and afraid?

"Stop it," he said. Feeling sorry for himself wasn't going to solve anything. He needed to take the bull by its horns. He needed to pay attention to what was around him and force himself to concentrate. That was the only way he was going to make his memory come back. And the first thing he needed to do was find out what was missing. He was quite sure something was gone, but he didn't know if it was gone from his head, or if it was gone from the house. Once he figured that out, he'd feel a whole lot better.

He hurried down the hall to the living room. Everything seemed okay there. The baby grand piano was a little bit dusty, but it looked fine. The couch was where it belonged, and so was the green velvet love seat and the small table with the phone.

What else?

He headed back to the bedroom. That's where all the important things were. All his important papers. All Laura's important things. Her poems and all that.

That's right. Laura's poems? Is that what he was looking for?

It didn't seem like that was true, but it could be. He should find them while they were still on his mind. Otherwise, he might forget and they'd be lost forever.

He went to the desk to see if her poems were in there, but all he found was bills in the drawers. Lots and lots of bills. Bills from the phone company. Bills from the gas company and the water company. He threw them all on the floor and kept searching for Laura's poems.

Suddenly, he stopped and looked at the pile of bills on the floor. Was he supposed to have paid those bills? Laura had always paid the bills. But what about when she died? Wasn't he supposed to do it then? Did *he* do it? He must have done it, but he couldn't be sure.

He picked a few of the bills up and looked them over. Some of them had handwritten dates, and another kind of number in Laura's handwriting. Those had to be the old ones that *she* paid. But what about the rest? Maybe he had paid them, and he just hadn't made the same kind of note as Laura had. After all, if the bills hadn't been paid, things would be turned off, wouldn't they? The lights would be off, along with everything else. He went to the light switch and turned it on. Yes, there was light. So far, so good. And it didn't feel too cold in the house, so maybe the heat was still on. Or maybe it wasn't time for heat yet.

Anyway, as long as things were turned on, maybe he could worry about the bills later when his mind was a little clearer.

After placing all the bills neatly on top of the desk where he'd be sure to see them later, he glanced around the room wondering about the other thing he'd been trying to find. He saw Laura's cedar chest and wondered if it was in there. When he got on his knees and opened the chest the smell of India came out. "It's still there," he cried. He loved that smell of India. It made him wish he could be there right now, out by that tree with the pretty woman in her pretty sari. Was he sorry he had looked at her bare breasts? No, he wasn't sorry, he was glad. Glad he'd seen the golden glow of her skin in the evening sun. Glad she'd made him feel so aroused and alive.

He continued to dig through the chest, not sure what he was looking for. But maybe if he found it, he'd know. It had to be in there somewhere. He dug down past the baby clothes and doilies, down past the little blankets, a pink one, a yellow one, and a blue one. He held the blue one to his face, and it smelled like it had been in there too long, so he took them all out and put them in a stack on the floor.

As he leaned into the chest again, he caught a glimpse of something way down in the corner. When he pulled it out, he saw it was a tight stack of papers tied up with a red ribbon. He held the papers to his face and the scent told him immediately what it was. It was those love letters Laura sent to him when he was in India. He turned the bundle over in his hands, remembering how excited he'd get when the sergeant came in the barracks with the mail from home. When there was a letter from Laura, he'd grab it and take it outside where he could be alone while he read it. Those letters meant the world to him back then.

He scooted back, so he could lean against the bed, and untied the red ribbon. As he held up the first envelope, he hesitated. Did he really want to bring back all those memories? He was already feeling sad. Maybe they'd just make him feel sadder. No. Those were happy times. He loved the whole world back then, except maybe the Japs and the Germans.

He pulled the pink fragrant letter out of the envelope and held it up to the light.

July 17, 1942

My dearest Arni,

It's only been a few months, but it feels like you've been gone forever. I miss you so much, I don't know what to do with myself. Last night, I felt so lost, I couldn't stay in bed anymore. I snuck out and ran down to that little tree house where we used to meet. Remember? When we were kids? Well, at least I was a kid. Maybe you still think I am. Anyway we had that bucket on a string that we used to dip water from the irrigation ditch to cool the cherries we stole from Mr. Anderson's orchard. Then we'd sit up there for hours and talk or just listen to the wind in the leaves and the chattering birds. You called me your little Lori. Remember? And I called you Arni. It was because we knew we were different with each other than we were with the whole rest of the world and because we knew each other's secret heart. Do you remember all that?

He set the letter in his lap and closed his eyes thinking of his little Lori and the way she looked back then. She was so pretty with those colorful beads in her hair and that soft white blouse that he could see through when the sun was just right. She was so full of passion, it scared him. He'd never felt anything like that before. But she was so young then and so—

He sighed and went back to reading.

Do you know what, Arni? The old cherry orchard doesn't have cherries anymore, and the wood platform in the tree hut is getting old and full of slivers, but the metal bucket is still there, like it's waiting for us to come back and use it too cool the cherries again. It was so strange. I climbed up to what's left of the platform, and I lay there and watched the full moon through the branches and leaves, and I thought about you. The moon was so ghostly white and beautiful, it made me cry. Did you see that moon, Arni? Did you look up at it and miss me like I was missing you?

Sometimes, I don't know how you feel. You said we'd get married when you come home, but when you write, it's all about India and how much you love it there, and how much you wish you could stay there forever. It makes me feel so far away from you. And then there's the war. I don't know what I'd do if you didn't come home. If your plane crashed or something . . . I'm sorry. You said you were safe, but when I can't hear you and see you and touch you, it feels like you're just a dream I made up. Are you a dream? If you are, please don't wake me up, Arni. Don't ever wake me up.

I love you more than you can imagine,
Your little Lori

He whispered, "Oh Lori, I miss you too. I'm afraid. I feel like I'm floating away, and there's no one here to stop me."

He closed his eyes, and thought about being up there in the tree house. He and Lori went there all the time. It was a place to hide from the world. A place to hide from his friends who were always calling him a grave robber. No, not a grave robber. A cradle robber. Their endless kidding was the reason he stopped seeing her. The reason he hurt her. He shouldn't have cared what they said. She was a better friend than they were. She cared what he thought. She loved him.

As he folded the letter and put it back in its envelope, he told himself not to think about his little Lori. It was too painful, and it didn't do any good. She was gone now. And so was that other girl.

What other girl?

There was another one, he was sure of it. But who was she, and why did she go? Was he mean to her too? Is that why she left? No. He shouldn't think about that.

He ruffled through the envelopes desperate to find something that would tell him the truth about what he was trying to find. He came to another letter in handwriting he knew. It was his *own* writing, wasn't it? Yes. Probably one of those letters he sent to Lori. Maybe there was something in there about his happy times in India. He hoped so. He could use something like that about now.

August 28, 1942

My dear Laura, Lori, Love (I do remember our special names, of course, I do.)

I'm sorry I'm so slow to answer. We've been very busy, but I think about you all the time. I'll try to remember all the things you said, and answer the questions you asked in your last few letters.

Yes, I do get off base sometimes. Mostly I go out to the countryside by myself or to the river or jungle. Those places are all very peaceful and special to me. I can almost forget about the war. It's true what you said. When I'm out there, I think I'd like to stay in India forever. It feels so natural, like I should have been born here in the first place. Do you know what I mean? It's only because when I'm here, I don't feel the weight and responsibility to be some person other people want me to be. My father, for example. And without that pressure, it's easier to understand who I really am. What I find is that I want to live a natural life, something like Adam in the Garden of Eden. A life without good and evil. Without guilt. Without judgment. But then I guess that would mean I couldn't have children, because Adam and Eve couldn't have children until they were thrown out of the Garden. That's a problem because I love the children here. They follow me around, like I'm some kind of movie star. It's wonderful. So, I don't know. I guess I want the knowledge of the Tree of Life, but why does it have to be so controlling? Why did Adam and Eve have to put on clothes and hide their bodies? Why did they have to become so ashamed of what is most natural? I don't understand that? Do you?

There are people living in the jungle here, just across the border in Burma. They don't have cars, or stores, or fancy houses and clothes. They don't even wear clothes most the time, neither the men nor the women. Well, unless they come to work for us, then they have to wear clothes. But otherwise, their lives are so beautifully simple. There's something about that simplicity that really appeals to me. I want to live like that. I really do.

I don't know if any of this makes sense, but if anyone can understand me, you can. You always have.

As for the war, I can't really talk about it. Some guys heard that might change, so maybe I'll be able to tell you more. I wish I could tell you what I feel about the war. Sometimes I have dreams, that I'm out in that Burmese jungle, looking for the enemy with fear in my heart, but that's not how it really is. I wake up sweating and feeling strangely excited. But you don't have to worry. It's not going to happen. I'm safe. Maybe too safe.

Anyway, I've got to sign off now. Got to get some sleep. It's early to bed and early to rise around here.

I love you Lori.
Aaron

When he finished the letter, he read it again, more slowly this time, concentrating on every word. He remembered that part about the people in the jungle and how it seemed like they were living in the Garden of Eden. If he could go there now and live in that garden, he wouldn't pick the forbidden fruit. He didn't want that kind of knowledge. He didn't want to know about death, or good and evil, or any of that stuff. If he could just live with his Eve forever, that would be enough.

He threw down the letter and stared at the wall. "Stop dreaming. Eve is gone, and so is the other one. All you've got is this empty house." But wait. He had that place in the desert, didn't he? That's right. His place in the desert. He should go down there right now. If he was down in the desert, everything would be fine.

Suddenly, he remembered what he'd been looking for the whole time—his truck. He needed his truck so he could go down to the desert.

He tried to remember where he'd lost it, and then he remembered the mean man who threw him in the ditch and took off with his girl. Then the rain came, and he walked and walked until the air raid started. Then Sarah came and drove him home and that's how he got here.

So where was his truck? It must still be down there in the desert. He had to go get it. But how could he do it, if he didn't have his truck? He was going to have to figure that out.

Chapter 29

Aaron was out in his garden, sweating as he pulled up weeds. He loved being out there in his garden more than he loved anything these days. It was sad to see that the peas were done, but it wouldn't be long before he'd have strawberries. He found a couple of partly ripe ones and popped them into his mouth. Then, he headed into the house for a drink and a stop in the bathroom.

When he came back out into the hall, he heard a noise. He spun around and saw a ghost of himself from the past. Or maybe it was an old memory that had escaped his head and was trying to be real. That kind of thing happened sometimes. So maybe that's all it was.

The ghost stood perfectly still, like it was waiting for him to say something. But he didn't know what it was, so he didn't know what to say. He kept quiet.

"Dad? What's wrong?"

Dad? So, it wasn't a ghost, it was Michael. But how could Michael be there? Wasn't he out in . . . that other place? He tried to ask why he was there, but the question came out as a croak.

"I came for a visit, Dad. Aren't you glad to see me?"

"Uh, sure, I am. How'd you get inside here?"

"You didn't answer when I knocked. So I used the key. I thought I'd better come in and see if you were okay. *Are* you okay? After what Sarah said, I wasn't sure what I'd find."

"Sarah? What does she have to do with anything?" He realized he was gaping at the boy like an old idiot, like he'd lost his mind somewhere. But who could blame him for that? How could he know he was going to turn around and see Michael standing there in his hall? He hadn't seen Michael in years. So why was the boy coming around now? Did he want something?

Michael came closer. "Didn't she tell you I was coming?"

"Who?"

"Sarah."

Oh no. Had Sarah been telling stories about him forgetting things? He tried to cover. "Well, I guess I did know something about . . . what you said. I just didn't know it would be so . . . quick."

"I would have come sooner, but I had to get things set up at work. Summer's on, you know. People are taking their vacations."

Aaron eyed him. "I see. So, what did you want?"

"What?"

From the quick dark look on the boy's face, he knew he'd said something wrong. "Uh, I mean what are we doing here?"

The boy shook his head and shrugged. "I don't know, Dad. Maybe you should get dressed before we do anything else."

Aaron looked down and was shocked to see that he was completely naked. How did that happen? Hadn't he just been out in the garden? He gave a wave of his hand over his head to show it was no a big deal, then he strolled down the hall to the bedroom, trying to act like there was nothing odd going on. So what if he was naked? It was his place, wasn't it?

He closed the bedroom door and put on pants and a shirt. While he was putting on his socks, he tried to sort things out. Something told him Michael was there for a reason, and it probably wasn't good. Did Sarah put him up to it with some bad story? Was she trying to get him in trouble with Michael, like he was always in trouble with her?

He went out and found Michael sitting on the couch in the living room. He went over and stood in front him and tried to say the right thing. "Thanks for coming, son. It's been a long time. A very, very long time. I'm really glad you could make it."

Michael put on a defiant look that Aaron knew by heart. A look that said the boy was ready for combat.

"Well, Michael, you can try to beat me down, but I know why you're here."

"You do?"

"Yes, I do. Sarah sent you. You two have been conniving against me, haven't you?"

The boy choked back a cough. "What are you talking about, Dad? Sarah and I are *not* conniving. She hardly ever calls me. In fact, no one around here ever calls me."

His words sounded like an accusation. "What's that supposed to mean?"

"It means, sometimes, I wonder if you ever even think of me."

"Sure I do. I think all the time."

Michael flapped his hand like he was chasing away a fly. "Ah, never mind. It's stupid."

"Who's stupid."

"I mean, worrying about all that. I shouldn't do it."

"Maybe not, but don't call me stupid. I'm not stupid. Did she tell you that?"

"No, Dad. She didn't. Forget it. It doesn't matter."

"I can't forget it. Tell me why you said what you said."

"Are you kidding me? Shit, Dad, you don't want to get into all that, do you?"

Something was terribly wrong. They were talking, but their words were flying past each other. If he didn't put a stop to it right now, their words might never meet up again. "What are you saying, son? Please tell me. I don't understand."

The boy stared at him. Then, his face changed from being mad to some kind of look Aaron was pretty sure he had never seen him show before. Was it sadness? Was the boy feeling sorry for him? He didn't need anybody to feel sorry for him. He threw up his hands. "If you're gonna do that, go away."

"Do what, Dad? I didn't do anything."

The boy was up now, and for some reason, he was pacing the floor. Aaron looked him over. He was tall. That meant he wasn't really a boy anymore. He was a man. All grown up. How did that happen? Did he take a leap forward, somehow? No, he couldn't do that. Michael had just been gone, so he hadn't seen him do it.

He got in step with Michael's pacing, but neither of them spoke. Then Aaron remembered, this conversation wasn't about being a man, it was about people trying to take charge of his life. He grabbed Michael's arm. "I know that you and Sarah have been planning something. Don't pretend you don't know what I mean."

"I'm sorry, Dad. I *don't* know what you mean. Why don't you tell me."

"I'm talking about doctors and rooms without keys! I'm talking about Miriam and the way they did it with her, and the way you want to do it with me!" He realized he was yelling, but he didn't care. He had to get through to the boy.

Michael shook his arm free. "Calm down, Dad. I'm not going to do anything like that. Why are you so paranoid? Is that part of what's going on?"

Aaron didn't remember saying anything about being . . . whatever the boy said. What did that word even mean? Had he ever heard it before? The boy was probably just trying to act smart so he could get the upper arm. He yelled, "I'm not stupid. Why don't you just shut up, if you can't say anything nice."

Michael looked like a cat ready to spring, and that brought out the tension in Aaron too. From now on, he realized he was going to have to be very careful what he said. Maybe he should stop saying anything at all. He sat back down on the couch with his mouth closed tight.

Michael came and sat on the couch too, but he kept his distance, like he was afraid he might catch something. A silence took over the room. It was so loud and lasted so long, it was hard for Aaron to remember how it started. Then, the happy sounds of the birds outside the window broke through and everything changed. Those birds made Aaron feel a little more hopeful that things might work out.

He started to say, "I wish—"

But Michael broke in with, "I think—"

Their eyes met and Michael said, "What do you wish, Dad?"

"I wish . . . Well, I wish we could go back and . . . I don't know, start over with things. I feel like I failed somehow . . . I mean, with you." He knew he'd better not say anything more or he'd start crying.

Michael stared at him. His eyes were angry, but Aaron didn't know what he'd done to make them go like that. Had he said something he didn't mean again? He'd seen those dark angry eyes of Michael's before. But when was it? He tried to trace it back, and then he remembered, and the blame came piling down on top of him. It made him feel like he couldn't breathe. "It's your mother, isn't it? You think I killed her. You think it was my fault she died. That's why you never come, and why you never want to see me."

Michael shook his head. "Are you kidding, Dad? I wasn't thinking about that at all." He rubbed his forehead. "Listen. I just came here to find out what's going on. I mean, how did you end up out there in the rain in the middle of the night? What happened? Do you remember?"

His voice was gentle now, but his words were accusing. Aaron jumped up from the couch, but that made him feel dizzy, so he had to sit back down. He could tell Michael was still waiting for an answer, and that he wasn't going to budge until he got it. "Well, I'm . . . I'm not sure what exactly happened. To my truck, I mean. Besides, she might be lying."

"Dad, why do think she'd lie about that?"

"Because she . . . she wants to take over my life. She wants to put me in that house . . . so she doesn't have to tend me."

"That house? What house?"

Aaron waved his hand in the air while he tried to think how to say it. "You know, *that* place. The place they put the people who sit around all day. You know, like Miriam."

Michael shook his head. "Dad, I'm not here for that. I'm just here to see what's going on, and to see if you're okay."

Aaron nodded several times to show the boy he was fine. "I *am* okay. I really am. I promise."

Michael didn't look so sure. "Sarah said you were out there in the rain all night and that you think there was some girl with you. Was there a girl?"

Aaron couldn't believe it. Michael had said it. The girl. That's the thing he'd been missing the whole time. His girl with the funny hair and the pretty smile. He grabbed Michael's arm and yelled, "Where is she? You have to tell me!"

Michael pulled away from his grip. "Who are you talking about, Dad?"

"My girl. Where is she? I want her back!"

Michael shook his head.

Aaron knew that meant he wasn't going to help find her. He had to convince him how important it was. "Please, Michael. We've got to go find her before that man hurts her."

"What man, Dad? Are you saying there was a man too?"

Aaron leaned closer and whispered, "Yes, there was. The dirty one. The one that wants your girl the whole time. And then he throws you out and just goes ahead and . . . takes her."

Michael nodded. "Hmmm . . . sounds like you're thinking about that man you caught dancing with Mom out at Saltair. Is that what it is?"

"Aw, I don't know anything about that." Maybe there was something in what the boy said. A long time ago. But he wasn't about to admit it. Not when they were already piling up the evidence against him.

"It was your own fault, Dad. Mom told me how you dumped her when your friends said she was too young. You just dropped her flat, with hardly a word. Why *wouldn't* she find someone else to dance with?"

"She told you that?"

"Yes, she did. And she told me how you went after the guy and pushed him in the Great Salt Lake. Now that would have been somethin' to see."

"Rub it in. Rub it in. What do I care?" Suddenly, Aaron's head felt hot, and he was feeling confused. "I mean, what are we talking about here? Some guy?"

Michael shook his head. "You know, now that I'm here, I can see why Sarah is so scared."

"What do you mean scared? What's wrong with her?"

"Well, Dad, it's hard to tell where your mind is at any given moment. I don't know whether you're making things up, or remembering things from the past, or wishing you had a girl that you don't have."

"Oh *yeah*, what about you?" Aaron stared him in the eye, letting the boy know he meant business. "How come you don't have a girl, if that's what we're talking about? Is there something wrong here?"

"What do you mean, wrong?"

"I mean, I can't remember you having any girl. Do you have one?"

Michael got up and went and stood in front of the window.

Aaron wondered if he'd gone too far. He didn't want the boy to leave. Not now, when they were just getting things straight. "Don't go away, Michael. I wasn't saying anything mean. I was just saying, I know how lonely it can get when the house is really big and silent and there's nobody there."

Michael muttered, "Yeah, well, you got that right."

Aaron went over and stood next to him, and they both stared out the window.

"Maybe you *should* get yourself a girl, Michael."

"Yeah, sure."

"I had one, you know. In that hot water out there."

"Hot water?"

"Yeah. It was . . . nice."

"Well, I don't know about any hot water, but Sarah did tell me you were talking about a girl."

"She did?"

"Yes. And she told me how you ran your truck out of oil. How did that happen, Dad? That doesn't seem like you at all."

"I don't know for sure, Michael, but can you help me get my truck back? I really need it. I really do. Otherwise, how will I ever go save my girl?"

Michael shook his head and stared at his feet. "Listen, Dad. The truck is gone. Besides, I don't think you should be driving anymore. And neither does Sarah."

"Hey! Listen! You don't have the right to say that. I'm your father. I should be the one telling you what to do."

"I'm, sorry, Dad, the truck is gone. You might as well face it."

"So what? That's my problem, not yours. Now give it back."

"Sorry. No can do. That truck is a thing of the past." The boy let out a big sigh and turned away from the window. "Maybe we should do something different, Dad. You're getting kind of upset again."

The boy was right. They *should* do something different. It would be better than all this fighting and blaming. "Uh, like what do you have in mind?"

"I don't know. Maybe I should fix us some breakfast. How about French toast?"

"You know how to do that?"

"Sure, I do."

They went into the kitchen, and even though Michael didn't talk the whole time he was cooking, the kitchen smelled nice with the sweet smell of warm maple syrup and whatever else he was cooking. It wasn't a bad silence. In fact, it felt like something had softened a little bit between them. Maybe things would get better now.

After they'd both finished off their food, Aaron wiped his mouth with the back of his hand. "You know, that was good. I haven't had one of . . . those in a long time."

Michael finished whatever he was drinking and said, "Well, what should we do now, Dad?"

Aaron didn't know. Why was he asking him? When the boy was little, he always knew what he wanted to do. They'd go to the park, or he'd take the boy down to the creek and they'd hike around. That gave him an idea. "Remember that creek?"

Michael nodded. "Sure I do. Me and my friends spent half our lives down there. Do you want to go to the creek?"

Well, that's exactly what he wanted to do, but he tried not to sound too excited. "Sure. That would be okay. Let's do it."

They put the dishes in the sink and headed out the door and up the paved road to where the trail started. Michael took the lead, and that was fine with Aaron. Let the boy feel like he was the boss for a while if that's what he needed.

When they got to the trailhead, Aaron pushed his way to the front. "You're going to love it down there. I'm sure the water's roaring over the dam with all that rain we had."

"Really? It rained?"

Well, maybe it hadn't rained. But it seemed like it did. He remembered it coming down like cats and dolls, hitting so hard it hurt his head. He just about froze to death out there. But maybe—

"The creek mostly gets high in the early spring," Michael said. "I remember hiking down here one time when the water was roaring down from the spring snow melt. It was so wild, it scared the pants off me."

Aaron stopped and looked back at Michael. "That's right. I was out there. Remember? I was up to my neck, and then—"

Michael frowned. "You went out in that wild water? I don't remember that."

"Well, maybe you were too young."

Michael seemed to want the lead again, so Aaron followed him down the last narrow part of the trail to the creek. As soon as he saw the dam and the cement spillway, he realized Michael was right. It *hadn't* rained. There was plenty of water, but it wasn't wild, and it wasn't pouring over the dam into the spillway. It was nice and calm, gurgling over the rocks with the sun shining down through the cottonwood trees.

Aaron pointed downstream. "I think it's that way."

"What is?" said Michael.

"The place I thought we were going."

"Sure. Doesn't matter to me."

He led Michael though the dappled light, breathing in the earthy smell of the dirt. There was nothing like a stream trail. That smell. The coolness in the air. The light. He loved everything about it.

They followed the narrow trail until they got to where the big pipe came down from the water treatment plant. Aaron stared at it thinking there was something funny he wanted to tell Michael about that pipe. He couldn't remember what it was, so he said, "Okay. We can go back to the dam now, if you want."

Michael shrugged. "Okay. Fine. Whatever."

When they were almost back to the dam, Aaron remembered something. It was the thing he was most scared about. Maybe if he told Michael about that thing Sarah had up her sleeves, he could make her stop. He pointed to a big flat rock in the middle of the stream not far below the dam. "How about we sit there. I've got something I want to say. I mean . . . if you've got the time."

Michael nodded. "Sure. I've got time."

They sat down on the rock, and Aaron tried to think how to set things straight. He glanced up at the dam, and then at the sky. Then he looked in Michael's eyes and said, "Sarah's wrong."

"About what?"

Aaron scowled and tried to focus on his words. "It's not true what she thinks. It's just that I . . . I can't find my words sometimes. That's all. They go some place where I can't find them, but then they come back."

Michael nodded. "Sure, that's understandable. I can't find words sometimes. But I think Sarah's worried about more than that. It has more to do with that last trip of yours down south."

"What trip?"

"You know, with the truck."

Aaron threw up his hands. "It was one thing. Just one lousy thing. Can't you give a person a second break?"

"It's not about second breaks, or second chances, Dad. It's about being safe."

"I am safe! I'm right here. I'm safe and that's it." His voice was too loud, and he realized that probably wasn't going to work. If he wanted Michael to be on his side, he'd better pipe down.

Michael met his eyes. "I guess you know she wants you to live with her."

So that's what it was. She'd told him about that. "I'm not going to do it. So you might as well just tell her to stop. I've got a perfectly fine house."

Michael nodded. "I can understand why you'd want to stay here. This is a beautiful place. It's familiar to you, and you're living in the house you and Mom built together. "

Now, he was getting somewhere. "That's right. We built it with our own hands. And you helped."

"I've always liked the house. Out here in the country near the mountains. The creek close by down here. And good clean air. I wish I had more of that in California."

Aaron nodded to keep him going.

Michael frowned. "I can tell you, it's nothing like this where I live. Los Angeles is, well, crazy. It feels tight. Too many people. Too much traffic. Too many brains. It wears me out sometimes."

"Why don't you come home then? Get yourself a girl and come home. You can both live with me."

Michael chuckled. "Oh, *that'd* be good."

"Why not?"

"California is where my job is, Dad. I've got to work. Make a living."

Aaron could tell the boy's voice had an edge to it again. But why? He'd just asked him to come home. That's all.

Michael took off his shoes and socks and put his feet into the water. But he pulled them out real quick. "Jeez, that's cold."

Aaron laughed. "That'll get you goin'."

"Yeah, it's like an ice cream headache of the feet."

Aaron wasn't sure what that meant, so he kept quiet. He watched in silence as Michael patted his feet dry with the top of his socks, and then he put his socks and shoes back on.

When he had the boy's attention back, he said, "So, what does Sarah want, Michael? Do you know?"

Michael shrugged. "She just wants you close so she can make sure you're okay. And she thought you might like having other people around."

"I can't do it!"

"Why not?"

He tried to think how to say it. "I need to be my own man, Michael. Can't you understand that? I need to be free with myself."

Michael nodded, but he still didn't look convinced.

He tried again. "If I lived over there, where would I be? I'd be hiding myself all over the place, trying to get out of her way. It's not good, Michael. It's not good for anyone."

"Well, she wants you there. That's all I know. And I feel like I need to support her."

"I've got my bed where I am. And all my things. My piano. My books. And there's your mother's things too. I can't give those up."

"Of course, you don't want to give up any of that, but you don't have to. You can take it all with you."

"I can?"

"Sure."

Aaron looked around and waved his hand toward the landscape. "What about this? Can I take it too? Can I take my mountain?"

"What mountain?"

"That one up there where the gods are."

"Oh, Mount Olympus? Is that what you mean?"

"Yes, that's the one."

"Well, no. I guess you can't take the creek or Mount Olympus, but you can always come back for a visit. They're not going anywhere."

Aaron thought about that, but it just didn't work. "No, I can't do it. I want to have my own place and do what I want to do."

Michael looked frustrated, but so what? He wasn't the one losing his life. If he let Sarah and Michael think they were in charge, they'd put him away before he could blink.

They both stared silently at the water for a while, then Michael said, "Well, she also talked about you moving to that other place."

That set Aaron on his guard. "What kind of place?"

"The house just down the street from her. You know, the one with the trampoline in the backyard. She said you liked that house. Said it reminded you of the place you grew up in. Why don't you just buy that one? Then you could live on your own, and she'd be close by. You could have your cake and eat it too."

Cake? What cake? He didn't like cake that much, but he did remember that house. It had that bouncing thing out back, and it was true, it did remind him of the house he grew up in. He liked that part. It'd be better than being trapped in someone else's room. But he still wasn't sure. "What would I do with my place here?"

"Well, you'd sell it."

"But it's our house. We built it with our own hands."

"I know that, Dad, but we've got to solve this. I've only got a few days before I have to get back to work."

"But you've only been here a few minutes. I've hardly even seen you."

"Listen, Dad, There's nothing I can do about that. I've got to get back to work. Sarah wants you to be closer to her, and I need to support her on that. That's all there is to it."

"Please, Michael. Don't make me do it."

Michael threw up his hands. "Make you do it? Are you kidding? When have *I* ever made *you* do anything?"

"But you could stop her, if you wanted to. You're . . . you're bigger than she is."

Michael laughed at that. Then he picked up a rock and threw it downstream, hard.

Aaron tried to think how to explain that he just wanted to live his own life. If Michael didn't want to help, he might as well just go back to wherever he came from. He picked up his own rock and threw it as hard as he could. It hit a big rock downstream and bounced back, almost hitting Michael in the head.

Michael glared at him. "That's great, Dad. Just great. Hit me with a rock, why don't you."

Aaron was pretty sure Michael was upset about more than the rock. It was like his face had gone back to that hard angry place. Well, so what? "Look, Michael, if you've got something to say, say it. I'm sure I did some wrong things with you, but we can't fix it, unless we know what it is."

"Fix it? It's a little late for that."

"Please, Michael. Tell me what I did that was so bad. You don't come to see me, and then you do, but you've got . . . razors in your eyes half the time. It hurts when you look at me like that."

Michael hid his eyes with his hand, but his words still came through. "Look, Dad. Why don't we just let sleeping dogs lie? It was a long time ago."

"No! I don't want them to lie! I want them to tell the truth. If you're going to breathe fire, show me where the wood is."

"Come on, Dad. Stop it."

"Come on, come on. Give it to me. Tell me why you stayed away so long."

"Fine. But don't say you didn't ask for it."

"I am asking. I'm begging. I'm down on my knees."

Michael shook his head, and got a look on his face like he wanted to escape.

Aaron couldn't let that happen. "Come on, son. Tell me what you're thinking."

The boy's eyes got all wet. "It's just . . . I can't forget what you did to Mom."

"What? What did I do?"

"You really don't know, do you?"

"No. I don't."

"That's right. You never did get it, and now you're going to wiggle out of it by forgetting the whole thing. She loved you to the end, you know, but she didn't have a chance with you. You were so—"

He waited for it, but Michael looked away and went silent.

"What? I was so what?"

Michael stayed mute.

Aaron didn't want him to stop there. Not when they were so close to breaking things loose. "Come on. Spit it out. I know I did a lot of wrong things. I found those words she wrote. They told me everything."

Michael stared at him. "So you found her poems, did you?"

"You knew about those? And I didn't?"

"She always wrote poems, Dad. It's hard for me to believe you didn't know that. I think you just didn't care."

"How could I care when she didn't tell me?" The bad feeling from the poems came rolling back. All the sad things she said. "It was . . . unbearable, Michael. She wrote all those terrible things, and then, she left without giving me a chance. I didn't know about any of it. Honest, Michael. She never told me a thing."

Michael scowled and shook his head.

Aaron couldn't understand why everybody thought he was so bad. He had always tried to be a good man. A good father. A good husband.

A good money-maker. He had tried hard to be *all* that, but somehow they all thought he'd failed.

He touched Michael's knee, then quickly pulled back his hand. "Please, son. If you have anything left for me, tell me what I did that was so bad."

Michael looked at him through his tears. "It's just that you couldn't see her, Dad. You had no idea what a special woman Mom was. Those poems of hers were really good. Publishable. I know they were. And that's just one thing she hid from you."

"Hid from me? But why? Why did she hide things?"

"Because you weren't interested. You didn't want her to be anything except your wife."

"That's not true, Michael. I loved her. I wanted her to have the whole world."

"Yeah, right." His look was cruel.

"It's not my fault, Michael. It's not. I just didn't know."

Michael stood up and stared down at him. "Look, I don't think we should do this, Dad. It was a long time ago. It doesn't matter now." He hopped across to another rock, and then continued to hop rocks until he was in the dry spillway by the dam. He turned back and said, "I'm sorry, Dad. Are you coming?"

"I guess, I am. There's nothing left for me here."

As they headed up the trail, Aaron's head was reeling. Everything had turned bad. Sarah wanted to take his life, and Michael wanted to hate him. He might as well go away some place where they couldn't find him. He could hitchhike to the desert, and nobody would have to worry about him anymore. They could have their lives, and he could have his. That would be the best thing for everyone.

Chapter 30

When they got back to the house, Michael went straight to the shower. Aaron wondered if it was because he felt dirty, or because he was upset and didn't want to talk anymore. It seemed like it was probably that last thing.

Not knowing what else to do while he waited, Aaron went to his bedroom to take a quick rest. He lay on top of the quilt and stared at the ceiling, worrying about what Michael had said about Laura. Was it true that she wanted more from life than he gave her? It seemed like some of the poem things said that too, but how could it be true? He loved her, didn't he? He wanted everything for her. So why would Michael say he didn't? And why would Laura have even talked to him about that? It didn't seem fair. He had never said bad things about *her* to the children.

Had she made it so Michael could never forgive him? What if he went back to wherever he came from, and he never saw him again? That thought was so sad, he didn't want to believe it. There had to be some way out of it. He'd just have to talk to Michael again and see if he couldn't solve it. But why was he taking such a long time in the shower? Was he trying to use all the water? Or did he just not want to come out?

The waiting became unbearable, but finally Aaron heard the water go off, and he hurried out into the hall.

After a few minutes, Michael came out, fully dressed and smelling like aftershave. "Dad, I'm going to go see some old friends I haven't seen in a long time."

"But Michael . . . I was hoping—"

"Hoping what?"

The boy seemed impatient, so he backed off. "Never mind. I'll . . . say it later . . . if I remember." He shouldn't have said those last words. They were just more evidence that he was forgetting things.

Michael looked like he might stay and talk, but then he waved his hand over his head and headed for the door. "Better get going. They'll be waiting. Don't wait up, Dad. I'll be late."

After he watched Michael drive away, Aaron went and stood in the middle of the living room wondering what he was going to do with himself now. He couldn't stand to think that what Michael had said was true. He was sure Laura was happy sometimes. They had a lot of fun together. The whole family had fun. He was sure of it. So why did Michael want to make it all sound so bad?

He went to Michael's old room and stared at his bed. It looked so small now that he'd seen how big Michael was. He was all grown up and set in his ways. What would happen when he and Sarah got together with their ideas? Would they gang up on him? Would they put him in that place with Miriam? That scared him more than anything, because he'd seen it. He knew how it was in a place like that. If they put him in there, he'd be trapped forever.

"Shut up! Just shut up!" he yelled. If he didn't stop thinking about that kind of scary stuff, he'd go crazy.

He hurried into the living room and sat down at the piano and pounded the keys. Maybe the loud sounds would silence his mind. He pounded the high notes, and he pounded the low notes, but it didn't help. He still felt scared.

Next, he tried yelling, but all that did was make his ears rings. Or wait, maybe it wasn't his ears. Maybe it was the phone. Maybe it was Michael calling to say he was ready to talk. He rushed to the phone and picked up the receiver. "Hello? Hello? Is that you, Michael?"

There was nobody there.

When he couldn't think of anything else to do, he went to bed. He lay there for hours, watching the light and the shadows move around the room. The house was so deadly quiet, he thought he could hear his heart beating. Was there something wrong with his heart?

He tried to trick himself into going to sleep by taking long deep breaths, but that just made his chest feel strange. Like it was too small for his lungs and his big beating heart.

The room got darker, and he pulled the covers up to his chin. Then, he was too hot, so he pushed them down. Why couldn't he just go to sleep? Why was it so hard?

He closed his eyes tight, and told himself not to move a muscle until he really *was* asleep.

He woke when he heard a sound in the house. Or was it the dream? No, there it was again. He was sure he could hear someone moving around the house. Was it robbers? Had they come to kill him in his bed?

Staring into the darkness, he tried to think if there was anything he could use to protect himself. There was a baseball bat in the garage, but he couldn't get to that.

Now, he could hear water running in the kitchen and someone was opening the cupboards. They *were* stealing things. Maybe he could make it to the laundry room, if he was quick. There might be something in there he could use to protect himself. Or maybe he could hide under the dirty clothes.

He went to the door and opened it a crack and listened.

Good. They were still in the kitchen.

Staying close to the wall, he slid along it to the laundry room. He went inside and grabbed the first thing he saw, the broom. Then he tiptoed back out into the hall and pressed himself against the wall.

It wasn't long before the villain came down the dark hall toward him. When he was right in front of him, Aaron lifted the broom and brought it down hard on the robber's head and yelled, "Get out! Get out! Or I'll whack you again!"

"Dad! Dad! What in the hell are you doing. It's me. Michael."

"Michael? My Michael? What are you doing here?" Aaron lowered the broom, feeling confused. Had he made another mistake?

"Jeez, Dad, didn't you remember I was here for a visit?"

"What? Me? Sure I remember. I mean, it's your fault, sneaking around my house in the dark."

"Damn," whispered Michael.

Aaron struggled to find the light switch. When he got it turned on, he saw that Michael's forehead was bleeding. "Oh no, what have I done? I'm sorry, son. It's just that I thought—"

"You thought what? That I was burglar? That I'd come to murder you in your bed?"

"Well, yes. I did think something like that. I mean, who wouldn't?"

Aaron followed Michael to the bathroom and watched him splash cold water on his wound. The blood swirled down the drain, and it seemed like there was quite a lot of it.

"Do you have any antiseptic, Dad? I doubt that broom was clean."

Aaron pulled all the drawers open, looking for a bandage or something else that would help. There was nothing there but old toothbrushes and used razors. "I'm sorry. I don't seem to have anything."

Michael grabbed some toilet paper and held it against his head. "Maybe I've got something in my suitcase. I'll go see." He headed down the hall, then turned back. "Go back to bed, Dad. Get some sleep. I'll be okay."

Sleep? How could he go to sleep after what he'd just done? He'd whacked his own son in the head. But maybe he should try to sleep. If he didn't, he might do something else that he'd have to be sorry for.

He went back to bed and tried.

Something woke Aaron up, but he kept his eyes closed and listened.

"Daddy. Are you awake?"

He knew it was Sarah's voice, but he kept his eyes closed. He was trying to call back a dream about Laura.

"Daddy, why don't you get dressed and come into the kitchen so we can talk."

He opened one eye. "Talk? What about breakfast? I'm hungry."

"I've fixed us something. Come on. We can eat while we talk."

She left the room, and he got up and got dressed. Maybe she'd made some of that French stuff again.

When he entered the kitchen, he saw Michael. What was he doing there? Is that what they were going to talk about? Something about Michael?

Sarah sat him down at the table next to Michael and brought them both a steaming plate of scrambled eggs and toast. The juicy smell made his mouth water.

He was about to dig in when Sarah started up. "Dad, we've decided. You have to sell this house and move closer to me."

His fork went flying out of his hand and clattered across the floor. He didn't care, he felt like throwing his plate down there too. "I'm not doing it!"

Sarah picked up his fork, washed it, and brought it back to him. "Daddy, Michael and I talked. We're worried. It's not safe for you to stay here alone anymore."

Aaron looked back and forth between them. "What do you mean? It's as safe here as it ever was."

"Think about it, Dad. You don't have a vehicle anymore, so you can't get anywhere. And with my job and the kids, I can't get here every day. That's a problem."

"No, it's not a problem. It's fine with me if you're not here."

"But what are you going to do if something happens and you need help? Or if you need something? Food or—"

"I'll just get in my truck and go get it."

She gave Michael a schemer's look, then came back at him. "You don't have a truck anymore, Daddy. Don't you remember? It got ruined. That's what I'm talking about. You can't remember things very well anymore. It's not safe."

"Don't worry. I can get a new truck."

"No! You are not going to get a new truck. Not after what happened to the last one."

Sarah gave Michael another look. It was a look that said she wanted him to get on board with her plan.

Michael nodded and leaned forward. "You know, Dad. This house is pretty big for one person. And the older it gets, the more work it's going to take to keep it up."

"So what? I don't mind work."

"I know you don't, but I think you should sell it now when you can get the best price"

Sarah jumped back in. "Daddy, you should think about what happened last night. Look what you did to Michael. Look at his forehead. You could have hurt him really bad, and it's all because you didn't remember he was here. That's not good."

He looked at Michael. "I'm sorry, son. It was . . . an accident."

"I know, Dad. It's okay. I should have realized you might not remember I was here."

"That's right. What's wrong with you? You should have remembered that."

Sarah held up her hands to stop them. "We don't need to talk about that. What we need to talk about is selling this house."

Michael nodded. "She's right, Dad. We need to get this settled. I've got to get back to California tomorrow."

"Well, what's stopping you? Nobody's twisting your arms. Go ahead and go. Then maybe I can get back to what I'm doing."

Sarah put on her sad dog look. She reached out and took his hands in hers. "What *are* you doing, Daddy? I mean, what do you want to do with the rest of your life?"

"What do you mean by that?"

"I mean, think about the future. Where do you want to be in five years? Do you want to still be rattling around here by yourself?"

Rattling around? Was she trying to confuse him? Of course, he didn't want to be rattling around by himself, but what could he do about that? No woman was going to take him now. He was too old and too sad and too . . . forgetful.

Michael stared at the ceiling, and Sarah sat back in her chair and sighed.

While they were taking their intermission, Aaron knew it was time to make his move. "Look, I'm fine right where I am. You can both go home now. I need to get back to work."

Sarah jumped on that. "You don't have any work."

Her words felt like an accusation. Did she think he was lazy, that he wasn't working hard enough, not earning enough money? He could call around tomorrow, after the weekend, if it *was* the weekend, he could get some jobs. There were plenty of jobs. He still knew lots of people that needed things done, people that knew how well he did things. Who was she to say he was lazy?

He didn't want to talk anymore. The whole conversation was making him feel hot. He got up and went to the sink. He filled a glass with water and gulped down the entire thing. Then, he spun around and pointed at them. "I don't know what you two think you're trying to pull, but I'm not going to take it."

Sarah hurried over and took his hands. "I'm sorry, Daddy. This is hard for all of us, but we're really worried. We want to help you. We love you, and we're trying to do what's best for you. Think about it. What would you do, if you were in our place?"

He could see she was going to sweet talk him now, but it wasn't going to work. He sat back down at the table and folded his arms across his chest. She could sweet talk all she wanted, but he was going to keep his bull by the horns.

She went behind him and squeezed his shoulders and then down his arms. It felt good, but he wasn't going to give in. She ran her hands down his back, and started pressing here and there. It showed him how much pain he had stuck in there, and it made him feel like crying.

She brought her mouth close to his ear. "What would *you* do, Daddy, if you loved someone and you were worried that they might get lost or hurt?"

He tried to force his words past the ache that had moved into his throat. "I'd . . . I'd just leave him alone."

Sarah squeezed down his arms again, but this time it scared him. Why was she trying to take him away from himself.

She whispered, "No, you wouldn't, Daddy. You always take care of people. Even people you don't know. You pick up hitchhikers and take them wherever they need to go. You always went to see Miriam, even when she didn't know you anymore. You're a kind and concerned person. You'd want to help."

He realized what she was saying. "You think I'm like Miriam, don't you? You think I'm . . . like that."

"No, Daddy, I don't think that, but I do think you have some memory problems. And the doctor says it could get worse. Don't you want to decide things while you still can?" She leaned closer, and he felt her hair brush the side of his face. "Who knows, maybe it's not true. Maybe when you hit your head down there in the desert, it just set you back temporarily. But it's been awhile, and it's not any better. We need to take care of things now, just in case?"

Just in case? In case of what? What was she implying?

She went back to her chair and sat down, smiling like she'd won, but he was pretty sure she hadn't.

"Think about it, Daddy. If you move into that little house close to me, you'd still be in your own space. You'd still be the man of the house. The king of your own castle." She smiled again. "And I'd be just up the street in case you needed me. I'd make you nice things to eat. You could eat at your own place, or join me and the kids any time you got feeling lonely. I could give you some nice back rubs too." She smiled. "I'm pretty good with my hands, you know."

Her sweet talking was getting sweeter, and he wasn't sure how to escape it. Meals anytime he wanted them sounded pretty good. And actually, that last part, about the back rubs, sounded pretty nice too. His back and neck could use some squeezing sometimes. Maybe she was right. Maybe his memory was getting worse. Maybe he was going to forget everything he ever knew. Maybe he would get lost. Miriam got lost that one time, and it took them days to find her. No one even knew where she'd been or what she'd been doing the whole time.

He turned to Michael for help, but Michael wouldn't meet his eyes. So that's how it was. The boy was going to let Sarah do the dirty work. Well, let him. Pretty soon he would go back to wherever he came from and she'd be in charge anyway. It was clear, Michael wasn't going to be any help to him.

Aaron got up and went to the window. Everything in the yard seemed worn out and worried, like he was. He didn't want to cause Sarah trouble, but how could he leave his house after all this time?

He turned around and faced the two of them. "I need to think."

Sarah nodded. "Yes, Daddy, please. Tell us what you're thinking."

A sob escaped him. "You want me to give up everything."

She put her hand over her eyes, and he realized she was crying too. It meant he'd done what he didn't want to do. Why was he making it so hard on her? After all, she was more important than his house. She was more important than anything. A father should take care of his daughter. He should do everything possible to make her happy.

The problem was, the only way he could do that right now was to not want so much. He'd have to give up his house. That wasn't so hard, was it? She said he'd get another one, a smaller one. It would make things simpler. And living a simple life is what he'd always wanted anyway. So why not sell the house and be free of it? In fact, why not get rid of everything. Maybe that's exactly what he needed. A fresh start. Maybe now was the perfect time to do it.

Chapter 31

Sarah and the two big moving boys swirled around him like frenzied dancers, waltzing through the rooms, packing up all his things. Even the kids had a little dance, Annie twirling around the rooms with his pillows. Sam marching down the hall with tall stacks of his books. They put everything in boxes and carried it all out to a big truck that had been parked in the driveway all day.

Aaron's heart cried out. Don't take those things. They're my life. They're all I've got left.

Nobody cared about that. They just kept doing it.

Sarah went back and forth to her car where she was putting his things that could break. His lamps. Laura's glass knickknacks. His fragile dishes. She packed pillows around everything, and when she ran out of pillows, she used his towels and his socks. Even his underwear was fair game.

He followed her and did his own dance of trying to stay out of the way. He thought maybe he should help, but why should he? Those were his things they were taking.

When they started in on his clothes, he tried to grab them and put them back in the closet. It didn't do any good. They ended up in a box anyway. When they started emptying Laura's cedar chest, he'd had it. "Don't touch that stuff!"

He picked up an empty box and threw it at the big boys. When he picked up another one, they went off to get Sarah.

She hurried into the bedroom shaking her head and looking upset. "Dad. Leave them alone. They're just putting the stuff in boxes so the chest won't be so heavy. Don't worry. It's okay."

What did she mean, don't worry? What if those things never made it back into Laura's chest? And how would he know if they had? He couldn't be expected to remember all that.

He stood in the corner watching the boys. He tried to make a list in his mind of everything they took out., but it was hopeless. He'd never remember all that stuff. It was going away, and it might never come back. All of his stuff from India. The pictures of the babies and their little blankets. Those letters tied up with the red satin ribbon.

That's right. Those were important letters. They were the ones he and Laura sent back and forth in the war. He grabbed the bundle from the big boy and ran from the room. Not knowing where else to hide them, he stuffed them down inside his shirt.

The letters whispered to him after that. And when he went into the bathroom, he thought he heard Laura say, "Why are you doing this, Arni? Why are you letting them take away our home?"

Her blame made him want to hide, but there was nowhere to do it. Even the big stuff had already been taken. He stood in front of the mirror staring at his sad worried face. Was that man really him? He tried to wash the worry off by splashing it with cold water, but it didn't work. Laura was still there, blaming him. "I'm sorry, honey. There's nothing I can do to stop them. It's not my fault."

When he left the bathroom, she disappeared. She went out the door with her plants, out with her photographs and record albums of old waltzes and fox trots. Every single thing about her ended up inside a box and got taken away.

Now, all that was left were the strange marks and different shaped squares in the carpet where the furniture used to be. Every single room had a sad emptiness that made him want to cry. Pretty soon it would be like he and Laura had never lived there, like they'd never made love in their bed, and never raised up their children there.

The big boys came marching back in. This time, they were after his piano. His heart broke all over again as he watched them turn the baby grand on its side and pull off its legs. It was like they thought it was some kind of animal that had to be hamstrung to keep it from running away. Aaron wished *he* could run away, but he was hamstrung too. He didn't have a car, or a truck, or any way to get anywhere. If he took off on foot, someone would just come and catch him and put someplace where he didn't want to be. That's why they locked up Miriam, because she was always trying to run away.

Sarah came hurrying into the living room. "Dad, how about we take some of that old stuff in the garage straight to the thrift store?"

"What stuff?"

"You know. All those board games, and the ping pong table."

"No!" he yelled. "You're not taking my ping pong table."

She shook her head and frowned. "But Dad, nobody's played ping pong in years."

He yelled, "How do you know?"

"Well, because it's all covered with dust."

Maybe it was, but so what? A good game of ping pong might be exactly what he needed to take his mind off of all the bad things that were happening. "Put it in the truck. I want it."

Before she could argue, he turned away and headed down the hall, but then he remembered something he hadn't seen go by. He turned back around. "Where is it?"

"Where's what?" she said.

"My bank."

"Your bank? What bank?"

"You know." He showed her the size and shape of it with his hands.

"Oh. You mean that big wooden box you made to keep all your silver coins in?"

"That's right. Where is it?"

She shook her head. "I don't know. I haven't seen it. Did you hide it somewhere?"

"No. I didn't hide it?"

"Are you sure?"

"Well, no, I'm not sure. How could I be sure?"

Sarah sighed. "Well, I guess we're going to have to look for it. Where's Sam?"

Aaron threw up his hands. "How the hell should I know?"

She went down the hall and came back with Sam. "Dad, do you at least know where we should start looking?"

"For what?"

"Your bank with the silver coins."

Aaron tried to think. "I don't know. The last time I saw it, it was in the closet."

"Which closet."

"My closet."

Sarah looked doubtful. "I don't think that's where it is, Dad. We emptied that closet."

"It can't be empty. My bank's in there."

"Sam, honey, why don't you go take a look."

Sam came back a few minutes later with the big wooden bank in his arms. "It was there, Mom. Hidden way in the back. Where it's dark." He set it down on the floor and a cloud of dust came up. "What have you got in here, Grandpa? It's really heavy."

"That's for me to find out, and for you to not know."

Aaron picked up the bank and carried it out to Sarah's car. He put it in the front seat, and when she came out he made her lock it inside the car. "I don't want anyone taking it while we're not looking."

Sarah shrugged and locked the door. She looked back toward the house. "Well, Dad, I think we're about ready to go."

When he heard that, he panicked. He raced inside the house and went from room to room, looking for something he could hold on to. When he got back to the kitchen, he tried to remember something that had taken place there, anything at all, but there was nothing left to remind him. Even Laura's flowered blue apron was gone from the pantry door. That apron had been there forever, and now it was gone, along with everything else from his life with Laura.

It scared him to think what would happen without those reminders. Would his mind just close down and stop trying? He realized that's what had happened to Miriam. When they put her in that place, she didn't know where she was, and she didn't recognize any of the things around her, so she just gave up. That's why she'd sit for hours staring at the blank wall, as if she was already gone. What if that's where he was headed now?

He ran outside, waving his hands and yelling, "Bring it all back. You've got to bring it back."

The big boys stared at him.

Sarah came out of the garage. "What's going on, Dad? What's wrong?"

"You've got to make them bring it back. I can't leave here. I just can't. It'll be a disaster."

"Dad, it's too late for that. You've sold the house. We've got to get you moved to your new house. You said you were on-board with this."

He held out his arms to her, pleading, "Please, I can't be on board. Can't you see what's going to happen?"

Sarah wrapped her arms around him and whispered, "It's okay, Daddy. Nothing bad is going to happen. I love you, and I'm going to take really good care of you."

"But what if I can't remember anything?"

"I'll help you remember. I always will."

She stepped back and brushed her hands off on her pants. "Now, then, I think we've done enough for today. Don't you? I'll come back tomorrow and clean up."

That's when Aaron knew it was over. He was never going to see his place again. The past was leaving, and there was nothing he could do to stop it.

He followed Sarah out to the car where the kids were already waiting in the back seat. He got in and put the bank on the floor and pressed his legs against it to make sure it stayed put. He wasn't going to lose track of his silvers. There was a good chance he would be needing them, and real soon.

Chapter 32

He felt like crying as Sarah pulled out of the driveway and headed up the street to the main road, but what good was that going to do? She wasn't about to turn around. He felt like something was dying inside him as he watched the houses and streets of his little town go flying by. Then the church and the neighbor's turkey farm went by, followed by the cherry orchard where they all used to go foraging for asparagus every spring. Everything was disappearing behind him. Pretty soon the whole town would be gone.

Sarah drove down the big hill and across the flats, and when she turned north, he looked out the side window and saw Mount Olympus towering in the distance. Was that going to disappear too?

Sarah touched his arm and he jumped. "I'm so excited, Dad. It's going to be great fun having you almost next door to us."

He frowned. "It is, huh?"

"Yes. I think it will be really good for the kids to have you around. I'm happy about that."

That surprised him. Why did she think he'd be good for them? Nobody had thought that way about him in a long time. He liked the idea, though. Liked to think he was good for something.

Annie called out from the back seat. "Look Grandpa. They're right behind us."

He looked back. That's right. That big truck had all of his stuff. If they took off, he'd lose everything. He'd better keep his eye on that truck.

They got on the freeway, and the cars and trucks whizzed by like they were going to a bad fire. Why did they have to go so fast all the time? It gave him the feeling they were all going to end up in a big pile.

After continuing on for quite a while, they finally they got off the freeway. Aaron took a deep breath and thought, thank God, that's done.

They headed down a narrow two-lane road, past dead fields and tall scary oil towers. How did those get there? Had he seen them before? He was about to ask Sarah, but she stopped the car.

She patted his arm. "Well, here we are, Dad. Your new house. Now, you take it easy and let me and Sam and the movers do the work."

"What do you mean? There's nothing wrong with me. My arms aren't painted on, you know."

"I know, Dad, but it's been a long hard day."

He stayed in the car while she went with the kids to open the front door. The big truck backed up into the driveway and the whole big moving dance started up again, in reverse.

He sat where he was and looked at his new place. Was he really going to live in that little cottage? It would be like going back in time, wouldn't it? Back when he was a child and they were poor and his father was always angry or upset. Little Stevie was there and so was Miriam. And mother. Everything was so familiar, it kind of scared him. What if he got stuck back there in time and he couldn't get out?

The warmth of the sun coming through the windshield felt nice. He closed his eyes and leaned his head back against the seat. Maybe he should take a nap for a few minutes. Then he'd wake up and get busy helping.

Just as he was dozing off, he heard a noise. He turned his head and saw Annie's pretty little smile outside the glass.

He rolled the window down, and she gave him a solemn look. "Are you okay, Grandpa?"

"Sure, I am. Why wouldn't I be?"

"Well, I was just wondering if you were ever going to get out of the car."

"I'm not sure I want to. It's real nice and warm in here. Do you want to join me?"

She opened the door and took his hand and gave it a gentle tug. "Come on, Grandpa. I want to show you something really special."

He couldn't resist such a tender invitation. He picked up the box with his silvers. "Okay, but you have to help me find a place to hide this."

Annie got a shine in her eyes. "Oh, I know a perfect place. That's just where we're going."

She led him across the lawn toward the back of the house, stopping whenever he needed to rest. When they got to the back door, she put her finger to her lips and whispered, "Shhhh. I'll make sure nobody's looking."

As she stood on her tip-toes peering through the window, a breeze came up and lifted her strawberry hair. It caught the sun and made it look like fire.

He gasped. Hadn't he seen that exact thing before? Some other girl with fire in her hair? He wanted to remember who that girl was, but Annie turned around and said, "Come on, Grandpa. It's safe now."

She opened the door, and he followed her across the kitchen. He saw stairs and knew exactly where he was. Those were the stairs up to his and Stevie's old room in the attic.

He followed Annie up, stopping to rest the heavy bank against the wall now and then. When they got to the top and Annie pushed open the door, he was shocked to see what was there. The ceiling and the walls were all painted dark blue. Who did that? It wasn't blue back when he and Stevie lived there. Why would it be blue now?

Annie gave him a mischievous smile. "Come inside, Grandpa. I'm going to show you something."

He went in, set the bank on the floor, and sat on top of it to rest. Annie ran and pulled the curtains across the windows on both ends of the room. Then she went to the door and closed it, and the room got very dark.

She whispered, "Are you ready?"

He peered through the darkness and said, "Well, I guess so."

She must have flipped a switch because the ceiling came alive with stars, blinking on and off, like real stars twinkling in a dark sky.

She came and lay on the floor beside where he was sitting on the bank and stared up at the lights. "This is my favorite room in your new house, Grandpa. Do you like it too?"

"Yes, I do like it. I always did. It's my bedroom." He stretched out on the floor beside her and whispered, "They're not real, you know. They weren't here before."

"I know that, Grandpa, but we can pretend, can't we?"

He nodded. "Sure we can. It won't hurt anything."

She snuggled closer. "Grandpa, do you think we could sleep up here under the stars sometimes?"

"I don't see why not."

She rolled onto her side and propped her head up on her hand. "Can we do it tonight?"

He laughed. "Okay by me."

She sat up all excited. "Oh boy. Oh boy. I'm gonna go tell Momma."

Annie ran out of the room leaving him staring up at her twinkling stars. There was something mysterious and calming about them, and he could understand why she liked them so much. But still, he'd rather have real stars, the kind you could see in the desert when it was really dark and there was no moon and no one around to take your attention away. He missed the dazzling stars in the desert sky. He was going to have to get down there real soon, if he could just work out a plan.

He stood up. Except for the blinking lights, it was dark in the room, but he caught the silhouette of his bank and remembered he was supposed to hide that. But where could he do it?

When he pulled back the curtains, he saw a sliding door that ran the length of the wall right below where the ceiling slanted down. That's right? He remembered a closet like that from before. It was the perfect place to hide things. In fact, he used to hide special things in that closet all the time. That's where he hid Sarah Larkin's scarf that time he saw her drop it. She was a pretty girl, but she didn't even know he existed.

He carried his bank over and set it on the floor inside the closet. Then he sat down and used his feet to push it in deep. That should do it. Nobody would think to find his coins in there.

When he stood up, he saw the artificial stars again. "Better turn those off. The girl won't like it if they wear out."

Next, he went downstairs to see what all the people with the big voices were up to.

The kitchen was a disaster area and so was the living room. There were boxes stacked all over the place. The stereo was in the middle of the room, facing the wrong way. The love seat looked forlorn, like it didn't know where it belonged. Everything was a big mess.

He spun around looking at it all, feeling irritated and anxious. Then, he saw the piano over in the cove by the bay windows. They'd put its legs back and the wood was glowing a rich golden brown in the afternoon sun. That's where he wanted to be. It was the perfect place for the piano and not a bad reason to start playing again. He should remember that, and do it.

Sarah stopped what she was doing and came over. "There you are, Dad. I wondered where you'd gotten to."

He threw up his hands. "Who's gonna clean up this mess?"

"Well, Dad, I guess we'll do it together. But it's too much for today. We've got your bedroom set up so you can sleep, and I put a few things in the bathroom and the kitchen that you'll need. Come on, I'll show you your room."

She led him through a door off the living room. His bed was pressed up against one wall, and his old oak dresser was squeezed in against the other wall. He caught a glimpse of himself in its murky mirror and was dumbfounded by what he saw. His hair was all frazzled, and he looked like he could be a hundred years old. How did he get looking like that so fast?

He leaned into the mirror and tried to pat down his hair, but it wouldn't stay put. He turned to Sarah. "What happened to me?"

"What do you mean?"

"I'm so old."

"You're not old. You're just tired. It's been a long day."

"It has?"

"Yes. And you've just moved into a new place. That's hard on anyone. But it's going to be okay. I really think you're going to like it here."

"I am?"

"Yes. I'm sure of it."

She smiled and pointed to the lamp table next to his bed. "Look. I've put your wedding picture there, along with Mom's poems. I thought you'd like that."

"Oh good. I thought her poems were lost." He picked up the binder and opened it to the first page. The ink was kind of smeared like it had gotten wet. "Oh no. What happened? Did someone leave it in the rain?"

"You had it inside your shirt when they took you to the hospital. Remember?"

No, he didn't remember.

He flipped through the pages, scared of what he'd find. Some of the other pages were smeared, but he could read most of the words. It didn't look very good, but at least he could still read the poems. They weren't completely ruined.

He put the binder down on the table and gave it a pat, then he picked up the wedding picture. Oh no. Someone had tried to ruin that too. There were big ugly words all over the front of it. Now why did they do that? Trying to ignore the words, he traced his finger over Laura's beautiful face, and then he looked at his own face. They were so young and handsome back then, so full of love. What happened to all that? Did it get ruined too?

He held the photograph up to his face so Sarah couldn't see him cry. It was useless to cry. That wasn't going to bring Laura back. Nothing was going to do that.

As he put the photograph back on the table, he remembered the letters inside his shirt. Those should be there too. He took the letters out and put them next to the blue binder. Then he stood up, feeling angry for some reason that he didn't quite understand. He looked at Sarah. "So, what are we supposed to do now?"

"Well, let's go see if those moving guys have finished unloading the truck. When they're gone, I think we should go to my house and fix something to eat. And I think you should sleep there too. Just until you get used to things, you know, until you have the lay of the land."

He stared at her, wondering how she could come up with so many words at one time, and when he didn't answer, she gave him some more words. "Does that sound good?"

No, it didn't sound good. "You get me here, and then you want me there. Where am I supposed to be?"

"Anywhere you want to be, Daddy."

"I'm not so sure about that."

He glared at her and headed back out to where the piano was, hoping he could escape the sad angry feeling that was growing inside him.

Sarah caught his arm. "Dad, you can sleep here, if you want to. But if you do, Annie wants to stay with you. And Sam too. In fact, maybe we could put out the mattresses from the other beds, and we can all sleep on the floor. Wouldn't that be fun?"

He shook his head and stared at her. "Sure. Let's have a party. Invite the whole world."

Chapter 33

As he stood on the porch and watched the moving boys drive off in their big truck, he got a bad feeling that maybe they hadn't unloaded everything. If they took off with some of his stuff, how would he know it?

Sarah came out. "Come on, Dad. How 'bout we go have some dinner?"

He shrugged. "I guess we might as well. I can't get that truck back anyway."

"What truck?"

"Never mind. It's gone."

Sarah went back in the house and got the kids, and they all drove up the street to her house.

She cooked, while Aaron sat at the table taking in all the noise and confusion. Is this how it was going to be? Kids talking in loud voices like they were *outside* playing. Pots and pans clanging? It made him feel like finding someplace to hide. It had been so noisy all day, he was desperate for some peace and quiet. Or maybe what he really needed was to just be alone with his own brain for a while. He'd been confused all day, slipping between the past and the future, not knowing quite where he was going to land.

Finally, Sarah carried steaming plates of food to the table, and the kids quieted down as they dug into their spaghetti and peas. Aaron hoped that the tension in his throat would recede enough that he could eat without everything getting stuck on the way down. He never had much use for spaghetti because he didn't really know how to eat it without getting the tomato stuff all over his chin and his shirt. He watched Sam to see how the boy did it. He had it down: he'd spin the noodles around on his fork and stuff it all into his mouth real quick before it had a chance to fall off. Aaron decided to give that method a try. It worked pretty good.

Annie kept looking at him with her shiny eyes, like they had a secret between them. Maybe she was still thinking about those ceiling stars she found. Or maybe she had another special thing she wanted to show him. He winked to let her know he was on-board, but he hoped it could wait until tomorrow. Right now, he was too tired for any more secrets.

By the time they finished eating, he was ready to go home, but Sarah wanted him to help with the dishes while the kids went off to do their homework.

He dried the dishes, but as soon as they were done, he said, "Okay, I'm going home now."

She looked surprised. "Really?"

"Yes. I need to be alone with myself."

She wiped down the counter and hung up the dish towel before she turned around and met his eyes. "Do you really want to sleep in that house alone?"

"Well, why not? I'm not scared of the dark, you know."

"I know, but what if you wake up and you don't know where you are?"

He threw up his hands. "Look. I'm a big boy. I can take care of myself."

She stared at him, and he knew he was going to have to take that worried look out of her eyes or he wasn't going to get anywhere. He took her by the arm and led her to the living room, and they sat on the couch. It took him a minute, but then he thought he knew how to explain. "Listen, you can't watch me every little minute. I like it here, but I need some room. I'm used to that."

"I know, Daddy. It'll take you some time to get used to having us around, but I thought maybe because this is your first night—"

"I don't need any time. I'm fine."

"I want to believe you. I really do. But what if you're wrong? What if you forget something crucial, or you go wandering off, and I can't find you again?"

"If I go wandering, that's my business. You don't have to stop me. I've got legs. I can use them if I want to."

Now she had tears in her eyes, and he was sure he was the one that put them there. He hadn't meant to do it. He understood what she was saying about wandering. She was afraid he'd get lost and end up wandering around a field screaming for help like Miriam did. But he wasn't like Miriam. He was stronger. He knew how to work with himself, how to be calm in a new situation, even if he didn't know exactly where he was. He'd done that a lot when he was out in the desert, hadn't he? Wandered around. Got lost. And he'd found his way back every single time. He'd be fine. If she could just let him be alone for a second, maybe he could find out if he really *could* be alone in his new house. And if he could, he'd feel a whole lot better.

He stood up and headed for the door waving his hand over his head, without looking back. "Okay. See you later."

Sarah called after him, "At least let me walk you down there. Wait just a minute, and I'll tell the kids where we're going."

No, he wasn't going to wait. He needed to go now. He went right out the front door, but when he got to the sidewalk he wasn't sure which way to go. Maybe she was right. Maybe he'd better wait for her.

When Sarah came out, he pretended to be looking at the stars.

"Here, you forgot this." She handed him his sweater. "It's kind of cool. You better have it."

He took his time putting his sweater on so that she could take the lead. When she turned right, he told himself, okay, that means you've got to turn right. Remember that. It's always right to turn right. He smiled, thinking that was a good trick he could use to remember in the future.

As they walked along, he tried to memorize the houses and the trees. It wasn't easy. They were tract houses. They all looked pretty much the same, especially in the dark. He gave up trying to do it until they came to a house with an apple tree in the front yard. That might be something he could hang onto. Remember that apple tree.

After one more house, they arrived at his little cottage. He saw the big pine tree and knew that was the best thing to remember. There was no other tree like that. And he knew that tree from before when they lived there the last time, didn't he?

Sarah said, "I've put my phone number right next to the phone, Dad. The phone is already working, and so is the gas and the electricity, so you don't have to worry about any of that. Now you be sure to call me if anything happens." She shook her finger at him like she thought he was one of the kids. "Are you listening, Dad? I don't care what time it is. If there's any kind of problem, anything at all, you call me. Okay?"

"Blah blah blah."

She stopped dead, and from the shocked look on her face, he knew he was in trouble again. Well, he didn't give a damn. If this was going to be his new house, he was ready to go in and start living in it. He held his hands up to warn her off. "Okay. G'night. Sleep tight. Don't let the bug bite you."

He hurried up the sidewalk and up the porch stairs, but when he tried the door, it was locked. "Oh for crying out loud." He turned back to Sarah. "Where are the damn keys?"

"They're right here." She showed him the keys, but she held them back. "Why are you always cussing and talking so mean? You never did that before. What's wrong with you?"

"Nothing's wrong with me. What's wrong with you?"

Her mouth turned down, and she shook her head. "See what I mean? Why can't you just be civil? I'm doing the best I can to help you."

He felt reprimanded, but he knew if he let her treat him like a child, that's how she'd be doing it from now on.

They stood on the porch and stared at each other until she finally gave in and unlocked the door. Once they were inside, he grabbed the keys from her hand.

"What are you doing, Dad?"

"They're mine, aren't they? This is my house."

"Yes, it is. I'm glad you know that."

"Of course, I know it. What do you think I am, stupid?"

She plopped down on the couch which was parked in the middle of a bunch of boxes. "Look, Dad, I'm sorry. I know it's a hard time for you. It's just that I'm . . . exhausted. We spent all day getting you moved, and now I've only got one day before I have to go back to work. Tomorrow, we're going to have to get as much of this unpacked and set up as we can."

He didn't have anything to say, so he just looked around. What was in all those boxes?

Sarah let out a big sigh and stood up. "Okay, let's get you settled."

He shook his head. "No. I can settle myself. Go home."

"Are you sure?"

"Yes. I am. Now go."

She looked reluctant, but then she came and gave him a hug. "Okay, Daddy. I'll leave. But remember. I love you. Please, let's try to make this work."

He thought she was trying to coddle him, so he kept his arms down at his sides. "I do remember. If I forget things, it doesn't mean I'm completely gone, you know."

She nodded. "I know. I know. But—"

"But what?"

"Nothing. Never mind."

He went and opened the door so she'd know it was time for her to go.

She headed down the steps to the sidewalk, and after stopping once to look back, she kept going.

He stood on the porch keeping his eyes on her until she was completely out of sight. Then he looked up at the stars. It was such a nice night, he decided to stay outside for a while. He sat down on the top step and took a deep breath of the cool air. It was good to finally be alone. The silence of the night and the sweet twinkling light of the stars was soothing. At least those stars were where they were supposed to be, even if everything else had changed. He should remember, life was like that. Always changing. Always carrying you along, making you older, when all you really wanted to do is to stay where you were and be young.

He looked at the big pine tree, still trying to remember if it had been there before. It seemed like they had planted it when he was young, and it had grown up. The same as he had. He wished he could remember if that was true, but it didn't really matter. It was a nice tree, and he was glad it was there.

The street was quiet now. No cars going by. That was good. Maybe all those houses weren't as busy as he thought they'd be. Maybe he'd be able to breathe okay, once he got used to this place.

He lay back on the porch and let himself drift. The air was kind of cool, but he didn't mind. He was often cold in the winter when he came back from doing stuff with his friends. Like that night they rode their homemade sleds down the snow-covered street under a full moon. What a great night that was. One of the best of his life. Wouldn't it be great if he could go back there.

The memory made him happy, and he closed his eyes as he remembered other times, like swimming nude in that pond in the woods with the boys. They always swam nude back then. Nobody cared. Life was free like that. Life was grand.

He thought he caught a whiff of cinnamon, and he decided he'd better go inside. Mother was probably waiting with some cinnamon toast and milk. She was always waiting when he came home late. She'd take him in the kitchen, and he'd tell her all about the fun he'd been having.

He got up and went inside and turned on the light, but his mother wasn't there waiting. There was nothing but a big mess of boxes all over the place. It took him a minute to realize this wasn't the past, it was the future. It was the place he was going to be living from now on, whether he wanted to or not. But maybe it wasn't so bad.

As he walked around the house, he wondered what to do with himself. The TV wasn't plugged in, and there was nothing he could do about the boxes tonight because he was too sleepy. Maybe he should just go to bed.

Once he found his bedroom and he was undressed and in bed, he wasn't sure he'd be able to sleep. Not in that unfamiliar room with the moon shining in through a different window. Even his old bed felt strange. Maybe it was just the smallness of the room that made him realize how big the bed was without Laura. He missed Laura.

The furnace came on, and he closed his eyes and listened. The sound of it reminded him of how he used to hold his breath to make sure Laura was still breathing. She hardly breathed at all toward the end. Sometimes he'd get scared that she was dead, and he'd wake her up just to make sure that wasn't true. Then he'd feel bad that he'd done it, but he didn't want her to die alone in her sleep not knowing that he was right there to give her comfort. Did he give her comfort? He gave her that last bath, didn't he? He held her in his arms. At least he did that much.

After the furnace went off, he held his breath like he did back then, wishing with all his heart that Laura could be there beside him. Even if it was only her spirit, or whatever was left of her.

Then he heard it. Yes, there it was. Just the slightest whisper of her breath. He focused on the sound, and for just a moment he was sure it was Laura. But the sound grew louder, and he realized it wasn't her after all; it was just the wind brushing through the leaves of the big pine tree out front.

Chapter 34

Aaron woke up in the dark wondering where in the hell he was. His bed felt right, but it was pushed up against the wall on one side, and the other side was too close to the dresser. The other thing he noticed was that the air had a nasty sweet smell like somebody had sprayed that stinky cover-up stuff everywhere. He hated that smell. And what was that terrible light blasting in through the window? That wasn't right. The moon was supposed to give off white light. This light was bright yellow. Like some kind of stupid light bulb that shouldn't be on.

He got out of bed and went to the window to see where that bad light was coming from. It looked like some kind of porch light on the neighbor's place. But why was the neighbor's door pointing out at *his* yard? Didn't that mean whoever was over there could look straight into his bedroom? Straight into his life? That wasn't right. There should be a tall fence over there. Or some kind of thick bushes. Or trees. He was going to have to do something about that, but right now he had to pee real bad.

Holding himself as he went, he hurried into the next room, hoping that's where the bathroom was. But it wasn't. It was just a cold dark room full of boxes that he could barely see. As he picked his way through the boxes, his foot caught something, and he went sprawling across the floor. It knocked the breath out of him, and once he recovered, he found out he'd peed himself.

He started to sob. That was it. The last straw. Wetting himself like a child. He couldn't do anything right anymore. Couldn't even make it to the bathroom without wetting himself. He'd never done that in his whole life. Never. Now here he was, a grown naked man sitting on the floor in a puddle of his own pee.

What did it mean? That he'd lost control of his bladder? Was he going to start peeing himself all the time and have to wear diapers like a little baby? Would everyone know?

He slammed his fist into the wood floor. No! He was never going let that happen. He'd run away first. He'd shoot himself in the head.

One thing was for sure, he wasn't going to let Sarah find out about it. She'd try to take him to the next step. She'd try to make him move in with her, or even worse, she'd take him to that place where they expected people to wet themselves all day. He wasn't going there. No way. No way in hell.

As he went to find something to clean up his mess, he realized he hadn't really lost control. He'd just had to pee, and he got it knocked out of him when he fell to the floor. That's all it was. It could happen to anyone. He needed to pee and he fell. No big deal. He should stop worrying about it.

When he found the bathroom, he went in and pulled off some toilet paper from the roller thing, and took it back out and cleaned up the mess. He carried the soppy gunk to the bathroom and threw it all in the toilet.

After he cleaned himself up, he went back to bed, but there was that yellow light. No matter which side he turned onto, it was still right there. If he didn't get rid of it, he was pretty sure he'd go crazy.

He got up and grabbed some pants and a T-shirt to put on. Then he made it through the minefield in the living room and the minefield in the kitchen and out the back door with nothing more than a couple of stubbed toes.

The sky was brilliant outside. The stars. The moon. The dark blueness of the heavens. It took his breath away and made him want to float right up there like a balloon. But the grass kept him down. It was cool and wet on his bare feet, and there was a cool breeze in the air that sent shivers through his skin. It made him feel like laughing, or maybe crying.

When he saw the trampoline, he knew that's where he wanted to be. He pulled himself up onto the edge of it and sat there for a minute, getting his balance and his breath. Then he crawled out to the middle. The rubber was still a little bit warm, and it made him want to lay on his back and look up at the stars. He did that for a while, but then he started thinking he'd like to bounce. Maybe he could catch the moon, or a star.

He got up and steadied himself. Then did a few little bounces. That felt okay, so he did some bigger ones. Pretty soon he was throwing out his arms as he went up, feeling a sensation a lot like flying. He liked flying, but he was afraid to look at the sky while he did it. He might lose touch with the rubber and fly off. He didn't need any more disasters. He'd already gone down once and peed himself.

Remembering that fiasco, reminded him that he was about to do something else before he started going on the trampoline. But what was it?

He got off the bouncer and looked around. Nothing there told him anything, so he wandered around to the side of the house. That's when he saw the yellow light, and he knew that's what it was. He had to get rid of that damn light.

He hurried over and knocked on the side of the screen door. Nobody came, so he knocked again and put his ear up against the mesh of the screen to listen. It seemed like he heard someone coming, so he stepped back and almost fell off the little raised porch. Why was he stumbling around so much? Was he trying to break his leg?

The door pulled back, and he thought he saw a face behind the dark screen. He wasn't sure, so he asked. "Is somebody there?"

"What do ya want?"

The voice was a woman, and she didn't sound nice.

"Well, I was wondering if you could turn your damn light off."

"My what?"

"The light. The light. The damn light." He pointed at it, and it blasted away at his eyes. What did she think she was doing with a light like that, anyway? Was she trying to catch bugs or something?

"Better get away from here, you ol' bugger. I'll call the cops."

"The cops? What have they got to do with anything?" He stepped closer and peered through the screen. "I'm just asking for you to turn off your light. It's too big, and it's too bright. And it's too . . . burning yellow."

"The light's there to stay. It's to keep you away."

"But why? I haven't done anything."

"It's the middle of the night. I'd say that's something."

"Well, I'm trying to sleep, and I can't. That's why I'm over here." He sniffed at the screen to see if he could smell her, but he just got a snoot full of dirt. "Look," he said. "Just turn it off, and I'll go away."

She slammed the door, but she didn't do the light. It was still shining as bright as ever. It was so bright it made purple spots on his eyelids when he turned away. He was going to have fix it, even if she didn't want him to fix it.

Reaching up inside the glass case, he unscrewed the bulb real quick before it could burn his fingers. He dropped it on top of the hedge. Thank, God. At last, it was dark.

By the time he got back in his bedroom, the yellow light was blasting again. Damn it. What was she trying to prove? That she could do it more than he could? Well, it wasn't true. He'd stay out there all night if he had to.

He went back over there, and this time when he unscrewed the bulb, he let it cool first, then he pushed it down inside the hedge. He let it cool a little more, and pushed it down even further. There, that ought to do it. She was never going to find it now.

It wasn't until he was halfway across the lawn, that he heard the old crab's raspy voice. "Hey, old man. You come here again, and I *will* call the cops."

Waving her off with a flap of his hand, he headed back inside. By the time he had made his way through the debris and was safely in bed, the yellow light was back on. Damn. Now what was he going to do? She wasn't going to let him win, no matter what. So how was he going to sleep?

The only way he could do it, was to block out the light. He pulled the quilt over his face, but then he couldn't breathe. He tried his arm across his eyes, but that didn't work either. The light just snuck in around the edges. He tossed and turned and finally got his T-shirt and put it over the top part of his head and wrapped it tight around his eyes. It wasn't comfortable, but he thought it might work. And, finally, it did.

In the morning, he woke up and went out to the living room. There were boxes everywhere. He got dressed and headed out to the garage and found the trash thing. He dragged it around to the porch and wrestled it up the steps and into the house. He'd just put all the junk in there and drag it out to the street, and let the garbage guys deal with it. It was their job, wasn't it?

Before he started, he took the time to look in a few of the boxes. It was all just old stuff that nobody would ever want or need. He started dumping the boxes, one at a time, into the big black trash thing. When he'd gone pretty far, he came across a box that had a lot of pictures in it. Looking closer, he saw they were old photographs of the family. Pictures of him and Laura. Pictures of the children when they were young. Oh no! What had he done? Had he thrown away other important stuff like this?

He pawed through the trash barrel, finding lots of things that should have been saved. Some of his favorite books. His old leather wallet. His favorite old swimming trunks. What were those doing in there?

He pulled out the stuff he could reach and put it on the floor, but some of it was too far down. He was going to have to tip the damn thing over. He was just about to do that when Sarah came in the door. She took one look at the room and gasped.

Oh no. Why didn't he close the door and lock it? Now he was going to have to listen to her blaming him for everything he didn't mean to do.

Bracing himself, he faced her head on. "So what? It's mine, isn't it?"

"What's yours?"

"This stuff."

She cocked her head and lifted one shoulder and wiggled it around like she was already getting tense. "What are you doing, Dad?"

"I was just taking it out."

"Out?"

"You know, out of the trash thing. I was just putting it all back . . . down there." He nodded toward the floor.

"But why—"

He threw up his hands. "Look. I don't want to hear it. I made a mistake, and I'm sorry. Forget about it."

She forced a smile. "Okay. I can do that. Do you want help sorting it out?"

"Well, I wouldn't mind that. I mean, I don't know exactly what happened, so we'll have to do it all over again. I guess."

She came over and gave him a hug. "Anyway, good morning, Dad. Did you get any sleep?"

"Not with that damn light."

"Light? What light?"

"That damn yellow light she has."

"Who are we talking about, Dad?"

"You know, that old crab apple over there. She doesn't care if I sleep or not. She doesn't give a damn about anybody."

"Show me."

He led her to the bedroom and pointed toward the porch across the lawn. "She's got it right there, and she won't turn it off when it's night, no matter how many times I hid it."

"You hid it?"

"Well, I had to. Otherwise, she just put it back. It didn't work anyway. That's why I can't sleep."

Sarah stepped back from the window. "I think I'll go talk to her."

"No! Don't!" He grabbed her arm.

"Why not?"

"She's already watching me as much as she can, and I don't want any more of it. Just leave her alone."

"Okay. I won't talk to her if you don't want me too. But don't be causing her trouble. Okay? We can put curtains on the window if the light's too bright."

"I don't like curtains."

"Well then, what should we do?"

She rubbed the back of her neck like it might be getting tight because of him, but he didn't care. She was the one that made all these problems in the first place. He should have just stayed where he was. That's right. She took his house, and now he was stuck here. "If you hadn't done it, none of this would of happened."

"Daddy, please! Can't we just go get the living room cleaned up?"

"Sure. Sure. Sure. Do whatever you want. It's not your problem."

He left her standing there with her hands on her hips and went to the living room and started pushing things around with his feet. What was all that junk, anyway? He got down on his knees and started throwing things into boxes.

Sarah came in. He looked up and saw the morning light on her skin. That was nice. She had a pretty turquoise shirt on, and the light made it glow. He smiled. "I like that. It's good on you."

She smiled a little and looked at him like she had no idea what he was saying.

"I mean that top you've got. It's a nice color."

She smiled. "Oh. Thank you. I like turquoise."

"Me too. I wish I had one."

"Are you saying you want a turquoise shirt."

"I'd wear it, if I had one."

"Okay then. I'll remember that." She let out a little laugh and the room brightened even more.

He scooted back against the wall, and looked up at her. "You're a real beauty, you know."

"Really?" She did a little twirl and ended it with a curtsy.

He laughed "You really are. I can see it all over you."

She shook her head. "You're such an . . . enigma, Daddy."

"I am?"

"Yeah."

"Well, what is it?"

She didn't tell him what the word meant. Instead, she said, "A compliment like that deserves breakfast. Come on. Let's go up to my house, and I'll fix you something really nice for breakfast. Then we'll come back here and get this place all fixed up. Does that sound good?"

"Sure. Why not? It's too big of a mess around here."

Chapter 35

As the days and weeks—or maybe it was months—went by, Annie was Aaron's savior. She came every day at the same time like a clock that worked really well. She was the one who gave him something to do, now that he didn't have anything to do, now that the people who used to call him to do drywall jobs were all gone. It was probably because they couldn't find him anymore, because he wasn't where he was supposed to be. Why didn't Sarah realize that once he was lost, he'd be lost forever? She should have let him stay where he was before.

He looked around and realized he was sitting on the top step of the porch. Where was Annie? Did her clock get broken? Did she get tired of playing with her old grandpa? He couldn't blame her for that, but he missed her real bad and wished she'd come.

As he continued to wait, his mind went back to thinking about the work he didn't have anymore. Maybe he should call some of those guys. They might be glad if he did. He could do some work, and if they liked it, they'd call him back, and he could do some more work. He decided to go in the house and see if he could find any of their old phone numbers.

When he got inside, he couldn't remember what he was doing. He went to the kitchen to see if there was anything there to remind him. But the kitchen was cold, and that made him wonder if maybe the summer was over. Or did he just need a thicker shirt? Hard to say how things worked now. If he knew how long he'd been living in the new house, he might know what season it was. Where was his little Annie? If she was there, he could ask her.

He sat in one of the kitchen chairs and looked around. It seemed like the room was waiting for him do something, but he didn't know what it wanted, and that scared him.

Then, suddenly, the house felt too tight, like the walls were squeezing in. He had to get out of there.

He jumped up and hurried out the front door. He sat down on the porch and looked at the big old pine tree. He knew that old tree, didn't he? Sure, he'd seen that tree his whole life. Even when he was in high school it was there. They were like old best friends. He liked being friends with the tree. It made him feel like he was part of something, like he still had a place in the world. At least he had something that knew him, even if it was an old tree.

What was that? There was some kind of a big ruckus going on. He followed the sound to the backyard and saw children flying up and down on his bouncer. They were squealing and filling the air with so much excitement it made his skin shiver. How did they get their clothes to be all bright like that? All those reds and turquoise and blues? Even their skin was glowing pink in the morning sun. The way it all came at him made him feel like he was seeing a whole different world, a wonderful world where everybody was young and free.

He went closer to join them.

Right away, he saw that Annie was there. She was on the jumper thing going up and down with the rest of them.

She spotted him and yelled, "Grandpa. Grandpa. Come and bounce with us."

That sounded fun, but wasn't he too big for the rest of them?

Annie wiggled her finger at him. "Come on, Grandpa. It's fun."

He thought, sure, why not? He knew how to jump. And it was his jumper, wasn't it?

He climbed up, and right away all the kids got off. Why did they do that? Was he spoiling their fun? He looked at Annie to see what he should do.

"Go ahead, Grandpa. Jump. You can do it."

Of course, he could do it. He did it all the time when nobody was there. But this time, the kids were all looking at him like he was the big show. He wasn't used to being the big show.

He did a few little bounces, and a dark-haired boy that looked older than the rest of the kids started clapping his hands and yelling, "Jump, Grampa. Jump."

"Well, hold onto your horses, boy, I was just getting started."

He did a bigger jump, but evidently it wasn't enough for the boy. He just laughed and yelled, "Come on, Gramps. You can jump higher than that."

Then all the other kids chimed in. "Jump, Grampa. Jump."

Aaron did a few bigger jumps, but for some reason, he felt dizzy. He stopped jumping to try to figure out what was wrong.

The dark-haired boy laughed. "What's a matter, Grampa? All tuckered out after a few little jumps?"

Aaron glared at him. "I can do it as good as you can, smarty pants. Just watch me." He started to jump again, throwing out his arms and going high.

The boy yelled, "Come on, Grampa. That's little kid stuff. Try something hard. Do a flip, or somethin'."

Annie's voice piped in. "Leave him alone, Jordan. Can't you see he's getting tired?"

Aaron was happy to hear Annie stand up for him, but the boy wouldn't let up. "Ahh, he's just a big scaredy-cat." He turned to the other kids, and said, "Come on. Let's go do somethin' else."

Aaron didn't want them to go. He liked the kids. He had to show them he could do it. He yelled, "Watch this."

He started to jump, going higher and higher, working up his nerve.

The big boy got all the kids clapping their hands and yelling, "Flip, Grampa. Flip."

Annie yelled, "No, Grandpa. Don't do it."

The dizziness came back, but he wasn't about to let that stop him. He had to do it now, or he never would. He jumped one last time, throwing his arms above his head, going really high, and then he threw himself into a roll.

Phump!

He hit the rubber hard, landing flat on his face. At first, he wasn't sure what had happened. His head was spinning, and for some reason he couldn't breathe.

Then Annie was there with her eyes full of tears. "Grandpa, Grandpa, are you okay?"

He gasped for air while she rubbed his back and kept saying, "Are you okay, Grandpa. Are you okay?'

He wanted to tell her he was okay, but he wasn't sure if it was true, and he couldn't really talk.

She looked over at the dark-haired boy, and yelled, "Jordan, you're so mean. You shouldn't have made him do that. Now go home."

The boy shrugged and walked away.

Aaron wondered if Annie was right. Had the boy made him do it? He didn't think so. He'd done it for the kids.

He stayed where he was trying to remember exactly what had happened. Gradually his breath came back. When he managed to sit up, Annie held his hand and asked him again if he was all right. She looked all upset and worried. He didn't want her to feel like that, so he gave her a shrug and a goofy smile.

She tried to smile back. "Can you get down, Grandpa? Do you need help?"

He wasn't sure. Did he need help? Was he broken anywhere? He moved his neck and his shoulders around. No, they seemed okay. "I think I can make it."

He tried to scoot to the edge of the rubber, but it made him woozy, so he decided to wait for another minute or two. That's when he noticed the circle of children staring at him with big scared eyes. He smiled and waved. "Everything's okay, kids. Don't worry. I'm okay."

Seeing his audience made him wonder if he'd done it. He grabbed Annie's hand. "Did I do it? Did I do the . . . flipping thing?"

She smiled. "Of course, you did. It was great."

"Well, that's good then. I guess it was worth it."

He crawled across the rubber, and when he got to the side, he carefully climbed down. As soon as his feet hit the ground, the children turned around scattered away like colorful birds.

Annie took him inside and helped him sit in a kitchen chair, then she got him a drink of water. It was nice the way she was taking care of him, but she looked worried. "Grandpa," she said. "If we tell Momma what happened, she'll be really mad at me."

"We don't have to tell her, do we?"

"But what if you're hurt?"

He ran his hands over his arms and chest and his thighs. "Nope. I don't seem hurt."

She stood in front of him. "But maybe Momma should call the doctor to make sure."

"You shouldn't worry so much, honey. I'm fine. And besides, I don't like doctors."

She threw her arms around him, and said, "Grandpa, I love you so much. I thought you were hurt, and it was my fault. I shouldn't have brought those kids over here."

"I like those kids. I always have. They can come anytime they want."

"But Jordan's mean. He made you do it."

"Nobody makes me do anything I don't want to." He patted her head. "Well, maybe you could make me do things, but that's because you're my Annie."

She sat crossed-legged on her chair, and looked into his eyes like she had something to say.

"What is it, honey?"

"Well, it's just that, sometimes, I don't understand what Momma said."

"Uh . . . like what did she say?"

"She said you're forgetting everything now. But sometimes that's not true. Sometimes we have real conversations, and it's almost like it was before."

He shrugged and gave her a silly grin. "Don't ask me. I can't remember."

She giggled. "You're so funny, Grandpa."

"It works, doesn't it?"

"What do you mean?"

"You know. When you can laugh instead of crying all the time."

"I know, but I was being serious. I'm worried about Momma being worried. I think she wants you to do something you might not want to do."

He didn't like that. Were they hatching plans behind him? "Like what? What does she want me to do?"

"Well, she worries about you when she has to go to work. She doesn't like you to be alone down here."

He shrugged. "I'm not alone. I've got you."

"That's what I wanted to tell you, Grandpa. School's going to start before too long, so I won't be able to come as often. I know you'll get lonely, but there's nothing I can do. I have to go to school."

"Well, you can come when it's over, right?"

"Yes, but if you lived at our house, I could come straight home from school, and you'd be right there. You could help me do my homework."

"I could, huh?" Now he was pretty sure what they'd been hatching.

"I just want you to be okay, Grandpa. Sometimes things are hard. I mean, you know with Daddy gone, and Sam being mad half the time, and Momma being lonely. Well, actually, she's not so lonely now, because she's got Kevin. You know, her new boyfriend. Anyway, I just want everyone to be happy. And I like being with you. It's fun. That's why I wish you would come and live with us."

"It's fun for me to be with you too, honey, but I'm not going to do it. I'm fine right here. This is where I am, even if I have to be lonely sometimes."

They looked at each other in silence. But then he felt like the silence was too big, so he said, "Well, what should we do now?"

Annie shrugged. "I don't know. Do you want to go eat some strawberries?"

"Strawberries? Where are they?"

"In your garden."

"Oh. That's right. My garden. Sure, strawberries sound good. Let's go get some."

Chapter 36

Time was moving in a strange way. It seemed too slow. In fact, the only way Aaron knew for sure it was passing was because of the way the light changed in the house. When he was in bed at night, sometimes he wasn't sure whether the light was coming from the moon, or from that blasting yellow light from next door. That old crab face was always over there burning her light and watching everything he did. Sometimes he didn't mind. At least it meant someone was there, and that he wasn't completely alone.

On this night, he couldn't sleep. His brain felt like it was asleep, but he was pretty sure the rest of him was awake. He was tired of being in bed, so he decided to get up whether it was morning or not.

After he got dressed and went to the bathroom, he came out wondering what to do with himself. Maybe he was supposed to eat something. He went to the kitchen and looked in the cooler majig to see if it would tell him. There were morning things in there, eggs, milk, and some kind of red gooey jam stuff. None of it looked very good. He pulled out the bottom drawers and saw some old vegetables and a few apples. None of that looked good either, so he just put some tomatoes on some bread and ate that with a glass of milk. Once the eating part was done, he went outside to see what the day looked like.

The first thing he noticed was that the grass was too long. It shouldn't be like that. It was his job to take care of it, so why hadn't he done it? He went to the garage and pushed the cutter thing out on the lawn. But when he pulled the cord it just sputtered. He yanked it a few more times, but it just kept making the same sputtering noise. He gave it a kick and tried once more, but it didn't work. What was wrong with the damn thing? He stared at it, shaking his head in frustration.

"Wait a minute," he said. "Maybe the gas is all gone." He unscrewed the cap and looked down into the hole. "Yep. Dry as a bone."

He went to the garage and found the gas can, but it was completely dry too. Shoot! Now, he was going to have to go take care of that. He went out front and started off down the road with the can, but then he remembered he'd better take some money. He went back to the house to get that.

His old leather money holder wasn't on the dresser where it was supposed to be, and it wasn't in any of his pants pockets either. The only thing he could see was a little dish of change on the dresser. It seemed like he had more of that change somewhere. Maybe some even bigger ones. In fact, he should have a whole bunch of bigger ones somewhere. That's right. They were in that square box thing he made. Like a big . . . piggybank sort of thing. He'd better find that.

He went through the house opening drawers and cupboards. He looked above things and behind things, but he couldn't find it anywhere. When he finished looking, the whole house was a mess, and he still hadn't found his bank. It scared him to think he'd lost all his money. Did someone sneak in and take it when he wasn't looking?

No, he was there the whole time. That money had to be somewhere.

Suddenly, he remembered the room at the top of the stairs. It was the place he *always* hid his best stuff, even when he lived up there before with Stevie. Maybe the money was up there.

He hurried up the stairs, and when he opened the door and turned on the light, he saw stars shining down from the ceiling. He stared at them for a long time, trying to figure out how they got up there. But he wasn't looking for stars, he was looking for money. His silver money. That's right. His money was made out of silver. They were those special old silvers he'd been saving for most of his life.

He saw the closet. That must be where they were. That's where he put all his good stuff.

After he slid the door open the whole way, he got down on his hands and knees. He crawled way back in where it was dark, moving his hands back and forth. Finally, he felt something. That could be it.

He lugged the thing out, and saw he was right. It was his money box. There was so much money in there, he could buy whatever he wanted. But what did he want to buy? What did he need?

As he thought about it, he realized what he really needed was his freedom. And to get that, he needed his truck. He was sick and tired of not being able to go someplace else. If he had his own truck, he could go anywhere he wanted to. He could even go down to the desert. That's right. He could drive his truck down to the desert, and nobody could stop him.

He laughed out loud. He'd found the right answer. He should go out right now and buy a truck. Then he should drive down to the desert where he belonged.

Holding the box tight against his chest, he carried it downstairs and put it on the kitchen table. The problem was, there was no way to get the money out except through that one little slot where you put the coins in. Now why would anybody build a box like that?

He wondered if the coins might come out if he held the box upside down and shook it, but when he tried that, it didn't work. All it did was make his arms ache. Maybe he could pry it open. He got a knife and tried to push it down into the seams, but he'd built it too tight. It looked like he was going to have to break the damn thing open.

He was pretty sure he had a big box breaker thing out in the garage, so he went out and found it, brought it back to the kitchen, and put the box on the floor. He gave it a good whack, but the darn thing didn't break. He spit on his hands and raised the big hammer over his head and brought it down really hard. It missed the bank and almost hit his foot, and now there was a big dent in the floor. That wasn't good. Maybe he'd better take the whole operation outside.

After carrying the box out to an old patch of sidewalk in the backyard, he went back and got his hitter. He raised it high over his head again and brought it down as hard as he could. This time it worked. The box shattered, sending coins flying all over the place, even into the deep grass. Now he'd done it. He was going to have to search for every one of them. He got down on his hands and knees and crawled around gathering up all the coins he could see, but he didn't have anything to put them in. He went into the house to get something, but the only thing he could find was an old flowered pillow case. It wasn't exactly the right thing to hold a bunch of silvers, but it would have to do until he could find something better.

After putting the coins he'd gathered up into the bag, he looked around in the grass for others. He was sure there had to be some hiding, but the only way he was going to find them was to cut the tall grass.

He carried the heavy bag into the kitchen and put it on the table, and then he went to get the grass cutter. As soon as he saw it sitting on the lawn with the gas cap off, he remembered that's where this whole rigmarole started. The grass cutter wasn't going to run because it was out of gas. He shook his head in disgust. "I'm just like a squirrel in a damn treadmill. Ahead of myself and still half behind."

If he had a truck, he could use it to go get some gas, and then he could go down to the desert where the air was clean, and he wouldn't feel so lost.

He went and got his bag of money from the house and headed off down the street. But then he stopped. Where could he find a truck? It seemed like he'd seen some cars and trucks for sale on the other side of the big wide road when he was in Sarah's car. But how could he get to the other side? He didn't think he was fast enough to dodge all the cars. There must be another way to get over there. He decided to just start walking. He'd get there eventually.

The pillow bag with his silvers in it was heavy. Maybe if he put some of the coins in his pockets, his pants could help with the work. He loaded up both front pockets with coins, and then put some in his back pockets too. The bag was lighter now, but he worried that some of the coins in his pockets might fall out as he walked. That wouldn't be good. He didn't want to leave a trail like Hansel and Gretel. He laughed at that idea.

After a while, he came to a different part of the street where the big fast road was on one side, and there were dead grass fields and towering oil things on the other side. He hated those oil things. They made the air smell so thick he could hardly breathe it. Sometimes he thought that was the reason his brain was so foggy. Were they doing him in?

Holding his breath, he hurried past the fumes, and before long, he came to the place where the street went under the big road. He hurried through there, and saw that the other side was just like he hoped it would be. There were lots of cars and trucks lined up in rows, and some of them had for sale signs on them.

He held the heavy bag of coins tight against his chest with both arms and pressed on, waddling now, because the coins in his pockets were trying to pull his pants down. When he finally got to the first car lot, the only cars he saw were all shiny and nice. But he wasn't looking for nice cars; he was looking for a truck. If he didn't get a truck, how would he be able to carry all of his work things? Besides, those shiny cars were probably too pricey for him. It could be everything was too pricey, and he was just chasing the goose, but he wasn't about to give up without trying.

Hoping to find some less shiny cars, he walked further down the street. But after a while, he felt tired, and he sat down on the curb to rest. Some of the coins rolled out of his pocket onto the side of the road. When he bent over to get those, others fell out. Finally, he got them all picked up. He looked around and saw a grimy fellow over in the bushes eyeing him. He didn't like the looks of the guy and decided he'd better move on.

He got up and hurried away, but then he stopped and looked back. The guy had made him think of his father when he was out of work and things were so hard. The whole family could have easily ended up out on the street, instead of moving into that sad shack. Maybe he should go back and help that guy. A few coins weren't going to cure anyone's problems, but they might help a little bit.

He went back and took six of the silver dollars from his pockets. He held them out to the man. "Here, you can have these."

The guy looked up at him all blurry eyed and confused. "What? What'd ya want?"

Aaron held the coins closer to the man's face, and smelled the alcohol on his breath. "Here. Take these."

The man took the coins and stared at them like he wasn't sure what they were. Then his eyes got all wet. "Thanks, man. God bless you."

Aaron was about to give a lecture on not spending the money on booze, but he realized the man needed freedom to decide things for himself, no matter how bad off he was. That was the thing that made you a man, wasn't it? The thing that made you so you weren't like the animals.

He wished the man good luck and headed off to find his truck. He didn't get far before he thought of something and stopped again. Hadn't he'd known a sorry-looking fellow like that before? Some guy with a bad leg and a bad mouth. Who was that? And when did it happen? He searched his mind, trying to come up with a picture of who the man was. Then suddenly, he could see him quite clearly. They were in the desert, and he and the man were sitting in hot water. But then what happened? Was that man still down there, waiting?

It seemed like he was supposed to have gone back for that guy, but he hadn't done it. Why not? Was that one of the things he forgot to do?

And now, it seemed like there was somebody else that was missing down there. Somebody he should have found, but he didn't. Somebody who might be in really big trouble. It was a girl, wasn't it? It was that girl that loved him. They'd been in the hot water too. But then somebody came and took her, and it seemed like it was *his* fault. Was it his fault?

Now he knew he had to hurry and get a truck so he could get back down there and find out what happened to those people, and make everything right.

He went along and pretty soon he came to a place with lined-up cars that didn't look quite so new. And there were some trucks there too. He knew he'd probably have to bargain to get one of those trucks, and he'd have to stay strong. Those used car guys could twist your arms real fast.

Sure enough, a slick-haired guy with big thick glasses was coming straight at him. "How do ya do, sir? Lookin' for a good car?"

The way the guy was staring at his bag of coins with his big magnified eyes made Aaron feel like a sitting duck. Maybe he'd better get moving before he got roped into something he didn't really want.

The guy put on a big smile and waved his hand toward the cars. "You know, you look like a Caddie sort of man. Am I right, or am I right?"

"Uh, no. Not really."

The guy squinted. "Okay, then how 'bout you tell me what you're lookin' for."

Aaron could feel the rope being thrown. He stood tall and spread his feet so he'd have better support. "What I need is a truck."

"A truck, you say?" The guy pulled at his chin as if he was pulling on a beard that he didn't have. "What kinda truck ya lookin' for?"

"Well, I'd mostly like to have a Chevy."

The guy's eyes lit up. "Well now . . . I think I might have just the ticket for you."

"I don't need a ticket. I need a truck."

"Haha. You're a funny guy. I like that." He took Aaron's arm. "Come with me. I'll show ya what I've got."

Aaron shook the man's arm lose, but he followed along. He might as well see what was there, before he tried somewhere else.

They went way out to the back of the lot where there were weeds growing everywhere, and the cars and trucks were even dirtier than the ones out front. That made Aaron suspicious. Was this guy trying to sell him a dog? He prepared to make himself tough, but then he saw the faded blue pickup. He gasped. "Where'd you get that?"

"Get what?"

"That blue Chevy." He pointed. "That's mine."

"Yours? Is that right?"

"Well, it was, before I lost it. How did it get here?"

Aaron hitched his pants up and hurried through the weeds to take a closer look. The paint was more faded than he remembered, and it was kind of scuffed up in places, but not too bad. He walked completely around the truck and saw that it didn't have any really bad dents, and none of the windows were broken. That was good. They'd taken pretty good care of it. The main question was, did it still work? He turned to the slicked-haired guy and said, "Can we start it up?"

For a second, the guy looked unsure, but then he put on a big smile. "Sure, we can. Just a sec. I'll go get the key."

Aaron couldn't believe he'd actually found his old truck. It was like some kind of a miracle. Now, he could go down to the desert and find his people and do what he should've done before.

He set his bag of coins in the truck bed and wiped the dust off the side window with his sleeve so he could see inside. The bench seat wasn't in very good shape. The stuffing was coming out in some places, but so what? The truck wasn't as new as it once was. He'd just have to put a blanket over the tears.

The man came back with the keys and got in. "Now, you gotta know, this truck's been sitting here awhile, just . . . uh . . . waitin' for you. It could take a little coaxing to get it started."

"Okay, well, I know how that goes."

The man turned the key, but the truck just sputtered.

Aaron remembered he'd just heard that sound. Where was that? He tried to think, and then he realized it was that mower thing. And the problem with the mower thing was that it was out of gas. So maybe the same thing was wrong with his truck.

He told the guy with the big eyes to move over, so he could try it himself. "I've got to see how it feels."

He got in and turned the key and pumped the gas, and it sounded for a second like it was going to hold, but then it didn't. What did it mean? "Are you sure it's a good one?"

"Are you kidding? It's a real good one. It's your good old truck, isn't it?"

"That's right, but it doesn't sound right."

"Well, like I said. It's been sitting awhile."

"How long?"

"I don't know. When did you lose it?"

"Um, maybe a year. I think. Or longer. Maybe a real long time. Anyway, I'm not going to do it, if it won't start."

"Oh, it'll start. Just let me get my guy out here. Let's start doing the paperwork, while he gets it going."

Aaron hesitated. It felt like things were moving too fast.

The guy took hold of Aaron's arm. "Look, mister, if you don't grab this little jewel right now, someone is sure to grab it. You better act fast, or you'll lose your own truck all over again."

"Well, all right," said Aaron, "but I'm not going to do it if it won't go. That's all there is to it."

"Sure. Sure. No problem. We'll get 'er goin'. Don't you worry about that."

Aaron followed the man to some kind of trailer thing, and when they got inside the guy spoke to a greasy looking kid who had his feet up on the desk. "Go out there and get that blue Chevy truck going. Jump it, or whatever you have to."

The kid nodded and raised his eyebrows at the seller guy like they were having a secret. Then the kid looked at Aaron and grinned. That made Aaron feel like something was going on. Did they think he was a sucker? Maybe he should take his coins and go somewhere else. That's when he realized he didn't have his coins. Where in the hell were his coins? He looked all around the little room, but they weren't there. Did he set them some place, or had these guys got a hold of them somehow? He squeezed his eyes shut and tried desperately to remember where he might have put them. Where was I? What was I doing?

It took him a minute, but then he remembered. Of course, they were out with the truck. That's what this whole thing was all about, wasn't it? He had to go back to the truck.

When he opened his eyes, the two guys were staring at him like he was some kind of nut. He didn't care, he had to go get his coins. He hurried out the door, and the two guys came following after.

The seller guy said, "What's going on, sir? Is there something the matter?"

"I need to go back to my truck. Where is it?"

"It's right over there."

They all went together, and Aaron frantically looked for his coins. He looked inside the truck and outside the truck. Finally, he saw the flowered bag in the back, exactly where he'd put it. He grabbed the bag and held it tight against his chest.

The seller guy said, "Whatcha got in that old pillowcase?"

"Uh . . . that's my business."

The man shrugged. "Sure. I was just . . . uh, wonderin'. So, what do you say? Should we get go back inside and do that paperwork?"

By now, Aaron was feeling worn out, but he knew he needed his truck to get down to the desert, so he had to keep going. They went back to the trailer, and the man got some papers out of a drawer. He put them on his desk, and sat down. "So, what's your offer?"

Aaron stayed standing. "What?"

"I mean, how much have you got to spend on that fine truck?"

"Uh . . . I don't know . . . exactly."

"Well, if you don't, who does?" The guy smirked.

Aaron wished he had counted his coins before he got there. Now, he was going to have to do it in front of the guy, and he'd probably try to take everything he had. He decided to turn the tables. "Uh, how much will you take?"

The man said, "How 'bout we see how much you've got there, and then I'll see if I can make you a deal. I could be wasting my time, if you don't have enough."

"I could be wasting my time, too," Aaron said. "Maybe I'll just go somewhere else."

"And what about your truck? You think you're ever gonna find it again?"

No, Aaron didn't think he'd find it again, so he wasn't sure what to do. He was still trying to decide when he saw the Chevy truck pull up in front of the window. So it was going. That made a difference, but he still wanted to bargain. "Can you clean it up?"

"You bet we can." The guy got up and yelled out the door, "Hey, kid, wash that truck up. And hurry!"

Aaron knew he was going to have to make up his mind, or forget it. He sat down with the bag of coins on his lap. When he took out a few of them out and set them on the desk, the guys magnified eyes got even bigger than before. It told Aaron he had to be careful. If he took out all his coins, he probably wouldn't have any left when the whole thing was over.

He took out a couple of handfuls and put them on the table, but that was no way to count. He was going to have to do it better.

The guy leaned forward with his own idea. "How about we stack them up in tens, so we know what we've got?"

"Well . . . okay. That might work."

The guy reached over and made a stack, and said, "Here, make some more like this."

Aaron did what the man said, counting the stacks out loud. He got to twelve, but the guy coughed, and Aaron lost track of where he was and had to start over.

The guy helped, and finally, between the two of them, they managed to stack up a lot of the coins.

Aaron said, "What about that? I think it's about right."

"You kidding me? You can't buy a nice truck like that for a few stacks of coins?"

"Well, how much do you want?"

The guy picked up a few of the coins and looked each one over carefully. "These are quite old, aren't they?"

"Yes, but that doesn't mean they're no good. In fact, I'm pretty sure they're worth a whole lot more than they're worth."

The guy said, "Well, it's still not enough."

Aaron said, "Okay, I'll give you two more stacks, but that's it." He counted them out and waited.

The guy stared at the coins for a minute. Then he took off his glasses, cleaned them on his dirty shirt, and then put them back on. He frowned.

"Well, seein' as how you want that truck so bad, I'll let you have it for what you've got."

"What I've got? I can't do that?"

"I mean, what you've got there on the desk."

Aaron was surprised. Maybe he'd judged the guy wrong. He hadn't even taken out all of his coins. He still had a quite few in the bag, and all the ones in his pockets.

Aaron stood up, ready to go get in his truck, but the guy said, "Wait a minute. You've gotta sign the contract."

"I do?"

"Yeah, right here." He pointed to a red X on the page.

Aaron signed it, being careful to make the writing clear. He didn't want the guy saying he couldn't read it. He stood up. "Is that it?"

"Not quite. I'm gonna need your name and your address right here. You know, to send you the title." He pointed to another place on the paper.

Aaron sat down again and filled in his name, and said, "Uh . . . I'm not quite sure about the other one."

The guy frowned. "You don't know where you live?"

"Well, I used to, but I don't think I've been there that long."

The guy looked down through his glasses, and said, "Hmmm . . . are you in the phone book?"

"I don't know. I might be."

"Well, let me look it up." The guy looked at Aaron's name, and then he grabbed a big book from behind the desk. He flipped through the pages and pointed to a number. "Is this it?

Aaron looked at it and shrugged.

"Well, do you live right over on the other side of the freeway?"

"Yep, I believe I do."

The guy wrote something on the page, and then said, "Are you alone over there?"

Aaron wasn't sure why he needed to know that. Was he trying to find out about Sarah. He decided to not answer.

"Hey bud, I asked you if anyone lives with you over there?"

"No, they don't. I live by myself."

"Well, okay then. That's good. I guess we're all set."

Aaron stood up. "I'm glad to hear it. I'm getting good and tired of all this."

The guy smirked. "Yeah, I bet you are. Let's go see if that kid's got your truck ready for ya."

They went outside, and Aaron saw that the truck wasn't exactly shiny, but it was clean. The engine was chugging a bit, but it was running, so that was good. Maybe everything would be all right.

He climbed in, put the truck in gear, and drove away from the car lot. It felt wonderful to be in the driver's seat again. Now, he could go wherever he wanted to go. But then he looked back and saw a cloud of black smoke chasing after him. "Oh no. Is that me?"

Chapter 37

When the black smoke kept coming out of the truck, Aaron knew he should turn around and go get his money back, but he couldn't make himself do it. The freedom the truck gave him was too strong. He couldn't give it up now, not when he knew how much joy he'd lose. It was going to take him down to the desert, and that's where he needed to be.

After a few dead-ends, he finally found his way onto the freeway, feeling like a sneaky boy driving his dad's truck without any permission. But why should he feel sneaky? It was his own truck, wasn't it? He knew how to drive it just fine, even if the steering thing did feel a little hard. That heavy feeling it had was probably just because he wasn't as strong as he used to be. He'd have to do more driving and get that strength back.

The lanes on the freeway were wide open, which told him it wasn't too early, and it wasn't too late. Everyone had already gotten wherever they were going, which is exactly where he wanted them to be. Even though he had all the room in the world, he decided to stay in the slow lane while he made sure he remembered everything he was supposed to do; like pushing in the clutch and shifting at the same time. There was a grinding sound when he did it the first time, but that wasn't his fault. The stick thing was sticky. The second and the third time, he had to cram the stick into place. That worried him a bit, but at least he was getting up some speed. Now, all he had was one more shift, and he could forget about the shifting part and just drive until he got to the desert. He pressed the clutch, ground it into gear, and moved over to the fast lane.

Now, he was flying, and it felt great. Well, great, except for those lumpy coins he was sitting on. Why didn't he take those out of there before he got going?

He let off the gas and tried to get some of the coins out of his back pocket while he was still driving. The car behind him blasted its horn. It scared him, and he jerked the wheel and almost hit the center wall. He got himself straightened out, but now he was so nervous, he had to get back over in the slow lane and try to recover.

As he crept along, he wondered if he should be driving at all. Was he too far gone to do it? No. He wasn't that bad. He just needed to pay attention and not do anything stupid. If he wanted the coins out of his pockets, he should stop and do it. The thing was, he didn't want to stop.

As he continued to drive, he wondered why the truck was making that strange kind of chugging noise. Was there something wrong with it, or was it *him* doing something wrong again? He glanced in the rearview mirror and saw that the black smoke was even thicker than before. Oh no. Did it mean the truck was going to die? Couldn't it please just hold together until he got to the desert?

He decided the smoke might just be telling him that he needed to do the stick thing again. That made it chug a little less, so he decided to do it again, but that wound it up too high. He put it back where it was before, and now he was worn out.

Maybe he should just go home and forget about the desert for now. It wasn't so bad back there, was it? Yes, it was bad. It was boring and sad now that the kids didn't come to bounce very often anymore. If he stayed where he was, he was going to have to spend every day of his life waiting for something to happen. He hated that. It would be better to drive the truck off a cliff than to wither away in boredom. He should just keep going and see where it got him.

He went through the last part of the shifting thing again, and the truck picked up speed. That was good. Now he could get back into the fast line where he'd wanted to be in the first place. The cars honked as he crossed lanes, but he didn't care. Let 'em honk, if that's what they liked to do.

When he got settled into the traffic, he looked around to see where he was. But he wasn't sure. It seemed like the buildings on the sides of the freeway were getting thinner, and that meant he must be getting somewhere close to being out of town. The only problem was he was starting to feel a little dizzy. Maybe that black smoke was coming inside the truck and taking all the air. He tried to roll down the window, but it seemed stuck. He tried harder, and all of a sudden the truck was scraping against the center wall making a terrible screeching sound. Then, he screeched too when he tried to get off the wall and found out the truck wouldn't do it. The steering wheel had gotten so frozen up, it wouldn't move at all.

The only thing he could do was slam on the brakes. The truck jerked several times, and then came to a stop against the wall. He sat there shaking and wondering what the hell had happened. Did he do something wrong again, or had the truck just given up its ghost?

After he recovered a bit and wasn't shaking quite so bad, he looked around. There were cars and trucks roaring by really close, and not one of them stopped to help. "What's wrong with you?" he yelled, shaking his fist at them. "I'm stuck here in the middle of the road in a broken-down truck. Doesn't anyone care about anybody anymore?"

He sat there waiting, feeling the quake that came with every vehicle that went by. He thought sure somebody would eventually stop to help, but nobody did.

Finally, he gave up. He was going to have to find his own way out of the situation. He waited until he couldn't see any cars coming up from behind him, then he grabbed his bag of coins and got out. He hurried around to the back of the truck. His head was hurting now. It made it hard to think, but he knew he had to come up with something. He thought about running across the freeway, but he realized the first thing he had to do was get those damn coins out his pockets. If he didn't, he'd lose his pants halfway across.

He leaned against the concrete wall, and unloaded all of the coins into his bag. Now, maybe he could get across the lanes without showing off his bottom.

It felt safer behind the truck, so he stayed there for a bit, waiting for a gap between the cars. But it never came. He decided if he was going to get anywhere, he was going to have to walk along the dividing wall. Then, if the traffic ever died down, he could race across to an exit, and he'd already be part way home. There was no way he could go to the desert now. His truck was ruined again, just like before. The whole situation upset him so much, all he wanted to do was go home and crawl into bed. Then, maybe if he got feeling a little better, he could figure out another way to get to the desert, and hopefully, the lost people would still be there.

He walked as fast as he could, with cars and trucks screaming by on both sides of the concrete wall. They were kicking up so much dust it made his head spin. There was a bit of room where he was walking, but the cars were still close enough for him to feel the heat off their engines, and their gas fumes were making his head feel real funny. Was he going to pass out? And what would happen if he did that? Would he fall into the traffic and get killed? Would his body be left next to the wall forever, flattened and drying out like a damn run-over cat?

Maybe he should have stayed with his truck. It might have been safer there. He looked back, but he couldn't even see it now. How long had he been walking? Hours? It seemed like forever.

He stopped and sat on the wall to rest and watch the cars. It was like none of the drivers could see him. Why? Was he invisible? He held up his hand to check, and it seemed like he was still there. So why couldn't *they* see him? And why didn't they stop?

After staring at the blur of cars for a long time, his mind got blurry, and he wasn't sure how he'd gotten himself where he was. It seemed like he'd been driving, and then his truck crashed, or something, and somebody got hurt. But who was it? He was pretty sure they needed his help, but he wasn't sure where they were, or how he was going to find them.

It wasn't doing any good to worry about that right now. He was in a bad place, sitting on a wall with all those cars flying by like he didn't exist. It made him feel like the whole world was against him. And now, he needed to pee. But how in the world was he going to do that?

He looked around for some place to do it, but there wasn't any place. He decided he didn't care if anyone saw him, he wasn't going to stand there and pee his pants like a little boy. They weren't looking at him anyway. Probably if he crouched a little bit and faced the wall, nobody would even notice.

He had barely started to pee when he heard a siren. When he looked up, he saw red lights coming toward him. Oh no. Why did they come, just when he didn't want them to come? Would they arrest him for doing it out there on the freeway? He should have tried to hold it back, but how could he hold it? He was too tired and too cold and too scared to hold anything.

The white police car with the twirling lights stopped just as he finished peeing. A tall officer in a brown shirt and a brown hat got out and came and stood in front of him. He had his hand on his hip just above his gun. "What in the hell do you think you're doing?"

Aaron looked at the ground and said, "I'm sorry. I couldn't hold it anymore. I've been out here too long?"

"Well, what are you doing out here in the first place? Are you crazy?"

"Uh . . . I don't know. Maybe."

"What do you mean, you don't know?"

The officer looked mad. Aaron was sure he was going to be arrested, but what had he done to deserve that? He was just lost and cold and hungry. Suddenly, he couldn't hold himself together anymore. He slid off the wall onto the ground and started sobbing. "Please sir, can't you just take me home?"

The highway man helped him up. Aaron grabbed his bag of coins and the officer took him to his car and put him in the back seat in a cage.

Then the officer stood by the door and said, "So, where is it you live?" His voice was softer now, and quite a bit kinder.

"Back there. You know, back up there by the—"

"By the what?"

"The . . . mountain."

"Which mountain would that be, sir?"

"I don't know. I just don't know, and I don't know why I don't know!" He was crying again, and he didn't want to be crying. It made him feel like a baby, but he couldn't stop. He didn't know where he lived, and he didn't know if he ever did know. The only place he remembered was the one place where he lived with Laura, but that wasn't right.

The man said, "Well, how about we get off this freeway, and then we can talk about it."

"Yes. That would be good. I'd like to get out from under all these cars. I need that."

The policeman got in the front seat of the car and drove along talking to some squawky voice. Aaron twisted the top of his bag of coins and put the bag on his lap so he wouldn't lose it.

He tried to listened to the conversation between the policeman and the squawking voice upfront, but he couldn't understand a damn thing. Were they talking about taking him to jail? He already felt like he was in jail, what with the car's black bars all around.

The longer they drove, and the more he had to listen to the squawking voice, the more anxious Aaron got. He looked for the door handle, hoping he could jump out and run as soon as they got to a safer place. But there was no door handle. How in the world was he ever going to get out, if there wasn't a door handle?

He was starting to panic, but then they got off the big highway and left the flying cars behind. A little bit later, they pulled into a nice park with quite a few trees. The officer got out of the front and opened the back door and gave Aaron a bottle of water. Then, he took out a notepad, and said, "So, what's your name, sir?"

"Aaron. My name's Aaron." He gulped some of the water.

"And, your last name?"

"Uh . . . you can just call me Aaron." No use giving him all the answers.

"Do you happen to have your wallet on you, Aaron? That might help us."

Aaron patted his pockets, but there was nothing there. "I don't seem to have it."

"It's not in that bag you're holding onto so tight?"

"No. That's just got, uh, my other stuff. Nothing, really." He wasn't sure why he didn't want the man to know about his coins. But that other guy had taken most of what he had, and he didn't want to lose anymore. That was the only money he had, as far as he could remember.

The officer scratched his head. "Well, is there someone we can call to help us out here?"

"You can call Sarah. I mean, no, don't call her. She'll be mad."

"She's your . . . wife?"

"No. No. She's nobody. I just got . . . confused." If he could only remember where he lived, then Sarah wouldn't need to know anything about anything. He could just go home, get some rest, wake up, and pretend like he'd been there the whole time. It would be easy to forget what happened. In fact, he already wasn't sure what *had* happened.

The policeman lifted his hand and said, "Well, sir. We've got to do something. We can't just sit here all day. Are you hungry?"

"Yes. Yes. I'm very hungry. Maybe if we can eat something, we can think better."

"Okay, then, Aaron. We'll do that."

The man didn't ask any more questions. He just closed Aaron's door and then drove for a while and then stopped. It looked like they were at some kind of eating place. The man led Aaron inside, and they sat down at a table. A friendly girl came over. She smiled and said, "What can I get you gentlemen?"

Aaron didn't know what to get, so he looked at the officer and shrugged.

"How about we get two cheeseburgers, some French fries, and—" He looked over at Aaron. "What do you want to drink?"

Aaron tried to think. "Uh, I'm not sure. Milk?"

"*Milk*? Or a milkshake?"

"Sure, a milkshake would be good. I haven't had one in about a hundred years."

"Chocolate?"

"Sure. Why not?"

The officer smiled at the girl and said, " A chocolate milkshake for him, and I'll have some coffee."

While they waited for their food, the officer asked friendly questions, like how long had he been rattling around this old world?

Aaron said, "Not as long as I want to."

The officer laughed. "Well, that makes sense. I guess the same is true for me." He squinted one eye, and said, "I'm thinking you're what, about seventy-five? Seventy-six? I'm pretty good at telling a person's age."

"You're not bad."

The guy eyed him, and said, "Hmmm . . ."

"What do mean by that?"

"Just wonderin'."

"What?"

"If I were to ask you what year it is, what would you say?"

"I don't know. Does it matter?"

"Not really."

Aaron turned it around. "What year would you say it is?"

The guy laughed. "Good one. You're quick."

Aaron laughed too and then got serious. "You're a nice man. Thank you for saving me. I don't know what I would have done without you."

The girl came with the food. Just smelling it made Aaron's mouth water. He ate fast, and slurped his milkshake. But then he realized he was making himself a pig. He said, "Sorry, I guess I was hungry."

"No problem. I'm hungry too. It was past time for my lunch."

When they finished eating and the girl had taken the dirty things away, the man looked at Aaron and said, "So, what are we going to do with you?"

"What do you mean?"

"Well, how are we going to get you home, if you don't know where home is?"

Aaron tried to think what to do. "Uh . . . maybe if we just drive, I can see if I see anything. Would that work?"

The man shrugged. "It might. Which way are we supposed to drive?"

That stumped Aaron, but then he thought of something. "Which way is the desert?"

"Which desert is that, Aaron?"

"Uh, the nice red one. With all the red rocks and everything."

"Well, that's mostly south, I'd say."

Aaron nodded. "Okay, then, go the other way."

"The other way?"

"Yes. Up past . . . uh, Moroni and all that."

"You mean past the Mormon temple?"

"Yes, up that way, only more."

"North?"

"Yes. That's right. North."
"Okay then. Let's do that."

Chapter 38

They headed back out to the police car, and this time Aaron got to sit up front where he could see better and didn't have to feel like a criminal going to jail. As they drove along, he looked from side-to-side, trying to spot anything that looked familiar. The problem was, he didn't know where he was, so he didn't know what was supposed to be there.

The officer looked over and said, "Anything?"

All Aaron could do was shrug and keep looking. They went a ways, and he was pretty sure he should be seeing something he liked, but he missed it, so he didn't say anything. He kept searching for familiar things, and then he spotted something he was sure he knew. It was the State Prison with its watching tower and its tall wire walls. He nodded toward it and said, "I'm glad you didn't put me in there."

The officer looked surprised. "You thought I might?"

"Well, I didn't know for sure." Aaron grinned to show he might just be joking.

They drove and drove until they got to a place where it was so busy along the sides of the freeway, Aaron wasn't sure if he'd ever been there before. There were cars parked everywhere, and different colored signs wanting you to buy this, and buy that. Either they'd gone crazy with the building, or it was just one more thing he'd forgotten.

It scared him. What if he'd forgotten where he lived, and he could never remember? Would they put him in jail and leave him there until he did? And if he never *could* remember, would they take him to that lost memory place where they took Miriam when *she* forgot everything?

He hated that thought, so he tried to think about something else, and then his mind went blank and everything became really quiet. He felt like he was floating. The road was stretched out before him like a ribbon, and he was floating above it, hardly feeling the bumps or the spin of the tires against the road or anything. It wasn't a bad feeling: it was restful and nice.

He looked out the side window and saw the world flying by, and that's when he realized they were close to the place where Sarah and Michael went to school. That meant they were close to the road that went up to the house where they all lived by the mountains. He pointed and was about to tell the officer to turn there, but then he knew it wasn't right. The children were gone, Laura was gone, and so was the house. If he ever forgot that, it would mean he'd forgotten everything, and then he'd be doomed.

The officer touched his arm and said, "So Aaron, tell me, what kind of work did you do?"

The question caught him off-guard and brought him back to where he was. "Oh, I'm just an old mud slinger."

"Really? What kind of mud did you sling?"

"You know, drywall mud. Walkin' on stilts, spottin' nails. All that stuff. I trained a lot of those guys."

"I see."

"What about you? What do you do?"

"Excuse me?"

"I mean, oh, that's right. You're doing it right now, aren't you?"

"Yes, I am. I've been doing this for quite some time now. I enjoy it . . . mostly." He got quiet, and then he said, "So, you been here your whole life, Aaron. I mean in Salt Lake?"

"Sure, pretty much. All except for the war. That's when I lived in India."

"Really? That sounds interesting."

"I loved it, but it was big, you know, the peaks and all that when you had to fly over into China. Sometimes, you didn't know if it was going to do it or not."

"If it was going to do what?"

"You know, if we were going to get the plane to get over it."

"That sounds scary."

"It was, but I was , you know, alive too. Like you are when it all matters, and you're not sure exactly what's going to happen."

The officer nodded. "Yes, I know about that. It's happened in this car a few times." The radio squawked something, and the officer picked up the thing and talked back, to somebody named Roger That."

Aaron wondered who that was, but he didn't ask.

The officer put the radio thing back on its clip and glanced at Aaron. "So what was going on over there?"

"Over where?"

"In India. I didn't hear about any war over there."

"You didn't?"

"Not really."

"Well, the Japs were there. They were trying to shoot us down, but that didn't matter. We did it anyhow. The Chinese needed gasoline, so we had to fly it across, and try to land. Anyway, if it wasn't all blown up. Sometimes we couldn't do it, so we used the parachutes."

"You dropped gasoline down in parachutes? That sounds dangerous."

"It really was. But the mountains were the biggest thing. You had to get over them, even with the clouds and the rain and the lightning, or whatever else was there to get you. If you couldn't do it, you couldn't do anything, and you might as well go home."

"Which mountains?"

"You know. The Himalayas. The biggest ones in the world."

"That's right. They are big. The mountain climbers like to go up there."

The radio squawked real loud. It sounded almost like a bird that was dying, and Aaron had to cover his ears with his hands to try to shut it out. When it was finished, he took his hands away, and the officer said, "So, that was World War II, right?"

"Yes. That's the one."

"I wonder why I never heard about that part of the war. I mean, we studied it in high school."

"Not very many people knew. It was a top secret. I couldn't even tell Laura what it was, until later. We could write some things, but some of it got blocked out, or we just knew we shouldn't do it."

"So, you were a pilot?"

"No. Mechanic. You know, I kept the planes up and watched over the stuff in the back when we were flying. We flew those C-47s. Great planes. They held a lot of stuff. And they were steady. And so loud inside, you couldn't hear yourself think. But it was exciting, and I liked it."

"I *bet* it was exciting."

Aaron nodded. "It really was. But nobody cares."

"No?"

"Well, not when you try to tell 'em. They act like they're listening, but then they get tired real fast, like they have someplace else to go. Even Michael didn't want to hear it. I thought he would, but he didn't."

"Who's Michael?"

"He's my boy, but he's not here anymore."

"I'm sorry. What happened?"

"He went away, and now he doesn't want to come home."

"He moved somewhere?"

"That's right. Out by . . . the big water, or whatever it is. Out by—"

"California?"

"Yes, that's it. I wish he could come over here sometimes, so we could be more, you know, like *we* are."

"What do you mean?"

Aaron shrugged. "You know. Take a nice drive, like this. Talk about things. Nobody does that anymore."

"Yeah. I guess not."

The officer stared out the front window, then looked at him like he wasn't sure if he should say what he wanted to say, but then he did. "You know, you remind me of my father."

That surprised Aaron. "I do?"

"Well, not so much physically. It's just that he's going the same way as you are."

"As me?"

"You know, forgetting things."

"That's not good."

"No, it's not. I was wondering if you could tell me what it's like, so I can know how to talk to him better. It's hard for him to talk to me."

Aaron wanted to help, but what could he say that the officer would understand? "I guess, it's kinda like . . . maybe like cotton. Like mushy mush when you try to find it. And then sometimes you don't even know what it is. That's the scary part. It's like the whole thing is just . . . gone, and you don't even know where you started."

"That must be really hard."

"Well, sometimes it's okay. Like when the colors get so strong, and the beauty gets so real, it makes me want to cry. I don't know why it does it like that, but it's the part that makes me want to stay there and never come out."

"I never would have considered that."

"Well, maybe it's not true. It's just that—"

"No, I can see how it could be like that. Like flying over those mountains, right?"

"Yes. That's it. Exactly."

"What is that experience? Can you describe it?"

"I'm not sure. It's just . . . sometimes it gets really quiet, and if I'm not afraid, I can see things real bright."

The officer looked at him and nodded. He was quiet for a minute, and then he said, "What else? What do you think a man like my father needs?"

Aaron stared at the tall yellow grass flying by next to the freeway and thought about how to answer. "I guess, the main thing is to understand. Nobody wants to be stupid or get locked up."

"And what if he takes off and gets lost?"

"Who?"

"My father. The one who's forgetting things."

"Well, if he's lost, he's probably trying to find something, or go some place and nobody will take him."

"Hmmm. That makes sense, but what if he takes off without asking anyone to take him? He could get hurt. I can't let that happen, can I?"

"Why can't he do what he wants to do? He's a big man, isn't he? He just wants his freedom sometimes, that's all."

The officer frowned. "It's not safe for him out in the world when he can't remember things. Is it? I mean, there's got to be a way to keep him from doing that."

"Why can't he do it? He's not going to hurt anything." The officer sounded like Sarah now, and the way he was going made Aaron mad. He yelled, "So, what are you going to do? Lock me up?"

"No. No. Of course not. I'm sorry, Aaron. I shouldn't have said anything."

Now Aaron felt bad. He shouldn't have yelled, but he couldn't call it back because he couldn't remember what he'd said. Hadn't they just been talking about something important? Something about when everything was okay? No, not that. It was the other side of it, how they wanted to lock everybody up just because they got lost sometimes and forgot a few things. He had to remember to never get lost. And even if he did, he had to be sure to not let anybody know that he was lost.

Would this man lock him up if he knew he couldn't remember? He seemed like a nice man, so maybe he wouldn't. They were driving all over the place and talking, like they were old friends. Maybe they were old friends, and he'd just forgotten. No, he'd remember something like that. Wouldn't he?

He was feeling really confused now, like he'd been thinking too hard, and now his brain was tired. He needed to rest. But how could he rest when he was riding in a strange car with a man he wasn't even sure he knew?

The officer touched his arm. "I want to thank you, Aaron. You've helped me understand why my father is always so angry."

"I have?"

"Yes. It's like you said, he just wants his freedom. When I try to take that away, he gets angry, even though I'm just trying to protect him. It's a hard one."

"Yes, it is hard."

They both got quiet, and Aaron started thinking about the problem of people not remembering things. What would happen if they all got put together? Would it help them to be with people who knew what it was like? He wasn't sure that was true. Maybe everybody would just sit there, trying to find words, and if nobody could find any words, there would just be dead silence.

The officer broke through his thoughts. "Well, I guess we'd better get back to the business at hand. Have you seen anything?"

"What kind of thing?"

"I mean, are we getting you any closer to home? Have you seen anything familiar?"

Aaron looked around. "Uh, I don't know. I mean, I forgot what we were doing."

"Yeah. Me too. Sorry. I shouldn't have distracted you. Anyway, we just passed the exit to downtown, you know, where that Angel Moroni is, on the Mormon temple, like you said."

"Oh, that's right. Moroni."

"You said we should go further north than that. So maybe you should start paying close attention and see if you recognize anything."

"Okay, I will."

They went a little further, and then he *did* see something he knew. It was that place where the whole side of the mountain had been scooped out, making it a big sore spot on his eyes. It was a sad and ugly place, but he was pretty sure it meant he was getting close to where his house was. He pointed. "I know that part. They've messed it all up."

"Yeah, they have, but at least it tells you where you are. Right?"

"I think so. It's probably just a little bit further."

"Okay, we'll take it slow, and you tell me when you see something else."

The thing started squawking again, and the officer talked to it, saying something about Beck Road, and I-15, and how he was going to call in his 10-20 later. The radio squawked back, and then kept quiet.

Not much farther on, Aaron saw something that he was sure he'd seen before. It was the place where he'd gone to get his truck. That's right. He was supposed to go to the desert, and he got his truck so he could go, but then it broke, and that's why he was here right now with this officer and why he wasn't in the desert. But he couldn't let the officer know about all that. He didn't know about the truck, and he might want him to go back and get it. But the damn truck wasn't any good. It was a dog, and it was a dirty dog that sold it to him. He was going to have to go back and get his money from that dirty dog, but maybe he should rest first because it was probably going to take a whole lot of yelling. At least the truck place had told him he was almost home. He pointed. "I think that's it. I was over there before I did anything else."

The officer drove off the freeway, and Aaron knew exactly where he was. He pointed to the tunnel where he'd gone through under the big freeway that morning. "Go under there, and then go a little further in the same way."

The officer did it, and then Aaron saw the oil things with their smokestacks. That told him he was getting closer. They went a little further, and then he saw his house. It was right there where it had been the whole time. He pointed at it. "That's it! That's it! That's my house. You can drop me off right here."

They pulled up in front of the house, and Aaron got out. But then he remembered his coins. When he leaned back in to grab those, the officer said, "Do you mind if I come in for a minute, Aaron? I'd like to make sure everything's okay."

Aaron wasn't so sure he wanted him to come in. If he did, he might find out about Sarah, and then he'd want to talk to Sarah, and then the cat would get out of its bag. He was about to say, no, but he realized it might make him seem suspicious and unfriendly, so he said, "Sure. Come on in. I'll get you a drink."

Chapter 39

Once they were inside the house, Aaron wanted to get his coins hidden so they'd be safe. He said, "Watch yourself. I'll be right back." He went to his bedroom and stashed the bag in the bottom drawer of his dresser.

When he came back the officer was holding his stack of little memory notes that he kept by the phone. "Hey. What are you doing with those?"

The officer quickly set them down. "Oh, sorry. Some of them were on the floor. I was picking them up."

That was strange. Why would they be on the floor? Had someone been messing around in there while he was gone?

The officer walked around the room and ended up by the piano. He looked at the family photographs, then pointed to one and said, "Is this your son Michael?"

"Yes, it is."

"He's quite a handsome man, isn't he?"

Aaron smirked. "Well, I would guess so. He looks like me."

The officer laughed. "You're right. He does." He pointed to another one. "And this is your daughter, Sarah?"

"How do you know her?"

"I just remember you mentioned her name."

"Yeah, well, she's not here." Aaron didn't like the officer getting all snoopy about Sarah. She was the one that held all his keys, and if those two ever got together, who knows what they'd hatch? He went over and turned her photograph face down on the piano.

The officer smiled. "Nice place you've got here, Aaron. Do you mind if I look around?"

"I guess so." The whole thing made Aaron nervous. Why did the man need to look around like he owned the place?

He went in the kitchen and turned back to face Aaron. "It really is a very nice house."

Aaron shrugged. "It is?"

"You don't like it?"

"Well . . . it's not as good as the one we had before, but then I built that one. Anyway, me and Laura did, and I—" He stopped talking. Why was he telling a stranger about all that? He didn't need to know about that house or about Laura. He didn't really need to know anything, did he?

Aaron went to the kitchen window and stared out. He kept his mouth closed tight to make sure he didn't reveal anything else.

The officer came and stood next to him. "Oh, you have a trampoline."

"That's right. I do."

"You jump on that thing?"

"Sure, I do. The kids jump. I jump. Everyone jumps."

"The kids?"

"Yeah. The whole kit and caboodle. I'm the favorite kid on the block."

"I bet you are. You like having them around?"

"Sure I do. Kids are beautiful. The freest ones in the whole world."

"Yes. They are, aren't they? But do their parents know they come here to jump?"

Aaron put on his guard. "Why do you want to know that?"

The officer shrugged. "Just seems like it could get a little, uh, wild out there with no supervision."

Aaron growled. "There's nothing wrong with them. Leave 'em alone."

The officer stepped back. "No, no. You've got me all wrong. I was just imagining them flying every which way. Wouldn't want anyone to fall off and get hurt, would we?"

Aaron shook his head in disgust. "We're not as dumb as you think. We know how to do it."

"Yeah. I guess you do. Sorry." The officer walked around the kitchen and then turned and faced Aaron again. "So, Mr. Young. I was just wondering. Do you have anyone you can call if you ever need anything?"

"I don't need anything." Aaron went to the counter and got an apple from the bowl and bit into it. Then he threw one to the officer.

The officer was quick and caught it before it hit him. "Well, it's good to have someone you can call, isn't it? Just in case. Like the song says, everybody needs somebody."

"Don't worry. I've got somebody."

"Sarah?"

"Sure. Why not?"

"I'd like to meet Sarah. I bet she's nice."

"Nice enough, but she doesn't need a boyfriend."

The officer chuckled and shook his head. "Well, I'm not looking for a girl. I don't think my wife would like that." He held up his hand. "Look, Aaron. I'll be straight with you. I'm not trying to pry into your business.

I like you. You're a good man, and I just want to be sure you have somebody you can call if you need anything. That's all. Is Sarah someone like that?"

Aaron relaxed a little and nodded. "Yes, she is. And I've got Sam and Annie too. They take good care of me."

"Okay, but just in case, I want you to have this." He took a little paper out of his shirt pocket, wrote something on it, then held it out. "This is my card. It has my phone number at work. Right here." He pointed. "And I've written my home number on the back." He showed Aaron the back of the card and handed it to him. "You keep this handy. Okay?"

"Okay. I can do that." Aaron turned the card over in his hands, trying to read the small print. He pointed to the front. "Is that your name?"

"That's right. Lieutenant John Howard. I guess I never told you that, did I? Sorry."

"That's okay. I probably wouldn't have remembered anyway."

"And you're Aaron Young. Right?"

"Sure. That's what I said, didn't I?"

"Well, no. You didn't say, but I saw it on one of your little notes by the phone."

"You did? Why were you snooping in those?"

The officer let out a sigh. "Well, I guess it's time for me to get back to work. They're probably wondering where I am."

"I guess so. You've been here . . . quite long."

The officer headed for the front door with Aaron right behind him. When they were outside, they shook hands and the officer said, "I've enjoyed talking with you, Aaron. I really have. Thank you."

Aaron nodded. "I've enjoyed it too, uh, what was your name again?"

"John. John Howard. It's right there on the card."

"That's right. Well, see you later . . . alligator."

The officer chuckled and Aaron chuckled too, even though he was already feeling sad about the officer leaving. It seemed like they'd had some nice time together, traveling around and talking. He didn't get a chance to do that very often.

As he watched the man walk out to the street, he felt like he was losing a friend. He called out. "Don't forget to write."

The officer waved. "I won't. Bye Aaron."

"Bye."

Aaron went back in the house and closed the door. He looked around for a safe place to put the officer's little name card and decided to put it in his pocket. That way, he'd have it no matter where he was.

He went to the kitchen for a glass of water. He was just finishing it off when he heard a knock on the door. He hurried to open it, thinking the officer had forgotten something and come back. But it wasn't him. It was Sarah, and she had that look on her face that said she knew something about something, and she didn't like it.

Aaron hurried back into the kitchen, trying to get away from her, but she followed and said, "I met your friend."

"Uh . . . what friend?"

"You know. Your Highway Patrol friend."

Aaron shrugged and pretended like he didn't know. "I'm not sure what you're talking about."

"Dad! I've been calling you all day. When you didn't answer, I decided I'd better leave work and come see what was wrong. Luckily, I got here just in time to meet your friend."

"I don't have any friends, and I don't know what you're saying."

"Well, he knows you. He said you were out on the freeway by the middle divider, peeing on the wall."

"He said that?"

"Yes, he did. What in the world were you doing out there?"

"Maybe you'd better go ask him."

"I'm not asking him. I'm asking you. How did you even get out there? There's so much traffic? You could've been killed, Daddy. Don't you know that?"

Aaron could see she was as mad as a hornet. It made him feel betrayed. He thought the man was his friend, but he must have been faking the whole time. And now that he'd spilled the beans, Sarah was standing there accusing him with her big green eyes and there was no way he could escape her.

She pulled out a kitchen chair. "Come on. Sit down. We need to talk."

Aaron folded his arms across his chest and stayed right where he was. "I don't need a talk."

"Please, Daddy, we have to figure out what to do. It's not safe for you to be running around like that. And how did you get that far away?"

Aaron zipped his mouth and looked past her.

She got an exasperated look on her face and did a little spin around the kitchen, then came back to him with a smile. "Maybe you just needed a little adventure, huh? Something to break the boredom? Something to cause a little stir?"

He waited to see if the smile was real or not. Maybe she was just trying to trap him.

She came closer, and he saw teas in her eyes. "You can trust me, Daddy. I want what you want, but I have to know you're safe. You can understand that, can't you?"

Her tears were real, and they were the thing that always did him in. Nothing was worth that. She was his daughter, and he was supposed to protect her and make her happy. But how was he supposed to do that? He didn't even know why she was crying.

He remembered she wanted him to sit down, so he did it, hoping that would help. She sat down too. She leaned forward and put her hands on his knees.

The sad look in her eyes was too much for him, so he looked away. "Okay, what do you want?"

"Just for you to be happy and safe. That's all."

Was that true? Is that really all she wanted? He could easily give her that. "I'm happy," he said. "I'm as happy as a . . . bird, or whatever it is."

"Are you sure?"

"You bet. Why wouldn't I be? I've got everything, don't I?" He hoped he'd made it sound true.

"But if you're so happy, why were you out on the freeway? Were you trying to go somewhere?"

He chewed on his thumbnail, not knowing if he should tell her.

"Is there some place you want me to take you?"

He shook his head. "I don't know if you can."

"Why not?"

"Because . . . I don't know if it's real." Now he was the one with tears in his eyes. He wiped them away and said, "I'm sorry. It hurts me."

"Hurts you? What hurts you?"

"You know. Those people I can't help."

"What people? I don't understand."

"I can't remember who they are. I just know they're waiting. And they need me."

Sarah took his hand in hers. "I wish I knew what you meant, Daddy. If I did, maybe I could help."

"It's down in the desert. That's all I know."

She seemed unsure. "Are you talking about your property down there?"

"Yes, that's it. That's where they are. Will you take me?"

"You're not talking about Mom, are you?"

"Who?"

"Laura. Your wife, Laura."

"She's gone, Sarah. It's hard, but you've got to live with that."

She looked away and sighed. Then she looked back at him. "I know that, Daddy. It is hard. But I was just trying to figure out who you meant by 'your people.'"

"What people?"

Sarah sat back and let out another big sigh, the same kind of sigh as that other man did. Why was everyone always sighing at him all the time? "What's wrong with you, Sarah?"

She wagged her head. "Nothing's wrong, Daddy. We're good." She shrugged. "I guess." She laughed. "Hey, how about let's go up to my house and fix something to eat?"

"Right now?"

"Sure. Why not?"

"I don't know. I thought we were going somewhere. Weren't we?"

"Yes, well, that can wait until tomorrow."

Chapter 40

It seemed like a day had gone by, or maybe it was a week, and then when he was just out of bed, Sarah showed up at the door with a tall man wearing a brown shirt and a badge with some kind of star on it. For some reason, the man seemed familiar. When they got in the house, the man smiled and shook his hand. "Hello, Mr. Young. How've you been since I last saw you?"

The words told Aaron he was supposed to know the man, but he didn't think he did. Maybe he was Sarah's date, but they didn't act like dates. The way their eyes went back and forth made them look like a couple of schemers. That told him, he'd better keep on his guard.

Sarah said they should sit down. The man sat on the couch with Sarah, but Aaron stayed by the door, thinking he might need a fast exit.

Sarah looked over at him. "They found that truck of yours, Dad."

"What truck?" He tried to think if he had a truck. It seemed like he had one once, but then he didn't. Maybe it was the one that went bad in the desert. Were they going to take him down there to get it? That would be nice. He'd been wanting to go to the desert.

"Do you know what I'm saying, Dad?"

"Uh, not really. Why don't you tell me."

"We're talking about that truck you bought and left on the freeway."

Did he do that? He remembered something about driving a truck, and maybe leaving it somewhere, but that's because it wouldn't go. He decided he'd better play dumb, or Sarah would try to make a molehill out of the whole thing. "Uh, why would I do that?"

He went and sat in the chair across from the couch. He crossed his legs and acted as innocent as he could.

"That's a good question. Why would you do that?" Sarah looked at the man like she needed his help.

Now, Aaron thought maybe he *did* recognize the man in the brown shirt from somewhere, but he wasn't sure where it happened, and he wasn't sure if they were friends or not, but he seemed pretty nice.

The man smiled like he'd read his thoughts. "I rescued you from the middle of the freeway and brought you home. Do you remember that?"

"Uh, not exactly." That's what he said, but maybe he did remember something about driving around, and all that.

"Well, I took you out of there, and we went and had a nice lunch. You had a chocolate milkshake. You remember that, don't you? You said it was the first one you'd had in a long time."

"That's true. I never really liked milkshakes all that much. That kind of sugary thing will kill ya."

The man looked at Sarah, and they both smiled.

Sarah said, "Dad, do you remember buying that truck?"

"I might. I did have a truck once, but it was no good."

"You bought it just across the freeway. A few blocks from here. At that used car place? Do you remember doing that?"

"A used car place? Do they sell trucks too?"

"Yes, they do. They said you bought the truck, and your name is on the title. How did you buy it? I mean, where did you get the money?"

That's when he remembered everything. That old shyster took his silvers. He should have gone back and got his silvers when the truck died. "Where was it?"

"Where was what?"

"That truck? I've got to take it back and get my silvers."

"Your silvers? Oh no, are you saying you spent your silver dollars on that truck?"

Now, she was shaking her head and looking at him like he was some kind of dumbbell. But all he did was get a truck. How could he know it was no good? Anyway, he didn't want to talk about it, he just wanted to go get his silvers before the man had them all spent.

"Dad, did you spend *all* your silver dollars on that truck just to leave it on the freeway?"

So what if he did? It wasn't his fault. It was that old cheater's fault. Besides, the silvers belonged to him, didn't they? He could spend them, if he wanted to. Even if he made a mistake, it was his right. Who could stop him? Besides—

Words were shooting around in his head, but he didn't want them to come flying out. Sarah would just turn them upside down and throw them back at him in a way he couldn't catch. He didn't need that. What he needed was to go get his silvers.

He stood up and headed for the door, but Sarah came and grabbed his arm before he could get there. "Where are you going, Dad?"

"I've got to go get those silvers back."

She held his arm and looked at the man. "Do you think we can get his coins back? I mean, the guy obviously took advantage of my father. He had to know something was wrong with him."

Aaron jumped on her. "What do you mean, something's wrong with me? What are you saying?"

"I'm sorry. I just meant that you can't always remember things."

"Well, so what? I remember he stole my silvers, and I'm gonna go get 'em." He tried to get loose, but Sarah held tight.

The man stood up and came over to help. "Why don't you let me see what I can do, Mr. Young. I'll try to get your coins back."

That gave Aaron some hope. "You think you can do it?"

"I'll do my best."

Sarah and the man made some kind of secret with their eyes, and then the man said, "You two have some things to work out, and you don't really need me here to do it. I think I'll be going."

Aaron reached out toward the man. "But what about my silvers?"

"I'll check the situation out, Mr. Young, and let you know what happens." The man looked at Sarah. "I'll give you a call, and if you need me, you've got my card."

Sarah nodded and opened the door for him. Aaron stood in the door and watched as the man went out and got into a police car.

"What's going on?" Aaron said. "What's that policeman doing here? Is someone going to be arrested?"

"He just came to tell you about your truck."

Sarah pulled him inside and closed the door. "Let's go in the kitchen and get something cold to drink. We need to have a conversation."

"About what?"

"Come on. Let's get something to drink first."

They went in the kitchen, and Sarah poured each of them a glass of orange juice. They sat down at the kitchen table to drink it.

When their glasses were half-gone, Sarah leaned forward in the way that always meant something was coming. He tried to duck it, but it came anyway.

"Dad, I think we need to make some changes."

He sat up straight. "Changes? What kind of changes?"

"Well, I think you're rattling around here too much on your own. Don't you get lonely?"

"Not really." He thought about it. "Well, maybe sometimes."

"I've been thinking you should move in with us."

"I'm okay where I am."

"Maybe so, but wouldn't it be more fun if you came and lived with us? We could sell this house and—"

"No! This is my place. I don't want to sell it."

"But it's not like the nice house you built with Mom. This is just a house. You don't even like it that much, do you?"

"What do you mean, I don't like it? I've been here the whole time, haven't I? I've got my stuff here."

"There's plenty of room for you and your stuff at my house. It would be nice. And the kids would love it."

"No!" Aaron jumped up and spilled his orange juice down the front of his shirt. "Now, look what you've done." He ripped off the shirt and threw it on the floor. He ran outside and grabbed the hose from where it was running in the garden. When Sarah showed up, he yelled, "Go away!" And then he gave her a good squirt in the face.

She tried to get closer, but he kept her away with more squirting.

"Fine. Fine," she yelled. "You can stay here, for now. But I can't leave it at that. I can't have you running off all the time. That police officer told me I've got to do something about it."

He gave her another squirt, this time full force in the chest.

"Dad, stop it! Now, put that down and come over here and talk to me."

He gave her a glare. "Why should I?"

"Because we've got to figure this out. I wish I could quit my job and stay home with you, but I can't. So what are we going to do with you?"

Now that she was asking him, instead of just telling him, he felt a little better. He took his finger off the hose and let the water flow down. "We don't need to do anything, Sarah. I'm fine. I really am."

"I know you think you're fine, and most of the time, you are. But sometimes you do crazy stuff."

"Like what?"

"Like buying that truck. You saved those coins your whole life, and then you just gave them away for a truck that wasn't worth a nickel. You're not happy about that, are you?"

He scowled and looked down at the water spilling on his bare feet.

Sarah stepped closer. "Listen, Dad, maybe if you had someone here with you during the day, it would work. You'd have someone to talk things over with before you do things. Wouldn't that be better?"

He nodded. "You mean, your mother?"

"What do you mean?"

"Like we used to talk things over."

"Yes. If only she was still with us. She'd know what to do, and she'd be here with you all the time. We need to do something like that."

"Like what?"

"You know. Get somebody to be with you. So you don't have to be alone while I'm at work and the kids are at school. Wouldn't that be nice?"

He shook his head. "I don't think I need it."

"Well, we could at least try it, couldn't we?"

She came and took the hose from him. "Come on, let's turn this off and go back inside. I've got to dry off. You drenched me, you little rascal." She gave him a quick squirt and laughed. "Now you're wet too, and we both need to dry off."

He grabbed the hose ready to make a good old water fight of it, but she ran away and turned the water off. When she came back, she took his arm in hers. "Come on, Daddy. I want to talk to you inside."

They went in the house and sat at the table again. Sarah looked him in the eye and smiled. "You know, I was going to talk to you about something else."

"Like what?"

"Kevin and I were thinking of taking the kids on a little vacation before they go back to school. Maybe up to Yellowstone, or something. Do you think they'd like that?"

"Sure, they would. That's what we did, didn't we?"

She nodded. "Yes, we did. It was a lot of fun, with Old Faithful and the bears and everything."

"I love those bears."

"Me too. Anyway, I was thinking that might be a good time for us to try out having someone here with you. You know, in case you need anything while we're gone."

"I don't think I need anything."

"I meant, company. Someone to talk to and get your groceries. Whatever you need."

"I don't need any of that. I've got my garden."

"Well your garden's coming to an end for the year, Daddy. You'll need food."

He didn't like it, but he knew he had to ask. "How long will you be gone?"

"Just a week or so."

It made him nervous to think about Sarah being gone for so long, but what could he do? If she needed a vacation, she should do it. "Don't worry, honey. I can take it."

"I know, but I'd feel better if I knew you had someone here . . . you know, just in case. How about if I check around? If there's someone who lives close by, maybe it won't be too expensive."

"Well, just so long as you don't try to pull any strings without me."

"I'd never do that, Daddy. You know that. I'll let you know what I find out."

Chapter 41

Aaron sat in front of the piano trying to remember a song he used to know. It went something like "some chanting even . . . you'll be finding strangers . . . you'll be seeing . . ." How did it go?

He ran his fingers lightly across the keys, feeling their cool smoothness, then he put his hands where he thought they should go and started to play. It sounded wrong, so he moved his fingers to a different place and tried again. After a few more adjustments, the notes seemed right, so he started to play the whole thing and sing along. "Some enchanting even, when you find a stranger. You may find a—"

Oh no! Was that the doorbell? Shoot, and just when he was about to find his song. He ignored the bell and went back to playing. "Now where was I? Some enchanting stranger, when you see a . . ." Dang, it was already gone.

He slammed the lid down and went and yanked open the front door. Sarah was standing there with some woman he didn't know. He thought maybe they were friends, but that didn't seem right. The woman was too old for that, and she seemed kind of frowny.

Sarah said, "Hi, Dad. Can we come in?"

He shrugged and stepped back. "Uh, yeah. Sure. Why not?"

As soon as they were inside, Sarah nodded toward the woman and said, "Dad, this is Mrs. Bodham."

He smirked. "Bottom?" He leaned to the side to see if she had a nice one. "Not too bad."

"Dad!"

"What?"

"Can't you just say hello?"

He stood up straight and said, "Ello," making it sound like an English parrot. An English parrot? Where did that come from?

The woman laughed and her eyes brightened up. "Hello, Mr. Young. It's very nice to meet you. How are you today?"

"Well, I'm pretty busy. How about you?"

"Fine. I'm really fine."

She didn't look fine, she looked nervous. But if that's what she wanted him to believe, it was okay with him. He shrugged. "So, what are we doin' here?"

Sarah nodded toward the woman again. "Mrs. *Bodham* is going to keep you company while we go up to Yellowstone."

"We're going to Yellowstone?"

"No. Not you. Me and Kevin are taking the kids up there for a little vacation before school starts." She smiled and nodded toward the woman. "Mrs. Bodham is going to keep you company while we're gone."

So that's what this was. Sarah was bringing him a babysitter. He took a step back. "I don't need a damn watcher hanging around all the time."

Sarah came and took his arm. "That's not what this is, Dad. She'll only be here during the day. To keep you company. You know, so you don't get too lonely. Remember how we talked about you rattling around this house too much by yourself. Well now, you won't have to do that."

He cocked his head and pretended to listen. "I'm pretty sure there's nothing rattling right now." He closed one eye and listened again. "Nope. Can't hear a thing. You can take her home. Bye now." He tried to herd them toward the door.

Sarah just laughed, and the woman laughed too.

They both seemed real happy, but he was tired of them gawking at him, so he went into the kitchen and tried to make himself busy with the broom.

Sarah and Mrs. Bumbum must have gone into his bedroom. He could hear them talking in there, and then he heard them laughing. What in the hell were they doing? He didn't need people poking around and laughing at his rooms. What was so funny anyhow?

He was about to go chase them out when they came into the kitchen.

Sarah pointed at various things and said, "And this is the kitchen."

Aaron said, "Of course, it's the kitchen. Anybody can see that. There's the . . . cooking thing over there, and the cooler thing. It's a kitchen."

They stared at him, so he stopped talking. Why were they looking at him like that? Did they think he was dumb? Well, he *wasn't* dumb. He knew exactly what was going on. Sarah was bringing in old Whatserbottom, and she expected him to just stand there and go along with it. It made him nervous thinking about a stranger being in his house all the time. She already had questions in her eyes that he knew he couldn't answer. So why was Sarah doing it? If she wanted him to be with somebody, why didn't she be with him herself? "Please, Sarah, if you think I need a watcher, why can't you do it?"

Sarah came over and took the broom away from him and leaned it against the wall. Then she gave him a big hug. "You know, I love being with you, Dad, but like I told you, we're going on this little vacation. It's been a long time since the kids had a vacation. And besides, I want them to get to know Kevin a little better. See how that works."

She looked at the timer on her wrist. "Oh dear. I'm late for work, I've got to get going, Dad." She turned to the woman. "Mrs. Bodham, why don't you two get to know each other today. I'll stop by after work, and you can give me a report."

The woman shrugged and gave Sarah a weak smile. "Okay. Well, I wish I had more experience with this sort of thing, but I guess I'll learn."

"You'll be fine," Sarah said. "Here's my card with my number.'" She pulled a little piece of paper out of her pocket and gave it to the woman. "You can call me at my office if you have any questions or concerns. Sorry, but I've got to go now. Bye." She gave Aaron another quick hug and hurried out the door.

So now, Sarah was gone, and he was stuck with a woman he didn't know. What was he supposed to do with her? Fix her dinner? He wasn't even sure he had any food in the house.

They stood still, looking at each other until finally the woman said, "Well, I guess I'll go out to my car and get my stuff."

"Sure. Sure. Go ahead."

Aaron followed the babysitter into the living room, and as soon as she was outside, he rushed over and locked the door. Then, he pressed himself flat against the wood of the door, so she couldn't see him from the window.

After a minute, the doorbell started ringing and the woman started yelling to let her in.

He didn't care how much she yelled, there was no way he was going to open that door. No use getting anything started when he didn't want it in the first place. He put his mouth up to the crack in the door and yelled, "Go home! Find your own things to do!"

She stopped banging, but then he heard her pleading. "Please, Mr. Young. I can't leave you alone. I need this job. You can understand that, can't you? My husband is sick. We need the money."

That made him feel bad. Maybe he *should* open the door. But why? He didn't want her there. She should go find her work someplace else.

No matter how long he kept her out there, she wouldn't leave. She just kept pleading in that sad, whiny voice, "Please, sir. I can't lose this job. You have to let me in."

Finally, he got so worn out from listening to her, he unlocked the door and swung it open. She fell into his arms, and everything she had went spilling across the floor.

He pushed her back and set her up straight and looked at the stuff on the floor "What's all that junk?"

"Uh . . . just some books and knitting and stuff. You know, things to keep me busy while I'm here." She got down on her hands and knees and picked everything up and put it all back in the big woven basket she'd brought.

He shrugged. "Fine. I've got my own stuff to do."

He left her on her knees and hurried through the kitchen and out the back door. Let her do whatever she was going to do. Maybe if he stayed outside, he could forget she was there.

The first thing he saw was his bouncer. That's what he needed. If he did some bouncing, maybe he could forget all the bad stuff that was going on. He climbed up and crawled out to the middle. After doing a few baby bounces, he pushed his feet hard into the rubber and went up high. He let out a little gasp as he felt the thrill of rising. That thrill always made him feel like a kid again. Like he was out somewhere doing fun stuff with his friends, and with Stevie. That's right. Stevie was always there. But where was Stevie now?

The thought scared him. He came to a quick stop, wondering what happened to Stevie. Was he gone? Did he get sick and die like Laura? Did he go the same way as Miriam? It scared him that he didn't know the answer. What if Stevie was alive, and he'd just forgotten him? No. He wouldn't do that. He would *never* forget Stevie. They were more than brothers, they were friends. But why wasn't he here?

He scrambled off the trampoline, knowing he had to go find out what happened to Stevie? But how could he do that? Did Sarah know where he was? She might know. He'd better go find her and ask.

As he headed across the grass to the house, he saw someone peering at him through the glass in the door. What was that old crumpled face doing in there? She wasn't supposed to be in his house. He put his nose against the window and pulled a mean face to try to scare her out. It didn't work. She just pulled her own mean face.

He did another one, this time squinting his eyes and showing his teeth like he was a ferocious lion.

She did the same thing back, and then she yanked the door open so fast he almost fell in on his face.

He caught himself and yelled, "What'd you do that for?"

"Turnabout's fair play." She laughed. "Anyway, I thought we were playing a game."

"A game?"

"Well, you're the one that started making faces."

"I was just . . ." Suddenly, he felt really hot, and he wasn't sure what they were doing. He pulled off his shirt and went to the kitchen sink and splashed cold water on his face and chest, trying to cool down. Why was he so damn hot?

When he turned around, the woman was staring at him.

"What?" he said.

"Well, you made a big water mess there, didn't you? It would be nice if you'd clean it up."

He looked at the floor where she was pointing and shrugged. "How'd that get there?"

"Hmm," she said. "So that's how it's going to be, huh?" She got that frown back on her face. "Listen, Mr. Young. I think we can be friends. Don't you?"

"I don't know. Who are you?"

"You really don't know?"

He shrugged. "If you don't want to tell me, I guess it's none of my business."

"I'm Mrs. Bodham. Don't you remember? Your daughter, Sarah, introduced us."

"Sure, I remember that. But she didn't say why you're here."

"She said I'm to take care of things while she's gone. She said you have to listen to me and do whatever I say."

He wasn't so sure that was true. Why should he have to listen to this woman when he didn't even know who she was? He decided to get away from her as far as he could. He turned and dashed into the bathroom and locked the door. He'd just stay in there until she went home.

There wasn't much to do in a bathroom, so he fiddled around, combing his hair, brushing his teeth, pushing his curly white eyebrows up and then back down. Then he realized something had happened to his hair. It had turned white, and he didn't even know it. He looked closer, turning his head right and left. That's when he saw that the hair in the back was still brown. It was like it was hiding back there, while the white hair was in front, trying to make him look old. But he wasn't old. In fact, he felt younger than ever. He decided he'd go with the brown part of his hair, and let the white part do whatever it was going to do.

He was tired of looking at the old man in the mirror. Besides, what was he doing in the there anyway? He didn't need to use the bathroom, so he might as well go out.

When he opened the door and stepped out into the living room, he saw that woman lying on the couch with her nose in a book. She had her big dirty shoes on his couch.

"Get those off!" he yelled.

"What? Get what off?"

"Those shoes. Didn't your mother teach you anything?"

"Oh, sorry." She sat up and took off her shoes. Then her face got sad. "Look, Aaron . . . can I call you that?"

"That's my name, isn't it? Don't wear it out."

"Well, Aaron. I'm really hoping we can be friends. I mean, as long as we're both going to be here together all day, we might as well try to get along. Isn't that right?"

He gave her a half shrug.

"Maybe we could do something together to pass the time. You know, like put a puzzle together or something. I could bring one."

"What kind of puzzle?"

"You know, a jigsaw puzzle. I think I have some nice landscapes at home. Wouldn't that be fun?"

He didn't know if it would be fun or not. It used to be fun. "Well, maybe."

"Okay. I'll bring one with me tomorrow." She let out a sigh. "So, what about right now? Is there something you want to do?"

"Not really."

"Well, why don't you tell me about yourself?"

"Why don't you tell me?"

"Well, okay. I can do that. Let's see . . . I'm married, but my husband got sick and lost his job recently, so that's why I'm working. The kids are gone. They moved out of state, and we don't see them very much. You know, except maybe at Thanksgiving, or Christmas."

He could see he was going to have to listen to her for a while, so he plopped down on the loveseat by the phone. "Who are we talking about?"

"My kids."

"Oh. I have kids too, you know. There's my daughter, Sarah. And there's . . . oh yeah, Mikey. He's somewhere else. I don't know who's got him."

"Do you miss him?"

"Sure, I do. I miss every last one of them. My girls. My Sarah. And all the rest of them."

"You have other daughters besides Sarah?"

"No, she's the only one. I think. Well, there's the other girl, and there's my Laura, but they're gone."

"Laura? That's your wife?"

"Yes, that's the one."

"Sarah told me about her. I'm sorry."

"What'd she tell you?" He didn't like people talking about Laura behind his back. They didn't understand anything about it.

"She said how young she was when she passed. It must've been really hard."

"Passed? What are we talking about?"

"Your wife, Laura."

"Laura? What about her?"

"I'm sorry. I was just—" The woman rubbed her forehead and looked away.

"What's wrong with you?" said Aaron. "Did you forget something?"

She looked surprised. "Uh, no. I didn't. I . . . actually, I guess I'm not so good at this."

"Why not?" He still wasn't sure what they were talking about, and he was getting tired of playing the guessing games. He pointed toward the bedroom. "Look, I'm going to go and lay down. You can let yourself out."

He went into the bedroom and closed the door. Now what? He opened a drawer. Nothing in there but socks. He took them all out, folded each sock over, and then put them all back. He went through some of the other drawers and refolded everything. When he was done with that, he sat on the bed and looked at the stuff that was on the little table. There was a picture of him and Laura in her wedding dress. It was a nice picture, but it had a big mess of black writing on it. Who did that?

He picked up the picture and ran his finger over Laura's white dress. His Laura. His love. That's what the words said, but she was gone now. He kissed her face on the picture and set it back down on the table. Then he picked up the blue binder that was there. He wasn't sure what was in it, but he thought maybe it was Laura's. He opened it up and discovered the whole thing was full of words, some of them typed, and some of them in squiggles he couldn't read very well. As he glanced through some of the typed ones, he saw Laura's name on the top of the pages. That told him the words were Laura's words just like he thought. He sat on the bed and looked for something that was short that he might be able to understand. There were some words about the moon. That might be good.

This Lonely Moon
by Laura Young
July 28, 1944

Oh my love,
If I could fly this lonely moon
I'd meet you in your bamboo bed, and we'd make love
While the wild Rhesus monkeys shriek upon the roof

Come morning,
We'd wander out to the Brahmaputra River
To swim with your swollen albino snakes
And feel their slippery skin against our flesh

He felt like the words were saying something important, but they were hard to hold on to. He read the whole thing again, and this time, he realized the bamboo bed must be that one he slept in when he was in India. And he knew those monkeys too. They were up on the roof of the temple, shrieking at him like he'd done something bad. Then he remembered something else. There were naked people on those temple walls, nasty people doing nasty things to each other. He knew he shouldn't look at them, but he couldn't stop doing it even though it made him feel dirty all over. And there were pictures of snakes on the walls, and there were snakes in the river too. He wished he could see those river snakes again and swim with the albino ones. They were so white. He could almost feel the slither of them against his skin. It was scary, but it was nice too. They were so big.

Thinking of those nasty pictures and the big snakes gave him a warm feeling down below in his own snake. He pulled his pants down and stretched out on the bed and touched it for a while. The pleasure that washed over him got all mixed up with a painful ache of sadness. What happened to his girls? Those pretty girls that held him in their arms, and touched him with such gentle skin it made him want to melt himself inside them. How could anyone say that was dirty? It wasn't dirty. It wasn't bad, like they said. It was just wanting to be loved in that special way, so he could feel his worth, and have his own place in the world where he could be free. Isn't that what God wanted for him too? It had to be what God wanted. Why else would He make him feel the way he was feeling?

His eyes filled with tears, and for the first time, he felt like he understood the whole thing. All that dirty stuff, wasn't dirty at all. It never was. It was just a man wanting to have his own—

Wait. What was that?

He listened.

Someone was knocking on his bedroom door. It was quite soft at first, but it got louder.

He didn't want to answer.

He stayed perfectly still, but the knocking was still there. Then, suddenly, a woman came bursting into his room.

He tried to hide himself with his hands, but it didn't do any good. She took one look at him, and started yelling, "What in the hell's going on in here, Aaron!"

"I . . . I—"

"That's a dirty thing to do, Mr. Young. Why would you do that when you know I'm right here?"

"Uh . . . uh . . . It's *my* house, isn't it? Yes, it is my house! Now get out of it! I don't want you to be here!"

Chapter 42

Aaron couldn't get away from Mrs. Busy Bottom. Everyday she woke him up with her banging on his front door. If he didn't let her in, she'd come in anyway. Then she'd be sitting there with her dirty feet up on his couch, watching him all day with her judging eyes. It made him feel like a little kid that was going to be in trouble no matter what he did. But he wasn't a little kid. He was a grown man, and a grown man should be able to do what he wanted to do in his own house.

Today, he'd gotten up early to see if he could get something done before she got there. He finished his business in the bathroom and poked his head out the door to see if she was there.

Nope. No sign of her. So far, so good. Maybe he could eat his breakfast in peace without her telling him how to do it.

He went into the kitchen and turned on the stove and put some water in a pan with the oatmeal. Then he decided it would be good to add some strawberries. He headed out to see if his garden had any left.

As soon as he stepped outside, he heard it. It was one of those planes he knew. A C-47. Yes, he was sure that's what it was. He'd know the sound of that engine anywhere.

He ran to the front yard to see if he could spot it. No. Too many trees. Maybe in the street. He ran out there and looked all around the sky.

There it was. Flying north. But where was it going? Were they going to drop their bombs? No. They weren't bomb droppers. They were supply carriers. They were going to take their supplies into China. He knew that. He'd done it a million times.

The whole great thing came roaring back, and he could almost feel the rattle of the plane, the drone of it, sitting back there smelling the gasoline. Getting light headed, but not so much from the gas, but from being so high. That was the thing that made your head float. Flying that high, with the whole big wide jungle down below. The bare-faced rock cliffs. The wild winter storms. Every bit of it filled him with life.

If only he could get back over there again. Be with his friends. Guys like Old Pritkin. Or Pinkman. Whoever it was. He was a great pilot. He saved their lives so many times. And Town . . . something or other, that radio guy. He was good too. They were like the three musketeers, Flying the Hump. Oh that was a great time.

A car came roaring at him, blasting its horn. He jumped off the street, but he didn't want to give it up. He could still see a speck of the plane, so he stayed on the sidewalk and followed along until it was completely out of sight.

When it was gone, he felt let down. Like he had almost caught a ride to the past, but it was too fast for him. And now he was going to be stuck where he was forever. Why did life have to be like that? He was as ready for excitement as anyone else, so why didn't it ever come? Did they think he was too old to need excitement anymore?

Anyway, the plane was gone, and it probably wasn't coming back, so he might as well go home before the old babysitter came and found out he was missing.

He turned around, and went straight back the way he thought he'd come. When he saw the house, he did a little skip, feeling proud. He hadn't gotten lost at all, so why was everybody always telling him to stay home? If he knew how to get home, he could go wherever he wanted to, and no one could stop him.

As he was going up the steps, he smelled something bad coming from the house. What in the hell was that? Was the place burning down?

He went in and found the kitchen all full of smoke. "Oh no, did he do something bad again?"

There was a pot on the stove. It was black, but it was still cooking. He grabbed the pot to get it off the flame, but it burned his hand, and he dropped it on the floor. Now the whole mess was down there, and there was still that little round fire burning on the stove. He turned the knob that he thought worked it, but the fire just got bigger. He tried some of the other knobs, but it just made more little fires. The whole thing was making him hot and sweaty and scared.

Finally, he got all the knobs turned off, and he told himself to calm down. So he'd burned up a pot. So what? Anybody could do that.

But what if that old Bumbum lady told Sarah? That wouldn't be good.

He was about to clean up the mess when he heard the old banger pounding on the door. Oh no. She was already there. What was he going to do?

He swooshed the pot and the goop under the table with his foot, then he ran to the bedroom and tried to squeeze under the bed, but it was too tight. Then he saw the closet, and he dove in there and closed the door.

Almost immediately, he heard her come into the house and start yelling. "What the hell's going on in here, Aaron? Aaron, where are you? What did you do?"

When she came into the bedroom yelling his name, he was too smart to answer. He held his breath and waited while she stormed around. If she couldn't find him, maybe she'd think someone else had burned up the pot, and she'd go try to find them.

It sounded like she was in the kitchen now, slamming things around and yelling curses with his name. If he came out, she'd burn him with her hot eyes, and he wouldn't know what to say.

He wondered if he could get outside before she saw him. If he went quick, maybe he could do it. He could hide in the garage. Or maybe he could go out to the street and hitch a ride. That would be the best thing to do. Get as far away from her as he could.

She was still making noise in the kitchen, so he crawled out of the closet. He crept to the bedroom door, and carefully peeked around the corner. Good. She wasn't there. He tiptoed toward the front door, holding his fingers over his mouth to make sure no words slipped out. When he was almost safe, he heard her coming behind him. He ripped the door open, hurried down the steps, and raced across the grass toward the street.

He had almost made it when his toe caught on a lump of grass, and he went sprawling. He crawled away as fast as he could, but she was right there. He got a hold of a tree and held on for his dear life, but she grabbed his foot and wouldn't let go. He kicked at her, but she held tight.

"Stop it, Aaron! You're acting like a child!"

Her voice was big, but he didn't care. He held onto the tree and wouldn't let go. She kept pulling on his foot, but he wasn't going to let her have it. Maybe she'd get tired and go away. But what if she just went and told Sarah? Maybe she'd try to blame the whole thing on him. Well, so what? Let her tell. He didn't care. He'd just say she was wrong.

The big bum wouldn't give up. She told him he'd done something bad, and that he needed to go back in the house and fix it.

He didn't want to go back in the house. It was all stinky, and the bad air burned his eyes. Mostly, he didn't want to be in there with her bossing him around and yelling what he should be doing all the time. He kept holding the tree, but she was strong and kept pulling his foot.

Finally, he got tired of it all and let go He turned and glared at her. "Why can't you just leave me alone?"

The blame in her eyes made him feel guilty and lost and just plain sad. But what could he do? She was the one in charge, and he wasn't.

He stood up and let her take his arm. She helped him up and led him back into the stinky house.

She took him to the sink in the kitchen and pointed at a black pan full of water. "Look at that! What did you think you were doing? You could've burned the whole house down."

Aaron shook his head. "I didn't do it. I was asleep. I was . . . uh . . . having a dream."

"Asleep? So this pan got burned by someone else?" She didn't look convinced.

"I . . . I was . . . out in the garden. That's it. I was out in the garden."

"Is that right? So I guess we've got gremlins, or something, in here doing things like this?"

"Yes. That must be it." He didn't believe in gremlins, but if she did, well let her.

She shook her head and plopped down into a kitchen chair. Her scraggly brown hair made her look exhausted. "I don't know, Aaron. What am I going to do with you?"

"You don't have to do *anything*. I get along just fine without you. You should go home."

"Believe me, I'd like to. But I can't go home. Sarah's paying me to keep an eye on you. You know that. She told you I was going to be here."

"I don't remember that."

She narrowed her eyes into slits. "You don't remember that, huh? Well, that's very convenient, isn't it?"

He tried to think what she meant by that word, but it didn't make any sense to him. He decided it wasn't worth worrying about. He gave her a mean look and stomped his foot toward her, hoping it would scare her and make her leave.

She just sat there giving him a dark look, but then, suddenly, she tossed her head, and everything changed. "Come on now, Aaron. I'm not mad at you. We're friends aren't we? I know you didn't mean to burn the pan, you were just . . . confused."

Her voice was softer, so maybe she wasn't mad anymore, and he couldn't remember if they were friends or not. Maybe they were.

She frowned and said, "Now, listen to me, Aaron. I'm sorry, but I've got to go out for a while today. My husband's got a doctor's appointment, and I have to take him because there's nobody else that can do it. I hope it will only take a few hours, but you know how it is with doctors. They're always late. Anyway, I don't want you getting into any more trouble. You understand? Don't try to cook anything, and just stay inside. And don't you go wandering off somewhere. If you do, I swear I'll lock you in next time. Do you understand me, Aaron?"

No, he didn't understand. How could he understand when so many words were being thrown at him at the same time?

"Say you understand, Aaron. I need you to understand." She came over and grabbed his chin and moved it up and down, making his head say yes.

He tried to get his chin away from her, but she held it too tight.

Finally, she let it go. "Okay. So I'm going now. Remember, you mind your P's and Q's, and don't you dare do anything else stupid." She headed out of the kitchen, then turned back and said, "And don't you worry. I'll be back before you know it. Then we'll do something fun. Okay?"

She didn't wait for his answer, and the next thing he knew, she was gone.

For some reason, he was completely exhausted. That's how the babysitter always made him feel. It was probably because he had to work so hard to try to make her happy. He couldn't just relax and enjoy himself like he used to. He might as well go to bed.

He went and lay down with his head under his pillow and tried to remember all of the things that had just happened. He wanted to understand why he felt so sad, like something important had been lost. But he couldn't remember what it was. It was too late. Everything inside his head had already crawled away into the cracks. There was nothing left but dark scary silence.

Chapter 43

After a little rest, Aaron pushed the pillow off his face and listened.

Not a sound. That must mean the babysitter was gone, and he could do whatever he wanted to do. But what should he do?

He got out of bed and wandered around the house looking for something fun. There was nothing there, and besides the house was so stinky he couldn't stand it. He went out back and stood with his hands on his hips and stared at the sky. Why was it so washed out? It was a strange milky white color, with hardly any blue. Had the heat burned it dry? Had it scared away all the clouds, and all the birds, and all the butterflies?

Darn it. Why was it always so hot? Wasn't summer supposed to be over? Someone said it was just about over, didn't they?

He took off his T-shirt and hung it on a post and looked around at his garden. The heat had gotten to all his garden plants too. They didn't look green, like they were supposed to be. It was more like they were all sad and wilted and most of the food was gone. Still, there might be some good things if he searched hard enough.

When he looked around, he spotted a ripe tomato he'd somehow missed. He went over and picked it and gave it a big kiss. He sunk his teeth into it and sucked the juice out, Then he ate the meat and even the skin. That was good. He must have been hungry.

Now his hands and his lips were all sticky, so he went around to the back of the house where the hose thing was and turned it on. The cold water felt great on his face, so he put some on his head, and on his chest, and his feet. When he looked down, he saw how brown the grass was. But wasn't it just green? He was sure it was supposed to be green. Maybe he'd better go get the sprinkle thing and try to bring it back.

He went and dragged the hose around to the side of the house where the grass was the brownest and screwed the sprinkle thing on it. Then he went and turned the water back on.

When he came around to see if it was working right, he saw the magic. The drops were flying every which way, capturing little bits of sunshine and making tiny rainbows in the air. It was almost like the water was laughing, and those tiny rainbows were calling him to come into the water. Well, why not? He got out of his pants and ran into the water like the rainbows said to do.

He stood naked and shivering in the cold drops, feeling the icy sharpness of each one as it hit his skin. How long had it been since he felt something as wonderful as that? It was so refreshing and real, it made his mind feel sharp, almost like it was young, without any confusion.

When he ran out of the water to get his breath back from the cold, he remembered another time he was in the sprinklers like that. It was his birthday, wasn't it? That's right. His mother had made him German chocolate cake. Then his father came home and found him running naked through the water. The next thing he knew his father had him by the arms and was spinning him in circles so fast it felt like his head was going to fly off. Then suddenly, he was sitting on the ground with a dizzy head, and his father was gone.

He never understood whether his father was playing with him, or if he was trying to scare him for being bad. He was afraid of sprinklers after that, afraid of having that kind of fun without clothes. But now here he was doing it again, and he felt free and wonderful. He liked that. A person ought to be able to be free and have fun once in a while.

Bracing himself for the cold, he ran back into the water and right out the other side. And then he did it again, each time gasping when the drops hit his skin. It felt really good, but it was almost painful, like his skin wasn't used to being touched, like it had been too long since he'd felt anything as real and intense as that. He wanted to hold onto the feeling, so he raced in again and stood smack dab in the middle where the squirting was the hardest. He closed his eyes and let himself feel as much of it as he could, the icy coldness of it biting his skin, the delicious sensation of being free.

His feelings were all mixed up. He didn't know whether to laugh or cry, or just throw his arms in the air and thank God for the blessing of being alive. That's all he ever really wanted, to be alive, and to feel free, and to be happy.

He opened his eyes, and suddenly, like magic, a little girl appeared. She called out to him. "Can I play in your sprinkler too, Mr. Grampa. Can I? Can I?"

Before he could answer, he saw other little girls and boys coming to join in. Not a one of them waited for him to say yes or no. They just stripped off their clothes and came squealing into the rainbows.

He laughed and threw out his arms. "Come on in. The more you are, the merrier."

It was thrilling. There were kids all over the place, running into the rain and running back out. Where did they all come from?

Aaron ran too, and the children started to follow him, like he was that pied piper guy in the books. He laughed out loud. That pied piper. He hadn't thought about that guy in years, and now here he was feeling just like him.

But then he decided, he didn't want to be the piper. He wanted to be like the children, fresh from heaven, and as beautiful as they were. It was like they were in that Garden of Eden place, and if they could all just stay there, they could be happy and free and let God take care of everything else.

He held up his arms and said, "Let's go," and they all went running into the sprinkler together. Then just as he was coming out, he heard a terrible roar. When he turned to find out what it was, he saw the old bear from next door. She was running at him full speed with a long thin switch in her hand. She got to him and whipped his arms so hard, he let out a cry. The switch hurt real bad, but it hurt him even more when she turned and yelled at the children to go home. They must have been as scared of her as he was because they all grabbed their clothes and went running away.

"Why did you do that?" he said. "They weren't doing anything wrong. We were just playing in the rain."

The old howler whipped him again, this time on his legs. She yelled, "You're a dirty old bugger. A dirty old man."

What did she mean? He wasn't dirty, he was clean. Hadn't he just been running in the rain? The rain was as good as anything else to make yourself clean.

He wanted to explain it to her, but he could see she wasn't going to listen. She kept whipping him and pushing him towards his house. When she'd driven him inside, he turned back real quick and pushed her out. Then he slammed the door and locked it.

She didn't go away. She stayed out there, shrieking like she'd gone crazy. "That's right. You stay in there, you old buzzard. I've called the cops. You bet, I have. They'll be here any minute. I'll tell them all about you and what you've been doing."

The cops. He didn't want the cops. Why did she call the cops? He didn't do anything wrong, did he?

He ran through the house looking for a place to hide. Maybe if they couldn't find him, they'd think he was gone, and they'd leave him alone.

When he saw the piano, he thought it might work. It was long and wide, so maybe he could hide under there. He got on his hands and knees and crawled way under it, clear to the back wall.

Pretty soon, he heard pounding on the front door, and there were big voices demanding to know if he was there. He wasn't about to answer. If he just stayed put and kept quiet, he was pretty sure they'd go away.

But the old witch wasn't going to let that happen. He could hear her out there telling them how she was sure he was in there and how she'd been watching the whole time. They banged the door even louder, and then, finally, they crashed it open.

Aaron held his breath and closed his eyes, hoping he could make himself disappear. But he wasn't sure it was going to work.

He could hear the old witch storming through the house saying, "He's gotta be here. We've just gotta find him."

Finally, she did find him, and she started yelling, "Here he is! He's under the piano, and he's still naked as a jaybird, just like I said."

Aaron opened one eye and saw her down on her haunches with her mean eyes and her ugly mouth all twisted up.

Then he saw the big men with uniforms crouch down where they could see him too. They told him to come on out.

No way! He wasn't going to do that.

They crawled in and grabbed his feet. When they started to pull, he wrapped his arms around a piano leg and held on with everything he had. They kept jerking on him, until the whole thing started to move. Oh no. If the piano slid and ruined the wood, he'd be in big trouble with his father. Maybe even bigger trouble than he was with the cops. He'd better let go.

As they pulled him out, his butt grabbed the floor and tore at his skin. It hurt a whole lot, but he wasn't about to cry. No one was going to say he was a baby, no matter what they did.

They stood him up, and he started kicking and swinging his fists, trying to get free. It didn't do any good. They held him tight, and they locked his hands up behind his back so he couldn't fight anymore.

The old witch was over by the door now, whispering to one of the cops in a secret way. The whole time, she kept looking over at Aaron with hate in her eyes. He couldn't figure out why she hated him so much. Blasting him all night with her big yellow light, and now she was acting like all the trouble was his fault, when she was the one that started it going in the first place.

The man with the witch must have gotten tired of listening to her because he told her to go home. He said she should bring him the names of the children later.

Why did he need the names of the children? Were they going to tie them up too? What for? They didn't deserve that.

He started yelling and wagging his head, hoping he could make them just think about him and not about the children. Maybe the kids could get far away, and nobody would be able to find them. If they asked him where they lived, he didn't know, so he wouldn't be able to tell them. That was good.

He stomped on the cop's shoe with his bare foot, but it just hurt his own foot. That was stupid. Why did he do that?

The cop gave him a glare. "You want me to tie your feet up too?"

"No. Not really."

"Well, then knock off your shenanigans, and let's get you dressed."

He told the other cop to go find some clothes. The cop did what he said and came back with some pants and a dirty white T-shirt that looked like a rag. Was he supposed to wear that dirty old thing?

They unlocked his hands, and told him to get dressed and to not try anything funny.

Aaron said, "I don't feel very funny. You're a mean man."

"What did you say?"

The man's voice was so mad, Aaron decided he'd better get dressed fast, whether he knew which way things went, or not. He sat on the couch and pulled the pants on and zipped them up, then he put on the dirty T-shirt thing. He wasn't sure if it was on right, but nobody else seemed to care if it was on right, so he didn't care either.

The man that had a hold of him said, "Shoes?"

Aaron shook his head. "I don't know. Where are they?"

Both men looked fed up with him, but it wasn't his fault he didn't have his shoes, and how could he go get his shoes when somebody was holding him back.

The man that got his clothes, left again and came back with some socks and those terrible black shoes that he hated. He wasn't going to put those things on, no matter what anybody said.

He put the socks on, then took the shoes and threw them at the wall.

The men jerked his arms together and put the locks back on. Then, they crammed the shoes onto his feet, not caring how much they hurt him.

They pulled him up and told him they were taking him to jail, and if he knew what was good for him, he'd better behave.

What did they mean, they were taking him to jail? He hadn't done anything wrong. Why were they taking him to jail?

Chapter 44

Being trapped in the back-seat cage of the police car, made him feel like a scared wild animal, an animal that didn't know what he'd done, or what they were going to do to him. He looked for a way to escape, but the windows had bars, and the part between him and the drivers had bars, and the doors didn't have any handles. How could a car not have any handles? Did that mean they were going to keep him inside there forever?

They drove and drove, until finally, they pulled up in front of a big fancy building. They took him inside and grabbed his hands and made his fingers all black and pushed them onto a piece of paper. Then they made him go stand up against a wall, and they took his picture one way and then the other way. He kept asking why they were being so mean, but they never answered.

When they finished taking his picture, they put him in front of a grouchy woman behind a thick window. She shoved a green plastic box through a slot at the bottom of her window and told him to give her everything he had in his pockets.

The only thing he had was a little white card with somebody's name on it. It seemed important, so he didn't want to give it up. He held it up to the window. "I've only got this one thing. I'd like to keep it, if you don't mind."

She scowled. "Put it in the tray."

He put the card in the green tray, wondering what he was giving up. If he needed it, would she ever give it back?

The woman picked up his little card. She glanced at it and gave him a sharp look. "Where'd you get this?"

"Uh . . . I'm not sure. What is it? Maybe you should give it back."

"What do you mean, what is it? It's a state trooper's card." She looked at it again, and scowled. "Oh, I get it. You've been in this kind of trouble before, haven't you?"

"I don't know if I've done it before because I don't what you're talking about."

"Don't give me that. You know why you're here." She shook the card at him and put it in her shirt pocket. "Don't think I'm not going to check this out."

He wondered what she meant, but then another man came and took him to a place where they wanted his belt and his shoes. He didn't care about that. He didn't have a belt, and the shoes hurt his feet anyway. They always had. He didn't care if they kept those shoes forever. If they were gone, maybe Sarah would take him to the shoe place so he could get some soft ones. That's right, Sarah. Where was Sarah? Why wasn't she there trying to help him?

Another man in a different uniform grabbed his arm and took him to another place and hooked him to a blue chair with a metal bracelet thing. The man went away, and there was nothing for him to do except stare at the blank walls and watch a TV that wasn't turned on. Why did they have so many blue chairs when there was nobody there to sit in them? It didn't make sense. In fact, the whole thing didn't make sense. Why would they build such a big new building when they didn't have any business? Did everyone go home?

All the sitting and waiting gave Aaron too much time to worry. And he was getting more and more scared all the time. Maybe they were going to keep him there. And if they did that, they might lock him up and take away the key. Maybe this was one of those places like they took Miriam to. It didn't seem quite the same, but it did have locks on the doors, and people in uniforms watching him like a hawk. They'd make sure he could never get out.

Thinking about all that made him so scared he started to shake. But maybe he was just cold. He wished he could go home and get something warm, but he was pretty sure they weren't going to let him do that.

He sat there shivering and thinking about all the bad things that might happen if he couldn't figure out a way to escape. Finally, after what seemed like forever, a new man came to get him. This man was dressed up in a suit with a tie. The suit made him look nice, but he didn't seem all that nice. He didn't say anything, and he didn't smile. He just unlocked the bracelet on Aaron's arm and took him down the hall to a small room with a long mirror on one side. Aaron was shocked when he saw himself in the mirror. Was that scared looking man really him?

The man in the suit told him to sit down.

Aaron did what he was told.

He could feel the tears building up in his eyes, and he quickly wiped them away with his arm. If the man saw he was weak, it would only go worse for him. He knew that. He'd always known that. A person had to be strong, or people would do whatever they wanted to do. He lifted his chin, and said, "I think you better let me go home now, or you might be sorry."

The man seemed too focused on his papers to respond. Aaron decided to take things under his own control. He got up and headed for the door, but the man got up real quick and brought him back and hooked his wrists to the chair the same way they did it before. Being hooked up like that made him feel like a dog on a chain. A dog that just wanted to be free so he could go home. He jerked at the chain, but it wouldn't give.

The man sat down and stared at him with a big frown on his face. That frown, and all the papers the man had, made Aaron feel like he was about to be given a hard test, and it wasn't going to be good if he failed it. The test started with the man wanting to know his name and where he lived and whether he was married, and all that. Aaron did his best to give him the right answers, but from the scowl on the man's face, he was pretty sure he didn't.

Next, the man took a piece of paper out of a brown folder and started saying some words about being silent if he wanted to, and how his words could be used against him, if he didn't have one . . . whatever it was.

He asked Aaron if he understood.

Aaron didn't understand, but he said, yes, hoping he could figure it out later.

The man said, "With these rights in mind, are you willing to answer my questions?"

"Sure. I'll do whatever you want. Then can I go home?"

The man pulled at his tie and looked him in the eye. "So, Mr. Young. Do you know why you're here?"

"No. I sure don't. I hope you can tell me."

"You don't know why the police came to your house and brought you here?"

Aaron closed his eyes and strained to remember, but it wasn't there. Maybe if he wasn't so scared, it would be easier. "I'm sorry. I don't know."

"So, you're saying you don't know why your neighbor called the police."

"Oh, that's right. It was probably that old snooper that called you. She hates me."

The man leaned closer. "Now, why do you think that might be?"

"I don't know." Aaron scratched his head, trying to think what it was. "Maybe it's that damn light."

"The light?"

"You know, blasting me all night, so I went over there and put it in the bushes."

"You put her light in the bushes?"

"Well, the yellow part. That's the only way I could get it to stop."

"So, you think that's why she called the police?"

Aaron shrugged. "What else could it be?"

"That's what I want you to tell me, Mr. Young."

A nervous laugh escaped him. "Believe me. I would if I could, but that's the only thing I know about for sure."

"Hmmm." The man leaned back in his chair and stared at him for a while.

It was nerve-wracking to sit in that hard chair with a man watching every move he made and the whole place being so quiet and scary, and a wild man in the big mirror sitting there looking as scared as he was. Aaron was sure he could hear his own heart beat, and listening to it made it beat even faster. Then, his mind started going fast too. How was he going to get out of here, if they kept on tying him down? He needed to go home real bad. And he needed to use the bathroom. If they didn't let him do it, he might have to go ahead and do it anyway, and that would be bad.

He wondered if they had a bathroom he could use, and he was about to ask, when the man loosened his tie and leaned forward again with his eyes all narrow and mean. "Mr. Young, can you tell me what you were doing at your house before the police came?"

"Uh, I'm not really sure." The man's eyes made him hot, and he would have loosened his own tie, if he wasn't tied down. But then he realized he didn't have a tie. All he had was that dirty T-shirt they gave him.

"Were there children at your house?"

"What?"

"I said, were there any children at your house, Mr. Young?"

Aaron thought about it. Children? Yes, there might have been some children. "I think they were there. Seems like a bunch of them showed up. It was fun."

"And what were you doing with those children?"

"Uh, I'm not sure. Probably just playing, like we do."

"Playing, huh? Like usual? Is that what you call it? Playing?"

"Well, it was kind of like playing. I mean . . . I think we were doing the water thing. Is that what it was?"

"I believe that's right, Mr. Young. There *was* water involved. But there was more too it than just playing in the water, wasn't there?"

"I don't think so. Children mostly just like to play. That's how they are. Don't you have any children?"

"I'll ask the questions here, Mr. Young." The man's voice was loud and sharp like a knife that wanted to cut him.

Did that mean he'd given the wrong answer? Was he going to fail the test and be in even more trouble? Aaron said, "I'm sorry. I'll try to get it better the next time."

The man stood up, and leaned forward with his hands on the table. "Mr. Young. I want you to tell me what you were wearing when you were playing with those children."

The glare in the man's eyes told him he'd better get this one right, or else. The problem was, the man was looking at him in such a scary way he'd already forgotten the question. "Uh . . . I'm sorry. What did you say?"

"I said, what were you wearing when you were *playing* with those children?"

Aaron shrugged. "Uh, I wish I could tell you, but I don't pay much attention to that sort of thing."

"You don't, huh? Are you telling me you don't pay attention to what you wear when you're around little children?"

"Well, I don't worry about clothes all that much. All that fussing around they do. Who cares what you wear?"

"So, you don't like wearing clothes? Is that what you're trying to tell me?"

"Well, I do it when I have to, but when it gets so hot in the summer, I don't mind . . . you know . . . shredding some . . . or whatever it is. Don't you?" He wished he could shred some right now.

"Never mind that. Did you take off your clothes in front of those children?"

"What children?"

"The ones you were playing with in the water. You've already admitted that you like to take your clothes off. Didn't you just admit that?"

The man's voice was so harsh, Aaron couldn't think straight, and now he needed to pee even more. He tried to remember what he was supposed to say, but all of a sudden his mind went blank. He grabbed his crotch and said, "I really need to pee, if you don't mind. I mean . . . really bad."

"After you've answered my question." The guard sat back down and waited for his answer.

Aaron shook his head, trying to clear it. "I'm sorry. I don't know what it is. I mean, what was the question?"

"Come on, Young. You heard me. Did you have clothes on, or not, when you were out there *playing* in the water with those children?"

"Oh, that's right. I remember now. We were running through the sprinkles. It was beautiful, with all those rainbows and everything. I love that. Don't you?"

The guard hit the table with his fist. "Now, look here, Young. How about you stop fucking around and give me a straight answer? You exposed your genitals to those children, didn't you?"

"My genitals?"

"Yeah, your genitals. Your dick. Your cock. You know what I'm saying."

Aaron couldn't believe his ears. "What? Me?" Aaron didn't like the way this was going. The man was getting dirty, and that made him feel dirty too. But that wasn't right. He wasn't being dirty with the children. "No!" he yelled. "You're wrong. We were just running through the sprinkles. That's all."

"Yeah right. So, can you tell me why a man of your age has a trampoline in his backyard."

"What do you mean, my age?"

"What are you, seventy? Seventy-five?"

"I'm not *that* old, am I?"

"Whatever, you're not exactly of an age to be bouncing on a trampoline."

"That's not true. I do it all the time."

"With the children?"

"Well, yes. They come sometimes."

"Isn't that how you entice them to your house? Isn't that why you have a trampoline?"

"What are you trying to say?"

"I mean, why would children come to an old man's house if he didn't have something like that to entice them." The man waved his fist in Aaron's face. "It sounds like you've done this sort of thing before. The children come over to your house to jump on the trampoline, and then what do you do?"

"I jump with them. Or, sometimes, I just stay off and make sure they're safe." He held onto his crotch even tighter, afraid he might lose control and pee in his pants. "I really need that bathroom now, if you don't mind."

"Yeah, sure. And then, you take them into your house. To *play*, right? Isn't that what you call it?"

The man's questions were making everything confused and scary. "I don't know. I guess sometimes we do play games. Or I give them things to eat . . . like strawberries, or grapes. Stuff like that. From my garden. Please, sir. I don't want to wet myself."

"More enticements, huh? Sweet, juicy stuff. Typical."

"Stop it! I don't know what you mean. Please. Let me go to the bathroom."

"Sure you do. You get the kids over there, and then you take them inside, where your neighbor can't see you. Then what do you do?"

"Nothing. We just . . . like I said, we play games and eat stuff."

"And you take off your clothes and touch them, don't you?"

"No! I don't!" Aaron tried to jump up, but the metal bracelet held him down. The man was getting so mean and dirty, he just wanted to run away. What was wrong with the man? Did he hate little children? Did he hate everybody? He decided to stop answering the man's questions. "I don't know why you're doing it, but you're a dirty man, and I'm not going to talk to you anymore."

"Are you kiddin' me, you pervert?"

"Pervert? That's not me. That's you. You think everything's dirty. Children aren't dirty. They're innocent and perfect. That's how God made them. That's why they're so beautiful."

The man's face got all red. He stood up and yelled, "You depraved old pervert. We're gonna put you away. Believe me, we've got a place for people like you. A place where no one will ever see you again."

He stormed out of the room, leaving Aaron trapped and shaking, and that's when he realized he'd peed himself. Oh no. Now what was he going to do? His pants were all wet, and they were going to send him to a place where nobody could ever see him again. What about Sarah? If she couldn't see him, what would she think? Would she think he was dead? He didn't want to be dead, and he didn't want Sarah to lose him. But what could he do? His pants were all wet, and they had him, and they weren't going to let him go. But why? What did he do to deserve that?

Chapter 45

Aaron sat in the puddle of his own pee trying not to look at himself in the big mirror. He knew what his face would say. It would say he was a big baby who needed a diaper. He was ashamed of his wet pants, even though he knew it wasn't his fault. A person can only hold it so long.

A big guard came in and took one look at the puddle and said, "Shit, man. What have you done?"

Aaron stared at the floor. "I told him I needed to go, but he wouldn't let me."

"Figures. That asshole."

The big guard unlocked his hand and took Aaron down a long hall and put him in a new kind of cage. He said, "Hold on. I'll go get you some dry clothes." Then he left, locking the big steel door behind him.

The new cage was so bleak, Aaron wondered why anybody would want to make a place like that. There wasn't a single thing that looked soft, just a steel bench hooked to the wall, and a steel toilet with some kind of steel sink above it, and a cold cement floor. There was no way out, except through that steel door. Why did he have to be in a cage anyway? He wasn't wild. He wasn't going to hurt anyone.

As he sat on the bench staring at the narrow band of glass in the steel door, a bad feeling grew inside him. What if he really did do something bad like all those questions said? What if he just couldn't remember? He tried to think what he might have done, but his mind kept coming back to the steel door, and how he was locked in, and how he just wanted to go home and crawl into bed where he could be safe.

Thinking of home made him think of Sarah. Where was she? She was the only person who could save him. If she came, she could tell them he was a good man, and that he'd never do anything to hurt anybody. But she wasn't there. Had she forgotten all about him? Had she forgotten her own father?

He jumped up and went over and started beating on the door. "Saaarah," he cried. "Help me. Get me out of here! They're gonna hurt me and take away the key."

He kept pounding and yelling until the big guard came back and opened the door. "Knock it off," he yelled. "That's not going to get you anywhere."

The guard pressed some cloth into his chest. "Here, take off your clothes and put these on."

It was some kind of ugly orange shirt and orange pants with big white stripes. No way he was going to put those things on. He dropped the clothes on the floor and folded his arms across his chest.

"Stop your nonsense, and put them on. Anybody who's gonna be here all night has to wear 'em. And besides, you need to get those wet pants off."

Aaron couldn't believe it. "Did you say, all night? I can't stay here all night. I have to go home."

"I'm sure you'd like to do that, but until someone comes and makes your bond, you're going to have to stay with us. Besides, if you wanna go to the cafeteria and get something to eat, you're gonna have to wear those clothes."

"Something to eat? You mean there's food in here?"

"Sure there's food. We're not going to starve you, are we?"

Aaron realized how hungry he was. And thirsty too. "So, I can eat if I wear those stripes?"

"That's right."

Aaron pulled off his T-shirt and pants and picked up the orange clothes from the floor and put them on. The whole thing was too loose and hung way down over his socks. How was he going to walk around without tripping? He threw up his hands. "Look. They're too big."

The guard shrugged. "Yeah, well, you're quite a bit smaller than most of the guys in here."

"That's probably because I'm starving. Can I have that food now?"

The guard looked at his watch. "Sure. They might still be serving, if we hurry." He took Aaron's arm and pulled him toward the door.

Aaron resisted and looked back at his clothes on the floor. "You forgot about my clothes. They need to be cleaned."

"Somebody'll take care of those. Now come along."

They went down a long hall and when they came to another hall, Aaron thought maybe he could smell food in the air. They kept going, and finally, the guard led him into a big room full of guys dressed in the same ugly orange clothes that he was wearing. Most of the guys were already sitting at long tables, eating their food and talking. Their noise was so loud it was bouncing off the ceiling in a crazy way that made Aaron's head feel like it was roaring. He covered his ears with his hands, and yelled, "Why do you have to talk so loud?"

The guard grabbed his arm. "What's wrong with you? Are you crazy?"

"No. Who said I was crazy?"

The guard pushed him in the direction of a long counter that looked a lot like the one in the cafeteria at the kid's school, but instead of nice ladies serving the food, there were big frowning men doing the job.

His guard picked up a tray and banged it down onto the counter. "Get yourself a plate. You don't have much time, so get on with it."

Aaron did what he was told and pushed the tray along the counter to each station where each of the grouchy men put different kinds of food on his plate. He was hungry, but he wasn't sure he liked the looks of what they were giving him. Some kind of white soupy stuff with a few big lumps in it, some half-dead string beans, and some limp looking carrots. Aaron told the big dark-skinned man that he didn't want any of those dead things. The man gave him a mean look and told him to keep moving. The last server in the line ladled some kind of yellow something onto his plate, and it got all mixed up with the white soupy stuff. He was pretty sure it was going to ruin everything, but the man looked so big and strong, he didn't dare complain.

At the end of the line, he got himself a little plastic spoon and a plastic glass full of water, then he looked around for a place to sit down. As he walked though the rows of tables, he couldn't find a friendly face anywhere. The few guys that even bothered to look at him seemed angry with him for some reason. Why would they be angry with him when they didn't even know him?

Finally, he spotted a little space between two guys. He headed there to sit down, but the two of them spread out their elbows so he couldn't fit. Aaron stared at them. Why did they do that? Were they all going to hate him before he could even get started?

He held up his tray and yelled, "Well, what am I supposed to do? I can't eat standing up, can I?"

Now, he had everyone's attention, but it looked like they all wanted to hurt him. He was about to make a run for it, but he saw a big friendly guy waving him over. "Come sit here, Pops. I won't hurt ya."

Aaron said, "Really? It's okay?"

"You betcha. Come on over here."

Aaron went over and sat down. He thanked his big blond-headed friend and got ready to eat. But how was he supposed to do it with that stupid little plastic spoon? After staring at it for a minute, he decided he'd better just go for it and see what it could do. He poked at one of the meaty-looking lumps that were hiding under the white soupy stuff. The lump jumped off his plate, slid across the table, and bounced down to the floor.

His new friend laughed and pointed at it with his own plastic spoon. "Hey, old timer, I see you got one of those Mexican rubber fish. It's a specialty around here."

Aaron got the joke and sniggered. "I guess so. But I've never seen one bounce that high."

The guy handed him a roll. "Here, you can use this to mop up all that crap they put on your plate."

Aaron quickly used the roll to soak up as much of the slop as he could. He stuck the soggy pieces of roll in his mouth, one at a time, then he wiped his lips with the back of his hand and burped. He looked at his friend. "So, what are we doing here?"

"Well, *I* was just in the wrong place at the wrong time. They caught me with some pot and said I was selling. It's not true, but you know how they are about marijuana in this state."

"I do?"

The guy pushed his fingers back through his long blond hair. "Hmmm . . . maybe not. So, what are you in for?"

Aaron shook his head. "I don't know."

His friend raised his eyebrows in a funny way. "Really? They just picked you up and threw you in the hoosegow for nothin'? That's not what I heard."

"Really? What did you hear?"

The guy leaned in and whispered, "I heard you were playin' around with kids?"

"Well, we were running through the sprinkles, if that's what you mean."

"I heard you didn't have your clothes on. Is that true?"

"They'd just get all wet, and then I'd be in trouble."

The guy leaned even closer. "Now, I want you to listen to me, my friend. You need to keep all that to yourself. You're already in big enough trouble here."

"Why? What did I do?"

"Nobody likes someone who messes around with little kids."

"But I don't mess with them. They're my little friends. That's all. They like to bounce on my bouncer."

The guy closed one eye and stared at him. "You don't know what's going on, do you?"

"No. I really don't. I was just—"

A bell rang. It was so loud it made Aaron jump and forget what he was saying. When he looked around he saw the room was empty except for the two of them. "Does that mean we're done with lunch?"

"Yeah, it does. Come on. Let's go outside. I'll try to protect you, but you've got to stay low key."

"Low key?"

"Yeah, try not to call attention to yourself."

They put their dirty eating things on the counter, and then they went outside to a playground with a tall fence around it.

Some of the orange guys were gathered in a circle smoking cigarettes. The way they stared at him and whispered made him nervous. Were they telling bad stories about him?

He followed his big friend over to the guys with a basketball. When they started choosing up sides, his friend got picked first thing, but nobody picked Aaron. Why didn't they want him? He knew how to play. If he could play the game and show them how good he was, maybe they'd like him a little better.

When the choosing was all done, some of the guys took off their shirts while the other ones didn't, and then they started to play. It looked like a lot of fun with everyone running back and forth, tossing up the ball, but all he could do was lean up against the brick wall of the building and watch.

He narrowed his eyes and watched the scene like it was a movie. It was nice how the sweat glistened on the guys' skin as they moved back and forth, following each other like a flock of birds, dipping and diving. The lively sound of their voices and their grunts and moans, made him want to play even more.

He moved closer and watched for a chance to get in, and when the ball finally got loose and came flying toward him, he grabbed it in mid-air and went racing for the hoop. By some kind of magic, it went in when he threw it up there. Then suddenly, he was the star of the show. Everyone was pounding him on the back and whooping him up.

"Way to go old man."

"What a shot!"

They let him play after that, and at first, it was nice. Then they started getting rough and knocking him around even when he didn't have the ball. He got frustrated and stopped. But then, his blond-headed friend threw him the ball and yelled, "Here you go, Pops. Take your shot. Don't let 'em stop you."

He ran toward the basket and flung up the ball, but it didn't even come close to the hoop. He was about to go back to his wall when one of the bullies came over and bumped into him harder than ever. Aaron couldn't take it anymore. "Stop it. Why are you doing that?"

"You got a problem, cocksucker?"

The foul-mouthed man gave him a hard push, and then he was on the ground and a fight started between the big bully and his big friend. The whole place went crazy with noise.

Aaron tried to see if his friend was okay, but the other guys pushed him out of the way with their feet and blocked his view with their legs. He knew he should get in there and help his friend, but he was so scared, he wasn't sure he could even stand up.

Just as he managed to get to his knees, he heard whistles and everyone went away. Now he could see his friend. One of his eyes was swollen and his face was all bloody and so was his yellow hair. The other guards left, but two of them stayed and grabbed his friend by the arms like they were really mad. Did they think he was the one that started all the trouble? That wasn't right.

Aaron thought he knew one of those guards, so he scrambled to his feet and said, "Don't blame him. He was saving my life."

The guard said, "He was, huh?"

His bloody friend nodded. "They went after this old guy here. I had to see what I could do."

The guard frowned. "Well, I guess that's up to you, but it's not gonna make you any friends around here."

"I know, but hopefully, I'll be out of here real soon. I've got somebody making my bail."

"I hope that happens, for your sake."

Aaron went to his friend's side. "I'm really sorry they hurt you? Why were they so mad?"

"Well, I don't think it's anything you can understand, Pops. You just better stay as far away from them as you can."

"Believe me. I want to."

The other guard took his friend away, and then his own guard turned to him and said, "Come on, Young. Let's get you to a cell where you'll be safe."

As they walked down the long halls, Aaron said, "Why did they want to hurt me in the first place? I didn't do anything to them. I just wanted to be in the game. That's all."

The guard muttered, "Nobody likes a child molester."

"A molester?" As the words sunk in, Aaron's head started to reel. "Wait. I'm not one of those. Why would they say that?"

The guard shrugged and shook his head.

They continued down the hall in silence until they came to another one of those steel doors. The guard said, "This is your cell. Don't worry. We'll keep you alone. You'll be safe."

Chapter 46

As soon as the door closed, all hope left Aaron. The cage was small and cold, like the other one, but this one had two beds, one on top and one down below. That must mean they were going to make him sleep there. The more he paced back and forth, the smaller the cage seemed to be. Why would they make a place like this for a man, a place where you were all alone, and nobody cared about you?

He went and pounded on the steel door. "Help! Please. I can't breathe in here."

No one came. He looked around the cage and tried to think how he got there. It was just a regular day, wasn't it? He was doing whatever he was doing, and then somebody came and took him, and now he was here.

Why didn't he know why it happened? It didn't seem like his brain had ever been this bad. Was it because he was scared? Well, who wouldn't be scared? He was alone in a cage, and they were saying bad things about him and trying to hurt him, and he didn't know if anybody would ever come to save him.

He went and sat on the shiny steel bench and folded his arms across his chest. He took deep breaths and tried to calm down, but he couldn't do it. The steel bench was too cold on his legs, and the slick floor was too cold through the thin stockings on his feet. He started to shiver. Then his heart started to pound, like it was trying get out of his chest. He had to do something fast to stop it.

The beds. Maybe the beds would be warm. It was one of those top and bottom things, like the kids liked to have. But which one was his? He tried to remember if he knew, but he couldn't find it, so he decided to go with the top one. At least he could hide up there if someone came in and tried to hurt him.

He climbed up there and got under the thin blanket with his orange clothes still on. He wrapped his arms around himself, but he still couldn't stop shivering. Why was he so cold and why did he hurt so much? It was like he'd been rolled down a hill and his whole body was beat up and broken. He didn't want to cry, but he couldn't help it. The tears were so crammed up inside his throat, they came bursting out in hard painful sobs. "I don't know what I did to deserve this. Please, God. Help me."

He wasn't sure God could hear him in a place like this. Maybe they'd locked God out. Maybe this was the place where the devil lived. It felt like that. Only cold instead of hot. Icy cold. Would the devil live in a cold place like this? Maybe not. Maybe the only ones living here were the evil people who took away his freedom. They had him locked up like a wild animal that couldn't be trusted. But why? Why couldn't he be trusted?

Maybe they thought he'd forgotten everything, and that meant he might do something wrong. But what could he do that would be so wrong that they'd have to lock him up? Why couldn't they just let him go home? He'd stay there, and he wouldn't do anything wrong. He yelled at the steel door, "Please. Let me out. I promise. I'll be good."

He listened, but no one answered. Maybe they couldn't hear him. Even if they did hear him, maybe they didn't want to help him. They didn't care anything about him. Nobody did. Even Sarah was gone.

That's right. What about Sarah? Where was Sarah? Shouldn't she be here?

Sarah was the one he needed more than anything. But how could he tell her to come when he didn't have a phone, and when he didn't have a letter or anything to write it with. Even if he could write to her, how could he explain everything when he couldn't even explain it to himself?

He pulled the blanket up under his chin and closed his eyes and whispered, "Sarah. Sarah. Sarah." Maybe if he said it enough times she'd hear him. No. He knew that wasn't true, but it was the only thing he had to hold on to.

His thoughts turned to Annie, and he tried whispering *her* name. "Annie. Please, Annie, can't you come save me?"

"Stop that!" he yelled at himself. "There's no use calling Annie. She can't hear you." How could she? He was caged up somewhere, and she wasn't there. Maybe no one was there. Maybe the whole world outside his cage was gone.

That awful thought got stuck in his head, and he couldn't stop it. The whole world was gone, and he was trapped in a cage. But what happened to the world? Did that Armageddon time come like they always said it would? Was it the true end of the world?

That didn't seem right. He'd just been with some people. They must still be out there. He sat up and listened.

Nothing.

He scrambled down off the bunk and went to the big iron door and peered through the little glass window panes. There was some kind of space out there, but nobody was in it. He hurled himself at the door, and yelled for them to let him out, but nobody came.

He put his ear against the door to see if he could hear anything, and then he went and put his ear against every cold wall in the room and listened to each one. There wasn't a single sound anywhere. Maybe he really was alone. Maybe they'd locked him in his cage and then something happened and everyone was gone. Maybe they'd never come back, and he'd die in there like a lonely starved dog.

His stomach felt like it had tied itself into a knot. When the knot started to move up into his throat, he hurried to the metal toilet and threw up. Terrible yucky stuff kept coming up until he was completely exhausted. He sat back on the cold cement floor and cried out, "Please, God, don't let me die in here. I don't want to die. Please, can't you save me?"

His whole body was trembling, and he knew he had to get warm. He crawled over and got in the bottom bunk and curled himself into a tight ball. As he lay there shivering, he remembered another time when someone locked him up. That time it was Stevie. They were playing a game, so maybe this was the same thing.

He squeezed his eyes closed and whispered, "It's okay. It's okay. It's okay. Stevie will come and let me out. I know he will. He just has to."

His whole body was full of pain, but he knew he had to try to get past it and sleep. It was the only way he was going to be able to wait until somebody came to save him.

He tried to sleep, but he was so hurt and so scared, he couldn't do it. How long had he been in here? Hours? Days? How was he supposed to know? He couldn't see outside, so he didn't know if it was night or day. There was just that same artificial light all the time. He hated that kind of light. It was just like that yellow light that old witch liked to blast him with.

That's right. It was that old snooper witch that got him. She did the whole thing in the first place. She called the people and they came and took him, and now here he was in this cage, locked up forever, and she was the one that did it.

He heard something and sat up quick. Was it voices behind the door? Was somebody there? Was the door going to open? He stared at it, begging it to be true. Could he make it happen? Could he?

Yes. He did it. The door was opening, and the voices were coming in. One of them belonged to that big guard he thought he knew, and the other one was a tall man wearing a brown shirt and a brown hat. He wasn't sure if he knew that one or not, but he thought maybe he did.

The man with the hat came over. He shook his head in a sad way, and said, "I'm so sorry this happened, Mr. Young? Are you okay?"

Aaron couldn't answer. He was so relieved to see somebody that liked him, his eyes filled with tears. He wiped them away, but they kept coming.

The man took his arm and helped him out of bed. "Come on, Aaron. Let's get you out of here. I'll take you home."

"Really? Do you mean it? I can go home?" He looked over at the big guard to make sure it was true.

The guard nodded. "That's right. We'll have to check you out of the system, but then you can go with your friend here, Lieutenant Howard."

"My friend?"

The kind man with the hat smiled. "Don't you remember me, Aaron?"

Aaron quickly nodded. "Uh, sure, I do. I mean, I'm really glad you came . . . and all that." He didn't care if he remembered the man or not, he just wanted to go home.

The guard handed Aaron his clothes, and they waited while he changed. His clothes seemed kind of dirty, but so what? He could put on some fresh clothes when he got home.

The two men let him out of his cage and took him down the long hall and gave him back his shoes. He took one look at them and said, "Oh no, not those. Don't you have any better ones?" Then he realized that kind of thing didn't matter. He just needed to get out of this place quick and go home.

His friendly man said. "They're *your* shoes, Aaron. Don't you like them?"

"Uh, yeah, sure. They're fine." He stuck them on his feet and said, "Okay. Let's go."

His friend held him back. "So Aaron, are those shoes all you had when you came in here? Did you have anything in your pockets?"

Aaron shrugged and said, "Uh . . . I'm not sure."

The guard went behind the counter. He sat there for a minute, then he stood up. "Nothing in the system but those shoes, Lieutenant. Oh, and your card."

"Well, I'm glad he had that. Who knows how long he would've been stuck in here, what with his daughter being on vacation. It must have been terrifying for him."

"I imagine so," said the guard. "Lucky for him, he had a protector."

"A protector?"

"Yeah, a big softy. A guy in here for selling pot."

"Well, I'm glad he was here, and I'm glad he was big."

The guard frowned. "Well, they still knocked him around a bit. He probably has a few bruises." He shook his head. "You know his living situation is going to have to change, or they'll have him right back in here. You gonna to talk to the daughter?"

The man with the hat said, "Yeah. I'll take care of that."

"All right then." The guard turned to Aaron and said, "Good luck to you, Mr. Young. I hope things work out. Don't let me see you back here."

Aaron gave him a salute. "No, sir. You won't."

His friend led him outside to a car. When Aaron saw it was one of those cars with a cage thing, he stopped dead.

"What's wrong?" asked the man.

"I'm not going back in a cage. You can't make me do it."

"It's okay, Aaron. I wouldn't do that to you. You can sit up front with me."

"I can?"

"Sure. You can."

"Okay, then, let's go." Aaron got into the front seat before the man could change his mind.

Once they were going, he turned to the man. "Thanks for saving me. You know, I thought I was a goner."

"I'm sorry I didn't come sooner. I didn't get the call 'til today."

"It's okay. I'm just glad you made it."

His friend looked worried. "Look, Aaron. I don't expect you'll remember this, but . . . well, never mind. I'll just talk to your daughter."

"No, tell *me*."

"Well, I understand that you didn't have any bad intentions when you were playing with those kids. I mean taking your clothes off like that. But . . . you just can't do that sort of thing. It doesn't matter what the circumstances are, there are people who will want to put you away, regardless."

"I promise I won't do anything."

"That's right. You don't want to get locked up in that place again, do you?"

"No. I really don't. It's a mean place."

"Well, then, you're going to have to listen to your daughter Sarah and do exactly what she says."

"Sarah? Where is she? I thought she was gone."

"She's waiting for you."

"She's going to be there?"

"Yes, I talked to her."

That worried Aaron. "Uh, do you know if she's like . . . mad, or anything?"

"Mad? Why would she be mad?"

Aaron tugged at the top of his T-shirt. "I don't know exactly. Maybe I did something wrong." He grabbed his friend's arm. "Did I do something wrong? Did I?"

The friend shook his head. "No. No. You didn't do anything wrong, Aaron. Don't worry. Everything's fine."

Aaron hoped that was true, but he had an aching feeling in his heart that somebody thought he was bad. He didn't want to be bad. There were enough bad people in the world without him being bad too.

They drove along in silence, and pretty soon they were going down a street Aaron thought he might know. Was he about to be home? Is that where they were?

It wasn't long before his friend pulled up in front of a house, but it wasn't his little white house. Why was he taking him there?

When the engine stopped, Aaron, said, "This isn't the one where I was before. What happened?"

"What do you mean, Aaron?"

"I mean, where's my house? It's not here."

"Oh. No, this is Sarah's house."

"It is?"

He was trying to remember if that was true when Sarah came running out. She got to the car and flung open his door and helped him out. She gave him a big hug and whispered, "Oh, Daddy. Are you okay?"

"Well, it was kind of, uh . . . rough, I'd say."

"I'm so sorry, Daddy. I never should have left you. Can you forgive me?"

He rubbed the places on his arms that hurt and thought about it. Could he forgive her? She should have come to save him, but she didn't. Still he needed her love right now more than anything, and she didn't seem at all mad at him. He said, "I'll forgive you, if you forgive me. But don't do it again. Please, Sarah. I can't take it. I got too scared in that place."

When they were inside, Sarah frowned and shook her head. She looked at the man who had saved him. "Look at him, he can hardly walk. What happened in there?"

"Well, it's not a good place to be, given what they thought he did."

"Unbelievable. They'd really go after someone his age, in his condition?" She gave him another hug. "I'm sorry, Daddy. I'm really sorry."

Her gentleness was so soft, it almost hurt him. He'd been far away from her, and now here she was, and she wasn't mad at all. In fact, she was the one that was sorry. So maybe it was true. Maybe he hadn't done anything bad.

Sarah and his friend took him to the couch, but before he could sit down, his friend took some little white papers out of his pocket and handed them to Sarah. "Maybe you should write his name on the back of my card, along with your address and phone number. Then make sure he keeps one in his pocket at all times. You know, just in case."

Sarah nodded. "Oh that's a good idea. I'll have them shrink-wrapped and pin them inside his pockets."

"Good idea." They shook hands on the deal, and then the man shook Aaron's hand and said, "Okay. I guess I'll be going. You be good, Aaron."

He was out the door before Aaron could say that he would.

Now that he was gone, Aaron turned to Sarah and was about to ask her about all that pocket business when Annie came running in. She flung her arms around him. "Oh, Grandpa. I'm so glad you're okay. I don't know what I'd do if anything ever happened to you."

He patted her head and said, "I'm okay. I'm okay."

He sat down on the couch, and she sat right next to him and kept looking at him with her sad eyes.

"Really, honey. I'm okay. I'm just happy to be home."

Sarah's boy came in and stood by the wall. He waved his hand a little. "Hi Grandpa."

"Hi there, boy."

The boy looked hurt. "My name isn't boy, Grandpa. It's Sam."

Aaron tried to cover his mistake. "Sure, I know that. Hi Sam. How are ya?"

"I'm okay, I guess."

"I'm glad to hear that."

Aaron noticed the man standing next to Sam, and he wondered if he was supposed to know *his* name too. He thought maybe the man had something to do with Sarah, but he was too tired to figure it out, so he let it go. It was just nice that they were all there, and not a single one of them looked mad at him. In fact, they all had such sweet love in their eyes, he wasn't sure what to do with it all.

He held out his arms. "It's like some kind of miracle. I mean, you're so beautiful." A tear caught in his throat, and he whispered, "I thought you were all gone."

Chapter 47

Aaron leaned his head back against the couch, feeling completely worn out. He told Sarah he wanted to go home and rest, but she wouldn't let him go. "I'm sorry, Daddy, but I can't let you be alone anymore. We've put your bed and your dresser in Sam's room downstairs in the basement. You can share that space with him until we decide what to do."

In the basement with Sam? He didn't want to sleep in the basement. "Who said you could do that?"

"Well, Daddy, either we have to move in with you, or you have to move in with us. And we're the ones with the most room."

She smiled like she wanted him to smile too, but he didn't feel like smiling.

"Why does it have to be either way?"

"Because that woman's down there, and I don't trust her."

Aaron nodded. "She's the one that got me, huh?"

"Yes. She did. We've got to play it safe, Daddy. She's got it out for you now."

"Safe and sorry, or else. Is that how it's gonna be?"

"That's right. Anyway, we don't have to think about that right now. I've got a nice surprise for you."

He worked up enough energy to smile.

"Just a minute. I'll go get it." She left and came back and gave him a package in white paper.

"What's this?"

"It's your present."

That was nice. He liked presents. He turned it over in his hands.

"Go ahead. Open it."

He pulled the paper off and saw some kind of picture on blue cloth. "What is it?"

"It's a turquoise T-shirt. Remember? You said you wanted one like mine."

"I did?"

"Uh-huh. Anyway, we found it up in Yellowstone" She pointed to the front of the shirt. "See, it's got this big elk etched on it in white, and Old Faithful going off. Isn't it nice?"

He touched the elk's antlers. "Yes. It really *is*."

Annie piped up. "We saw a live elk, Grandpa. And some bears in the river, even though they said there weren't supposed to be any bears anymore."

Aaron patted her knee. "You're a lucky duck, aren't you?"

She nodded. "I know. I really am." She touched his new shirt. "Why don't you put it on, Grandpa?"

"Sure. I could do that."

Sarah helped him pull off his dirty old T-shirt. She took one look at him and gasped. "Oh, Daddy. I didn't know you were so bruised up. It's awful." She frowned and turned toward the man that Aaron was wondering about before. "How could they do this to him, Kevin? How could they?"

The man shook his head. "They must have found out why he was in there. They're all criminals, but they've got their own sense of justice, and they like to deal it out."

Sarah frowned even more. "I'm gonna do something about this."

"Like what? The police were at fault. They should have known what would happen. But at the same time, it was your police friend that *saved* him." The man shrugged. "It might be best to forget the whole thing, and just make sure it doesn't happen again."

Sarah's frown got bigger. "How can you be so casual about it, Kevin?"

"I'm not casual. I'm practical. You need to realize what you're taking on here."

She threw up her hands. "Of course, I know what I'm taking on. But the responsibility is mine. There's no one else."

Aaron tried to follow what they were saying, but he felt a deep tiredness closing in. He touched Sarah's arm. "Please, I'm tired. Can't we—"

She straightened up. "Right. Grandpa's tired. We should let him rest. Do you want something to eat first, Dad? Are you hungry?"

"I don't know."

"Did you have anything today?"

He shrugged. "I'm not sure I can remember." He wanted them all to be there, but at the same time, they were making him really tired. Maybe if he could just sleep for a bit, he could wake up and be more like they wanted him to be.

Sarah said, "Well, let me make you a quick sandwich, and then you can rest."

She hurried off to the kitchen followed by her man. Aaron could hear them whispering out there. He cocked his head to try to hear what they were saying, but then Annie chimed in. "That's Kevin, Grandpa. Do you remember? You met him before."

Aaron shrugged. "I guess so."

"Anyway, he's Momma's new boyfriend. I like him, and we had a lot of fun on the trip, but sometimes they argue, and that's the part I don't like. I think maybe they're going to get married."

Aaron nodded, but he was so tired he couldn't keep his head up anymore. He let out a big sigh and let himself sink back into the soft cushions of the couch so he could sleep.

Later, when he woke up, there was no one around. He sat up, feeling scared. Was he alone? He didn't want to be alone. He was pretty sure he'd been alone too much lately.

He sat there wondering what to do, and then he thought maybe he'd go home. At least there he'd know where he was. But did he know how to get there? Yes, he could probably do it. He was pretty sure it was just down the road somewhere. He should go home and get some rest, then he could come back to wherever he was and someone would be there.

He made it to the front door and out to the sidewalk, but then he felt woozy, and he had to hold onto a mailbox that was there. Before he could get going again, Sarah came running out. "Where are you going, Dad?"

"Uh, I thought I'd go home."

She shook her head. "No. You can't do that. Oh dear, how am I ever going to keep you from running off?"

"I just wanted to go home. I'm tired."

"I know. I know. But you can't be alone anymore."

"I don't want to be alone."

"Well, then why did you try to leave?"

"I thought you were all gone."

"We were just out in the backyard trying to be quiet so you could sleep. If I hadn't gone into the house to use the bathroom and seen you leaving, who knows where you'd be by now?"

"Well, how could I know all that." Suddenly, he felt very weak, like all of the blood had gone out of his head. He leaned over with his hands on his knees, and took several big breaths.

Sarah grabbed his arm. "What's wrong, Daddy?"

"I don't know. I hardly have anything left."

"Come on. Let's get you to bed. I'll bring you that sandwich, then you can go to sleep and try to recover."

She took him into the house and helped him get down the stairs and into bed. When he was alone, he lay there wondering why he had to be in the basement. It was dark and cold down there, sort of like that cage they put him in before. Why were they always putting him in cages?

Somehow, he had to keep them from doing it. And it looked like he needed to be on guard with everyone, even his own Sarah. She might act nice, but she still wanted to lock him up, just like everybody else. Why couldn't he be free? He had some time left, didn't he? A few years, at least. Why couldn't he just go to the desert and be with his red rocks. He could live with the desert critters. They never cared how he was. They wouldn't try to cage him.

He knew it was the right solution. He was going to have to escape from his dungeon. If he had to walk the whole way, he'd get to the desert. If he was free, and he was in the desert, everything would be fine.

Chapter 48

With Sarah's good home cooking and lots of rest, Aaron started to feel like his old self again. It got easier and easier for him to make it up and down the stairs to the basement. In fact, when he was going up, he liked to take them two at a time, sometimes, just to prove that he could. Now that he was strong, he was ready to go home. He'd had enough of being in the way.

He found Sarah in the kitchen and told her his plan.

She said, "No, Daddy. We've put that house up for sale. You don't need it anymore. You're going to live here now. And when I'm at work, during the day, I've found a nice place where you can be safe. It's a great place. There are lots of nice people for you to talk to. And good food. They have field trips to interesting places like the zoo and museums. And you can even learn how to paint, if you want to."

"Paint? I know how to paint. I must've painted a thousand rooms." He tried to sort out all the other words she'd just said, but the only thing he knew for sure was that she wanted to put him somewhere. She was trying to make it sound good, but he knew what it was. She was trying to put him in one of those places like they put Miriam in. He lifted his foot, and put it down. "I'm not going."

"Why in heaven's name not? It'd be fun for you."

"I'm fine just doing my own life."

"Listen, Daddy. I took time off from work to help you get used to things here, but I have to go back soon. We can't have you staying here alone and probably running off. I'm sorry."

He knew what it really was. "I understand what I am. I'm the third wheel, and it doesn't work. You all have your own business, and I don't. You don't need me hanging around."

She came over and gave him a hug. "That's just not true, Daddy. We love having you here."

He pushed her away. "I don't know what to do with myself here!" It was true. He hated sitting around all day with nothing to do but stare at the walls. He might as well be in that place with Miriam staring at the walls, but he wasn't going to let her put him there, no matter how nice she tried to make it sound.

"That's exactly why I thought you might like that place I just told you about. You'd have—"

He stomped his foot down again. "Stop it! I know what you're doing!"

"What? What am I doing, Daddy?"

"You take the steps, and then you take the next one, and pretty soon I'm in the same boat as Miriam and we're going downhill." He was so scared of what she was planning and how hard she was pushing, he started to shake. He had to do something, but how could he make her stop?

He decided to stop listening. He turned his back on her and went to the kitchen window, trying to get his thoughts straight. First she took his house and put him in the basement, and now she wanted to go the whole yard and stick him in that bad place. He understood why. Sure, he did. She just wanted her own life. But he wanted his own life too. So why wouldn't she let him go home? Then they could both do it. No. She wasn't going to do that. She wanted to be the boss of everything. She wanted to put him in that place with Miriam where he'd never get out. Well, she could make all the plans in the world, he wasn't going in there with Miriam. Never. Not in a million years.

Sarah came up next to him, and they both stood and looked out the window. He knew what she was doing. She was cozying up so she could get him on her side. But it wasn't going to work. Still, maybe he'd better let her think it was going to work, then he'd make his getaway when she wasn't looking. Okay. That's a good plan.

He shot her a smile to make her happy. "Sure, why not?"

"Why not what?"

"Let's do it. Let's get it done. Then you can get on with your life . . . I mean, with your work and all that." He made her another smile, and he hoped it looked real.

She seemed a little suspicious "Are you sure?"

"Sure, I'm sure. Let's go."

"No. Not today. I've got an appointment for us to take a look at the place early next week."

"Okay . . . well, thanks for thinking of me. I guess I'll, uh, go look around downstairs. Or something."

"You're acting very strange, Daddy. What are you up to?"

"I'm just, you know, trying to—" He waved his hand in the air and left the kitchen heading for his room down in the dungeon.

As soon he was downstairs, he closed the door and listened to make sure she hadn't followed him. When he didn't hear her, he thought, okay, time to make a plan. What he needed was something to carry his stuff in. He looked around the room, but the only thing they gave him was his bed and his dresser.

He went to the boy's closet to see if he could borrow anything there. He slid the door one way and didn't see anything but clothes, so he slid it the other way. That's when he saw one of those bag things that the kids liked to wear on their backs to keep their books in. That might do it. He could carry his own stuff like that. Now, what would he need?

He took the back carrying thing to his dresser and started going through the drawers. The first thing he found was his new turquoise T-shirt. That would be a nice thing to wear down in the desert. The coyotes might like that big buck for their dinner. He smirked at his own joke and stuck the shirt inside his bag, then he looked through more drawers. Socks. He threw a couple of those in. Then he added some underpants, but he took them back out. He didn't want to make things too heavy.

He thought about taking one of his sweatshirts, but he was going to the desert. It would be warm down there, so he wouldn't need a sweatshirt. He might not need any clothes at all, if it got hot, but he'd better take some at least until he got there.

What else? As he went through the bottom drawers, he came across a rolled up pillow case. He lifted it out, and when he looked inside, he saw his old silver coins. Wow! There they were. He'd been looking for those silvers for a long time, hadn't he? But shouldn't there be more?

He tried to count how many there were, but he kept on losing track of where he was. Maybe it didn't matter. He had what he had, and it was better than nothing. At least, he could buy some gas.

After he stashed the coins in the bottom of his pack, he stepped back to think what else he'd need. That's when he saw the picture on the dresser. It was the one about him and his pretty Lori on their wedding day. He knew he'd want that, but it seemed too heavy. He took the picture out its frame, folded it in half, and put it carefully in the bag. Then he put the bundle of letters with the red ribbon in there. There was a blue plastic notebook thing sitting there. He wasn't sure what it was, but when he opened it up and saw all the words, he thought it was probably important. He pulled the metal rings apart and took out all the papers. Then he folded them up and put them in the bag with the rest of his good stuff. He closed up the top of the back bag and said, "Okay. That's ready."

Now, he had everything he thought he needed, but where could he put it until it was time to go? He had to hide it in a safe place and wait for Sarah to be gone. As soon as she was, he could get the bag out, and see if there was anything else he needed. Like maybe some food or something. But he didn't need to think about that now. He was too tired. He stashed the bag way under his bed against the wall, then he stretched out on top of the quilt to rest.

He tried to go to sleep, but he couldn't do it. He was too excited about going to the desert. He was also a little worried that he wouldn't remember where he had put his stuff. After he thought about it, he decided what he needed was a sign. But how could he make a sign that would tell himself what to do, and not tell Sarah at the same time? Think, he told himself. You've got to make your old brain do its best work. It's more important now than ever.

As he looked around the room trying to think what kind of sign he could do, he saw that old man in the mirror. It was strange how worn out and dusty he looked since they put him in the basement. Aaron hated seeing him that way, but he was always right there in the mirror, so maybe he could help him remember. He went to the boy's desk in the corner and found a pencil and some paper and took it back to his dresser. He thought for a minute, and then he wrote some words, and then a few more. When he was finished, it said,

Remember the desert.
It's warm down there and you can sleep under it.

That should do it. It was a good reminder. Nobody else would know what it was saying, but he would. It was the best he could do.

He stuck the paper with the words into the edge of the mirror frame where it would stay put, and then he poked at the reflection in the mirror. "Okay, old man. If you forget to remind me, you'll be real sorry. We'll both end up in that cage with old Miriam."

Chapter 49

Aaron woke up the next morning and realized he was still in his dungeon. It was dark and gloomy with just a little bit of light coming in through the small window up by the ceiling. It made his brain feel dark and gloomy too, and almost empty.

But wait! It wasn't completely empty. There was something in there that said he was supposed to remember something, something that was really important.

He searched his mind, but it wasn't there. Not even an edge of it. Nothing he could grab on to. So what should he do? If he didn't remember what it was, he was pretty sure something bad was going to happen.

"Think," he said. "If you can't figure this out, you're in trouble."

As he moved around the dark room trying to find something that would tell him what he was trying to remember, he saw the boy's narrow bed under the window. There was nobody in the bed, but the covers were pushed back in a way that showed how the boy got out. So, where was the boy now? Was he supposed to go find him? Is that what he was supposed to remember?

Maybe so, but before he did that, he needed to get dressed. He was cold.

While he was putting on his pants, he saw a dark shadow in the mirror. It was that man that liked to be in there. He stared at him and realized he was the one that was supposed to remember the thing he'd forgotten.

Aaron leaned in and glared into the man's dark eyes. "Did you do it?"

"Do what?"

"Did you remember?"

The man lifted his shoulders and let them drop. "No, I don't think I did."

"Well, that's just great! Now, what are we supposed to do?"

Aaron shook his head, trying to rattle things lose. And the man in the mirror shook his head too. That's when Aaron saw the note stuck in the frame of the mirror. Was that his note? He tried to read what the words said, but it was too dark.

He looked around until he found the light switch by the stairs. He went and flipped it on. Now the room was full of light. That was good, but why did he need it? He hated when he started to do something, then couldn't remember what it was. Now, he was going to have to start all over and try to figure it out. But first, he was cold, so he'd better go get a shirt.

He went back to the dresser and put a shirt on, and after he'd done up the buttons, he noticed the words on the paper that was stuck in the wood of the mirror. Suddenly, he knew that's where everything got started. Those were his words, and they were trying to tell him something.

He pulled the paper off the mirror and turned it towards the light.

Remember the desert.
It's warm down there and you can sleep under it.

What was that supposed to mean? The desert? He knew what the desert was, and of course, it was warm down there. That's why he wanted to be there. But what was the part about sleeping under it? How could you sleep under a desert?

After he read the whole paper again, he was pretty sure the words didn't make sense. But there was something about the part about sleeping under it. If that was the important part, maybe it was saying something about the bed where you sleep. A bed.

He looked at his bed and saw his pillow. There was something important about pillows. Well, for one thing, he used to keep his old silvers in that kind of pillow bag. Maybe that's what he was looking for the whole time. His silvers. They were hidden somewhere. Maybe the place where they were hidden was under the bed.

He got down on his hands and knees and moved his hand around under the bed. His fingers touched something hard. "Aha! Was that his silvers?"

When he pulled the thing out, it didn't look like his silvers bag. It was one of those blue bag things like the kids liked to wear on their backs. But there it was, so maybe that's what he was looking for. Now, was he supposed to do something with that bag, or was he just supposed to know where it was?

He stayed sitting on the floor and opened the bag. It looked like his stuff was in there. He took it all out. There was his nice turquoise T-shirt, some nice socks, and some folded up papers with lots of words. And there was that picture of his wedding with Lori. So why was all that important stuff in the bag? Was he supposed to keep it with him so it didn't get lost?

As he was putting everything back in his bag, he saw his turquoise T-shirt again, and he decided to wear it. I was a nice shirt, and it would make him feel good, so why not?

After he had it on, he put everything else back in the bag. He stood up and put the bag on his back. Now what was he supposed to do? He was hungry. He knew that. So maybe he was supposed to go upstairs and see if anyone had made any food.

The house was silent upstairs. He went into every room, but it was completely empty. Not the soul of a person anywhere. That didn't seem right. Wasn't there supposed to be somebody cooking breakfast?

He went to the kitchen to get his own food and found a big note on the refrigerator door. The words said,

Good morning Dad,
The kids are at school, but you were sleeping so good, I decided to slip off for a minute to get some stuff from the store. YOU STAY PUT!!!! I'll be right back and fix you a really nice breakfast.
Sarah

So, she wanted him to wait, did she? He couldn't do that. He was hungry right now. He took a banana and an orange from the bowl on the counter and sat down at the table. First, he ate the banana. That was good. Then he peeled and ate the orange, and that was good too. It was probably enough for right now. He could eat the real breakfast when Sarah came home.

He sat at the table waiting and staring at the warm yellow light coming through the window. It made him think of the desert. That's how the sun was in the desert, nice and warm and yellow. Maybe he should go down there. It would be warm all the time, and he wouldn't have to worry about what to do with himself, or being cold.

He stood up and felt the weight of the pack on his back, and that's when he realized he should go to the desert right now. He might as well. If he waited for Sarah to come home, she'd make him stay put. He didn't want to stay put. He was tired of doing that. Besides, didn't she say something about taking him to some kind of bad place? Yes, that was it. She wanted to take him to that bad place where Miriam was. That's exactly why he had the pack and all that stuff he'd put in it.

"Come on! You've got to get out of here before she comes back. Quick. Get your shoes on and go!"

He searched the whole house and finally found his good work shoes next to the front door. He didn't know how they got there, but he took them outside and sat on the step to put them on. Then he hurried out to the sidewalk. Which way should he go? It didn't matter, just go! He had to get as far away from here as he could. When he got to the desert, he could rest, and everything would be fine.

He started walking. Luckily, the street next to the sidewalk was almost empty of cars. No one could stop him now.

By the time he got to the big oil tower things, he'd only seen one beat-up old truck. It made him wish he had his old blue truck. He could really use it right now to get himself down to the desert, but this was no time to cry over sour milk. All he had to do is keep going, and he'd get there sooner or later.

He spotted the ramp up to the big road, and thought about going up there to hitch a ride, but he decided that wouldn't be good. Everyone would see him up there, and then they'd try to take him back to where he was before. He should stay down below where he could hear the big road, but he couldn't see it. That way they couldn't see him either. He'd just follow along with the car sounds in his ears, and when he got further along, he'd go up there and find a hitch with somebody that was going where he wanted to go.

As he walked across the lumpy ground through the bushes and trees down below the road, his mind got to thinking about the desert and how nice it was going to be when he got there. The first thing he'd do is take off his clothes and lay on one of those big old warm red rocks and get the ache out of his bones. Then, he'd go see if he could find some of that hot water. But he had to get there first, and to do that he had to keep his attention on the big road. He stopped to listen for its sound, but it wasn't there. Oh no. He must have gotten too far away from it.

He tried to think how to get back to the sound, but he wasn't sure. Those mountains in the distance were up there before, so maybe that was the right way to go. That was the only clue he had.

He kept his eyes on the biggest peak, and finally, he got back to the roar of the cars. "Okay. I'm back on my track."

The sun was a lot taller now, and it was making him hot and really thirsty. He could feel the sweat dripping down his face and inside his T-shirt. He started looking for water, but he was past all the houses, so he didn't know where he was going to find it.

Finally, he came to a kind of tunnel that looked like it went straight under the big road. He took it, and when he got to the other side, he laughed out loud because now he knew exactly where he was. He was at that place where they'd hacked out all the dirt from the mountain and hauled it away. It was a big ugly scar, and it always hurt his heart to see it, but this time it didn't hurt so much because it told him where he was.

He stayed on the same street until he saw the old hot springs swimming pool building. He knew that place for sure. It was where they used to take the kids all the time to swim. They all loved that place. What was it called? The name wouldn't come, but that didn't matter. He just kept going, and pretty soon, he came to a nice place with grass and trees. And they even had one of those drinking things. He hurried to it and bent over and took a long cool drink of the water. When he straightened up and looked around, he saw a pretty girl with blond hair and an older boy with dark scraggly hair sitting on a bench. Maybe they were going his way and they could take him for a ride. As he went over to ask, he noticed some kind of animal lying by the girl's feet. It had really long white hair. Even the ears had long hair. It was almost like the hair of a pretty girl, but it wasn't. Was it a dog? He'd never seen a dog like that, but it had to be a dog.

He went over and stooped down and ran his fingers through the strange dog's hair. It was soft and silky.

The guy cleared his throat and looked at Aaron like he'd done something wrong. "Hey, old man. What do ya think you're doin'?"

Aaron took a step back. "Uh . . . I just wanted to touch its hair. Is it real?"

The guy said, "What do you mean, real?"

"I mean, how did it get like that?"

The pretty girl smiled at him. "It's how Afghan dogs are. She's an Afghan."

"She is, huh?" Aaron didn't want to forget what he really needed to know, so he stopped looking at the dog and said, "Say, you don't happen to be going my way, do you?"

The guy scowled at him. "Your way?"

"I mean to the desert."

"What desert?"

"You know . . . the one with the red rocks."

"Moab?"

"No. I don't think so. The other one."

"How am I supposed to know what you mean? What desert?"

"Well, it's down by some town that's down there." He nodded in the direction he thought it might be.

"Saint George?"

"Yes. Yes. That's it. Are you going that way?"

"Well, we actually are going that way," said the girl. "We're going to Las Vegas to get married."

"Well, that's nice. Could you give me a ride down there."

"I don't know," said the guy. He was scowling again. "Why would we want to bother with you when we're heading off to get married?"

Aaron shrugged. "I don't know. I thought that's how it worked. You know, hitching and all that."

The girl touched her guy's arm. "We could take him, Bruce. Couldn't we?"

"No Karen. I don't want some old guy looking over my shoulder the whole time I'm driving."

She tugged on the guys arm. "Come on, Bruce. It wouldn't hurt anything."

He closed one eye and looked Aaron over. "Do you have anything of value in that pack? Anything you might want to give us for our efforts?"

"Uh, I'm not sure. Let's see." Aaron took the pack off his back. He pawed through his stuff and pulled out a pair of socks. "You can have these, if you want."

"Socks? Are you shittin' me?"

"Well, no. Not really. Uh . . . I do have this nice shirt I have on." He looked down at it. "But I think it's kind of a special shirt, and I'd like to keep it if you don't mind."

"I don't need your shirt, mister. I was thinking of a little thing called money. You know, money? Have you got any of that?"

"Oh, money." Aaron felt around in his bag to see if he had any money. His hand touched some things that felt hard and round. It had to be his silvers. But he didn't want to give his special silvers to this unfriendly guy. Why should he? He thought about it and realized that if he didn't do it, he might not get another ride. And then people would come looking for him, and he'd have to go back, and Sarah would put him in that place where he'd never get out.

He decided he could spare a few silvers. After all, he had quite a few of them, and it would be worth it if he could get to the desert. He felt around in the cloth bag and pulled out a handful. "I have a few of these you can have." He held them out and then pulled them back. "If I give them to you, you have to promise to take me the whole way."

"Let's see 'em."

Aaron handed them over.

The guy held a few of the coins up and looked at them real close. "They're silver? Real silver?"

"Yes. They're my silvers. They're worth a lot."

"Oh yeah? What's a lot?"

"Well, a whole lot. So will you take me?"

The guy looked at the girl, and she looked back at him, and finally, he stood up. "Okay. But I don't want you blabbering the whole time or doing any backseat driving."

"No. No. I don't drive from the back seat. Not ever."

"Okay then. Let's go."

They took him over to a big blue car that was all faded and had a bunch of dents on it. Aaron wasn't sure that old car could really make it all the way down to the desert, but what choice did he have? The guy had his silvers, so the deal had been made.

The girl helped Aaron and the pretty dog into the back seat. As soon as the girl closed the door, the dog gave him a big wet lick on the face. Then she started circling around until she found a black thing that looked like a balled-up sock. She lay down and tucked the sock between her legs and gave it a few licks, then she put her head in Aaron's lap and looked up at him with her big brown eyes like she wanted to be friends.

Well, he thought, this ride might not be as bad as I thought. I haven't had a nice dog friend in a long time.

Chapter 50

It was fun zooming along with a dog in his lap. He hadn't been with a nice dog since that old German Shepherd he had as kid. Boy, he loved that dog. They did everything together, until something happened, and his dog friend died. Tears filled his eyes as he remembered coming home from school that day and finding the dog's dead body out in the field. He never knew if it was his fault, or if someone else had opened the gate and let him out. All he knew is that his dog friend was dead.

His new dog friend must have known how sad he was feeling because she lifted her head and licked his hand. He stroked her long silky hair. "Thank you. You're a good girl."

Aaron heard voices and realized the driver and the girl were in the front seat whispering secrets. Were they talking about him? He cocked his head to listen.

The guy tipped his head backwards, and whispered, "I wonder if he has any more of those . . . you know what I mean."

"So what if he does?" said the girl. "They're his, not yours."

"Hey, I was just wonderin'."

"You leave him alone, Bruce, or I swear—"

"You swear what?"

"I swear . . . well, you wouldn't like it."

"Okay, okay, keep your panties on."

"That's exactly what I'll do, if you don't leave him alone."

Aaron had thought they were talking about him, but now they were talking about panties. Why were they talking about panties? He leaned forward to try to hear a little better.

The guy's eyes flashed in the backwards mirror. He yelled, "You listening to us, old man? Are you eavesdroppin'?"

Aaron wasn't sure what that word even meant. "Easeropin? What's that?"

"Sure. Sure. Play innocent. I know your type."

The girl pushed the guy's shoulder like she was mad. "If you don't want him to hear you, don't be talking about him."

The guy just gave her a scowl.

Aaron thought the girl was nice. She was pretty in a scrubbed clean kind of way. It made Aaron wonder what was she doing with a guy like that with such scruffily hair on his head and his face.

There was something about that guy that Aaron didn't trust, even though he couldn't lay his finger on it. He decided he'd better keep his eyes open and not let him get away with anything.

They kept going along, and after a while, Aaron noticed there weren't any buildings by the road anymore. That meant they must be pretty far out of town. That was good. It meant they were getting there.

A little bit later, they came up on that place where he always used to buy gas, and he said, "Aren't you going to do it here?"

"What are you talking about?" said the guy.

"Gas? Aren't you going to get the gas?"

"I don't need you telling me when I need gas, buster."

"Okay. Okay. I was just trying to help. Why are you so . . . crabby?"

"Yeah, Bruce," the girl said, "why *are* you so crabby?"

"What? What did you say?" The guy jerked the steering wheel so that the car swerved, and then he jerked it again.

All of a sudden the car felt too tight, and Aaron wished he had his old truck. Then he wouldn't have to listen to somebody being so mean. He could drive along all by himself, or maybe he could take his nice dog friend with him. That would be even better.

The car rattled along, bouncing every time it hit a bump too hard, but Aaron didn't say a word. If he felt like saying something, he put his hand over his mouth, or put his attention on stroking the dog's soft hair.

Sitting in the back seat with nothing to do made him sleepy. He tried to stay awake, but his eyes kept falling asleep by themselves. Then he'd wake up and worry that he'd been sleeping with strangers, but what could he do. It was hot in the car, and he was tired.

When he woke up again, the car was stopped at one of those rest places where you go to the bathroom. Nobody was in the car, which meant they were probably inside doing their business. He decided he'd better go do his business too, so he didn't have to ask for it later.

While he was in the bathroom, he realized the driver guy wasn't in there, and that made him scared that they might be trying to leave him. His stuff was out there in the car, wasn't it? And his dog friend was there. What would he do if he lost all that?

Even though he wasn't quite sure he was finished, he quickly zipped up his pants and ran outside. The couple and the dog were already in the car, and it looked like they were about ready to leave. He made a dash for it, and dove in the back seat. "Sorry, I wasn't sure I was going to make it."

The guy smirked. "I wasn't sure either. Hey, it looks like you peed on yourself."

"I did?" Aaron looked down and saw that his pants had a wet spot. How did that happen?

"Yeah, you did. Unless you got that water on your pants washing your hands. Did you wash your hands?"

"Sure. That's what I did. I always *do*, don't I?"

The guy rolled his eyes. "Well, I just hope you don't smell up the whole car."

The girl gave the guy a look, and the guy said, "What?"

They got out on the road again and drove and drove and didn't stop until the dog got restless and started doing those circles things on the back seat again.

The girl said, "Bruce, we need to stop and let the dog out for a walk."

"You just took her for a walk at that last rest stop."

"That was two hours ago. Look at her. She needs to get out again."

"Okay. Okay. I'll take the next exit."

The guy took the next exit and stopped the car in the middle of some juniper trees. The girl got out with the dog.

Aaron got out too, and took a deep breath. The air smelled sweet and clean and kind of familiar. It made him wonder if they were getting close to his desert. He saw some of those nice red rocks up ahead in the distance, and that meant they really were getting close.

He was walking around, stretching his legs when he saw something go flying by.

The dog went tearing after it.

At first, Aaron thought that the guy had thrown a ball for the dog to chase after, but then he saw it was that black sock thing the dog had.

The dog gently picked up the thing and carried it back towards the car, whimpering. As soon as the poor dog got close, the guy grabbed the sock from her and got ready to throw it again.

The dog went crazy, whining and jumping up and down, trying to get it.

The girl yelled for the guy to stop doing that, but the guy said, "Why? It's funny."

Aaron wasn't sure what was happening, but he knew his nice dog friend was in a frenzy. "What's going on here," he said.

"She thinks it's one of her pups," said the girl. "Bruce wanted his money, so he sold all of her pups too soon, and now she's confused. She thinks the sock is her pup."

The girl grabbed the sock out of the guys hand, but he grabbed it back, and threw it hard.

The dog went tearing after it again.

Aaron couldn't stand it anymore. He went and got the sock and the dog and helped her back inside the car. The poor thing whimpered and tucked her little sock baby down between her legs where her nipples were.

The guy grabbed Aaron's arm and spun him around. "What the hell do you think you're doing?"

"I could ask you that."

"Oh yeah? What business is it of yours?"

"You're being mean."

"Is that right? Well, old man, you want me to show you what mean really is?"

The girl got between the two of them. "Stop it right now, Bruce. I'm getting sick of this. If you don't knock it off right now, I'm leaving you. I swear, I will. In fact, maybe you should just take me back home right now and forget about us getting married."

The guy ignored the girl and glared at Aaron. "Now look what you've done, you old bastard. Well, fuck this. You can walk from here."

That didn't seem right. How could he walk from there. "Uh, I don't think I can do it. We're, uh . . . kind of in the middle of nowhere."

"That's your problem, isn't it? You can go back out to the road and hitch another ride, or walk from here. We're not all that far from where you said you wanted to go anyway, so go. One thing's for sure. You're not getting back in my car." He grabbed Aaron's bag from the back seat and threw it in the dirt. Then he turned back to the girl, "Get in the car!"

When she hesitated, he said, "I'm not screwing around here, Karen. Get in the car. Right now!"

The girl stared at the guy for what seemed like a long time. Finally, she turned to Aaron, and mouthed the words, "I'm sorry."

Aaron could see she didn't have any choice, so he shrugged and told her goodbye. He hoped she'd be okay, and he hoped she'd do what she said she'd do and not marry that mean guy.

As the car drove away, he saw his pretty dog friend looking through the window at him with a sad face. He sure did wish he could have kept her with him. She would have been nice company while he walked to his desert place, but it looked like he was going to have to do all his walking alone.

He felt a little scared standing there alone in the silence. Even with the junipers, here and there, and the red rocks in the distance, there wasn't much to hold on to.

But maybe it wasn't such a bad place to be. He loved the desert. He had always loved it, and at least he had those red rocks up ahead to show him the way. All he had to do was follow the red rocks until they got bigger. Then he'd be right where he wanted to be, in his red rock desert.

Chapter 51

As he headed toward his red rocks, it felt like there were butterflies going crazy in his stomach. He was alone, now. Completely alone. But he was where he wanted to be. The complete silence told him that. He couldn't see anything that had ever been touched by man. It made him feel like he was back in the Garden of Eden, living in that safe world, before everything went bad. But where was his Eve? Shouldn't his Eve be there?

The thought scared him. If he didn't have his Eve, he'd be lonely. Did he really want to be lonely forever?

A little bird shot by right in front of his face, almost hitting him in the nose. He stepped back, surprised, then he laughed. "Well, I've got you, haven't I?"

He turned his head to see if anything else was out there with him. He heard the wind whispering in his ear. It had a soft peaceful voice, and he realized that's what he'd been looking for the whole time. Some kind of peace where he didn't have to worry about things all the time. He wasn't quite sure what he'd been so worried about, but he knew he didn't like it.

As he walked across the red sand through the sagebrush, he kept his thoughts on what his eyes were seeing and his ears were hearing. The sun was turning the sky gold and making the long black shadows grow. It made the landscape up ahead dark and mysterious, like anything could happen. He told himself there was nothing to be afraid of. What was going to happen, would happen. The whole world was his now. Everything he could see and taste and smell was his. There was no one there to tell him it wasn't.

So why not call the birds out, and ask them to sing. Why not call out the coyotes and ask them how the desert had been doing all this time he'd been gone

He stopped and tried a few howls. Sure enough, he got an answer. Two clear yips and a long howl. Perfect. And it wasn't even entirely dark yet. The sun was just down, and the moon was coming up over the blue mountains on the other side of the valley. It made him feel like he was entering a world of pure beauty. For a moment, he thought he saw his pretty girl twirling across the desert toward him. But if she was there, all that was left of her was the pink dust of one of those spinning devil things.

Thinking of the devil brought a worry. What if he couldn't find any water? What if the devil had burned the ground so hot, there wasn't any water left? That would be bad. He was already thirsty.

But so what? If he was going the right way, and the red rocks were telling him he was, he would find water where it always was, in his river.

He kept going and there were red rocks all around him now, and a whole mountain of red rock up ahead under a full moon that was completely up now and shining on everything. There was even some pink in the sky and the deep purple blue of the light on the other mountain across the valley. Everything was exactly where it should be. He was almost home.